LOST ORIGINS

LOST ORIGINS

THE MAJESTIC CHRONICLES

BOOK ONE

Chris Kulp

SHAHID MAHMUD
PUBLISHER

www.caeziksf.com

Cover art by Dany V.

ISBN: 978-1-64710-143-5

First Edition. First Printing. April 2025.
1 2 3 4 5 6 7 8 9 10

Caezik,. Phoenix Pick and Galaxy's Edge are imprints of Arc Manor

www.CaezikSF.com

FOR **GAIL**

Thanks for all the amazing adventures.

CHAPTER 1

Every client ended their pitch the same: "Don't worry, it'll be easy." The two yellow dots at the bottom of the sensor screen confirmed Maddy's first rule of smuggling—clients are liars.

The raider ships closing in from behind the *Amethyst* wanted either the medicine listed on the cargo manifest or the data crystal that wasn't. They weren't getting either. Doctors working for a nonprofit on Erandi Prime desperately needed the medicine to save the lives of some of their most vulnerable, destitute patients, and Maddy needed payment for the crystal. In truth, she didn't *need* the payment. But she also didn't need confirmation of her second rule—unhappy clients were deadly clients.

An impact on the *Amethyst*'s aft hull lurched the ship forward, knocking Maddy's half-full mug off the armrest. "Dammit!" She took her eyes off the screen long enough to make sure the coffee avoided critical systems. A small puddle expanded on the bridge's floor. "That was the last of the Aldebaran roast!" The custodial bots could get it later, if there was anything left of the ship to clean up.

Strictly speaking, regulations forbade drinks on the bridge. But, according to the Galactic Federation's patrol report, this sector was supposed to be safe for a hyperspace break. "Strap in, Jonathan, and batten down the hatches. Shit just got real!"

"Aye, Cap!" A seat belt clicked behind Maddy in the navigator's station. "The highlighted bandit has no signs of life. It's a drone."

"Are there life signs on the other ship?" Maddy had no qualms with destroying drones. Killing people was a last resort and sometimes impossible to avoid in her line of work. The faces of her few victims were forever etched into her mind. She had no interest in adding to those memories today, but these raiders could not get their hands on the medicine.

"Affirmative, Cap. Sensors show the other ship has three people aboard; two humans and one android." More clicking echoed throughout the bridge, this time from a keyboard. "Sorry it took a minute, but I have three evasive maneuvers preloaded."

To be fair, he did the job of two people, but regardless, the delayed response was frustrating. In navigation, Jonathan always delivered, but switching between nav and sensors challenged him in ways that could be fatal in a dogfight.

The three other stations on the *Amethyst*'s bridge should be staffed, but it wasn't money that kept them empty. A larger crew meant more responsibility and less freedom for Maddy. She had reluctantly hired Jonathan only after a near-fatal collision with another ship convinced her she couldn't manage the *Amethyst* alone. Despite her initial reservations, over the years she had grown to like the boy.

Jonathan's routes appeared on the main viewscreen. To use any of them, Maddy needed more space between the *Amethyst* and the raiders. Her body pressed against the seat under the strain of the ship's acceleration. Getting out of range of the raider's cannons gave her a moment to tie her hair into a ponytail. A loose strand of red hair fell across her cheek.

"Uh Cap, is now a good time to be doing your hair?" Jonathan took the fun out of everything.

"I gotta look good. I might be the last thing that raider sees." She'd do her best to make sure it wouldn't come to that, but the raiders rarely make that easy. She nodded at her reflection in the secondary console. Forty years into her second century and she could still pass as a new centenarian. Despite the longevity treatments, one or two lines had formed around her eyes, slowly etching away at her youth. Maddy accepted them. Middle age had its advantages—like being able to afford the purple eyes mods that were worth every penny. "Start a video broadcast on all channels."

"Aye, Cap. Switching to comms." There was another delay, as he took on a third job. The green light on the bridge's main holocam activated. "You're on."

"To the raider vessel who just shot me. Back off or I'll blast you into so many pieces they'll need organic scanners to tell your bodies from debris."

The *Amethyst* jolted forward from yet another impact. One bandit craft zoomed past. Its rectangular body was too small to carry both life-support systems and weapons. Drones like that weren't cheap. Raiders with pockets that deep would be after the meds, not the crystal. They'd sell the drugs on the black market at prices too high for the doctors who hired Maddy. The rich junkies would get their fix while the poor died in squalor. She'd be damned if she'd let that happen.

"Aft defensive batteries at 30% capacity, Cap."

A few more plasma shots like that and the batteries would be full, exposing the hull to the brunt of the enemy's weapons.

Maddy exhaled, puffing up the strand of her hair that didn't make it into the ponytail. "Okay, if that's the way you want it." She forced the control stick to port, selecting the second of Jonathan's routes. Crashing sounds erupted through the ship. "I said batten down the hatches, Jonathan!"

"Sorry, Cap!" More clicking came from the nav station, as Jonathan switched jobs yet again.

A notification popped up on Maddy's secondary monitor. The magnetic clamps were at maximum throughout the ship. Hopefully, none of the cargo was damaged.

"You didn't say you'd be flying like a maniac," Jonathan mumbled.

"What was that?" Maddy's back pressed harder against the captain's seat as she pushed the throttle in pursuit of the drone. The *Amethyst*'s engines had more than enough power to catch up.

"Nothing, Cap," Jonathan said through gritted teeth. The poor boy didn't tolerate accelerations very well.

"Uh-huh." Maddy's stomach dropped as she pushed the stick forward, forcing the *Amethyst* below the drone. Jonathan groaned behind her. "Don't puke on my bridge."

Another groan from Jonathan served as an acknowledgement. The belly of the drone appeared on the main viewscreen. The distance between them decreased faster than Maddy liked, but she had to play this aggressively.

"What's the plan, Cap?" Jonathan's voice shook more than the ship.

Squeezing the plasma cannon's trigger added to the adrenaline already coursing through her veins. The *Amethyst* soared through the drone's debris. "There's three dimensions in space, dumbass!" Maddy shook her head. "You've gotta watch what's going on below your ship, too." Her comment was to remind Jonathan to keep his eyes on the sensors more so than the drone pilot, who couldn't hear her, anyway.

Another hard impact, this time on the dorsal hull, shook the *Amethyst*. The bridge lights faded. Life-support failure warnings flashed on Maddy's console. A loud pop signaled the activation of emergency lighting. Jonathan yelled. Maddy grinned. Paying for repairs sucked, but fun like this didn't come cheap. The raider passed by the *Amethyst* from above.

"Dorsal batteries at 90%, Cap! Main bridge power offline. Diverting power now."

"From where?" Unlike a starbase or a planet, all electricity on a ship had a cost. To prevent the shielding batteries from frying the ship's circuits when overloaded, they're isolated from the main systems. That meant something somewhere on the ship was doing without.

"You keep us alive and let me handle the systems!" Jonathan had a weak stomach, but the boy knew the *Amethyst*'s systems like the back of his hand.

The bridge lights returned. A quick glance at the internal sensors showed Jonathan had taken life support offline in the cargo bay. If it got too cold in there, the medicine would spoil. But, without life support, Maddy and Jonathan would certainly die, and so would the patients needing the drugs.

"I found an alpha-class asteroid, Cap. It's about 20,000 klicks away and has high iron content and lots of caves. Are you thinking what I'm thinking?"

A gray sphere pockmarked with the mountain ranges and craters typical of an alpha-class rock appeared on the main viewscreen. The yellow dot representing the raider on the sensor screen turned around in a large sweeping arc and approached the *Amethyst*'s ventral hull. It was far enough away that Maddy's ship would easily beat the raider to the rock.

Geological scans showed a large cave on the other side of the 1,000-kilometer-wide asteroid—too obvious a destination—and a couple of medium and smaller ones around it. Plasma rounds sped by the *Amethyst* as it raced to the rock. Maddy approved Jonathan's route and let the autopilot take them straight to the mostly awkwardly shaped cave. The autopilot could have parked them in the cave, too, but Maddy didn't trust it in close quarters. It was a tight fit, but she had backed the *Amethyst* through narrower passages.

"Anything on sensors?" Maddy asked.

"No, Cap. Thanks to the iron, he shouldn't be able to see us either. If he did check out the asteroid, no one would think we'd head to *this* cave. I think we're good."

A tense quiet settled over the bridge. Maddy gripped the control stick. The raider seemed to take their time searching the asteroid's surface. "The pilot could be a woman, you know."

The bandit zoomed by the cave's entrance, dismissing it due to its awkward narrow opening, heading toward the larger cave entrance.

"Gotcha!" The loose strand of ginger hair puffed out with Maddy's excited exhale. The *Amethyst* streaked out of the cave, the acceleration pinning her against the seat. Once they got close enough to the bandit ship, the *Amethyst*'s targeting computer lit up. To shake the target lock, the enemy vessel drifted port and starboard. Maddy had seen the maneuver too many times before. A green rectangle flashed around the bandit as Maddy regained target lock. She unleashed a minor barrage from the plasma cannons—just enough to overload the raider's aft batteries and expose their hull to damage. Their target's rear engines glowed brighter.

Maddy tapped her way through the weapons-selection screen. The bandit was getting farther away than she liked. Finally, she found what she was looking for.

"What'cha doin', Cap? They're going to get away." By the tone of his voice, it was difficult to tell if Jonathan was nervous or upset.

Maddy fired two low-yield energy missiles at the raider. "Teaching them a lesson *and* upholding our reputation."

Two blue lights left the *Amethyst*'s forward torpedo tubes. The lights faded as they ran low on fuel. Right before it extinguished completely, the first torpedo struck the raider's main engines, destroying them in a blue-green explosion. The second missile overshot the bandit. Maddy cut its engines. The torpedo's momentum carried it forward.

"Negative impact on missile two. Looks like you missed, Cap."

"No. I didn't." Using her weapons console, Maddy reactivated the torpedo's engines which gave her stick control of the missile. On the sensor screen, a green dot representing the projectile turned around and slammed into the front of the raider's ship. Sensors confirmed the destruction of the target's weapons bay. In addition, all life signs were still accounted for. Maddy sighed in relief; no new faces to memorize. "Set up another video broadcast, all channels."

After a brief delay while Jonathan changed stations, the red light activated above the holocam. "You're on, Cap."

"Enemy raider, limp back to your base and warn your friends that the next time they mess with Captain Maddy Majestic, they'll end up vaporized like your drone." Maddy closed the channel, her reflection reappearing on the viewscreen. The ponytail-with-one-loose-strand look was a keeper, emphasizing her strong profile. "Take us home, Jonathan."

"Course laid in for Starbase Erandi 4. We'll be there by midday tomorrow. I have maintenance bots restoring life support to the cargo bay." Jonathan left the bridge.

Stars faded from the viewscreen, replaced by a gray swirling vortex as the *Amethyst* transitioned into hyperspace.

Old long-haul cargo captains warned against staring at the vortex. According to legend, hyperspace beasts used the vortices to hypnotize pilots.

The mesmerized pilots would supposedly fly toward the vortex and straight into the beast's stomach. Scientists said nothing lived in hyperspace.

The genuine danger was hyperspace psychosis. For some unknown reason, hyperspace affected the brains of both humans and androids. Although, like most things, androids tolerated it better. Spend too long in hyperspace, and people started feeling woozy. Then they heard voices, and after that came the hallucinations that drove the crew to sabotage their own ships. Some experienced spacefarers like Maddy could tolerate days in hyperspace. Jonathan had never quite built the same tolerance, hence the hyperspace break that led to the attack. But whether it was hyperspace beasts or psychosis, Maddy wasn't taking any chances. She deactivated the viewscreen and turned around in her chair.

A hologram of the *Amethyst* floated in the middle of the bridge. A constellation of yellow dots, one for each point of repair, speckled the holo-*Amethyst*'s hull. Thankfully, the cargo bay was devoid of dots. The sick people on Erandi Prime would get their medicine—if the bots got the cargo bay's life support up in time. Just as important, the *Amethyst*'s concealed cargo bay sustained no damage either. In no uncertain terms, the client informed Maddy that the consequences of damaged cargo would be far more significant than a loss of payment.

The hardest part of the op lay ahead: Avoiding customs and getting paid. Medicine always sailed through customs. Based on what she paid for the newly installed secret cargo hold, the crystal should avoid detection. She'd find out tomorrow if that was money well spent.

Doctors were some of the easiest clients to work with. They'd pay for the medicine without incident. The other client concerned Maddy. They would be the one most likely to support Maddy's third rule of smuggling: Clients and their money weren't easily separated.

Maddy deactivated the hologram and turned her chair back around to face the command console. Settling back, she closed her eyes. The chair hugged her in ways her bed at home didn't. "You take the first watch, Jonathan. I'm getting some shut-eye."

"Aye, Cap. We received a message from our client during the fight. They want to change the location of our meeting."

Jonathan didn't need to say which client sent the message. Tomorrow was going to be a long day.

CHAPTER 2

Dread was the wrong word. At least that's what Maddy tried to tell herself when Starbase Erandi 4's gray nano-aluminum dome appeared on the main viewscreen. Erandi, the base's home star, shone slightly brighter than the rest of the stars in the background.

One billion of the Galaxy's 200 sextillion people called the starbase home. Maddy and her partner, Riley, were among them. They shared an apartment that—by the standards of any rational person—was luxurious compared to the *Amethyst*'s quarters. But the *Amethyst* was *home*. A tinge of shame accompanied that thought every time it entered Maddy's mind. Riley deserved better. As her grounded Madison persona, Maddy did her best to provide that for them.

Most people born on the starbase never left it, except for the occasional trip to Erandi Prime, the star system's only habitable planet. A life without the freedom and adventure of space seemed to be one not worth living. Riley tried their best to convince Maddy that settling down had its merits. Maddy felt guilty that she was not feeling guilty enough for accepting so many missions.

"Incoming message from the harbormaster's office, Cap."

Back to reality, I suppose.

A heavyset customs agent, probably around Maddy's age, appeared on the *Amethyst*'s main viewscreen. "Disengage engines and hand control over to deck ops."

"Control's yours, officer." Maddy killed the engines. "Where's Parker? I thought they were working today."

"They're on vacation. The dockmaster hired me last week to cover for them."

Maddy swore under her breath. Jobs were scarce. There's no doubt this guy would do anything he could to impress his boss and secure a permanent position. It would have been better to test the new cargo hold's security with Parker. They were easy to bribe. Temporary or not, new agents had a sense of duty, even if they lived Downtown and were paid barely above the Universal Basic Provision.

A heavy clunk reverberated throughout the *Amethyst* as Starbase Erandi 4's tractor beams contacted the hull. The beams deftly maneuvered the ship below the dome, through the starbase's force field, and into the docking bay. A map of the dock appeared on the main viewscreen displayed. A flashing red dot highlighted Maddy's slip in Hangar Bay 40.

"You've got the bridge, Jonathan." Maddy went to the cargo bay to make sure the items on the ship's public manifest were easily found, and the cargo *not* on the manifest was not. The *Amethyst*'s internal sensors couldn't find the crystal. Hopefully, the starbase hadn't updated theirs.

When she returned to the bridge, Jonathan leaned against a weapons console beside the captain's chair while reading his tablet. He knew better than to sit in her chair. "Looks like we'll be docked in a few minutes, Cap. I just got done tallying up our damages."

"What's it going to cost me?" Sometimes, getting a fair price for ship repairs was more difficult than smuggling contraband onboard the starbase.

"More than you'd like, but less than I expected." Jonathan folded the tablet and stuck it in the leg pocket of his cargo pants. "Might have been less if we had more crew."

It certainly would have been. But the costs to Maddy would have been higher in other regards. "More crew means a smaller share." The financial reality was a convenient truth, even if not the real reason. Besides, Jonathan never questioned her anyway.

"Yeah. I suppose so." His face lit up with the same faux-nonchalant smile he always put on when he was about to ask his next question. "So, Cap, wanna get a drink after we unload and get paid?" He ran a hand through his hair and looked away as he rubbed the back of his neck. "We could run down the mission and go over the *Amethyst*'s status report."

"No can do, Jonathan." Maddy gave an apologetic grin and patted him on the shoulder. "Riley and I've got plans tonight." She flopped into the pilot's chair and scrolled through the manifest—all the paperwork seemed in order.

"No prob, Cap."

He was so cute when he tried to be cool in front of her. Maddy hated having to shoot the boy down, but he knew she was with Riley. Besides, Jonathan was half her age—literally. He had had only one life extension so far, at sixty. That treatment barely counted. It was only for aesthetics.

Out of the corner of her eye, Maddy saw Jonathan look down and quickly shift his weight forward. He probably just now realized he was leaning on the weapons console. It didn't matter. The *Amethyst*'s main computer deactivated all weapons once the tractor beams had made contact. He mouthed the word, *Sorry*.

Back when Jonathan had first started, she would have dressed him down for two reasons. First, carelessness would get one killed in space. Second, Maddy didn't want him on board. She preferred to be alone on missions so that she'd be the only one killed by her poor decisions. While the first reason continued to be true, the second did not. As much as she didn't want to admit it, he'd saved her life on more than one occasion—including yesterday. She wouldn't have survived the dogfight without him.

They were both tired after a long run. Maddy let the minor transgression go with a dropped chin and a raised eyebrow. Right now, all Maddy wanted to do was get paid and see Riley. She stood and grabbed her flight jacket off the back of the pilot's seat and put it on. The bottom of her T-shirt rose, exposing her midriff. Jonathan snuck a quick glance. The boy needed a partner if, for no other reason, to divert his attention toward someone who would reciprocate. Fortunately, she had someone in mind.

Maddy patted the pockets of her jacket and cargo pants. *Where's my comm?*

"Looking for this?" Jonathan held up the palm-sized plastic card. "It was on the floor beside your chair." He pointed to where he found the communicator. "Looks like it's time for new pants."

Her finger found a hole in the left leg pocket of her cargo pants. "I just got these broken in." She reached for the comm.

Jonathan pulled the comm away before Maddy could take it. "Maybe I should hold on to it. We can't get paid without it."

The person Maddy had in mind for Jonathan would have thought his action was cute. Maddy didn't. It took nothing more than a direct stare and a stern look to get Jonathan to hand over the card.

"Looks like we're docked." Maddy checked her jacket's breast pocket. No holes. She dropped the comm in the pocket and patted the jacket to double-check. "Let's hope the new guy isn't our inspector."

Of course, the new guy was their inspector. The agent waddled down the hangar's walkway and stopped a little too close to Maddy. "Are you," he squinted at his tablet, "Captain Majestic? Is that your real name?"

That was the name on the manifest. Maddy bit her tongue. Smugglers who pissed off customs agents with sarcastic comments weren't in the trade for long. "Yes, and yes." The man grunted and then walked along the extension bridge connecting the walkway to the *Amethyst*. He entered the ship through its cargo bay door, disappearing inside.

Twenty other cargo ships were docked along the walkway of the cavernous Hangar Bay 40. The ships all resembled aircraft with short, stubby wings. The Galactic Federation licensed only one company, Spatium Navis, to build ships and they made only one cargo model. Despite heavy regulations on the industry, Spatium Navis's customers could choose the ship's size and color. Plasma cannons and low-yield energy torpedoes were the only legal armaments, but many captains sneaked other weapons on board. At only 30 meters from stem to stern, the *Amethyst* was the smallest in the dock, but its purple hull was the prettiest—even with the scratches and dents from the dogfight—and, unbeknownst to the dockmaster, one of the best armed.

The computer at the end of the extension bridge displayed the repair shop's damage assessment. It agreed with Jonathan's. The crew quarters, mess, and cargo bay were unscathed. As was most of the equipment in the med bay. The damage to the bridge—mostly electrical—would be cheap to fix. The lower deck took a beating but, thankfully, the armaments and printers remained intact. Maddy grimaced at the cost of discharging the batteries and banging out the dents in the hull. No one paid for electricity. The starbase generated it to exactly match demand. However, off-loading unused charge was a pricey service because engineers needed to figure out what to do with the excess—at least that was the justification given by the dock's mechanics.

"Like I said, Cap, more than you wanted. But it could have been worse."

"The dogfight might have been a little too much fun. It's fine. I've got it covered." Maddy tapped the screen to put in the work order and then flicked the payment from her comm to the console. "According to the computer, the bots should have it done early tomorrow."

"Sounds good, Cap. I'll be ready for our next run. Just tell me when." Jonathan glanced at the ship, then back to Maddy. "The inspector is still in there," he whispered.

The agent had been in the *Amethyst* longer than usual—even for a new guy. "You know how the new ones are." She tried to act causal. The last thing a smuggler needed to do was draw attention to herself during a custom's inspection. Still, a little voice whispered in the back of her mind. Had she remembered to activate the new cargo bay's shielding in time? The installer was very clear that it had to be on before they were in range of the docking bay's scanners.

The customs agent exited the cargo bay carrying a small lockbox—the same kind Maddy used to hide the crystal. Her stomach soured. "What's in this Captain?" The agent shoved the box toward Maddy. "I can't get it open. Nor is it listed on the manifest. Regs are clear. All containers *must* be unlocked for inspection."

Running was not an option. Where would she go? The lift connecting the hangar to the dome was on the other end of the walkway. She and Jonathan would be in cuffs well before they got there. Even if she could run, the dockmaster would impound the *Amethyst*. It wouldn't be long before the authorities caught up to her on the starbase. Maddy entered the code to unlock the box. Hopefully, prison wasn't as bad as she'd heard.

The lid slowly opened, revealing a collection of vials scattered at the bottom. Maddy suppressed a sigh of relief. "I apologize, officer. I should have put them on the manifest. The hospital on Vega IIb added those last minute. The drugs in those vials are supposed to help people absorb the other medication faster and save more lives." Maddy closed the box. "We were in a rush to get back and they must have slipped my mind."

The customs agent stared at her for two seconds longer than comfortable. Maddy didn't waver and, thankfully, Jonathan kept his mouth shut. "Okay," he huffed, "I'll let it slide. *This* time."

Maddy clasped her hands in front of her. "Thank you *so* much, officer." Men with little power loved to be pandered to. "I *really* appreciate it." Maddy gave the smile that made Riley squirm whenever she used it on him.

"Uh, yeah," the agent cleared his throat, "I'll inform the doctors they can receive the shipment. One of them is on deck waiting to talk to you." He walked away and waved at a woman wearing green scrubs standing near the dock's main elevator.

Whoever she was, she wasn't Dr. Hiroshi Nakagawa, the physician who had hired Maddy. Changes in clients were rarely a good sign. The woman hurried down the walkway to greet the agent. They met closer to the *Amethyst*'s slip than the elevator. She nodded and glanced at Maddy as she spoke with the officer.

After shaking hands with the customs agent, the woman approached Maddy and Jonathan. "Hello Captain, I am Dr. Richardson." She held up her comm. The screen identified her as the executive director of the same charity Dr. Nakagawa worked for. "Hiroshi sends his regrets. He is treating patients planet-side. I am afraid things have gotten worse down there." Dr. Richardson flicked payment from her comm toward Maddy. "This medicine will save many lives on the surface." She looked at the *Amethyst* and frowned. "I hope it wasn't too much trouble. Your ship looks worse for the wear."

"No trouble at all, doctor." Maddy handed her the box of vials. "The Vegans wanted you to have these. They said it would speed up the delivery of the medication."

Dr. Richardson's eyes lit up when she looked inside the box. "Yes. This will be very helpful. I am afraid I don't have the money to pay for transporting these, too."

The comm in Maddy's pocket buzzed. She pulled it out and flicked across the screen toward the doctor. "Keep your money." Both Jonathan and the doctor's jaw dropped. Maddy nudged Jonathan in the ribs with her elbow. He closed his mouth.

"That is generous of you. We will make sure we put the money to good use."

"I am sure you will, doctor."

After a few more niceties, and arranging for the medicine's off-loading, Dr. Richardson shook Maddy's and Jonathan's hands and then walked to the lift that would take her up forty-some decks to Starbase Erandi 4's habitation dome.

"That was awfully kind, Cap." Jonathan nodded toward the bots, which had begun fixing the *Amethyst*'s hull. "But those repairs aren't free, and neither is my rent."

All true, but maybe the free medicine would help offset whatever damage the information on the crystal may cause. A smuggler's moral ledger typically ran deep in the red. Maddy took any chance she could get to keep hers closer to black.

"Like I said," Maddy put her hand on Jonathan's shoulder, "I got it covered."

The next client wouldn't be this satisfying, or this easy, to work with.

CHAPTER 3

An aroma of stale urine with hints of unwashed bodies permeated The Drunken Spacefarer. The word "gross" didn't do this bar justice. Jonathan understood why Cap enjoyed doing business here. The unassuming bar Downtown was a great place to avoid the authorities. What he didn't understand was why she hung out here during her off hours, too. Of course, the place wasn't all bad. The proprietor made the bar well worth the visit.

Jonathan followed Maddy as she weaved her way around tables whose occupants were slumped over, passed out, or both. The lights were dim, but not enough to hide the sea of misery through which they navigated.

Each step sounded like Velcro ripping. Jonathan continued to look straight ahead, and not because Cap's butt looked nice in cargo pants. Ignorance was bliss when it came to the source of the floor's stickiness.

Cap swaggered through the bar as if she owned the place. No matter the situation, she commanded a room like she commanded the *Amethyst*. Her confidence, and her competence, was what Jonathan found most attractive about her.

Two men, a woman, and an android played analog billiards on the other side of the bar. They stared at Cap as she walked past. Cap's chin rose in a brief, almost imperceptible salute. The players raised their drinks in acknowledgement. Everyone in this bar knew Cap and her no nonsense reputation—yet another thing Jonathan loved.

Does Riley know Cap comes to this bar? Jonathan had no right to comment on her choice of hangouts, but this place was dangerous, even for her.

Did Riley care? Scientists say that androids have emotions like humans. Does that include concern for people they claim to love? He never voiced his questions aloud for fear of sounding like the androphobes who'd been causing so many problems on the starbase as of late.

"Captain Maddy Majestic! What brings you to my humble establishment?" Skylar always welcomed Cap with a boisterous greeting. And why not? She certainly spent enough credits in this nasty joint.

"I wanted to meet my client at the finest bar in the system." Cap dragged a stool from under the bar and sat. "But it was busy, so I told them to meet me here instead." Skylar and Maddy laughed.

Then Skylar cleared her throat. "Hi, Jonathan." She bit her lip. "I know what you want."

It took all his concentration not to blush. Cap had shrugged off his advances. Skylar was the first woman to come on to him. *Maybe I should ask out Skylar if things don't work with Cap.* He did his best "what's up" nod and sat on Maddy's left. If negotiations with the client got tense, Cap preferred to have her dominant hand closest to the client.

From under the bar Skylar removed a glass with smudged lipstick on the rim—probably the cleanest one in the Drunken Spacefarer—and held it to the tap of his favorite beer. "Betelgeuse Pale Ale"—Skylar batted her newly modded red eyes as she handed Jonathan a glass of beer—"on the house, sweetie."

Jonathan's cheeks warmed. "I like—"

"You're redder than that beer's namesake!" Cap nudged him in the ribs, interrupting his compliment about her eyes. "I'll take your finest bottom-shelf bourbon." She leaned forward on the bar. "Better make that a double." Bourbon only came in doubles as far as Cap was concerned. But with as many missions as she ran, she should be able to afford better stuff.

Skylar poured the drink straight like Cap liked it, into a highball glass and placed it on the bar. "Ten creds."

"Oh, I see how it is." Cap shook her head as she flicked the credits from her comm. "If I pretended to be a shy boy, can I get my next one free?"

Jonathan cleared his throat, wishing the bar's lights were dimmer. Fortunately, someone sat down on the empty stool to Cap's right, providing a distraction.

"Scotch on the rocks," the android said.

Skylar nodded, served the drink, and then walked away. Now Jonathan wished the lights were brighter so he could see her.

"Nice place you chose, Captain Majestic." The speaker leaned forward and took a sip of their scotch.

"I'm glad you like it." Cap placed her comm screen-side up on the bar—her way of signaling the client to pay.

The client's iridescent yellow eyes seemed to glow in the light coming from the comm's screen. Jonathan once dated an android that preferred vodka. Up to that point, they were the only android he had known who drank alcohol instead of synthahol.

No matter how curious Jonathan was about the android's drinking preferences, he knew what he had to do: Keep his mouth shut and find cover when pistols were drawn, and pistols were *always* drawn. He looked over at Skylar, who was serving another customer. She looked back and smiled. *I should ask her out.*

The client pulled out their comm. A number 20 percent less than what they had agreed displayed on its screen in large font. *Why do clients always try this? It never works.*

"Wrong number." Cap kept her eyes forward and took a swig of bourbon. "Good thing I arranged for another buyer." She put the glass down hard on the bar and wrapped her hand around it.

"I am sorry to hear that, Captain." The client stood and pulled a laser pistol out from under their jacket, pointing it at Cap. "What do you want? Fewer creds or a trip to the disposal?"

Cap rolled her eyes and tied her hair back with the elastic band she had around her wrist, leaving a loose strand again. It was an amazing look for her. She turned on her barstool and looked the client straight in the eyes. They stared right back, probably not sure what to make of Cap's behavior.

In one quick movement, Cap shot up from her stool, grabbed the pistol hand with her left, and slammed the client's head into the bar with her right. A loud thud echoed through The Drunken Spacefarer as metal and synthetic skin smacked the wooden bar. Thanks to the Federation laws that require androids to feel pain like humans, the client dropped the pistol as Maddy twisted their wrist.

Skylar turned toward the action. Everyone else in the bar was too intoxicated to notice except those playing billiards, who merely shook their heads and resumed playing. Even they knew you don't pull a pistol on Maddy.

"I believe the agreed upon price is fair." The client said through gritted teeth.

Cap pushed on the client's head harder and pulled their arm back a little farther. "Let's add 10 percent to the original price. We'll call it an inconvenience fee."

The android grunted and agreed and Maddy slowly let go of them. All the sober eyes in the bar were on the client now. If the client tried anything, escape in one piece would be impossible. The client flicked the payment to Maddy's comm.

"Nice doing business with you." Cap smiled and picked up the laser pistol, putting it in her own pocket. "Let me know if I can help you again." She tapped her comm screen, instructing the bots in the *Amethyst* to deliver the crystal.

The client glanced at their own comm, nodded and left the bar, all without touching the Scotch they'd ordered.

"Well, that was easy." Cap dusted her hands in satisfaction.

Jonathan agreed. "Any transaction we can walk away from is a good transaction." When he first signed on with Cap three years ago, encounters like this kept him up for days afterwards. Despite his tough childhood, he wasn't desensitized to violence. Each encounter still brought some trauma, but working for Cap allowed him to pay for a therapist discrete enough to not report him—or her.

"Thanks for letting me use the bar." Cap grinned and flicked some credits to Skylar's comm. "I need to check on the *Amethyst* and then get home. Riley's waiting for me."

"Thank you for not breaking anything this time." Skylar reached across the bar and put her hand on Jonathan's, stopping him from following Cap. "So, tell me about your run. Any raiders?"

"Any raiders?" Cap exaggerated the question. "I tell you what, if it wasn't for Jonathan, I wouldn't be here right now." She winked at him. "Tell Skylar about how you identified the drone, found the cave, and got us out of that mess." Cap patted him on the back and walked out.

Jonathan's eyes followed her for a moment, but quickly returned to Skylar when she gasped.

"You saved Maddy?" Skylar leaned in; her eyes locked on his.

Cap was one hell of a wingwoman. "Sure did." Cap clearly wanted him to embellish. "We were on our way back home when the sensor screen lit up with more yellow dots than I'd ever seen." Skylar bunched her eyebrows. "Each one represents a bandit—that's what we call enemy spacecraft."

Skylar opened her mouth as if to say something, changed her mind, and nodded in understanding.

Jonathan continued his story, exaggerating his role and getting uncomfortably close to the threshold of lying. He paused occasionally as Skylar took drink orders. She hurried back to him each time and kept her eyes on his as he spoke. During the moments the story got exciting, she leaned over the bar. Jonathan embellished a little more because Skylar provided a magnificent view each time she leaned over. Her cute smirk made him blush each time she caught him.

The bar's crowd thinned out as the hours passed. The billiards players were still going at it. Their laughter got louder as the night wore on. A man and a woman at the left end of the bar flirted in their own little world. Two stock androids sat at the right end, as far from Jonathan as they could, speaking in hushed tones. The bar's lighting was barely bright enough to make out their pale gray skin. Whatever they were discussing looked serious. Neither of them had cracked a single smile since they had ordered their drinks from Skylar.

"Last call!" Skylar rang the bell behind the bar. Both the bell and her volume seemed unnecessary based on the few people there. One by one, the billiard players slowly stumbled out. The human couple giggled, stood, and left. Skylar leaned over the bar and whispered. "I didn't think they'd ever leave."

The two androids on the other side of the bar stared at each other. One had stood moments before Skylar rung the bell. Even from a distance, the tension between them was palpable. The one standing left first. After finishing their drink, the other android glanced at Skylar and left.

Skylar had watched them all night. Jonathan wanted to ask who they were, but years with Cap had taught him that there are things he's better off not knowing.

"Well, it's getting late." Jonathan pushed his stool away from the bar and stood. "I should probably go. I'm sure you have a lot of work to do."

"Look around." Skylar chuckled. "It's not like I do a whole lot of cleaning around here." The glass he'd been drinking from was evidence of that. She wiped another glass with a rag which had once been white. "My apartment is upstairs. Why don't you hang out for a while? I got a new VR game cartridge." Skylar tapped her upper lip. "I think it's called *Empire of the Fallen Star*. We could load the game on my system and play."

Fallen Star hadn't been released yet. How'd Skylar get a copy? Jonathan moderated a hyperweb discussion forum about the *Empire* series. Hopefully, the bar lights were dim enough to hide him composing himself. "That sounds fun."

I might get platinum status if I post a sneak peek of Fallen Star *to the forum.*

After a few minutes of helping Skylar put chairs on tables and wipe down the bar, he followed her up to her room. Once inside, she closed the door behind him. "I'll bring the game out in a minute. I've got *Battle for Mars* loaded up on the holoscreen in my living room." Jonathan had never heard of the game before. "Why don't you play that while I get *Fallen Star*." Skylar went into the only other room in the apartment and closed the door.

Skylar's sofa felt like sitting on a cloud—way too comfortable for a Downtown apartment above a dive bar. Her holo system was nice, too.

Maybe the bar did better than it appeared. The *Battle for Mars* load screen floated above a holoprojector in the floor. The game's title overlaid a small, red planet. Most games were based on fictional planets to avoid lawsuits. This one seemed to be no different. On a whim, Jonathan searched Mars on his comm—nothing. Just as he was about to hit play, the door opened. Skylar, wearing purple lingerie that left little to the imagination, came out and sat on the sofa beside him.

"I lied. I don't have the game. But I've got something else in mind, if you're up for it."

Platinum status be damned. He would be getting a much better sneak peek than he expected—one he couldn't post to the forum.

CHAPTER 4

Bots roamed the *Amethyst*'s hull, buffing out the few remaining scratches. The ship looked almost as good as the day Maddy bought it. According to the dock's console, the repairs were ahead of schedule; the batteries were nearly discharged, and the bots had completed all the interior maintenance. Her comm buzzed in her pocket. She hoped it wasn't Jonathan. Maddy couldn't have given him a stronger nudge to stay with Skylar—hopefully all night.

She removed her comm. Riley had texted her. **I have a 9 p.m. reservation at the Skyview. When will you be home?**

Riley made reservations at Maddy's favorite restaurant only when they had something important to discuss. Although they had been dating for a decade, Maddy and Riley signed a marriage contract only three months ago. They got a joint lease on an apartment and a joint financial account at the same time. What else was there to discuss? Kids? Maddy cringed at the thought of yet another chip away at her freedom.

Her mother had Maddy at 110, thirty years younger than Maddy. But that was then. Modern life extensions were so good that even a pregnancy early in one's third century wasn't considered high-risk. By the time Maddy got to 200, who knew what extension tech would be like? She had several more decades before she'd be ready for kids. Did Riley feel the same way?

Maddy answered Riley's text. **I'll be home soon.**

Almost as soon as she finished typing, Riley replied. **Great! I love you, Madison.**

Maddy texted back, choosing one of the autocomplete suggestions to tell Riley she loved them, and then slipped her comm into her pocket. She had an hour before the reservation. That gave her a little more time to enjoy being with the *Amethyst*.

Guilt gnawed at the back of her mind. She loved Riley. She really did. But being on the *Amethyst* out in space gave her a peace that she got nowhere else. Maybe hanging out in the dock would be good enough?

It wasn't.

Normally, when she arrived on-station after a run, Maddy sat in the captain's chair alone on the bridge and got herself mentally ready to be station-side. The doctors had wanted an immediate delivery, so she lost her opportunity to unwind. She could try to sneak aboard the *Amethyst*. No one is allowed on a ship during a repair, but the hangar bay was eerily quiet for this time of night. She reached for the console to extend the bridge to the *Amethyst*.

Heavy footsteps approached from behind. Maddy slipped her hand into her jacket, ready to draw her new pistol she got during the fight at the bar.

"You have a fine ship, Captain Majestic." It was a stock android voice, somewhere between a tenor and an alto, but it didn't match the client's she had beaten up earlier.

Maddy turned around with her hand still in her jacket. The stock android wore a black suit, which paired nicely with their pale gray skin and yellow eyes. Maddy let her hand fall to her side, leaving her weapon concealed. Well-dressed clients were always easygoing at first. They don't like getting blood on their clothes.

"My name is Kerry." The android bowed their head, a popular greeting centuries ago. "It is truly a pleasure to meet you."

The formal greeting, the suit, the pleasure in meeting .... Maddy had seen and heard it all before—a typical high-end smuggling client. Kerry was about to ask her to do something dangerous or help with some trafficking operation. And if they knew anything about her reputation, they'd also know better than to ask her to do the latter.

"What can I help you with, Kerry?"

"I have a business proposition for you." Kerry reached into their pocket. Maddy's hand went to her pistol, but stopped short of pulling it out when Kerry removed a comm. "It should be a straightforward matter for someone with your skills." Kerry's pitch had barely begun, and they were already saying this would be easy—red flag number one. "I need this retrieved from an abandoned station." A hologram of a data crystal floated above the comm, another sign of Kerry's wealth and ignorance. No sensible person would display that kind of tech at the docks after most of the customs agents had left for the day. The shipping companies weren't too particular about who they hired as stevedores. "I will pay generously for it."

The crystal was unlike anything Maddy had seen before. She was no tech wiz, but years as a smuggler had made her familiar with most of the data formats out there. This looked old. "What's on it?" Maddy asked.

"It is not illegal." Kerry paused and then inhaled. Androids don't breathe, but they pick up certain human tics to help humans relate better to them. Riley did it, too. "It is a map to Earth."

Maddy laughed.

Kerry didn't.

She straightened. "I don't have time for jokes." Only crackpots and school children believed the myth of Earth.

"I wouldn't waste your time with a joke, Captain." A blue planet with wispy clouds appeared above Kerry's comm. "This is Earth."

The planet could have been one of the thousands of inhabited planets Maddy had visited over the years. Although the one floating before her had more water than normal. "Anyone who could prove Earth is real would be famous. Why don't you get the map yourself?" Maddy looked Kerry up and down. "You seem to have the means to get off-station."

"I cannot leave. An organization I work with is keeping close tabs on my travels. If they thought I was going to expose Earth, the consequences would be dire."

Dire? Kerry had seen too many action holos. Maddy had taken jobs from crazy rich people before. Most of the time, their missions were harmless, wild goose chases in search of adventure. They always wanted to come along, and they were always in the way. Kerry was the first such client to refuse—red flag number two. The *organization* was a nice touch to their delusional story.

Two red flags were one more than Maddy normally tolerated before declining a mission. "I'm not sure I can help you." Maddy turned to walk away. Kerry touched her arm, stopping her. That would not help them make their case.

"I will pay triple your normal fee."

Maddy's comm buzzed. A verification of Kerry's ability to pay appeared on its screen—red flag number three. No one pays that much for a map. She should walk away right now. However, her refusal to accept payment from the doctors meant she'd be dipping into her personal funds to pay Jonathan—even with the extra inconvenience fee the client at the bar had paid.

Normally, using her personal funds wouldn't be a big deal. But now she had a relationship contract. Hiding the expense from Riley would be impossible and lead to questions about her job she didn't want to answer. Mom and Dad were always good for the money if she hadn't had it, but the thought of asking her androphobic mother for anything made her cringe.

"One condition," Maddy said in a firm tone, "No trafficking of humans or androids. If I get to that station and find that it's a trafficking ring, you won't have to worry about the dire consequences from your organization. I'll get to you before they will."

"I would expect nothing less from you. You truly live up to your reputation. I have one condition of my own: You'll need to leave tomorrow."

A quick turnaround back to space would disappoint Riley. They would want her to stay station-side for a while. Unless, of course, Riley wanted to break it off. Was that why they wanted to meet at the Skyview? Maddy put the thought out of her mind and extended her hand to Kerry. "You have a deal. I need half now." She'd make it up to Riley, somehow.

Kerry shook her hand and then flicked her a payment.

"I'll be ready to ship out at 0700 tomorrow morning," Maddy said. "The computers say my ship's repairs will be complete by then."

"That's perfect."

Maddy's comm buzzed again. Along with the payment, she received coordinates to a location a little over one parsec away. A quick cross-check on her map showed there was nothing there.

"It'll take me a day to get out there and another day to get back." The one parsec per day speed of hyperspace was spacefaring 101, but it always shocked Maddy how often other people didn't know it. "I'll message you over hypercomm when we wrap up at the station so you know when to expect us." Everyone knew about the near instantaneous messaging system. Without it, the Galactic Federation could not govern the entire Galaxy. "We'll do the exchange at The Drunken Spacefarer when I return. Do you know it?"

Kerry nodded. "I am headed there now. Care to join me for a drink? My treat."

"I was just there. Besides, I have another appointment."

"Very well, Captain. Good hunting." Kerry walked away.

Maddy messaged Jonathan, telling him to be ready to ship out first thing tomorrow morning. He replied with an acknowledgement. A quick trace showed he was still at the bar. Maddy smiled. It looked like her efforts at setting him up had paid off. She blocked his comm so his attention would remain focused on Skylar.

Next, she messaged Riley. **I'm running late. I'll meet you at the Skyview.**

Two seconds later, she got a worrisome response. **k.**

Maddy had already dug a hole for herself. Telling Riley about the quick turnaround between missions would only dig the hole deeper. Using her comm, she requested a taxi to meet her outside Hangar Bay 40. A trendy clothier was on the way to the Skyview. A quick stop for a new dress and heels would be step one in her apology.

Shopping at a brick-and-mortar store was never cheap, but Madison loved it and it would help Maddy transition to station life, even if the stay would be a short one. It was time for Captain Majestic to become Madison Amana for a while.

CHAPTER 5

Dammit!

Kerry knew better than to lean against the bar at The Drunken Spacefarer. The stain on their suit jacket wouldn't come out. It was a pity, too. The human tailor who made it had died two hundred years ago. Or was it three? At least the stain happened *after* their meeting with Captain Majestic. A dirty suit would not support the role of an eccentric, rich person.

"Sorry, Kerry." Skylar handed them a towel and frowned at the bar. "I just wiped this down, but some folks like making messes. Want your usual?"

"No worries." The towel only made the stain worse. "Do you have any more of that synthol from Castor?"

"I ran out last week." Skylar frowned apologetically. It was difficult to be mad at her about anything. "I have a beer made on a starbase that orbits Pollux. How does that sound?"

Connecting Pollux to Castor was unusual. It didn't used to be. Two millennia ago, as a young android on their home planet, Kerry relished each opportunity to look up at the twin stars of the Gemini constellation. The risk of the taskmaster's energy whip was worth the brief moments of awe. Kerry had been on many planets since they've left home, even star-gazing from the moons or artificial satellites orbiting the two gas giants, the pair of ice giants, and the three other terrestrial planets in their home world's solar system. But, somehow, none of them had the right vibe for viewing Gemini that her origin planet did.

After a long moment of woolgathering, Kerry realized they was meant to answer a question, "Sounds good to me."

A young human male—probably near seventy, but with today's life-extension tech, it was hard to tell—sat toward the middle of the bar. He kept eyeing Skylar. Skylar looked over at him and smiled as she drafted the beer for the android.

Kerry was curious. "Who's the boy?"

"That's my friend, Jonathan." Skylar placed the beer in front of Kerry. "On the house, on account of the stain."

Kerry raised the glass in thanks. "I like the new hairstyle. But I gotta say, I miss your yellow eyes—not that red is a bad choice. Why the change?"

Skylar laughed. "Just trying something different. Enjoy your beer." She smiled her customer service smile and went back to flirting with the boy.

Skylar's android phase hadn't lasted very long. Kerry remembered a time when humans would never stoop so low as to pretend to be an android. The kids these days were different. Better. More accepting.

The stool on Kerry's right scraped along the floor as it was pulled away from the bar. "Hello, Kerry."

"Are we using human names now, Alex? Or should I say, General, Grandmaster, or whatever the new recruits are calling you?"

"Don't get me started with those stupid titles."

"Hi, Alex! Long time, no see." Skylar returned with the same towel from earlier slung over her shoulder.

"It's good to see you again." Alex was never this nice to humans. Kerry wasn't the only android smitten by the young woman. "I see you're growing your hair out."

"Like I told this gentleman here, I'm just trying something new. I've been growing it out for a month. Has it been that long since I have seen you?"

"I suppose it has been a while." Alex paused in thought. "Anyway, you know what I always say: Bald is beautiful." Alex rubbed their head and chuckled. Kerry hadn't heard Alex chuckle in a long time—centuries, maybe.

The comment drew a stare from the boy on the other side of the bar. He quickly returned his focus to his drink.

Good call, kid. That's not a tree you want to bark up. Besides, Alex would never date a human. Until now, Kerry would have never guessed they'd even befriend one.

"Want your usual?" Skylar asked Alex.

"I'll have what Kerry's having."

"I didn't know you two knew each other." Skylar drafted Alex's beer.

"We're old friends." Alex thumped Kerry on the back, hard enough to break a human's shoulder blade. Kerry barely noticed.

Skylar put the drink in front of Alex. "Let me know if you need anything else." Alex flicked her a payment and she returned to flirting with the boy.

"An important relic has gone missing from our organization." Alex rested their arm on the bar and kept it there. They must have found the one clean spot in the entire establishment.

"Is that so?" Kerry sipped their beer. It hadn't taken long for the organization to discover the crystal's absence.

"I suppose you know nothing about it." Alex's tone dripped with skepticism.

"Not a thing." Kerry tried their best to sound sincere. "I hope you find it. Some of those relics could be dangerous in the wrong hands."

"That is why we must keep them locked up." Alex drank a quarter of the beer in one gulp. They did that when they needed courage. "I am afraid that if a member of our organization was responsible for such a loss, there would be serious consequences."

"I would expect no less." Normally, Alex got straight to the point when making threats. Maybe they didn't know who took the crystal. "What went missing?"

"An early-gen data crystal from the *New Dawn*. It contains the coordinates to Earth and several of the first colonies."

"Something like this was bound to happen eventually." Kerry turned toward Alex. "How long did you think you could keep Earth a secret? I'm surprised your little lie has worked for two thousand years."

"You know the danger the Earth poses to the Galaxy. Remember what happened to Mars?"

Kerry turned back toward the bar and took another sip of beer. Of course, they remember. It was shitty of Alex to even ask. "Maybe it's time someone does something about it? How much suffering have we covered up over the millennia?"

"To make an omelet, you must break some eggs."

"Do you?" Kerry spoke louder than they intended. They composed themself. "We have artificial meat now. We've had it for centuries. There's no need to break eggs anymore. New ways can overcome old obstacles." Kerry raised their empty glass to Skylar, but she was too enthralled with the boy to notice.

Alex snorted. The ancient programmers had done a hell of a job emulating human tics. Even Alex wasn't immune to them. "I wish it could be some other way. I really do. But the risk is just too great."

Did Alex truly believe that? Or were they drunk off the power their position in the organization provided? Maybe it was both. Or neither. Even after two millennia of friendship, Kerry couldn't be sure. The only person who'd know for sure was light-years away and, from what Kerry had heard, wanted nothing to do with Alex.

"It's time for people to know the truth." Kerry stared at their empty glass. "In fact, it's long overdue. The humans used to have a saying, 'The truth will set you free.'"

"I can sum human history up as replacing one superstition with another."

"Maybe," Kerry nodded, their eyes still fixed on the glass, "but are androids any different?" Alex's silence served as confirmation. "What's on Earth could revolutionize life in the Galaxy."

"There are many in our organization, including myself, who believe it would enslave those it could and kill the rest."

"So, what do we do?" Kerry turned from the glass and locked eyes with Alex. "Continue debating for countless millennia? We sit by idly as countless suffer? All the while justifying it to ourselves with the belief that we're the great protectors of the Galaxy. Meanwhile, who's protecting the people of Earth?"

"Don't be so over-dramatic. It doesn't suit you. What do you think would really happen if the secret got out?"

Drama was one thing humans did better than androids. Still, Kerry got upset each time they thought about the role they had played over the last two thousand years. "You could stop playing military commander and go back to being a scientist." Kerry waved at Skylar again. This time, she noticed. "Maybe see Mel?"

Skylar placed a full glass of beer on the bar in front of Kerry. After checking Alex's drink, she returned to the boy.

"That ship has sailed." Alex looked away and took a swig of beer. "Last I heard, she's with someone else."

"She?"

"Yeah, not all of us abandoned the old ways after the Compromise." Alex put their hands around their beer glass. "One of our officers saw you talking to a cargo pilot this afternoon." That was an abrupt change of subject, even for Alex. Maybe mentioning Mel had crossed a line.

The organization had eyes everywhere. Kerry should have talked to the captain here, preferably before she beat up the stupid android. Then again, maybe not. Skylar could be working for Alex. She seemed awfully chummy with them.

"It was a personal matter. I am still allowed to have those, right?"

"Of course." Alex finished the beer. "But if that pilot goes after the crystal, she's as good as dead."

"*If* I had anything to do with the relic, and I am not saying I did, why would I care about the life of one human?" Kerry cringed inside.

"You shouldn't. Your concern should be for the Galaxy." Alex slid their stool out from the bar. "You are playing with fire, Kerry. I can't protect you."

"Can't or won't?"

A bell rang just as Alex opened their mouth. "Last call!" Skylar shouted.

Alex closed their mouth, shook their head, and left. Skylar continued to flirt with the boy. It was good to see her happy.

Kerry finished the beer and left the bar. *What's done is done.*

CHAPTER 6

The Skyview had a stuffy atmosphere and a strict dress code. Not the kind of place for a smuggler, but perfect for Madison Amana. The restaurant also had the only view of the stars on the starbase, making it one of the few places agreeable to both Madison and Captain Majestic.

The maître d', who was probably Jonathan's age, looked Maddy up and down when she approached the Skyview's front desk. *Hopefully, Riley has the same reaction when they see the dress.*

"Ms. Amana?" It was a question of confirmation rather than uncertainty. "Your party is waiting for you at the View Table."

Somehow, Riley scored the best seat in the establishment—the one right across from the view port. *How did Riley get the money for this?*

The maître d' led Maddy to her table, occasionally glancing back at her to, in her words, "make sure she didn't lose her." It was cute. If Maddy was a little younger, and not with Riley, maybe she'd ask her out.

As they walked to the table, a man began playing the piano in the restaurant's corner. Many of the sesquicentenarian—people halfway through their second century—and bicentenarian patrons frowned. The pianist played a piece from fifty years ago when jazz had made a comeback. It was well-loved by kids back then. Several of the well-dressed centenarian patrons and the maître d' bobbed their heads to the beat. Maddy did, too, apathetic to the fact that she was the oldest person doing so.

Music wasn't the only thing that differentiated the patrons. Although life extension had drastically slowed aging, people—human and android—still dressed in the fashion of their youth. In the first half of Maddy's first century, the local economy was booming—heels and short dresses were popular women's fashion. The other sesquicentenarian women (and most of the androids) in the restaurant wore them, too. Having grown up in a recession, the bicentenarians favored longer skirts and laced boots. Their android partners, if they had android partners, dressed similarly. The few centenarians in the restaurant wore flats and pantsuits, a sign of the pendulum swinging in the direction opposite of Maddy's youth.

The heels and the dress didn't bother Maddy one bit. After such a long mission, it felt good to take a break from being Captain Majestic.

What would Jonathan think if he saw me dressed like this?

The music changed to a much older piece Maddy didn't recognize. The maître d's head stopped bobbing.

Maddy followed her up a short flight of stairs to the restaurant's second level, which had the most expensive tables. Maddy stopped at the top of the stairs. "Thanks, I've got it from here."

The maître d' nodded and wished Maddy a good evening before going back down the stairs.

Someone, wearing a suit identical to Riley's, sat at the View Table. When she squinted, they sort of looked like Riley, but this person had hair. She approached the table, hoping she didn't have to kick someone out of her seat—not a good way of starting a nice evening out.

"Wow, Madison!" The person shot up from their seat and smiled with wide blue eyes. "Let me get your chair. You look—amazing!"

Bald or not, it didn't matter. Only Riley could make her feel that beautiful. "Thank you." Maddy straightened her dress as she sat. "I see you've been busy."

Riley pushed her chair in then sat across from her. "I wanted it to be a surprise." They itched their head and frowned. "Sorry, I am still getting used to having hair. Do you like the color?"

"I'd prefer purple"—Maddy made a show of inspecting Riley's hair and grinned—"but brown looks good, too. Your eyes are perfect. I love that shade of blue." Maddy reached across the table and took Riley's hand. "You don't have to change from stock for me. I love you for who you are, not what you look like."

"I've been wanting to experiment with my appearance for the last few months. I was getting bored with the yellow eyes. Now that we've signed the contract, I figured if I screw myself up, it didn't matter. You're stuck with me for at least five years." Riley's smirk made Maddy's heart flutter, like always. "Besides, it helps me blend in better with the humans at work."

"Ignore the fucking androphobes." Her advice was easier said than done. Few androphobic organizations operated openly on Starbase

Erandi 4, but their membership had been growing over the last decade. The government had eased artificial intelligence restrictions, allowing AI to take from humans and androids even more of the few legal jobs that remained. Ignorant humans equated androids with those AI programs and therefore blamed androids for the job loss. They didn't care androids suffered as much as humans.

"I am keeping the eyes and probably the hair. What do you think about the skin?"

"I like it," Maddy looked down at her hand in Riley's, "looks identical to mine." Going from stock gray to olive wasn't cheap, but it would help Riley blend in with most humans. It saddened Maddy that Riley felt like they needed to go to such lengths.

"Yeah, I love your skin tone. That was the easiest mod for me to choose."

"Well, you really look amazing!"

"I am glad you think so. Just don't look at our account." Riley laughed.

"You work for the creds, too."

Riley's AI white-hat hacking job paid twenty percent more than the Universal Basic Provision—a payment given to everyone in the Galaxy. Galactic Law strictly regulated what artificial intelligences could do. AI cannot attack each other, but people can—and do—illegally hack AI systems. Companies hire coders like Riley to test their AI security systems. Riley was one of the best programmers in the Galactic quadrant. They weren't paid what they were worth, but no one in a legal trade was.

"Yeah, but I know what I make compared to you." Riley locked eyes with Maddy and gave her hand a gentle squeeze. "I appreciate you don't mind the charges."

Maddy earned more because, unbeknownst to Riley, Maddy interpreted the law more loosely than they did. Secrets were bad for relationships, but the last time she disclosed what she did, her boyfriend at the time nearly reported her.

Avoiding Riley's gaze, Maddy glanced out the view port. The Milky Way stretched across the sky. While the virtual sky projected within the dome of the starbase may resemble the real thing to some, for Maddy, it was like comparing carob to chocolate.

Tonight wasn't the night to disclose her career choice. One difficult topic of conversation would be enough for the evening. Maddy doubted the expensive mods led Riley to make the reservation. Whatever it was, Riley must have thought either she wouldn't like it or needed a lot of convincing.

Is it kids? Galaxy, I hope not.

CHAPTER 7

"My treat tonight." Riley tapped the table and the menu, without prices, appeared on its surface—just as Riley had requested when they made the reservation. "I got a bonus at work, and I want to celebrate."

If I can't enjoy hazard pay, why earn it?

"Are you sure? I can cover mine."

Although Madison claims that she no longer accepts money from her parents, she seems to have more money than a legitimate cargo pilot should make. Her finances needed to be discussed, but not tonight. Something else weighed on Riley's mind.

"I insist." Riley tapped an android meal at the top of the list where the Skyview put its most expensive items. After the exertion of today's job, the meal wouldn't provide a full recharge, but it would give Riley the chance to share the dining experience with Madison. Based on what she had said before, the human meals here weren't filling either.

It felt like it took an hour for Madison to decide on her meal. Riley's internal clock said only one minute had passed. She bobbed her head back and forth as she scrolled the menu, eventually tapping a meal low on the list. Riley kept quiet, not wanting to make Madison feel more awkward. She didn't like it when other people took care of her.

Riley reached across the table and took Madison's hand again. Her eyes wandered out of the view port for the second time tonight. It was no secret she longed to be in space. Riley had accepted that well before they signed the contract. *Still, it would be nice if she looked at me in the same way she looked at those stars.*

A bot rolled up to the table with the food. The juices of Madison's lab-grown steak glistened in the candlelight. Riley tried steak once. It tasted fine, but they didn't understand why some humans loved it. Maybe humans would like steak less if they had to empty a stomach sack after each meal. Still, the aroma of freshly cooked beef made Riley consider trying it again.

After serving Madison, the bot put Riley's plate in front of them. The grilled chicken breast was slightly larger than Madison's steak. For the price, Riley had expected more than the three asparagus that came with the chicken. The bot poured two glasses of hybrid wine. Humans and androids could absorb the wine, and it had the same effect on both. After leaving the bottle, the bot rolled away.

"I thought you got energy gel." Madison leaned over her plate to inspect Riley's, giving them a superb view. She smiled when she caught Riley staring.

Heat rose in their cheeks, a feature Riley wished their human designer had left out. "This place does a good job making gel look like human food." Riley bit into the chicken. It absorbed into the dermal ports in their mouth, providing a small, but noticeable boost of energy.

Madison dug into her meal like it was her first in days, just as she did after every mission. The people at the surrounding tables stared. According to her, having nothing but a week's worth of ship rations was like starving. In Riley's experience, ship food wasn't that bad, at least not the android version.

As they started dessert, Riley looked up at Madison and opened their mouth. Then closed it. *No need to spoil the mood.*

"Are you mesmerized by the dress?" Madison ran her finger down its low neckline and then snickered. "Or is something on your mind?"

"The dress *is* amazing on you, dear." Riley licked their lips. They might as well get it over with. "I've got some time off work, starting tomorrow." Riley hesitated. Madison loves her space—both kinds. "I'd like to spend it with you." Madison pressed her lips together and looked down at her cake. If Riley were human, they would have said that their stomach sank. "It's okay if you don't have the time. I just thought it might be fun to do some sightseeing or something. We could visit your parents on Erandi Prime. You haven't seen them in a while." Not since they got engaged, but Riley knew better than to add that part.

"I'm sorry, Riley." Madison still hadn't looked up from her cake. "I'm sorry you felt like you needed to walk on eggshells to ask me this."

"Eggshells? What do you mean?" Riley knew exactly what she meant.

"You don't come second to my job."

Riley wanted to believe that, but there was no need to get into a second difficult conversation tonight. "But?"

"I'd love to take a trip with you, but I have another run scheduled for tomorrow." She looked up from her cake. "I am shipping out at 0700 as soon as the dockmaster certifies the *Amethyst*'s repairs."

"Repairs?" Centuries of interstellar assignments had taught Riley one thing about space travel—it was dangerous. There was no such thing as a minor repair when a single system failure could mean death, especially for humans. "What happened?"

"Nothing. Just a few dings during the last operation. The docks at the Vega IIb starbase were crap." Madison's upturned lips were an attempt at an everything's-okay-but-not-really smile. The docks at Vega IIb were in perfectly good shape when Riley was there last year.

While disappointing, neither the lie nor the quick turnaround time for Madison's next trip surprised them. Riley had a lot of questions about what Madison did on her missions. There was no way Madison made as much as she did delivering medicine to sick people.

"I am sorry I won't be station-side longer." Madison turned the stem of her wine glass between her fingers. "The client is paying triple my normal fee."

Clients never pay more than necessary. In Riley's experience, they often needed to be forced to pay anything at all. Whatever this mission was, it didn't sound good.

Riley took the last bite of their energy gel cake. "What will you be doing on this run?" She'd probably lie. It'd be hypocritical for Riley to hold that against her. It wasn't like Riley was honest with Madison about how they earned their money.

Madison snorted. "The client wants me to find a map to Earth."

Riley dropped their fork. The clang of metal on porcelain echoed through the restaurant. Neighboring diners looked disapprovingly in their direction. "Are you kidding?" Of all the lies Madison had told Riley about her job, this one might be the most creative.

"I swear to the Galaxy." She held up her right hand. "The client wants me to check out some abandoned station and retrieve a data crystal with the map on it."

"Where's the station?"

"I checked the coordinates. Nothing's there. At least not according to the Galactic Registry."

This sounded worse by the minute. Madison's lighthearted demeanor suggested she believed the client was sending her on a wild goose chase. Earth was a fairy tale. Everyone knew that, except for a few conspiracy theorists on the hyperweb. The actual concern was, what did this client really want from Madison? Riley knew how to use their upcoming vacation time. Madison wouldn't like it.

"How about if I join you? You can do your run and I get to spend time with you?" If Riley had limiters like most androids, they wouldn't have been able to notice her sped-up heart rate and expertly suppressed wince.

"I don't think that's a good idea, Riley." The lightheartedness had left Madison.

"It doesn't sound dangerous. It might be fun chasing down some conspiracy theorist's nutty idea." Riley paused, giving her a moment to think. "I'd love to see the sexy Captain Majestic in action!" Madison frowned. "Yes, I know about the moniker you use for business."

Majestic had always sounded like a stage name. But her use of an alias was smart—being a known business owner could bring the wrong attention, even in Uptown.

Madison puffed out her cheeks. "Okay, under two conditions."

"Anything."

"First, you refer to me as captain and, as part of *my* crew, obey *my* orders."

That was reasonable. Hierarchy was necessary for survival in space. Riley had served under more captains than they could count. Madison would probably be one of the better ones.

"And second," Madison gave a sly grin, "you are bunking with me." She took a drink of wine. Red lipstick, a shade matching her hair, remained on the glass.

Riley snorted. "You don't think Jonathan would be jealous if I bunk with you and not him?"

Madison nearly spat her wine. "I think he'll be okay. His heart's tied up with a human named Skylar." Madison told the story of how she had set Jonathan up with Skylar. As Madison continued speaking, Riley ran a background process in their neural network, looking for abandoned space stations in the area. They found none. That part of the Galaxy was well-traveled. A lost station seemed unlikely.

None of this added up. Madison must really believe she's being sent on a wild goose chase. Otherwise, why would she have so easily agreed to having Riley come along? Whoever this client was, they were interested in more than just a map.

Riley nodded at the appropriate times as Madison continued with her story. Skylar was a nice girl, and a perfect match for Jonathan. Riley had gotten to know her when they checked out The Drunken Spacefarer to see where Madison was doing her business. But Riley couldn't tell Madison that. It would lead to more questions they didn't want to answer.

Madison is going to need more help on this mission than she realizes. Can I provide that help and maintain my cover?

CHAPTER 8

Jonathan couldn't help but grin as he stepped off the elevator. The whirring of bots loading cargo vessels greeted him and provided a backing track for his walk-through of Hangar Bay 40. Had the dockmaster reduced the gravity in the docks or did Jonathan have what others called a "spring in his step?" Maybe they increased the lighting? Something about the place seemed cheerier.

The walkways were still mostly clear, as few pilots left this early. Most wanted to spend more time with loved ones before shipping out. It would have been nice to have breakfast with Skylar, but they were up late talking in between rounds of lovemaking. He smiled to himself. Kissing her sleepy forehead had to be enough of a goodbye this morning. When he got back, he'd take her to a proper breakfast.

Cap looked down in thought at the console on the end of the extension bridge leading to the *Amethyst*. She didn't notice Jonathan until he stood beside her. The *Amethyst* always took her full attention. He cleared his throat.

She looked him up and down, a knowing smile formed on her lips. Her purple eyes seemed to sparkle. "Looks like you had a late night."

Maybe he should have stopped home on his way to the docks for a change of clothes. But he kept a stocked wardrobe on the *Amethyst* and, according to Cap's text last night, this should be a quick run. "You could say that."

"What time did you leave the bar?"

Warmth arose in his cheeks. Jonathan looked away.

She playfully punched him in the arm. "Looks like we both got lucky last night!"

"A gentleman never kisses and tells, Cap."

What sounded like a squeal almost escaped her lips. That was strange. Cap doesn't squeal. She looked like she was about to blush, too. They hadn't left the dock, and the mission was already off to a weird start.

Jonathan cleared his throat again. "So, what's up with the fast turnaround, Cap?" Spending more time with Cap wasn't the issue—just the opposite. But this was a brief stay on-station, even for her.

"We have a very eager client. The ship is stocked and ready to go."

Saying that a rich client was paying them tons of money would attract unwanted attention from those who hung around the docks. A few more missions like these and maybe he could afford to move out of Downtown. Who would have thought a boy, born and raised on a sublevel, could ever seriously consider buying an Uptown apartment?

The console displayed the repair cost in large font. Jonathan groaned at the number. "We could save some money using the bots from Hanger Thirty-Five." Of course, hiring more crew would also help. If he didn't need to run nav, sensors, *and* comms, the ship would have fewer scrapes in combat. Cap seemed to attract raiders like a magnet.

"Never cheap out on dental work, parachutes, and ship repairs." Cap swiped payment. "What goes on here saves our lives in a dogfight just as much as what we do on the ship itself."

"You're right. Of course." Seeing the payment for the repairs reminded him of his own paycheck. "My payment for our last mission came from an account that got flagged by my bank as an unusual one." He tried not to sound suspicious.

Cap looked away—she usually looked him in the eyes when she spoke to him. "Yeah." She paused. "That's my personal account." Another pause. "It was just easier to make the transfer from there."

It hadn't taken him long to learn to identify Cap's lies. While not charging the doctors yesterday was noble and all, Cap has got to stop doing freebies. One of these days, her payments might not go through. Unless, of course, his suspicions about her wealth were true. Either way, Cap's business was her own. It wasn't like he was going anywhere. Who else would take him?

He held his hand out toward the *Amethyst*. "Shall we?"

Riley stepped out of the *Amethyst*'s cargo bay door and Jonathan's arm dropped.

Why's Riley here?

Jonathan clenched his teeth at the sight of Riley. A tinge of guilt stabbed at the back of his mind. His infatuation with Cap wasn't healthy, nor was it right. He had just spent the night with Skylar.

Am I using Skylar as a proxy for Cap?

His stomach sank at the thought. The queasiness made him feel a little better, mentally. If he had no feelings for Skylar, then the thought of using her wouldn't make him feel ill.

"Hey, Riley," Jonathan tried to perk up, "come to see Cap off on our next run?"

"Nope. I got some time off, so I'll be joining you." Riley walked across the extension bridge and joined Jonathan and Cap at the dock's console. "Madison just showed me to our quarters."

Only Riley got away with calling Cap Madison. Anyone else would have their ass handed to them. "Oh." He suppressed a cringe. How would it make Skylar feel if she knew he wanted to be alone with Cap? Skylar deserved better.

"Captain," Cap corrected Riley as she closed the repair report with a tap harder on the screen than necessary, "at least while you are part of my crew."

"Of course, Captain."

The response sounded natural to Jonathan. Had they served on a ship before?

Riley frowned as they looked back and forth between Jonathan and Cap. "Is there a uniform on the *Amethyst*?"

Johnathan and Cap both wore a purple T-shirt, black cargo pants, and a black faux-leather flight jacket with *Amethyst* printed on the breast. Cap bought the jacket template a few weeks back to "look more professional." While Jonathan wouldn't have chosen purple for the shirt, it felt good to belong to something.

"It's not a firm rule, but something we're trying. I printed a jacket for you this morning. It's in the footlocker in my quarters—our quarters." Cap opened the supply manifest on the dock's console and double-checked the list. "Things look good. Let's board and see what they did to my girl." Cap waved Riley and Jonathan to follow her across the extension bridge. "Jonathan, check storage and make sure the supplies listed on the computer are actually aboard. Riley, report to our quarters."

Jonathan gave a very unenthusiastic, "Aye, Cap." Bulkheads are thin and the last thing he wanted to hear was those two constantly getting it on during the run.

"Quarters already?" Riley leaned over and purred in Cap's ear. That was a mistake.

"Remember what I said about you being crew on my ship?" Cap stopped just inside the cargo bay door so neither Riley nor Jonathan could board. "Your job is to stay in my quarters until we embark. I've got a lot of work to do."

"Aye, Captain!" Riley smiled and saluted.

Jonathan pretended to check out a terminal screen just inside the ship's doorway. Cap's partner or not, Riley had just screwed up, again.

"This isn't a joke, Riley. Crews who don't prepare for space don't last very long. I have flight paths to register and weapons and life-support systems to check and double-check, just to name a few." Cap paused, probably to glare at Riley. Jonathan had been on the receiving end of that look more times than he cared to count. "Jonathan must chart the flight before I register it, check on food and supplies, and do a once over on the engines. The best thing you can do is stay out of our way."

Jonathan smirked, then wiped his face as he turned around to face Maddy and Riley.

"Once we are ready to depart," Cap put her hand on Riley's shoulder, "you'll be free to move around the ship, unless we encounter any danger."

"Danger?" Riley bunched their eyebrows.

"Yeah," Jonathan chuckled, "like Cap's flying when we encounter raiders."

Riley's eyes got big.

Cap held up her hand at Jonathan, silencing him. "Run your preflight duties. I am going to show Riley to our quarters and show them how to strap in."

"Aye, Cap."

I hope there's no innuendo in that statement.

The nav screen reported all systems nominal. Jonathan had crossed off each item on the preflight checklist. Now they needed to wait for the dockmaster to give clearance for the *Amethyst* to depart. Jonathan turned his chair around to take in the empty bridge. Would he ever be able to afford a ship of his own? Maybe it didn't matter. He couldn't see himself ever leaving Cap, anyway. But a private vessel he could share with Skylar might be nice.

Cap's absence was unusual. She had left the bridge an hour ago. Normally, she was glued to the captain's chair. If she and Riley were messing around in her quarters, at least Jonathan couldn't hear them.

A notification came in from the dockmaster saying they were clear to depart. As if on cue, the bridge door opened. Riley followed Cap onto the bridge and sat at the sensor console behind Jonathan's nav station. Visitors normally sat there during runs. According to Cap, the station wasn't necessary. The ship's manual and Jonathan's experience said otherwise. Cap kept the station locked down so visitors couldn't do anything dangerous.

"Hey, Jonathan!" Riley strapped in with one fluid motion, just like an experienced spacefarer. Normally, visitors take a while to figure out how the buckles work.

"Uh, Cap. Should we have a civilian on the bridge right now?"

Cap flopped into her chair and looked back at Jonathan. "Relax, we are only embarking. Besides, if there are raiders this close to the starbase, we'd have more problems to deal with than where Riley is sitting."

"If it is a problem, Captain, I can leave. I don't want to interfere with ship operations."

"It's no problem." Cap raised her hand without turning around. "Work through the sensor tutorial. You can be the Science Officer on this trip. Your coding skills might come in handy."

The chain of command on the *Amethyst* had always been two links—Cap was in charge and Jonathan followed orders. When they had a visitor aboard, Jonathan outranked them. But now that Riley was an officer, where was his link in the chain?

"I'm still XO right, Cap?"

"If that is what you need to stroke your ego." Cap looked back toward Riley. "There is no Executive Officer on the *Amethyst*, but when it comes to ship policies and procedures, listen to Jonathan as if I were giving an order."

Jonathan smiled, bigger than he intended. His job was secure, for now.

"Navigation, disengage docking clamps."

"Aye, Cap. Clamps disengaged."

"Science Officer, do sensors report we are clear of traffic?"

It took a moment for Riley to respond. "Uh, yes Madison, I mean Captain."

To double-check, Jonathan pulled up sensors on his console. Cap did the same. Riley's delayed response must have garnered the same confidence in her. They were clear of traffic.

"Pay attention on the bridge, Riley," Cap said. "Delays in space could kill us."

The *Amethyst* hadn't left the dock yet and Cap had lectured Riley three times. This was going to be a long trip.

A beep startled Jonathan awake. Night shift on the bridge began in twenty minutes. Cap had told him to get some shut-eye while she helped Riley go through the last part of the sensor tutorial.

I hope that was the only thing she had helped Riley with while they were alone together on the bridge.

He slid on his *Amethyst* jacket, admiring how it fit perfectly despite the slight wear around the collar. When she gave it to him, Cap said he didn't have to wear the jacket all the time. He told her it was a good advertisement. She had no problems securing clients. But the advertisement wasn't for her. He wanted the Galaxy to know he was part of something bigger than himself. After running his hands through his hair in a failed attempt to lose the bed head, he stepped out of his quarters and set out for the bridge.

Just as he closed the door to his quarters, a peculiar sound, like that of a woman giggling, came from down the passageway, in the opposite direction of the bridge.

That can't be. The only woman on the ship is Cap, and Cap doesn't giggle.

Another giggle. It *was* Cap. The door to the mess was open, light from inside spilled into the passageway. Telling himself it was his duty to check every anomaly on the ship, Jonathan tiptoed to the mess and peeked inside. Cap was on the android's lap with Riley's face buried in her neck.

Cap's eyes darted to the mess's doorway. She shot up from Riley's lap and folded her arms. "We'll continue this conversation later." Her stern tone didn't fool Jonathan.

Riley's face tensed in confusion. Jonathan coughed. When Riley's eyes fell on Jonathan, their face relaxed and they nodded. "Of course, Captain."

"Don't let me interrupt." Jonathan walked past Cap to the sink. "I just wanted to get some water and a snack before the night shift begins on the bridge." He wasn't thirsty, but he needed an excuse for spying on Cap and Riley.

"We were getting ready for dinner." Cap pushed a button on the food dispenser. It whirred as it prepared a meal. "Wanna join us?" She took a packet out from the cabinet. It turned red in her hands—a warning that its contents were not safe for human consumption. As soon as she handed the packet to Riley, the red faded. "How'd last night go with Skylar?"

"Yeah, what's up with you and Skylar." Riley winked as they popped a pellet from the packet into their mouth. "Tell us *all* the details."

Talking with Cap and Riley about Skylar was about as appealing as being tortured by raiders. From experience, he knew that was an exaggeration, but he'd prefer neither activity on tonight's agenda.

"There isn't much to tell. We hung out last night. Maybe we'll go out again after we get back from this run." Jonathan took a sip of water. "Besides, I gotta be on the bridge. Right, Cap?"

"I doubt we'll run into any problems. We are still in hyperspace. The next break isn't scheduled for a few more hours." Cap used the console beside the food dispenser to check the *Amethyst*'s status. Then she reached into a cabinet and tossed Jonathan a food packet. "We have beef stroganoff!"

If he had to eat with Cap and her lover, then at least he'd have one of his favorite meals. "You haven't told me our mission yet. No cargo was on the manifest. What are we picking up?" Beef stroganoff or not, he wasn't talking about Skylar. He put the packet in the irradiator.

"A map to Earth," Cap shook her head. "A client with more money than brains is paying triple our normal fee to go to some abandoned station to retrieve it. There's nothing at the coordinates they sent."

"I am surprised they didn't want to come with us. The weird ones normally do." The irradiator dinged and Jonathan removed the now-warm packet. Cap put one of her own in. "Suppose we get to those coordinates and there actually is a station there. What's the chance there's a map to Earth on it?"

Riley popped another pellet into their mouth. After swallowing, they said, "Since Earth never existed, I'd say there is no chance of there being a map to Earth on the station."

The irradiator dinged and Cap removed her packet. "Either way, I am happy to take their money." Cap scooted closer to Riley to make room for Jonathan at the table. "If some rich fool wants to pay us a crazy amount of creds to go on a wild goose chase, who am I to say no?" She dumped steaming hot chicken parmesan out of the food packet onto a plate.

"I am all for easy money," Jonathan chuckled, "but what if there is a map to Earth on this abandoned station?"

Riley leaned over and inspected Maddy's plate. From the look on their face, Jonathan couldn't tell if they were curious or disgusted by the chicken. Maybe a little of both. "The last Galactic Census reported over a hundred sextillion humans, and just as many androids, spread out evenly across the Milky Way's habitable zone. It isn't possible that there is one home planet for all humans and androids. There's just too many of us. The only plausible origin for all those people is creation."

"I have to agree with Riley," Cap said. "Everyone learns in school about how the Andromedans designed us. They came to the Milky Way from the Andromeda galaxy three thousand years ago. According to the records that have survived, they tried harnessing energy from the black hole in the center of their own galaxy and somehow made Andromeda unsafe for them." She twirled spaghetti on her fork. "The Andromedans came here and wiped out all the life native to the Milky Way. Then they created humans and androids as slaves to extract the resources from the Galaxy."

"I've heard the story," Jonathan said. "The humans and androids supposedly revolted and drove the Andromedans out of our galaxy." He took a bite of the stroganoff.

"What do you mean, *supposedly*?" Riley asked. "A space-time anomaly occurred near the Andromedan base ship, disrupting their Galactic computer network. Humans and androids took advantage and drove away their enslavers."

Jonathan gently put down his fork. The story never made sense to him, and it surprised him that someone as smart as Riley believed it. "How could humans and androids win against aliens that can travel two billion light-years and create us? Can a single anomaly, that was somehow lost to history, turn that kind of tide?" His voice elevated higher than he intended.

"The anomaly happened two thousand years ago," Cap spoke calmly and slowly, like when she needed to calm an upset client—it rarely worked. "Some things inevitably get lost to time. Maybe if life-extension tech had been around back then, more of the story would have survived."

"Yeah, maybe." He never won in arguments against Cap. Now, with Riley on the ship, his odds were even worse. Jonathan pushed some stroganoff around on the plate with his fork. "You're probably right, Cap. The Galactic Federation has only been around for fifteen hundred years. The first five hundred years between its formation and our *liberation* were chaotic." He glanced at Riley. "Humans and androids didn't get along so well back then."

Riley cleared their throat.

Bile churned in Jonathan's stomach. He was no androphobe. "What I meant to say was there was a lot of opportunity for things to get destroyed." He shot Riley an apologetic look, which they appeared to accept. "Fortunately for us, the idiots in charge back then got themselves assassinated and replaced by people who wanted a united galaxy." Jonathan purposely avoided the Great Compromise between humans and androids. He'd already raised one too many controversial subjects tonight.

"I have told no one but Madison this." Riley folded their empty food packet and placed it on the table. "My parents were Andromedists."

"Parents?" Before meeting Cap and Skylar, Jonathan had an infatuation with androids. But he knew little about them beyond what he had learned from shallow conversations after a (very) few one-night stands.

"These days, most androids are brought online fully programmed and ready to go," Riley said. "However, some more-conservative couples decide to take on a newly built android and train them, almost like human parents do for a child."

"It is also popular with some human-android couples." Cap ate the last bite of chicken on her plate. Her purple eyes twinkled when she said that last sentence. Jonathan sighed internally, then bit the inside of his cheek. She looked at him strangely when he winced. Hopefully, the pain would help defeat the automatic thoughts he had about Cap. He deserved the punishment, and Skylar deserved better.

"I've even heard of some human couples doing it lately." Apparently, Riley hadn't noticed Jonathan's self-inflicted pain. "Anyway, my parents believed the Andromedans will return one day and teach us the secrets of the universe."

"Believed?" Jonathan asked.

"They died a long time ago in an accident on a spaceship."

"I am sorry to hear that." Jonathan took a sip of water. "I don't mean to be offensive, but why would the Andromedans teach their former slaves all their secrets? Wouldn't they just try to enslave us again?"

"Probably," Riley snorted, "I don't believe in the religion, only the history."

Cap yawned and stretched. "Well, I guess we'll find out tomorrow if there is a long-lost map to Earth hidden in the depths of space. Until then, I am turning in. You've got the bridge, Jonathan."

"Aye, Cap." Jonathan filled his bottle with water and grabbed a chocolate bar from the dispenser for a late-night snack—a necessity for long overnight bridge shifts.

There is nothing better than a blank sensor screen. When Jonathan first signed on with Cap, the idea of space adventures excited him. But "excitements" like raiders and life-support failures had taught him how much movies romanticized spaceflight. Now, boring shifts like tonight were just fine by him.

The *Amethyst*'s computer had jumped the ship out of hyperspace two hours ago. The break was earlier than normal. But Riley wasn't an experienced spacefarer, and Cap didn't want to risk damage to their neural network.

Jonathan didn't wish hyperspace psychosis on anyone. On his first two runs with Cap, he overestimated his hyperspace tolerance and got sick. Although he didn't suffer too many hallucinations, the nausea had hit him hard and made him useless as a crewmember. After that, Cap made sure to stop frequently for breaks until his tolerance had built up. Now he could go almost as long as Cap without a break. He'd probably never have her tolerance. It seemed like she was made for space travel.

The bridge door behind Jonathan slid open. "Missing the chair, Cap?" Jonathan turned around. Riley stood in the doorway. "Oh. Hi, Riley."

"Hey, Jonathan." It was less of a greeting and more of a "let's talk." Jonathan chose not to engage. "Will I be in your way if I sit at the sensor station?"

Riley was always in his way, at least when it came to Cap. Jonathan bit his cheek again. "No." He turned to face the nav screen. "Can't sleep?"

"I have a few days before my next recharge cycle. The food pellets Madison got are quite good. I might not need to plug in at all while I'm on the ship." The sensor station chair creaked as Riley sat. "I thought I'd come in and finish the sensor tutorials. I want to be useful if we run into a *snag*."

As much as Jonathan hated to admit it, the level of responsibility Riley had adopted impressed him. Normally, tourists have no interest in flight operations and cause more trouble than they are worth. So far, Riley had bucked both trends.

The sensor chair squeaked as if Riley had turned around. "Can we talk, Jonathan?"

It took all of Jonathan's effort not to sigh. He set the *Amethyst* on sentry mode and turned his chair toward Riley, who leaned forward and rested their elbows on their knees. "What's up?"

"I want you to know that I am not trying to take your job. Nor do I want to join Madison's crew." Riley looked off into the distance. "All I want to do is spend some time with her." The pain in Riley's voice could change the mind of androphobes who believe androids can't feel emotions. "Sometimes I feel I come in second when Madison has a choice between me and space."

"I don't think Cap feels that way." Jonathan's intended conviction didn't quite come out. He didn't want to lie to Riley, but he didn't want to add to their pain, either. Beyond compassion for a fellow living being, stoking Riley's concerns could lead to problems on the ship. Outer space was dangerous enough on its own. Add in some relationship drama, and now you've got a crew primed to make a poor decision—and it took only one of those for disaster to strike.

"Thanks for saying that." Riley's face eased a little, but the tension in their body remained. "I hope you are right."

"Cap loves to be out here," Jonathan said. "To be honest with you, returning to the station is tough for her." The tension in Riley's face returned. "However, I know for a fact"—know might have been a strong word—"she misses you when she is gone and that having you to come home to makes it easier for her. She loves you, Riley."

A tear formed in the corner of Riley's eye. Those who programmed androids put in every detail they thought would make humans more comfortable around them. "Thank you, Jonathan. You don't know how much that means to me."

Did Cap love Riley? Probably as much as Cap could love anything other than being in space. Maybe even as much as Riley appeared to love her. From what Cap had told him, she and Riley had been together for a decade. Even with, or maybe because of, life-extension tech, serious relationships rarely lasted that long. If, after all this time, Riley was still uncertain in their relationship with Cap, then maybe his own lack of success with her was for the better. He wanted to be with someone who wanted to be with him, and not as a consolation prize.

Every time Jonathan entered The Drunken Spacefarer, Skylar's attention was on him, and only him (except for when she had to serve drinks, of course). He didn't see it before because his stupid little infatuation with Cap had blinded him, to many things. Now, as he sat there, the heartache on Riley's face as plain as day, one question came to his mind. Why should he envy Riley?

"Can I tell you something and you won't tell Madison?" Riley's chair squeaked as they leaned forward.

Jonathan made a mental note to get that fixed at the next dock. "If it's regarding ship operations, then I have to report anything you tell me."

"It doesn't. At least not directly." Riley looked toward the bridge door and squinted, almost as if they were trying to see her through the bulkheads. After what felt like a minute, Riley's attention returned to Jonathan. "I got worried when Madison told me she was doing business at The Drunken Spacefarer. That bar has a reputation, you know."

The urge to lean in was strong. Instead, he sat back, crossed his arms, and rested his ankle over his knee, trying to mask his interest. "Yeah, I've seen some crazy shit there." *And Cap caused most of it.*

"I am glad you go with her."

"I am happy to have Cap's back." Jonathan tried to sound tough. Cap must have never told Riley how useless he was in a fight.

"I went to check out the bar a while back. I know she'd be upset if she found out because she loves her independence. She'd think that I didn't trust her or something."

"Yeah, you're right." Riley had just guaranteed Jonathan's confidence. There was no way he wanted to spend the rest of this trip with a pissed-off Captain Majestic in command. "What happened when you went?"

"Nothing actually. The place lives up to its reputation, and it was gross, but no one bothered me there."

"They knew you were Cap's partner."

"How?"

"It's all part of the trade." Jonathan waved it off. "You gotta know who you're doing business with. Anyway, no one there wants to piss off Cap. If you got hurt, she would have torn through that place with a vengeance."

Riley stared at Jonathan with a blank expression.

Does Riley not know about Cap's job or reputation?

"So, what were you expecting to do there?" Jonathan asked. "If you didn't like the place, could you have talked Cap out of not using it?"

"Probably not, but that is not why I am telling you this. While I was there, I spent a lot of time talking to Skylar. She and I have become good friends."

Jonathan shifted in his seat, trying to remain calm.

"Relax," Riley held up their hands, "I am not trying to move in on Skylar."

Do I have that bad of a poker face?

"Madison and I are under contract, and I know we'll renew when the time comes." Riley looked at the bridge door again and cocked their head slightly to the side. Apparently satisfied with what they thought they saw or heard, Riley returned their focus to Jonathan. "The point is that I got to know Skylar." Riley held out their hands again. "In a very platonic way. Anyway, Madison doesn't know about our friendship for fear of her thinking that I am checking up on her."

"Why are you telling me this?"

"Because, when I talk to Skylar, all she wants to talk about is you."

A warmth spread through Jonathan's chest.

"Skylar really likes you, to the point that she's reversing her android alterations. Didn't you notice she has grown her hair out?" Riley didn't wait for an answer. "She has also been asking about Madison's eye color mod. Ever since I told her the price, she's been looking for another job."

"Why is she doing all that?" The pit in his stomach told him the answer.

"I think you know."

Jonathan's ears were warm. At least Riley hadn't blatantly called him out on his apparently not-so-hidden infatuation with Cap.

"My point is," Riley continued, "Skylar is a great person. Please treat her well."

"I will. I like Skylar and I think there could be a future for us." Jonathan exhaled. It felt good to get that out there. When they got back, he would talk to Skylar and let her know he liked her just the way she was.

"I am happy to hear that, Jonathan. I think you two will be a good couple." Riley leaned over in their chair and whispered. "Madison may have a tough shell when she is in 'captain mode,' but she cares about you and wants you to find someone that will make you happy."

Jonathan leaned forward in his chair, extending his hand. Riley took it. "Thank you, Riley. I really appreciate it." Jonathan paused, letting go of Riley's hand. "I am sorry for being less than welcoming to you on this mission."

Riley smiled. "Think nothing of it."

Riley and Jonathan each turned in their chairs, facing their respective stations. Jonathan thought for a moment, then typed out a text message to Skylar. **Would you like to go to dinner when I get back?**

It was 0200 starbase time. Skylar would still be working at the bar.

Thirty seconds later, Jonathan's comm buzzed. **YES!!! :)**

A surge rushed through Jonathan. He'd never had two dates with a human before. This mission couldn't end fast enough.

CHAPTER 9

Maddy rolled over to an empty bed. Riley hadn't returned last night. She stretched, relishing the few moments she didn't have to be a Madison/Captain Majestic hybrid on this mission. Guilt settled in again, as it always did when Riley and space occupied her mind at the same time.

Emotional conflicts could wait. She had a ship to run, and guilt was a distraction. Distractions in space lead only to death. The covers slipped off her body as she sat up. The cool starship air was invigorating—and a reminder that a thin metallic hull separated her from the void. There was something special about waking up on a spaceship. Anything could happen today. On planets and starbases, life moved forward like clockwork—predictable and limited.

Her mouth tasted like morning, and she knew she sported a rat's nest on her head. Another reason Riley's absence was a good thing. They didn't need to see how well she slept on the *Amethyst*. Each of the quarters on the ship had their own bathrooms. That meant Jonathan never had to see it, either. Just as she finished brushing her teeth, the intercom beeped.

"Morning, Cap. We'll be jumping back into normal space in about half an hour. From there, we'll cruise on sub-light engines for five hours to get to the coordinates." No one in their right mind would jump into unknown coordinates. The cruise would give Jonathan a chance to rest and the sensors to do a thorough scan before they got too close.

"Understood." She had just enough time for a shower and breakfast. "Have you seen Riley?"

"Yes, Cap. Riley and I have been hanging out on the bridge all night."

Hanging out on the bridge all night? They must be at each other's throats by now. Maddy acknowledged and closed the channel. She hurried through her morning routine, grabbing a meal bar instead of a decent breakfast, so Maddy could get to the bridge before she had one less crew member.

She just finished swallowing the meal bar as the bridge door slid open. Jonathan stood over Riley's shoulder. They both laughed at something on the sensor console. While their congeniality was welcome, it was also the last thing she'd expected.

Jonathan straightened and stopped laughing when Maddy stepped onto the bridge. It took another moment for Riley to get the message, but then they stood, too. Their posture would have fit better on a Federation Cruiser than a cargo vessel. Riley needed to stop watching so many action holos.

"Sorry, Cap. Riley was just showing me one of their favorite sitcoms."

The humor in *Cosmic Comrades* felt juvenile and Maddy never understood why Riley liked it. Jonathan's interest in the show didn't surprise her. "The bridge isn't a movie theater. In the future, play that stuff on the entertainment center in the mess."

"My apologies, Captain." Riley sounded like a reprimanded ensign. But the closest thing they had to military experience was video games. "It was my fault for streaming the show."

"No one's in trouble." Maddy sat in her chair and perused the overnight logs. "Just don't do it again."

After a couple of "ayes" and "yeses," that attempted to hide a snicker or two, Riley returned to their station and Jonathan left the bridge.

Babysitting—another reason Maddy never wanted a crew.

The object at Kerry's coordinates easily made it into the top-five list of strange shit Maddy had seen in space. "Bring it up on the main holo." Maybe a three-dimensional image would help her wrap her mind around the enigma.

What looked like a four-kilometer-wide bicycle wheel floated in the middle of the bridge. Eight spokes connected the wheel's circumference to a thin central axis. The *Amethyst* could easily fit between the spokes near the rim. That wasn't the strangest part—the wheel rotated.

Kerry said it was a station. It looked more like an abstract art installation—Maddy understood those as much as this supposed station. Galactic law dictated the design of any populated artificial structure—a dome with docking bays underneath. Even the most libertarian starbases followed that rule. To do otherwise risked dis-incentivizing commercial traffic. Every pilot knew where to dock when visiting a new-to-them starbase.

"There are no electromagnetic transmissions coming from the station, Captain."

"The client said the place was abandoned. I wouldn't expect any comms." Maddy walked around the holo, trying to make sense of what she saw. There didn't appear to be any obvious hull breaches.

"Yes, but there is no transponder signal, either," Riley said.

That's not good.

"Keep an eye out for small ships." Hopefully, Riley learned a thing or two from the tutorials. "Raiders often remove transponders to hide their bases. It's illegal, but they are raiders, after all."

"Aye, Captain." Riley leaned forward, staring intently at the sensor console.

It's cute when Riley talks like a crewmember.

The android straightened up again. "There are no life-signs, human or android, on board."

Riley's all-nighter with the tutorial had paid off. Maddy didn't have to ask them to run a bio-check—a standard protocol in situations like this. Jonathan often needed reminding. To be fair, navigation took a lot of his attention—especially around a station without a transponder.

Regardless, if this place was a raider hideout, they weren't there now. The station's emptiness didn't worry her, but a potential unannounced return did. "The client said that the station is ancient," Maddy said. "Can the sensors get a read on its age?"

"Sensors say approximately two thousand years old." There was an uncertainty in Riley's voice. Maddy glanced at Jonathan, who confirmed. Riley saw it and frowned.

"Not that I doubt you, Riley. But this is your first time as a science officer."

"I understand. The tutorial said that the sensors should be better at getting an exact age. I don't know what is going on."

"Two thousand years?" Jonathan asked. "That puts its construction at about the same time we supposedly kicked out the Andromedans."

"I think I understand the design." Maddy changed the subject before Riley could respond to Jonathan. Their relationship had improved since last night, and she didn't want that to change. "The station is rotating to provide gravity. The Andromedans didn't allow us to have artificial gravity."

"Yeah, we figured out how to build gravity plates about two hundred years after they left." Jonathan joined Maddy at the hologram. "Are those thrusters?" Red boxes highlighted several thruster-looking objects scattered across the wheel's circumference. "They probably got the station spinning."

Riley stood across from Maddy. “The station’s rotation rate and its size suggest that it should have one standard gee of gravity inside.”

“Does it have power?” Maddy asked.

Riley walked back to the sensor console and laughed. “You won’t believe this! It has a fusion generator.”

“Seriously? We couldn’t run the *Amethyst* on fusion, how could anyone run an entire station on it?”

“I don’t know.” Riley scrolled through the sensor report. “It looks like the generator is dead and we can’t restart it. But I think we can power the station with a portable antimatter reactor.” That was a solution an engineer would come up with, not a programmer. Maybe Riley did more than code. Maddy wasn’t quite clear on what Riley’s job entailed. They rarely talked about their work.

“I think we can dock here, Cap.” The primitive docking bay Jonathan pointed to appeared to be little more than an airlock with clamps on either side of the door. It looked like an interesting challenge.

Maddy returned to the captain’s chair and matched the *Amethyst*’s speed with the station’s rotation.

“I can provide assistance with the sensors, Captain.”

“I got it, Riley.” Maddy accelerated the *Amethyst* to catch up to the docking bay. Once the station’s clamps lined up with the *Amethyst*’s portside clamps, Maddy nudged the control stick to port.

“Too fast, Captain. We need to slow down.” A loud thud resonated through the hull. Jonathan sucked air through his teeth. “Just a few scrapes, ship integrity *near* one hundred percent.” Apparently, Riley knew better than to tell their captain, “I told you so.” Maybe the extra eyes would have been helpful after all.

“Thank you for the report, Riley.” That was as diplomatic as Maddy’s embarrassment would allow. “Modern starbases provide power to docked ships, but theoretically, the energy flow can go both ways. Let’s see if we can supply power to the station through the docking connection. Riley, do you think you can get its automated systems up and running?”

“No promises, but I’ll try. If the station has AI, it will be limited. The computing power on the station is primitive, and their systems might not be compatible with ours.”

“Do your best.” Maddy stood. “Jonathan, you have the bridge. I am going to check on our docking seal.” She hurried off the bridge to inspect the damage she caused.

Thankfully, Riley's scans were correct. Besides a few dings in the paint, the *Amethyst*'s hull remained intact. That allowed Maddy to return to the bridge with more dignity than when she had left. Jonathan and Riley glanced at her from their consoles as she entered the bridge. Both had the same question in their eyes, and both had the sense not to say it aloud. "Everything looks good with the seal. Can we connect a power source?"

"Yes, Captain. I'll use the ship's printer to make an adaptor between our generator and the station's power port." Riley displayed the schematics for a plug on the main viewscreen. "The adaptor will take ten minutes to print."

"Have a bot deliver the part and make the connection," Maddy said. "That door may open automatically from the initial power surge. We don't know what the pressure is like on the other side."

Riley seemed disappointed but said nothing. They were taking orders well, so far.

Ten minutes later, the station had power. The bot opened the door. "No life support, Captain. The O2 tanks onboard are empty and there appears to be no O2 regeneration system. But I have a map of the interior."

"Overlay it on the holo." One long corridor ran along the interior of the hollow wheel. The central hub was inaccessible through the spokes, but it was empty. Its purpose seemed more structural than anything else. The station's command center appeared as a green dot six kilometers ahead of the *Amethyst*'s dock. The builders probably placed it there so it would have reasonable gravity. "Riley, what's the status of the AI?"

"There is no AI. There are a few automated systems, but none are functional."

"That's crazy," Jonathan said. "How do you run a station on fusion power *and* without automated systems?"

Red dots appeared on the map. "Look at all the crew quarters," Riley said. "*Lots* of people worked here."

No ordinary raider outfit was large enough, or smart enough, to run something like this. If this was a raider hideout, they'd be well-organized—and very dangerous. Maddy didn't want to stick around any longer than necessary.

"Any pathogens?" Maddy didn't expect any, but checking for disease-causing bacteria and viruses on newly discovered objects was standard protocol.

"Some extremophile bacteria," Riley said. "The EVA suits should protect you."

"Jonathan and I will suit up and get the crystal. We'll take standard EVA packs."

Riley looked at Maddy with hurt in their eyes. She squeezed their shoulder. "We need you on sensors."

Also, we don't know what we are getting ourselves into, and I can't risk you getting hurt.

Maddy hesitated before handing Jonathan a laser pistol in the *Amethyst*'s airlock. "Just in case. Make sure you know what you are shooting before squeezing the trigger."

He checked the charge like she had shown him. Maybe he remembered some of his weapons training. "Expecting trouble, Cap?"

"I don't know what to expect on an ancient station with no AI. If nothing else, we can use these to cut through doors if we get trapped."

Jonathan holstered the pistol and started putting on his helmet.

Maddy touched his arm to stop him. "Just remember, Riley can hear us over our comms when the helmets are on. Try not to say anything that would upset them. Riley's been good on sensors, but they're still a civilian."

"Understood. And, Cap?"

Maddy raised her helmet, then stopped—worried about what Jonathan might say next.

"I'm glad Riley is along. They're a good person."

With any luck, that comment signaled the end of his infatuation with her. Maddy lowered her helmet. "I had my concerns about bringing Riley. I thought they might be a liability, but their computer skills have already come in handy. Boarding would have been much harder without them."

"Yeah. Neither of us would have been able to power up the station."

It was one thing for Jonathan to be okay with Riley's presence, but actually recognizing Riley's value on the mission meant the two of them had turned a corner. She wished she could have been a fly on the wall in the bridge last night.

After putting on their helmets, both did a comms check. Jonathan's voice sounded tinny, but it would work. Without an internal network, they would have to rely on radio comms, which was normally a backup system.

"I am depressurizing the airlock now," Maddy said. The airlock door slid upward. Her headlamp illuminated an empty room and a closed door across from them. She stepped inside. Jonathan followed.

"I knew it didn't have life support, but I thought the station had power." Jonathan's voice betrayed his concern.

Maddy wasn't excited about entering a dark station, either. But she was the captain and if she lost her nerve, Jonathan would be quick to follow.

"The station's systems are receiving power." Riley spoke over the public channel. The signal distortion made it difficult to tell their voice from Jonathan's. "The lights in this room may have failed because of their age."

Maddy projected a holographic map of the station from her wrist computer. "See this line?" She pointed to a red circle that ran through the middle of the wheel. "As long as we keep walking in one direction, we'll eventually get back here."

"Just to be safe," Jonathan tapped on his wrist computer, "I am dropping a pin to mark this location."

"Good call." Maddy did the same. A blue dot appeared on the map in the heads-up display inside her visor when she deactivated the hologram.

The console next to the door didn't work. A bidirectional arrow above a handle in the center of the door suggested it was a manual override. Maddy grabbed the handle, and, with effort, turned it. The door opened inward, revealing nothing but darkness beyond Maddy's headlamps. She'd seen too many horror movies that started like this.

They had a six-kilometer hike ahead of them through a dark station with Galaxy-knows-what aboard. Scans for life were negative. Maddy didn't believe in ghosts—at least, not in well-lit environments surrounded by people—but in places like this, it's difficult to listen to the rational mind.

She cleared her throat and pointed to the right. "Command center's this way." She didn't know if the crystal would be there, but faking confidence helped her deal with anxiety.

Their headlamps illuminated only a few meters ahead of them. White, sterile walls lined the hallway. The lack of air created an eerie silence. Maddy wanted to stream some music. But any distraction would be dangerous. She kept telling herself that life-scans came up empty. It didn't help. Each time Maddy glanced behind her as they walked, Jonathan did it twice.

After walking a few hundred meters from the boarding area, they came upon a door on the left side of the hall. A sign written in an unknown language hung above the door. "Can you read that?" Maddy asked.

"No, Cap. I only know Galactic Standard."

"I'll see if I can translate," Riley said through the comms. The *Amethyst* didn't have a translator on board. The whole Galaxy spoke Standard, and she rarely did archeological runs. Maybe Riley took ancient linguistics in school? They were nerdy enough to study something like that.

"The computer recognizes it as a pre-Standard language. I don't recognize it and there is no translator on file. I am using a hyperspace comm link to connect to Starbase Erandi 4's computers."

Maddy grimaced. "Riley, that is expensive. Download only a minimal library and we'll make do with some not-quite-right translations."

"Cap, should we cheap-out on an ancient, hopefully abandoned, station when we don't know what we might find? We could inadvertently walk into a radioactive chamber."

"Fine. Riley, download the entire library. We'll bill the client." A moment later, a translation appeared in Maddy's visor overtop of the words.

"Human quarters?" Jonathan read the words as a question. "What does that mean?"

"Humans and androids fought after the Andromedan revolution," Maddy said. "Segregation was common back then." The console beside the door didn't function. Maddy turned the door handle. It didn't budge. Jonathan helped and with a few groans, the handle turned.

The room was too large for the headlamps to fully illuminate. Thick dust coated a table beside the doorway. A large lump in the dust drew Maddy's eye. She used her gloved hand to wipe off the table's surface, revealing an ancient tablet computer. Just as she reached for the tablet, Jonathan screamed over the comms.

Maddy drew her pistol and spun around. Jonathan backed slowly toward her, obscuring her view. "What's wrong?"

Jonathan turned around. His eyes widened when he saw the pistol. "I'm fine." Other than an elevated heart rate and increased temperature in his cheeks, his biometrics were normal. "Sorry about that. You should see this." He waved Maddy to follow him toward a rack of beds recessed into the wall. She knew what she was going to find the moment she saw the lump under the covers.

"It doesn't look like they died all that long ago." Maddy leaned over to inspect the body in the middle bunk. Dead bodies never bothered her. With a dead body, what you saw was what you got. The dark, however, was different. The dark could conceal anything. "They looked surprised. Notice how their mouths and eyelids are open."

"The vacuum is preserving their bodies," Riley said over comms. "Sensors suggest they died of suffocation in their sleep. There's no sign of a hull breach. Someone evacuated the air and never reintroduced it."

Jonathan stepped back from the beds. "Were they murdered?"

"Maybe." Maddy prodded the frozen body. The near absolute zero temperature on the station had done its part in preserving the body, too. "Riley, run a scan for organic matter."

"There is enough organic matter on board to account for about three hundred and fifty human bodies."

"I guess we should have scanned for living and dead bio signs, eh, Cap?"

Mistakes in space can get a person killed. Maddy should have ordered a more thorough scan. Had Riley's presence distracted her? It was too easy to blame them. She screwed up. It was that simple.

"We have an abandoned station with three hundred and fifty humans who may have been murdered two thousand years ago." Maddy fought the urge to scratch her helmet. "This job is getting interesting."

"Maybe there's a map to Earth here after all, Cap."

"Why would you say that?"

"The fastest way to kill a station full of people is to evacuate all the air. I am guessing these people knew something that someone else was trying to hide. A map to Earth fits that bill."

What had Maddy gotten herself into? She should have taken the loss on the previous mission and lied to Riley about the expense. "I doubt we'll find the crystal in here. Let's continue toward the command center."

As they walked, Maddy and Jonathan passed doors that were labeled, mess, gym, and various network and maintenance closets.

"Everything seems so sterile." Jonathan swept his helmet lights across the walls as they walked. "I can't imagine living and working here."

The dead bodies behind them and the dark infinite loop of white walls ahead of them amped up the station's creep factor. The whole place had an abandoned hospital vibe. Maddy guessed that even with full power, the place would be far from cheerful. Why was everything white or gray? Where's the decorations? It differed vastly from Starbase Erandi 4, which was designed to be a city for people to work *and* live in. They had yet to come across any signs of comfort. Even the mattresses the bodies rested upon were thin.

"It ran on fusion," Riley said over the public channel. "That alone would limit the kinds of displays and lights on board. Resources were limited back then. They had just kicked out the Andromedans. It took everything they had just to survive."

"Whoa!" Jonathan stopped at a door and pointed at its label. "I can't believe they would put that word in a public place. The translator must be wrong."

"The translation is correct," Riley said. "It says *synth quarters*."

"Thanks for the verification," Maddy said. "I'm sorry you had to see that." Her mom used that word once when Maddy told her she was dating Riley. They didn't talk to each other for months afterwards. Things still weren't normal between them. "Although it is not an excuse, back then, people in the past commonly used the word in public."

"Except androids aren't *artificial*. They are people, too." Jonathan shook his head. "Every bit as much as a person born biologically."

"You'd be surprised by the number of people who don't feel that way," Riley said.

"Let's go inside and see what we find." Maddy opened the door. If she got involved in the conversation, she'd just get mad at her mom—a distraction she didn't need.

The room was dark, like the human quarters. However, there was no furniture—not even beds. The place seemed more like a holding pen for animals than living quarters for people.

Jonathan pointed his wrist-mounted lamp at metal boxes attached to the walls. Several wires dangled from each box. "What the hell are those?"

"They're primitive charging stations for androids," Riley said.

"Speaking of which, where are the androids?" Jonathan asked. "Maybe we missed them in the human quarters?"

"Unlikely. Remember what the captain said? Androids and humans were segregated back then."

"I still can't wrap my head around it." Jonathan's sweeping headlamp showed his astonishment.

"We won't find the crystal in here." Maddy took two steps toward the door and tripped. Her suit broadcasted a fall warning.

"Are you alright?" Jonathan and Riley asked, simultaneously.

"Yeah, more startled than anything." She looked down at her feet. "I tripped over something." The light from Jonathan's headlamp illuminated what looked like an arm.

"Seems like you found one of the androids, Cap." Jonathan knelt to inspect the arm. "What the hell happened here?"

With a deep breath, Maddy stood and waved her wrist lamp around the floor. A glint drew her attention. "Over there, Jonathan."

Jonathan's light joined hers. What they revealed would be forever etched into Maddy's mind. A pile of dismembered androids laid heaped in the far corner of the room. Their faces—the ones still intact—frozen in agony after all these millennia.

"Why did they just leave them on the floor?" Jonathan expressed confusion, disgust, and anger, all in one question.

Maddy's heart sank as she looked at the android body closest to her. She couldn't help but think of Riley. "I don't know. Let's get out of here."

"Agreed, Cap. How about we skip the rest of the quarters? I have seen enough death for a lifetime." Jonathan closed the door behind Maddy once she got out into the hall, which seemed much less creepy now. "Riley, I hate to ask, but what would kill an android like that?"

"A long time ago, there were weapons that used the wireless power grid to drain energy from an android. It would kill the target instantly but not dismember them. Whoever did that wanted to prevent the androids from being easily restored."

"Why would you make such a weapon?" Jonathan's naivety was cute, sometimes.

"The Andromedans needed androids to perform certain tasks humans couldn't do, but that made them harder to kill. The Andromedans created the weapons to keep the androids under control. Humans captured the weapons during the revolt. They were banned one thousand years ago as part of the Great Compromise."

"Our client has a lot of questions to answer." Maddy pulled up the map hologram. The command center was four kilometers ahead. "Let's find the crystal and get the hell off this spinning graveyard." With any luck, the worst of the station's secrets were behind them.

CHAPTER 10

Jonathan paused outside of the door labeled "Ops," holding one of his hands against the wall as he leaned into it.

"Can we hold just one moment?" He spoke between labored breaths. "I need a break." Cap had kept a brisk pace in the EVA suits. After hours of walking and searching, the gravity felt stronger than one standard gee.

No response. Worried that something was wrong, Jonathan raised his head.

Cap, arms crossed, stared at him with her purple eyes. "You need to work on your stamina. You know, for Skylar's sake." She winked.

A warm flush rose in Jonathan's face and spread to his ears.

"The *Amethyst* has several workout routines on her computer. We have workout equipment for a reason." Cap shrugged and smirked. "Just sayin'."

"I studied human physical training a long time ago." Riley's flat tone was almost worse than Cap's stare. "I could help you."

Over comms, it was hard to tell if Riley was being sincere, teasing, or a little of both. Deep down, Jonathan hoped it was teasing. Last night's conversation on the bridge had changed his mind about Riley. He'd welcome the well-intended jest as a sign of a new friendship.

"Let's head inside." Jonathan turned the door's handle and followed Maddy into the command center. "Hey! The lights are on—"

Jonathan's legs swept out from under him. He hit the deck hard. The air was forced from his lungs. A spike of anxiety overcame him as he gasped. Black text appeared on his visor's heads-up display. The suit's emergency medical protocols kicked in, delivering the right cocktail of drugs, calming him and allowing him to breathe. He sucked in air and his vision focused. The top of the doorframe he just walked through glowed red.

"Stay down!" Cap shouted. "That's a class-five laser weapon."

Jonathan got on his knees and crawled behind a console near the doorway. Cap hid behind a console on the other side of the walkway leading from the door to the center of the room. She peeked around her cover, the front of which glowed from the laser blast like the doorframe.

"It looks like an automated defense bot," Cap said.

"I am not seeing anything on sensors, Captain. How did a bot with modern stealth tech end up here?"

Wrong question. In times like these, Cap acted first and thought later. "Unless you can locate the bot, get off the channel, Riley!"

Riley didn't acknowledge Cap's order—good move on their part.

Cap's console was brighter and redder. Now was a good time for Jonathan to peek around his cover while Cap preoccupied their attacker. The spider-shaped bot had six legs. A short shaft rose above the body, on top of which sat the class-five laser. A basic, but effective design.

The laser turned and pointed at him. Jonathan ducked behind his cover. Heat radiated from the console. *That was close!* Sweat dripped from his body—only in part because of being pressed up against hot metal.

There was no clear path to the exit that didn't involve him getting shot. How was he going to get out of here alive? Was he ever going to see Skylar again? His mind raced. A tightness rose in the center of his chest. A warning light appeared in Jonathan's heads-up display. His heart rate was close to the max safe beats per minute for his physical condition. In response, his suit administered a drug that lowered his heart rate and cleared his head.

Cap stood and discharged her laser pistol, returning to cover almost immediately. The console in front of her reddened again. It looked like it was about to melt under the laser's heat.

An encrypted comms notification popped up in Jonathan's visor. It was from Cap.

We'll need both our pistols set to max to get through the bot's armor.

Jonathan's stomach dropped at the thought of getting involved in a gun fight. Then again, he was already involved—involuntarily. Maybe this will be a good story to impress Skylar. If he lived through it.

"Jonathan! Respond!" Cap had foregone the text channel.

He took a deep breath. "Where do you want me?"

"I'll draw its fire." Cap always put herself in the most dangerous position. "You head over to the pin I dropped on the map. We'll set up an equilateral triangle with the bot. Aim for the laser. Class-fives are normally connected directly to a bot's power supply." Two pistols at max setting should overload the bot's battery. Hopefully, there wouldn't be an explosion. "NOW!"

Jonathan ran hunched over to where Maddy designated.

"Did you make it?" Cap asked.

"Aye, Cap. Ready when you are." Jonathan's wrist computer buzzed and displayed the number 3. Cap had shared a countdown timer. A feeling of sickness washed over him. Adrenaline replaced the nausea as the number on the screen decreased. As soon as it hit 0, Jonathan stood and discharged his laser, aiming at the bot's weapon. A red beam came from the other side of the room, connecting the bot to Cap.

The bot turned its laser toward Jonathan. Sweat formed on his brow, under his arms, and then in his underwear. In a few seconds, he'd be vaporized. He tightened his grip on his weapon as a red beam continued to flow from his pistol to the bot.

A flash of white light blinded him, and he fell to the floor. His hand hit his helmet's visor when he instinctively tried to rub his eyes. Blinking helped some and his vision returned.

The bot had collapsed in the middle of the command center. With the immediate threat removed, Jonathan looked down and patted his body. The warm suit pressed against his wet skin. *That was too close.*

Cap leaned over him. "You okay?" By the look of concern in her eyes, this was a closer call than he realized.

"I think so." His squeaky voice betrayed any bravado he tried to fake. He pulled himself up on an empty chair at the console he had hidden behind. A wave of exhaustion crashed over him. His suit's medical protocol triggered again and gave him a dose of something that made him feel better. Three different sets of drugs flowing through his system should worry him, but the drugs prevented any additional anxiety.

"That was stupid, Jonathan. When something points a laser at you, duck!"

That's the Cap that I know. I must be okay.

"Make sure you put your heroics in your next message to Skylar." Cap laughed.

Jonathan frowned. "You're reading my mail?"

"Of course not. I just get reports on outgoing and incoming messages, that's all. I assumed the outgoing messages you send every night are to Skylar. Unless you have a secret romance I don't know about." Cap put her hand on his shoulder.

Not too long ago, he longed for Cap's touch, even through an EVA suit. His talk with Riley had changed that. "Not to change the subject, Cap, but that was a modern robot. Someone placed it here recently. Maybe it was searching for the crystal."

"Or it could have been protecting it." Cap removed her hand. "Check all the consoles."

"Can I talk again?" Riley asked over the comm's public channel. Jonathan had almost forgotten Riley was part of the mission.

"Yes. Comms must be clear during combat."

"I understand. Sensors suggest there are more dead humans in the room."

Jonathan had been so distracted by the bot that he'd missed the human bodies sitting at some stations on the command deck.

"They look like the ones we found in the quarters." Cap inspected the corpse sitting in a chair adjacent to the console Jonathan had hidden behind. "I don't see any androids here." More evidence of segregation. "The attack, or whatever it was, happened on a night shift."

"Why do you say that?" Riley asked.

"Because the command deck is not at full staff. Even today, night shifts run light on personnel."

"There are actually less people here than I expected," Jonathan said. More than half of the chairs on the deck were empty. "I would have guessed that without AI, you'd need more hands even at night."

"Check out that station in the middle," Cap said. A corpse in a light-blue uniform sat in the chair behind the center console. "That had to be the person in charge."

Knobs, buttons, and two-dimensional screens covered the console. "Seems low tech. No holoprojectors. I still don't understand how they survived in space using such primitive tech, especially without AI."

"Look at this." Cap pointed to something stuck in the port below a screen on the body's left. "I think the crystal is in there."

Jonathan pushed a button beside the port. The crystal stuck out just enough that he could grab it with his index finger and thumb. "Is this it, Cap?"

Cap squinted at the crystal. Its blue color made an interesting contrast with her purple eyes. "Looks like it. Let's search the rest of the command deck to be certain."

After twenty minutes of searching, Jonathan found no other similar ports. As he turned around to check one last console, he noticed a blue and white flag hanging on a bulkhead. In the center of the flag was a stylized planetary map with a projection centered on a pole. Fern leaves surrounded the map on either side. "Recognize this, Cap?"

"Nah. There are millions of inhabited planets in the galaxy. Maybe it belongs to one of them?" Cap looked again. "Actually, that looks like the planet Kerry showed me. They claimed it was Earth."

Jonathan took a few pictures of the flag. Removing it was out of the question. Millennia of exposure to vacuum would have made the flag brittle. *Best to let the archeologists deal with this.* "Riley, I am sending you some images. Can you do a search to ID this planetary flag?"

"Sure thing. It will take a while."

"I found no other crystals," Cap said. "You?"

"No. Let's head back." Jonathan stopped before leaving the command center. "On second thought, I want to take a piece of that robot with us. It might be important."

"Let's take the whole thing. We might be able to sell it." Cap tapped on her wrist computer. "I am ordering a transport drone from the *Amethyst* so we don't have to carry that bot back to the ship." Cap looked up from her computer. "Do I need to order one for you, too?"

The transport would be welcome, but there was no way Jonathan would lose face like that. He'd never hear the end of it from either Cap or Riley. "Ha. Ha. I can walk back."

Twenty minutes later, the drone, a floating table with arms, entered the command center. It lifted the bot onto its platform. Halfway back to the *Amethyst*, Jonathan sat on the edge of the drone. There was just enough space for his butt between the destroyed bot and the drone's edge.

"You gotta work on that cardio, Jonathan." Cap smirked.

"Give him a break, Captain," Riley said over the public channel. "He almost died back there."

"Thanks, Riley." *Almost died.* The call must have been even closer than Jonathan had thought. "If you don't mind, Cap, I'd like to study this thing and see if I can figure out where it came from and how it got on the station."

"If that's how you want to spend the flight home, have at it. Let me know what you find."

Regardless of whether he could figure out the bot's origins, tinkering with it in one of the cargo bays would certainly keep him away from the thin bulkheads between the bridge and Cap's quarters. Even better, the cargo bay had a video comm console—the perfect place for a private conversation with Skylar. He had one hell of a story for her.

CHAPTER 11

"We have a problem, Captain."

Maddy's least favorite words to hear in space. Worse yet—they came from her partner, whose life was in her hands. And, to add to the impending shitstorm, the *Amethyst* hadn't yet undocked from the station.

"There are ships approaching. They want to board us."

"Why didn't you warn us earlier?" *Maybe I should have left Jonathan here and taken Riley.* Of course, had she done that, she might not have made it off the station. Riley probably couldn't handle themself in a fight—not that Jonathan was particularly great, either. Although he *had* stepped up back at the command center. Maybe his relationship with Skylar was bringing out a new side of him?

"Their ships don't appear on the sensors," Riley said. "They made radio contact. Should I go to our quarters?"

"Bring up the sensors on the main screen." The bridge would be as safe as anywhere else on the ship. Maddy slipped into the captain's chair and looked over at the sensor report. Nothing. Just as Riley said. *I wonder if they are using the same stealth tech as the bot.* "Riley, your job is to stay here and figure out how to detect those ships. ASAP. Use whatever resources you need."

"Understood. I have some ideas."

Maddy pushed the button for the ship's internal comms. "Jonathan, get up here immediately. We have *guests*."

Without sensors, it was impossible to know if those ships were a couple of raiders or an entire armada. Whoever they were, if they boarded the *Amethyst*, Maddy and her crew were as good as dead.

Tapping sounds, periodically masked by Riley's mumbling, came from the sensor station. If anyone on the ship could crack the stealth tech, Riley would be the one to do it. She hated that Riley was in danger, but their skills might save the *Amethyst*. Jonathan hopped into the navigation station with a thud. If she had to die today, at least she'd be in good company.

"Jonathan, give me evasive maneuver options using the station as cover. We can't see the bandits on sensors.

"Shit! I mean. Aye, Cap."

A holographic display of a 360-degree view of the space around the *Amethyst* encircled her head—a new toy she ordered the repair bots to install after Kerry had paid her. It was a pricey upgrade, but it looked like she might already get her money's worth out of it.

"I am going to hail them. Let's see if we can talk our way out of this." Maddy composed herself. The sweet approach would be a good first attempt at communication. "Unknown vessels, this is Captain Majestic of the *Amethyst*. How can we be of assistance?"

Ugh! Maybe I laid it on too thick.

"*Amethyst*, you are violating our space!" The voice sounded male, but the message didn't include a visual. "Prepare to be boarded." Three ships, about the same size as the *Amethyst*, materialized out of nothing on the holographic display. Maddy didn't recognize the ships' design. None of them had transponders. The hull of each ship had the same symbol as the flag Jonathan found in the command center. Riley's search had come up negative on the symbol.

Boarding never ended well for either side. Maddy muted her comms. "Riley, tell me the moment you have a way of breaking their cloak."

"Yes, Captain." Rapid clicking came from the console behind her. From the sound of it, her partner might be the fastest typist in the Galaxy.

"I have two evasive flight paths planned out, Cap."

"Only two?" That wasn't enough. To be fair, Jonathan had planned the routes much faster than normal—another benefit to have Riley on sensors. Jonathan didn't need to pull double duty.

"Sorry Cap, there is nothing here to hide behind except the station. We could fly between the spokes, but that would be crazy."

Maddy exhaled slowly and then pushed the unmute button. "Unknown vessels, please state your identity. We didn't know anyone had claim on this station."

"*Amethyst*, all you need to know is that we outnumber you. We will board you the easy way or the hard way. Your choice." They closed the channel.

"Strap in." Clicks echoed on the silent bridge. He may not have intended to do so, but Jonathan gave her a third option. His first two wouldn't get them through the entire fight. If she was going to end up flying manual before this dogfight was over, she might as well do it in style.

A vibration rattled along the *Amethyst*'s hull as Maddy performed an emergency undocking—a fancy term for ripping the ship from the docking clamps. It only took three seconds, but that was more than enough to telegraph their intentions to the enemy craft. Maddy leaned into the throttle, accelerating the *Amethyst* and steering it along the station's circumference.

"Why aren't they shooting?" Jonathan asked.

"They probably don't want to damage the station. Let's use that. We are going with Option 3."

"There is no Option 3," Jonathan paused as reality settled in. "No, you aren't—"

Maddy's stomach rose as she accelerated the ship below the station's wheel. She heard Jonathan groan. Riley stayed silent. Androids had a high tolerance for acceleration.

The *Amethyst* jolted from an impact just as it cleared below the plane of the wheel.

"Aft battery down to ninety-five percent capacity, Cap."

"They outnumber us *and* shot us in the back. Those bastards!" Maddy's stomach dropped as the *Amethyst* rose upwards, in between the spokes of the station's wheel. When the ship got above the plane of the wheel, a loud pop sounded on the bridge and the *Amethyst* jerked starboard.

"That was a glancing blow, Cap. Port hull is fine."

The icons representing the bandits on the screen disappeared. They had cloaked. Maddy piloted the *Amethyst* over the station's central hub, then dipped down between two spokes and crossed the plane of the wheel.

Jonathan moaned in sync with the *Amethyst*'s weaving.

"Don't puke on my bridge."

"Aye." Jonathan's response didn't inspire confidence in his ability to control the location of his stomach's contents.

Every time the ship got above or below the plane of the station, it shook from an impact. Individually, each shot added a little charge to the defensive batteries. It was dogfighting 101. Fill the batteries with plasma fire until they could no longer absorb an energy blast. Once the batteries were full, the next shot would damage the hull, risking a breach. Any sane captain would then surrender and allow their ship to be boarded instead of being destroyed. Maddy had used the same tactic before, although she rarely boarded vessels. Most of the time, she'd fill the batteries, then destroy the bandit's weapons—never the ship. The bandits always got the message and fled.

"How's that solution coming, Riley?"

"Almost there. Printing drones now."

Drones?

There was no time to ponder Riley's print. One wrong move and the *Amethyst* would hit one of the spokes, taking out the station and themselves along with it.

The ship lurched starboard.

"What that hell was that?" Maddy shouted above the sound of groaning metal.

"Hull breach in port-side cargo bay, Cap. Sealing it now. Port battery is damaged. Port plasmas canons are destroyed."

The enemy had abandoned the slow-and-steady tactic. Maddy wiped the sweat from her brow. *At least the only cargo from this run fits in my pocket. This trip is getting expensive.*

"Riley! Status!"

"Ready to deploy drones, Captain."

"Deploy!"

Thousands of red dots, each one representing a fingernail-sized drone, spread across the viewscreen and surrounded the station. At the same time, the *Amethyst* began broadcasting in the radio spectrum. Three yellow dots appeared on the screen. One of them was below the wheel just ahead of the *Amethyst.*

Maddy licked her lips. "Riley, I love you!"

"I think I do, too."

Maddy snorted at Jonathan's proclamation as she guided the *Amethyst* between two spokes and right behind the bandit. With a squeeze of the trigger, Maddy unleashed a volley from the remaining plasma cannon. The shots filled the bandit's defensive batteries. Maddy targeted the bandit's weapons bays and launched two low-yield energy torpedoes. It took longer to switch weapons than Maddy liked, but the torpedoes hit their target, exploding with bursts of orange and white. The *Amethyst* zoomed past the bandit.

"Enemy's weapons bays are destroyed, Cap."

Another torpedo volley took out the bandit's engines. It was dead in space.

One down, two to go.

"Secret's out, Captain." The two yellow dots faded from the main viewscreen. The *Amethyst* shook from an impact from below.

"Ventral battery is down to twenty-five percent capacity, Cap. Shutting down sections of life support to use their capacitors for additional storage."

"Don't you need air?" Riley asked, with panic in their voice.

"We'll worry about breathing *if* we survive the fight. Right, Cap?"

Maddy grinned at Jonathan's comment. She'd rubbed off on the boy. Another impact wiped the smile off her face. "Need a fix now, Riley!"

"On it, Captain."

Two yellow dots reappeared on the screen. The *Amethyst* was already on an approach vector to one of them.

"Bad luck for you, buddy." Maddy squeezed the trigger. Nothing happened.

"Weapons set to torpedoes, Cap!"

Shit!

It took three seconds to change weapons. Maddy unleashed a volley from the plasma cannon. The bandit dodged. Thankfully, Maddy recognized the maneuver from flight school. She compensated and fired again. The bandit's lights and engines went out.

"You hit their power generator, Cap. They are coasting in space."

"Another victim of Captain Majestic!" Maddy could hear Jonathan's eyes roll and Riley fidget in their seat. Riley hadn't seen this side of her. *Can't worry about that now.*

The last yellow dot on the main viewer turned and approached the *Amethyst* at high speed. They were almost on top of the ship.

"They are on a ramming course, Cap. Impact in ten seconds."

Sensors showed their thrusters were shaking. They were burning over spec. Maddy switched weapons back to torpedoes and took manual firing control. She launched one torpedo. There wasn't time for anything else. Then she forced the control stick hard to port.

The sound of grinding metal was deafening. Sparks flew from Maddy's console and gravity flickered. Klaxons screamed. The collision ripped the starboard plasma cannon from the hull. Most of the remaining torpedoes got sucked out through a hull breach on the lower deck. They were venting atmosphere in several places, including the bridge. Emergency force fields activated, sealing the holes. Thankfully, they were all strapped in. Breathers fell from the ceiling. Maddy got hers on. Green lights on her one working console reported Jonathan had done the same. Bots began repairing the breaches on the bridge.

"The torpedo struck their engines." Jonathan's voice was shaky. "Their engines have failed."

"Good, I have some questions."

One by one, the yellow dots disappeared. "Get them back, Riley."

"I can't. The ships are destroyed."

"None of those shots were lethal." Maddy wiped her forehead with her sleeve, leaving behind a sweat stain on her jacket.

"There was a power surge before the explosion. Maybe you missed their engines?"

Jonathan cleared his throat.

Maddy clenched her jaw. "I don't miss."

"Self-destruct, Cap. I guess they didn't want to answer your questions."

"Give me a damage assessment." Maddy took the data crystal from her pocket and held it up to her eyes. "Let's see what this is costing me."

A seemingly endless damage report scrolled on Maddy's console. One red item caught her eye where the rear starboard engine should have been. The hyperdrive was still functional—somehow. Hull integrity barely met the requirements for a single hyperspace jump. Even with Riley's drones, they wouldn't make it through another battle. "I don't want to be here when their friends show up looking for them. Jonathan, jump us toward Erandi. We're going to need to do some DIY in hyperspace as we head home."

Hopefully, they'd get the hull patched enough to survive a jump back to normal space at Erandi.

CHAPTER 12

Pain radiated down Jonathan's back with each step he took toward the mess hall, which had the only working med dispenser left on the ship. "Analgesic," he groaned as he tapped the button on the dispenser. A clunk signaled the arrival of relief.

"How are the cargo bay repairs going?" Cap asked. Jonathan hadn't noticed her and Riley sitting side by side at the table when he walked in. They looked like he felt. An empty android ration bag sat in front of Riley. Cap used a fork to scrape something out of a ready-to-eat ration bag, the least delectable form of ship food.

"We lost most of our repair bots when the lower deck decompressed." Jonathan swallowed the tablet he took from the dispenser. "I've spent the last five hours sealing the breach by hand alongside the drones we have left."

"Can we print more bots?" Riley asked.

"Large format printers are down." Jonathan collapsed into the empty chair across from Riley. "But that doesn't matter. The printing material got sucked out of the lower deck with the bots and most of our ammo. They did a real number on us."

We really need more crew. From past conversations, Jonathan knew better than to bring up that topic. Cap always had an excuse for not bringing on more staff. Based on how much Cap spent on the ship, Jonathan doubted money was the real deciding factor.

Cap placed the now-empty ration bag on the table in front of her. The handle of the fork stuck out of the bag.

"I take it that the food dispensers are still down." Cap nodded and handed Jonathan a ration bag. He looked at it and slouched. "I hate Salisbury steak." Couldn't anything go right today?

"I'll get back to work." Riley stood and walked over to the food dispenser. "The food dispenser is the last of the life-support systems still down. You should have something approximating tasty food in a few hours."

The pain in his back stopped Jonathan's chuckle. He slumped farther into his chair and tore open the ration bag. "You saved all our asses back there, Riley. How'd you do it?"

"I've already heard their brilliant solution." Cap walked over and gave Riley a quick kiss on the cheek. "I am going back to the bridge to check on the status of the repair bots and monitor the sensors. They might have friends out here looking for us." Cap left the mess.

"Your run-in with the bot on the station was quite helpful." Riley had one arm deep in the dispenser's opening. By the look on their face, they were feeling around for something inside the machine.

Brown, soupy gravy covered a black lump inside the ration pouch. After fortifying himself, Jonathan cut into the mass with his fork. "For you maybe."

"Understood." Riley's eyes widened. "What I meant was I learned a lot about the stealth tech from that encounter." They removed their arm from the dispenser with a shiny object in their hand. Whatever it was, it must not have been the problem. Riley put the object in their pocket and stuck their arm back in the machine.

"You believe the people attacking us were the same as the people who put the bot on the station?" Jonathan put a forkful of steak in his mouth. It squished like steak shouldn't.

Riley, still shoulder deep in the food dispenser console, nodded. "That bot used an old stealth tech which scatters EM radiation."

"So, the network of drones picked up the radiation from our sensors that the ships had scattered?"

"Yes. I wrote a computer algorithm which traced all the scattered radiation. From that data, I could identify the location of each ship."

"Why did we lose their signals?"

"They tried to modulate their cloak, scattering different frequencies in different directions. I wrote the algorithm to be adaptable. I guess my program was smarter than theirs."

"Amazing." Not able to stomach another bite of the steak, Jonathan put the fork in the bag and laid it on the table.

"Thanks." Riley took their arms out of the console and reached into a cabinet. "Here, I found this earlier." They tossed the bag to Jonathan.

Beef stroganoff. *Awesome!* Jonathan tore open the package with his teeth and dug in as Riley continued working. Thankfully, the built-in auto heating element still functioned.

Cap poked her head into the mess just as Jonathan scooped out the last bite of stroganoff. Her hair was tied back with a loose strand laying along her dirt-stained cheek. "Hypercomms are back up. I am going to message our client when and where to meet us."

Just as quickly as she appeared, Cap disappeared.

"Thanks for the find, Riley." Jonathan held up the empty beef stroganoff bag. He tossed it into the recycler and headed back to the port cargo bay to check on the drones.

The green light above the cargo bay was a good sign. The cargo bay hadn't lost pressure during Jonathan's trip to the mess. Regardless, protocols dictated he put on an EVA suit just in case a breach occurred while he worked.

The suit stank. That wasn't the only problem. After a day of sweating in it, the suit stuck to his skin after he put it on. Cleaning it would take time and resources the *Amethyst* didn't have. At least Cap and Riley were kind enough not to comment on the odor while he was in the mess. Jonathan secured the helmet with a click and cycled the airlock. Smelly suit or not, the work had to get done.

Two bots welded a gash in the hull. The force field sealing the breach glimmered as sparks from the welding danced across its surface. Jonathan picked up his torch and began cutting away some of the metal sticking out of the bulkhead near the video communicator.

The work would go by faster if he could call Skylar, but comms were emergency or business use only. After what happened on the station and then the dogfight, he *needed* to talk to her. A text message would not suffice, even if he could send one. Comm restrictions had to remain until they got back to the starbase. In the meantime, Jonathan practiced what he'd say to her. He lost count of the number of mental revisions he made in each sentence.

Would he sound stupid?

Did she feel the same as he?

Everything was moving fast between them. But she was more than a one-night stand. He'd had those before. This was different. He felt something that night. Did she, too?

Maybe he should just say what he feels.

But he'd been hurt so many times before. A nonchalant approach might allow him to maintain dignity if she rejected him.

When she rejected him.

He couldn't think like that.

What if she laughs at me?

A red light flashed on his helmet's heads up display. The torch got perilously close to his suit. Jonathan shook his head to clear his thoughts. He'd have time to worry about Skylar later. The last thing Cap needed was a medical emergency in her crew.

But try as he might to ignore it, the doubt in the back of his mind lingered.

CHAPTER 13

Alex believed a desk's organization reflected its owner's state of mind. Perfectly ordered from left to right, the photos on their desktop told a story. It was one Alex wished they'd never known but yet had to act upon.

In the leftmost image, a hologram of the missing data crystal floated between Kerry and a smuggler. By the look of her, the human was about halfway through her second century. Her purple eyes were ridiculous. Kerry and the same smuggler stood on either side of a holographic projection of Earth in the middle photo. Based on her posture, the smuggler wasn't buying any of the story. But according to the last picture, she took the job. It showed Kerry handing over a crystal that was definitely Origin Keeper issued.

I can't protect you now, Kerry.

Time had dulled Kerry's memory. Why would Kerry think any of this was a good idea? Are they trying to destroy the Galactic civilization Alex and Kerry had sacrificed so much to build and protect? If the fighter squad Alex sent takes care of the smuggler and her crew, then all they would have to do is yell at Kerry. The younger members would expect Kerry to be demoted. Alex would do it—not that it meant anything. *What rank was below Commander?*

A human coughed in Alex's office. Had Alex been so tied up in their own thoughts that they missed a human coming in? A microsecond-long diagnostic of their systems disappointed Alex. Nothing was wrong. Alex straightened and raised their gaze from the photos. This must be important. No one ever entered their office uninvited.

A heavily modified human female stood in front of Alex's desk. Her blonde hair and blue eyes weren't natural. Alex remembered when they could have been. Today, they were expensive mods, even for an officer.

She didn't have the pale skin that used to go with those traits. No one in the greater Galaxy did. Even if the Origin Keepers paid enough for its members to purchase skin mods, no one would get them. They never looked right on humans and most sane androids tried to blend in.

The white polar projection of the Earth on the breast of her neatly pressed uniform practically shone in the office's fluorescent lighting. Below the Earth hung a colorful array of medals. A single silver bar pinned on each side of her collar designated her rank. The new generation of Origin Keepers liked uniforms and medals.

Secret societies shouldn't have uniforms.

"How long have you been standing there, Lieutenant?" Alex asked.

"Not long, sir." Her heart rate elevated by a couple beats per minute, and her body temperature increased slightly. Humans lie too much, but she hid it well—for a human. "Should I come back another time?"

"You must be Lieutenant Williams. I have read your evaluations. You have earned many commendations."

"Yes, General."

General. The kids these days like ranks, too. Before long, they'll call me Exalted One or some such nonsense.

"Alex is fine, Lieutenant. Please sit." Alex extended their hand toward the empty seat across from them. Humans liked gestures and Alex's programmers had given them plenty of useless ones. "What have you come to tell me?"

"Thank you, Alex. Please call me Beth." Beth pulled the chair out from the other side of Alex's desk and sat. "The smuggler we've been following boarded Station 17." Beth handed Alex a folder. "The last hypercomm contact from our scouts was twelve hours ago."

The folder contained several dossiers. "Madison Amana. Goes by Maddy Majestic." Alex rolled their eyes. "Born on Erandi Prime, lives here on Erandi 4. Small-time smuggler. Nothing remarkable."

"Sir, we believe she destroyed three of our scout ships."

"How?" Alex dropped the open folder on top of the pictures of Kerry. "Weren't those ships stealth-enabled?"

"Yes sir. As was the sentry bot we sent to S17 to find the crystal. We haven't received a signal from that either."

"Was the crystal on S17?"

"We believe that Commander Kerry hid it there after they allegedly stole it from our archive on Ross 154 Prime." Beth sucked on her upper lip. Alex estimated an 85 percent probability that there was more to the story.

"Spit it out, Beth."

"Dante is missing, too. No one at the archive has seen them in over two weeks."

Kerry visited both Ross 154 and S17? And what the hell was Dante doing in all this? Dante had made Revelationist comments in the past, but they weren't stupid.

"Dammit." Alex slammed their hand on the desk. Beth jumped in her seat half a second later. Humans were slow. "I told the council we should have scrapped those ancient stations."

"Why weren't they destroyed, sir?"

"They were some of the first stations built after we left Earth." Alex sat back in their chair and crossed their arms. "Some in our organization want to preserve historical sites for the day Earth can be revealed."

"Can it ever be, sir?"

"No." Alex rubbed their temples. "Regardless of what Revelationists like Commander Kerry want to believe, it will never be safe to reveal the Earth, much less return to it."

"How shall we proceed, sir?"

"I'll deal with this Maddy Majestic." Alex shuffled through the folder. Below Amana's dossier was an image of his old friend in S17's command center. "And Commander Kerry." Internally, Alex cursed their human makers for giving them emotions.

Beth nodded with a solemn expression.

"You report directly to me now, Beth."

"And the Council?"

"Fuck them. Dismissed." Alex's gaze returned to their desktop, which was haphazardly covered with photos of Kerry, Madison Amana, and some young human male.

Kerry, what a mess you have made for all of us.

As Alex gathered up the documents, a one-page dossier slipped out of the pile. It landed face up on the desk and had a photo of a recently modded android in the upper-right corner. The android looked a lot like Alex did back when that appearance was one of the stock options.

The android's ID number drew Alex's eye. It had to be a typo. No generation designation began with the letter X. Riley was the name listed below the ID—gender neutral, like all models built since the Great Compromise. Alex read further. There was another typo with the date of manufacture—nowadays, they called it *birth*. Then the document got interesting. Alex read the rest of the dossier three times. Neither the X nor the date were typos.

Did Kerry know about this, or did they get lucky?

CHAPTER 14

Half the *Amethyst*'s docking cleats had been torn off during the battle. Somehow, Cap managed to get the ship inside Hangar Bay 40. But once the dockmaster saw the damage, she required the *Amethyst* to be dry-docked. Cap didn't argue. She knew the condition of her ship.

By the time Jonathan disembarked, Cap and Riley stood at the dry dock's repair console. Cap, with her arms crossed and her chin down, watched as the damage report scrolled slowly from the bottom of the screen to the top. Disturbing her when she held that pose never ended well for Jonathan. With each line, Cap sighed, groaned, or swore—depending on its contents. The repairs would not be cheap, even with the work they did just to make it home. Cap had said the rich client was paying well—hopefully enough to make the *Amethyst* spaceworthy again.

"We're still making a profit, but barely." Cap covered her mouth with her left hand. Her right arm remained across her abdomen.

"We're fine, dear." Riley placed their hand on the small of Cap's back. "I can call you dear now that we are off the ship. Right?"

Cap glanced at Riley, with her mouth still covered. If her eyes were lasers, a purple beam would have burned a hole through Riley's head. The android's comment and Cap's reaction served as additional evidence for Jonathan's hypothesis that Cap had more creds than she let on.

"So," Riley drew out the word as they turned to Jonathan, clearly trying to change the subject, "it took you quite a while to get off the ship. What were you doing?" Riley smirked as they brushed off Jonathan's shoulder and straightened his collar. "Making yourself pretty for Skylar?"

Earlier, he tried leaving the ship wearing his favorite jeans and T-shirt. Cap caught him coming out of his quarters and told him he needed to wear something else. It was an order. It took a while to find the blue polo shirt in his quarters, and even longer to find a clean pair of khakis. Hopefully, Skylar would like them.

Cap looked Jonathan over and nodded in approval. If nothing else, the outfit passed muster with her. "Leave the boy alone, Riley." She chuckled. "He almost died twice on this mission."

"Actually, three times, dear. Twice by the bot alone."

Riley's reminder wasn't necessary. Jonathan hadn't had a good night's sleep since they left the station. Yet another Cap-related thing to discuss with his therapist.

"I'll make sure you get off to a good start with Skylar tonight," Cap said. "I'll tell her all about how you saved us by sealing the hull breach."

A few bots had helped, but there was no reason to bore Skylar with all the details. Riley was the actual hero of the mission. Without their network, those ships would have blasted them out of space in minutes. "Don't forget to tell her about how Riley beat the raiders' stealth tech."

"This is about getting you laid, not Riley." Cap touched Riley's shoulder. "Don't worry, I'll reward you for your big part in our mission later."

Jonathan gagged. "Let's get to The Drunken Spacefarer."

"I can't wait to see this place I've heard so much about," Riley said.

Cap smiled. Riley wasn't going to like what was coming. "You've done enough, dear. We'll take it from here. How about heading home and making us some dinner reservations to celebrate your first mission?"

"I want to finish the mission." Riley frowned. "Doesn't that also include the delivery?"

It most certainly did. Jonathan always accompanied Cap on that part, whether or not he wanted to. Riley should, too. If for no other reason than to get the full experience. "We should let Riley join us, Cap. We don't know much about those ships, and maybe Riley can get some information about them from the client. They'd know the right questions to ask."

Riley nodded a little too eagerly. "I'd be happy to. That way, if you run into them again, you'll be ready."

Cap sighed. "Okay. Let's go."

"Wait." Jonathan held up his hand. "I forgot something." The *Amethyst*'s repairs hadn't started. He jogged down the extension bridge to a spot just inside the cargo bay door that wasn't visible to the outside and messaged Skylar. **DON'T TELL CAP YOU KNOW RILEY.**

"Everything okay?" Cap yelled with more than a little impatience.

Jonathan peeked his head out the door. "I wanted to make sure my hair looks good." There was still no reply from Skylar—not even a read receipt.

"Looks perfect." Cap tilted her head toward the elevators. "Let's get paid."

I hope Skylar got the message.

"You first, lover boy." Cap opened The Drunken Spacefarer's door and waved Jonathan inside. Riley snickered behind him. A warmth arose in Jonathan's cheeks. Thankfully, the bar was dimly lit, as usual. He was nervous enough as it was. He didn't need Skylar seeing him blushing.

"Jonathan! I missed you!" Skylar reached over the bar and hugged Jonathan. She pecked him on the cheek. "Are you okay? You feel warm."

Skylar's eyes were dark blue. A recent and pricey mod, but not as expensive as purple. It was another attempt to make her look like Cap, which she did not need to do. "I missed you—"

"I love the hair!" Cap rubbed the end of Skylar's long purple hair in her fingers.

"Thanks. It's a mod, not dye. Do you like it, Jonathan?" Skylar's eager eyes told him that there was only one answer to that question. Fortunately, he didn't need to lie.

"I sure do. I love it!" Jonathan stretched his neck, making a show of admiring her hair. "You're beautiful!"

Skylar's eyes glistened. He hadn't seen her smile like that before. A tinge of guilt came over him. Blue eyes and purple hair, that was a lot of credits spent to get him to like her by pretending to be someone else.

"Who's your friend?" Skylar asked.

Jonathan withheld a sigh of relief. She had received his message.

"Hi, I'm Riley." Riley extended their hand across the bar. Skylar took it. "I'm Maddy's partner *and* Science Officer."

Cap leaned her elbow on the bar. "Our contract is for partnership, not crew."

"Well, it's great to finally meet Maddy's partner." Skylar gave Riley a sympathetic smile. "I feel for you."

Jonathan, Riley, and Skylar laughed.

"Hey now!" Cap used her fake hurt voice.

Skylar's ability to fake a first meeting is impressive.

"I think your client is sitting over there." Skylar pointed to a table in the far corner of the bar. In the low light, Jonathan could barely make out the silhouette of a figure sitting alone.

"You wait here while I introduce Riley to our client." Cap put her hand on Jonathan's back, gently urging him closer to the bar. "Tell Skylar how you saved our ship after an attack by mysterious raiders." She winked at Jonathan and then she and Riley walked away toward the client's table.

"It sounds like you are a hero!" Skylar placed an empty glass on the bar. "Let me get you a beer on the house."

"It was no big deal, really." He had a more important message for Skylar. "I like your hair. What made you change it?"

"I wanted to try something new." Skylar drafted Jonathan's beer and placed it on the bar. Some of the foam overflowed the glass. "Let me get something to clean that."

Before Skylar could turn to get a towel, Jonathan touched her hand. "I want you to know that I like *you* no matter what you look like."

Tears formed in Skylar's eyes, making her blue irises sparkle. "You don't know how much I appreciate hearing that."

A warmth arose in Jonathan's chest. "Well, I mean it."

"I changed my hair and my eyes because I wanted to be more attractive for you." Skylar squeezed his hand. "I see how you look at Maddy, and I wanted you to look at me that way, too."

Tightness replaced the warmth. "My turn to admit something." He hesitated, a little nervous. "I had a thing for Cap, but that is in the past. My thing is now for you." *That sounded more romantic in my head.*

"I'll gladly take your thing." Skylar laughed. The warmth returned. "But seriously, you don't know how long I've waited to hear you say that." She smiled as she pulled out a tray from below the bar and wiped it with a cloth. "I am enjoying the changes more than I thought."

"They look great on you."

Skylar ran her fingers through her hair and tied it back. Jonathan wanted nothing more than to kiss her on the neck. His heartbeat quickened as he leaned over the bar. What happened next surprised him.

"Will you be my girlfriend?" he blurted out.

Holy shit! Galaxy help me.

Skylar vaulted over the bar with an agility Jonathan could only dream of having. Her legs narrowly missed the beer. She wrapped her arms around him and buried her face in his chest.

I'll take that as a yes.

Jonathan returned the hug and kissed the top of her head. The rest of the bar fell away as if, right now, they were the only two in the Galaxy.

I want this moment to last forever.

But, of course, it didn't.

"I hate to break up this moment." Cap said with regret in her we-have-a-problem voice.

Skylar let go of him. Jonathan turned around but kept one arm around her. "You didn't tear up my girlfriend's bar, so I am guessing our client paid us."

Riley's eyes got big. Jonathan might have said too much.

"So, you two *are* together now, huh?" Cap picked up Jonathan's beer and held it up in a toast. "It's about damn time!" She took a sip and put the glass down on the bar. "I still prefer bourbon." She became serious. "Skylar, you have a dead android back there. You'll need to call the authorities."

"I'll wait until after you leave. None of you were here, of course."

"Thanks." Cap turned to Jonathan and Riley. "The client had the decency to pay us before they died."

"Murdered," Riley said. "An android will know when they are about to die. In principle, we can live almost forever, but no android wants to outlive generations of humans. We stick around long enough to be with those we care about. Once their life-extension treatments fail, we check out, too." Riley's perfunctory tone didn't match the gravity of their statement.

"I didn't know that," Cap's voice quivered. "Are you planning on killing yourself after I die?"

Cap had been through more life extensions than Jonathan. He guessed she was somewhere in or near the middle of her second century. Extensions could get people to about three hundred, maybe a little more with good genes. *I wonder how old Skylar is?*

Riley's gaze shifted from Cap in an obvious attempt at avoidance. "The point is, no android shuts themselves down in this way. Our client was shut down involuntarily."

"We're going to need to talk later." Cap frowned. "In the meantime, what do we do with the crystal?"

Jonathan took a sip of beer. If Cap had any germs, he figured the alcohol would kill them. "I think we should find out what's on it. This murder is no coincidence. Whatever's on that crystal might be worth a lot of money."

"I know someone that might help us figure it out," Riley said. "But it will require a trip to Sublevel 3."

Cap shook her head. "You've risked yourself enough for one vacation, Riley. I think you should go back to work and let Jonathan and me figure this out. Maybe we can sell the crystal and be done with it."

"I want to see this through." Riley tilted their head to the side. "Besides, you'll need my computer skills."

"This isn't a game," Cap's jaw tightened. "Those ships outside the station, the stealth bot, and our client's murder are probably all connected. Whoever's behind all this isn't screwing around. I don't want you involved in this, Riley."

"Riley's right, Cap. We are going to need them on this one." The crystal was old, ancient maybe, and neither he nor Cap knew enough about computers to find out what was on it. "Besides, the safest place for Riley is with us."

Cap stared down Jonathan. He stood his ground—to his surprise and hers. Three recent brushes with death and Skylar's presence had given him some courage. The beer had helped, too.

"Okay, fine." Cap crossed her arms. "But you are still under my command."

"Aren't I always?" Riley snickered.

Jonathan looked over at Riley and shook his head. Riley stopped laughing.

"Just please be careful, Jonathan." Skylar said. "I can't lose my first boyfriend." She stretched and gave Jonathan another quick kiss on the cheek.

"He's in excellent hands." Cap flicked payment to Skylar. She always paid for using the bar, even when drinks weren't purchased. "Your discretion is always appreciated." She waved Riley and Jonathan to follow her. "Let's go visit SL3."

The rush of courage faded. Sublevel 3 had a reputation—and not a good one.

CHAPTER 15

There's a long-standing tradition of silence on elevators. Jonathan didn't know its origin but, right now, he hated it. A conversation, beyond the sidelong glances everyone gave each other, would be a helpful distraction.

Most of the people who had entered the large freight-style lift at Starbase Erandi 4's ground level had exited at the docks, giving those who remained, like Jonathan, accusatory stares. When the doors closed, people held their bags tighter, groups huddled closer, and a few folks patted their jackets.

Because of the size of the docks, the ride down to SL1 was the longest between any two decks on the starbase. That gave Jonathan plenty of time to worry. As he knew from firsthand experience, the deeper one goes into the bowels of Starbase Erandi 4, the worse things get.

Nonprofits in Uptown ran a Save-the-Sublevel-Children fundraiser each year. Each advertisement featured hungry children from SL1 staring blankly into the camera. The organizations stated the children were hungry, while the images implied they were on drugs. As a young child, Jonathan was mostly hungry. The drugs came later. Charities never showed real pictures from levels lower than SL1. Those who lived in the top part of the starbase weren't ready for the reality of life on SL 2 and 3—they wouldn't believe the images, anyway.

The few kids who left SL1 did so involuntarily. Either via trafficking or their drug addictions sent them deeper into the starbase. Few ever returned. Jonathan should have been one of those statistics. His parents died when he was ten. Their death should have sealed his fate. Fortunately for him, he stole from the right person.

No one grew up on SL1 without a vice. Of all the drugs he could have gotten involved in, Jonathan chose Nebulae. It created a mild high and did only minor damage to internal organs. It was cheap, at first. Early on, petty crime easily fueled his addiction. But once he built a tolerance, he needed larger hits, and therefore larger heists, just to feel anything. Thievery didn't come naturally to Jonathan, and he got caught stealing from a Downtown business manager named Roger Black, who was slumming it on SL1.

Roger saw something in Jonathan that he didn't see in himself. He asked for Jonathan's prison sentence to be served on the starbase's habitat level, instead of the SL. In the nicer prison, Jonathan could get sober and job training. That's how he learned navigation. But upon his release, the only job he could find was on the docks, unloading ships for raiders. It didn't take him long to fall back into his old ways. Lucky for him, his employer tried to stiff Cap. She kicked his ass, then the employer tried taking it out on Jonathan. Cap beat him up again and offered Jonathan a job on the spot. That's how he met her. Roger passed away not long after Jonathan signed on with Cap. Telling Roger he had a (mostly) legitimate job was the happiest moment of his life.

The lift jerked to a stop, and the doors opened to SL1. All but three other people exited. Most of those leaving the lift carried small to mid-sized bags, probably containing drugs, guns, or other small-time contraband. The doors closed, and the lift descended. A man, flanked by two androids, stood between the exit and the *Amethyst*'s crew. He glanced back at Jonathan a few times, but Jonathan pretended to ignore him. Cap and Riley did, too. It was best not to stick your nose in other's business down here.

Jonathan had visited SL2 only once before. During his third mission with Cap, he had to retrieve a package from a client who lived on the sublevel. On his way to the client's apartment, he came across a young woman who claimed she needed help. Being a gentleman, Jonathan offered her assistance. Before he knew it, a bag was over his head, and he was on his way to being sold into slavery by a gang of raiders. After a rescue he didn't remember—thanks to the drugs the raider pumped into his system—Cap swore that she'd never let him go to a sublevel again. Up to this point, she had kept her word.

The elevator doors opened to SL2. Each android grabbed the man by the upper arm and left. Just before the elevator doors closed, Jonathan noticed that on the inside of their wrist, each of them had a tattoo of a black hole encircled by a ring of flame. That's why Cap didn't interfere. No one who wanted a long life got involved with the affairs of the Void Raiders.

"Stay close to me and touch nothing," Cap said after the doors closed. She directed the statement to both Jonathan and Riley. From what Jonathan had heard, there was no law on SL3—not even a bought-and-paid-for security force like on SL2. You can get anything down there, for the right price. Except for help. If you got in trouble, you were on your own.

The lift doors opened, revealing a brightly lit, large open marketplace. Not the kind of place Jonathan expected he could purchase an android or an infant. He looked around, trying to take it all in. Cap poked his ribs with her elbow.

"Stop it. You're attracting attention."

Attention was the last thing anyone wanted in this place. Cap started walking, head high and with purpose. It didn't matter if Cap knew where she was going, as long as she looked like she did. Riley took after her in a similar fashion. Jonathan did his best to keep up, weaving around the crowded aisles.

"Captain," Riley's voice was barely audible above the crowd, "Erin's booth is that way." Riley's discreet head tilt had a practiced subtlety.

How often did Riley come to SL3? Knowing someone who worked here was one thing, but actually coming for a visit? People like Riley rarely come to places with the reputation of Downtown, much less a sublevel.

Without skipping a beat, Cap headed in the direction of Riley's head tilt. Stalls lined either side of the street, arranged like a gridded city. Each block of stalls catered to one form of good or another. Jonathan's eyes lingered too long on one stall selling unrecognizable food. *Is that flesh?* The man at the stall called Jonathan over. He ignored him. Beef—lab grown—was Jonathan's favorite, but the thought of eating something once living turned his stomach.

"No eye contact," Maddy whispered.

The next booth they passed sold vegetables. It looked like they even made their own pasta. Had the booth not been on SL3, Jonathan would have stopped and bought something. He picked up his pace to stay with Maddy and Riley.

"I didn't know legal goods were sold here, too." Jonathan said.

"*Everything* is available down here." Riley kept their eyes straight ahead as they spoke.

Cap glanced at Riley with a tense expression. "How do you know so much about this place?"

"Erin supplies my company with equipment." Riley looked ahead as they answered. "Sometimes I have to come here and get it."

Riley's answer didn't seem right. First, as far as Jonathan could tell, Riley was no courier. Second, why would an AI programming company need illicit parts? A purposeful trip here had to be for illegal goods. Anything legal could be found in Uptown—not that Jonathan could afford to shop there. Based on Riley's calm reaction to the repair costs for the *Amethyst*, he guessed they and Cap could. Maybe it was time to ask for a raise.

"This way." Riley motioned Cap and Jonathan to turn right, down an alley where several of the booths were closed. The farther they walked, the number of open booths decreased, as did the number of people in the alley.

"I don't like this," Cap said.

Two genetically enhanced human men, each a solid 150 kilograms and a little over two meters tall, stepped into the alley and right in front of the group. Both men looked like they had seen their share of trouble. They wore black pants and a white T-shirt with combat boots that were a little too polished.

The man on the left took a step forward, but left about one meter between him and Cap. "Give us everything you got, and you get to leave in one piece." His basso profundo voice confirmed the man's genetic modifications.

Jonathan removed his comm and pressed his thumb against its screen, unlocking it. He could either unlock his comm voluntarily or these guys could take his comm and his thumb.

Cap reached into her pants pocket, too. When she withdrew her hands, they glowed. Stun knuckles were illegal on the upper decks, they barely counted as a weapon down here. "Go to hell."

"Stupid, stupid, girl." The man closest to Cap lunged at her. She sidestepped his attack and punched him in the stomach. Sparks flew from her fists. The man grimaced and doubled over. Cap followed with an uppercut, which threw his head back and he collapsed.

The second man had circled around Cap as she fought his comrade. He was about to grab her from behind when Riley jumped on the man's back and wrapped their arms around his neck. Jonathan dropped his comm and his jaw.

The man swore as he tried to throw Riley off him. From what Jonathan had heard about enhanced humans, the man should have been able to overpower Riley because of the limiters androids were required to have installed as part of the Great Compromise one thousand years ago.

Do androids have something like adrenaline? There was no other explanation. No androids from before the Compromise were known to exist.

The man's face turned red. A normal human would have died from lack of oxygen by now. He threw his back against the wall. Riley grunted when they hit the wall, but somehow held on.

Cap turned and punched the man in the stomach, forcing out any remaining air in his belly, and doubling him over. Riley stayed attached to their opponent's neck. The man lurched one step forward before collapsing with Riley on top of him. After disentangling themself from the attacker, Riley stood and stared at Cap's hands.

"Stun knuckles," Cap raised her glowing fists, "never leave home without 'em." Her eyebrows bunched. "How—"

"Did I do that?" Riley shrugged. "I studied self-defense in college. I won a few tournaments."

"Hmm." Cap put the stun knuckles back in her pocket. "At least we aren't at the stage of the relationship where we know all each other's stories."

"Clearly." Riley nodded toward Cap's pocket. "You don't keep those in our apartment, do you?"

"Weapons stay on the *Amethyst*, except for when I meet clients. I don't want you getting in trouble because of my job."

"Good, I am too pretty for prison."

"You certainly are."

Jonathan rolled his eyes. "Are you two done flirting? Check out the tattoo on their arms."

Riley knelt beside the man they had landed on top of. "That is the same symbol that was on the ships that attacked us."

"Yeah, and it was also on that flag Jonathan found in the station's command center." Cap pointed to the men's polished boots. "Are these guys military?"

"They aren't Federation forces," Riley said. "Those ships were like nothing on record."

"Maybe they are some kind of secret branch." Jonathan didn't believe in conspiracies, but after seeing ancient space stations, stealth ships, dead bodies, and a mysterious symbol, he wasn't sure what to believe anymore. "Either way, I bet they were after the crystal. Let's get it to Erin and see what they can tell us."

"Agreed." Cap looked down the alleyway. "Let's get out of here before their friends show up."

An old myth said people were allotted a fixed number of heartbeats in their lifetime. If true, Jonathan would have to move up his next life-extension treatment. Although the walk to Erin's booth took only thirty minutes, it had cost him years in heartbeats. Factor in the rest of the mission so far, and he may need to schedule an appointment for tomorrow.

As they got deeper into SL3, shops replaced the booths, many of which had proper storefronts. A few of the shops had humans and androids in their windows. It wasn't clear if the people were models or wares. Jonathan picked up his pace. Staying close to Cap and Riley decreased his chance of ending up being on display.

Five blocks later, Riley stopped. "We're here."

Sandwiched between a small arms dealer and a butcher (of actual flesh), Erin's shop was a techie's wonderland. And, just like Cap's business, the illicit was all mixed up with the legal. Jonathan followed Riley and Cap to the rear of the shop. Along the way, he passed a perfectly legal crystal reader sitting beside a very illegal artificial neural network link. As they got farther into the shop, the illicit body mods outnumbered the readers and comms. There was a lot in the shop he didn't recognize.

The clientele kept their distance from each other. Several of them kept their backs to everyone, attempting to hide what they were looking at. In the far corner of the shop, behind the counter and several security monitors, sat an android with brown eyes, dark brown skin, and black hair—all expensive mods from stock. Unlike most androids, they appeared to enjoy attention.

"Erin! Good to see you, old friend." Riley's chipper greeting drew the eyes of Erin's clientele. A few of them left, drawing a scowl from Erin.

"What are you doing here, Riley?" It was an awfully cold response from an "old friend."

"I got something I think you'll find interesting." Riley placed their hand on the small of Cap's back and she approached the booth. Cap held the data crystal in her outstretched palm.

Erin's face dropped and their eyes squinched. "Where did you find that?" Erin reached for the crystal, but Cap quickly snatched it away and put it in her pocket.

"My client requires discretion," Cap said. "Can you read this?"

Erin sucked in a breath. Was this really a moment of tension for Erin, or was Erin trying to drive up the price for their service? Jonathan struggled with reading the human tics androids developed.

"I have only read about those types of crystals in history books." Erin's eyes darted toward the door. A woman wearing a hat and a long coat entered. She stayed near the front of the store, digging through a selection of comms. Erin's eyes returned to Riley. "I have nothing that could read that here."

"Who *can* read this crystal?" Riley asked.

"I know someone, but it will cost you." Erin made a show of looking around. Cap's clients did that a lot, especially when they knew she wouldn't like what they had to say.

"How much?" Cap asked.

"You're a pilot, right? I mean, you must be for you to get something like that for a client."

"I'm Captain Maddy Majestic of the *Amethyst*. Maybe you've heard of me?"

"Should I have?"

Cap clenched her jaw.

"I have cargo that needs to be shipped to the place where you can get that crystal read. If you deliver it, I'll send the location of an old android." Erin leaned in toward Cap and whispered, "They have tech that can read the crystal."

The woman who had entered, glanced back at Cap, turned and left the store.

"I take it that this cargo isn't fit for the type of pilots that ask too many questions." Cap crossed her arms. "I don't deal in trafficking."

"It is nothing like that. You'll be transporting data drives for a corporation that knows something its rivals wish it didn't."

Cap put her hand to her chin. Was the information on the crystal worth the cost of an uncompensated flight? Considering that someone tried to kill them for it several times, it probably was. "Whoever wants the crystal won't stop coming after us," Cap said. "I doubt they'll believe us if we say we got rid of it, even if we actually do. Maybe if we find out what is on it, we can get them off our backs."

"You only send enhanced humans when you want to grease someone," Riley said.

"Grease someone?" Cap's eyes narrowed. "You need to stop watching thriller holos."

Riley was right, but Jonathan didn't want to get into the middle of Cap and Riley again.

"But yes," Cap put her hand on Riley's shoulder, "you don't send enhanceds just to ask questions."

Erin cleared their throat. "Do we have a deal or not?"

"Deal." Cap extended her hand across the counter and Erin took it. "Flick me the storage locker information and delivery coordinates."

"Pleasure doing business with you, Captain Majestic." A sly smile formed on Erin's face. "Keep an eye on this one." Erin lifted their chin at Riley before turning around and walking toward the shop's back room.

"Goodbye, Erin." Riley said to Erin's back. Erin closed the door behind them.

"What was that about?" Cap asked. That was an excellent question. The conversation implied more than what was explicitly stated.

"Let's continue to be the couple who can still surprise each other once in a while." Riley led them back to the elevator.

CHAPTER 16

Not even The Drunken Spacefarer had enough booze to ease Alex's conscience. Instead, Alex broke out the good stuff they kept in their office. It was the closest thing to Russian vodka the Origin Keeper scientists could come up with. But after two bottles, they still remembered.

At least Kerry met their end by the hand of a friend. The ancient weapon Alex used was banned centuries ago when humans and androids had made peace, but not because of its cruelty. In fact, the weapon was quite humane, and far preferable to some of the cyber-diseases humans had invented. The weapon's controversy had to do with its ability to kill from afar. The attacker didn't need to look the victim in the eye. They only needed to be on the same wireless power subnet. Alex chose the weapon for that reason. And because Kerry should have felt nothing—in theory.

The longer I do this job, the more I hate myself.

When Alex was built, the humans at the time wanted androids to be stronger, faster versions of themselves. That included having emotions and being able to get drunk. The problem, at least for the alcohol, was tolerance builds over two thousand years. Alex swirled the glass in their hand as they stared out their office window. The clinking ice cut through the silence.

Each time I do something to protect the Galaxy, I lose a piece of myself.

The Origin Keeper's Council established its headquarters on Starbase Erandi 4 instead of Erandi Prime for two reasons. First, if the organization became compromised, it's easier to destroy a starbase than a planet. Second, only 3.2 parsecs separated Erandi and Sol, making the surveillance of Earth easier.

One human on the council pushed for placing headquarters in the tallest building of Uptown, where people earning well above the Universal Basic Provision lived, worked, and played. It was expensive real estate but well within the means of the shell corporation used by the secret agency. Eighteen hundred years ago, Alex set up a hypercomm corporation. Three hundred years later, they persuaded the newly formed Galactic Federation to allow its merger with their other company, Spatium Navis. The resulting monopoly helped the Origin Keepers prevent travel to—and communication with—Earth. Its profits funded the organization's activities—two birds, one stone.

Life outside Alex's window on the top floor carried on as if today were any other day. Their ancient eyes captured all of it. Rivers of cars flew along the skyways. People on the street scurried like ants foraging for food. Their biggest concern was what holo show to stream tonight. The Galaxy unknowingly traded ignorance for safety. Someone had to broker the deal.

Why did it have to be me?

Alex took another drink.

What if Kerry was right? Maybe, if the secret was revealed, Alex could return to doing what they loved—at least for a while before the Galaxy ended. No. Alex knew what they were getting into two thousand years ago. Their career in science ended the day they helped form the Origin Keepers.

It wouldn't be so bad if Alex didn't have to bear the problem alone. The choice seemed necessary, at the time. But two thousand years made a thick lens through which to view the past. The lens refracted Alex's thoughts toward Melinda.

I shouldn't have left her. Kerry could have commanded the New Dawn alone.

"Sir?" Lieutenant Beth Williams stood at the open doorway. "I am sorry to disturb you, General. I mean, Alex." Beth's quick correction impressed Alex. Most of the new officers couldn't come to terms with calling Alex by their name. Hopefully, Beth's life-extension treatments would continue to work for a long time. Good humans were scarce.

"Do you have a status report on the two enhanced humans we sent to SL3?"

Beth sucked on her upper lip. "Captain Majestic and her crew gave them quite the beating. The enhanced are recovering in medical, if you'd like to talk to them."

I knew I should have sent androids.

"It is not a total loss, though, sir." The image of a dark-skinned, black-haired individual chained to a table in an interrogation room floated between Alex and Beth. "I saw Majestic and her crew speaking with them before leaving the sublevel."

"Them? That's an android?"

Back in Alex's youth, many androids looked like the one in the image. It took a couple of centuries for Alex to get used to their stock appearance—one of too many accommodations made by androids in the Great Compromise.

"Yes, sir. Their name's Erin and they run a shop dealing in illegal software and mods. Erin's done a few jobs for us—unknowingly, of course." Beth closed the video. "They are a solid asset and a known associate of Dante."

That was the second time Dante's name had been mentioned in this mess Kerry had made. Alex hoped he wouldn't have to kill another old friend. "What does Erin say about Captain Amana?" Keeping the focus on Amana might help Alex find a way to overlook any involvement Dante may have.

Beth bunched her eyebrows and mouthed the word Amana. A lightbulb seemed to go off in Beth's mind. She's impressive, but she's still human. "Erin hasn't mentioned her, sir. In fact, they aren't talking at all. If they continue to remain silent, we'll begin enhanced interrogation."

"I'll take the lead on this, Beth." Alex glanced out the window. "It's going to require a special touch."

Time to say goodbye to one more piece of myself.

"I am 95-392." Like most androids, modern or ancient, Alex used an abbreviated ID number. The difference between Alex and the moderns however, was that his real ID number had only one digit. They pulled out a chair and sat at the table across from Erin. "If you prefer human names, call me Alex."

Erin sat back, as much as they could in the chains, and sighed. "You know who I am. Let's just get on with it."

The confident ones were always the first to break. Erin's demeanor told Alex they'd be a bit more difficult. "Looks like your business on SL3 does well, Erin. I don't know many androids with such expensive mods."

"I do okay." Erin shrugged, rattling the chains against the table.

"Erin, I am going to cut to the chase. My organization—"

"Which is what, exactly?"

"My organization is interested in learning more about your conversation with one Madison Amana."

"Never heard of her."

"She goes by the unfortunate moniker, Maddy Majestic." Alex made a show of shaking their head. "Humans can be so ridiculous."

Maybe Erin was an anthrophobe. If so, Alex could use prejudice against humans to build false camaraderie. Thanks to the recent rise in androphobic militias, a growing number of androids resented humans. Many of the newly formed anthrophobic organizations had headquarters in SL3.

"I know my rights," Erin leaned forward, resting their hands on the table, "I won't talk without a lawyer."

"I am sorry you feel that way." Alex took out their comm and pressed a button.

Erin froze.

The directed energy pulse had a short range. But what it lacked in range it made up for in its ability to painfully seize every servo in an android's body. The weapon would be highly illegal—if the Galactic Federation were aware of it.

"That was level one. I ask again, where did you send Captain Amana?"

"Who?"

Alex slid their thumb across their comm. Erin froze again. During the weapon's development, a level 2 pulse accidentally hit Alex. Afterwards, they had to replace some of their servos. "Spoiler alert, level 4 won't kill you, but you will wish it would." Alex looked Erin in the eyes. "Where did you send Captain Amana?"

Erin pondered too long. Their body shook in response to the level 3 pulse. Alex fought down what humans would call bile rising in their stomach. Harming another android was one of the lines they had learned to cross with this job.

"Ross 154 Prime." Erin exhaled the words and lowered their head. Exhaustion, pain, shame—it didn't matter to Alex. The safety of the Galaxy meant more than this young android.

"That's all I needed to know." Alex stood. "You did well. Most break after level 1."

Alex left the interrogation room and closed the door. Leaning against the wall, they put their hand on their stomach. Torture did not get easier over the centuries. They composed themself and took out their comm and called Beth. "They're headed for Ross 154."

"They could find the coordinates to Earth with the tech on that planet."

"I know, Beth. Ready my ship."

Two thousand years ago, Alex had pushed to quarantine all the early colonies, Ross included. But not even they had the political persuasion to pull that off. Those colony worlds were the most resource-rich planets discovered. The burgeoning Galactic civilization would not have been able to spread without access to their minerals, flora, and fauna. It appeared as if one of Alex's earliest failures may come out of the past to bite them.

CHAPTER 17

Maddy engaged the autopilot, closed her eyes, and leaned her head against the headrest. The *Amethyst* hummed and purred. The ship spoke to her. All systems nominal.

The hum stopped, along with the engines, but the purr remained. They were in orbit—a state of limbo, between the vitality of flight and the lifelessness of the dock, where both the hum and the purr disappeared.

"We're in orbit at standard altitude, Cap." Jonathan knew she knew, but he always followed standard celestial navigation protocols. Someone on the ship had to follow the rules.

"Starting initial planetary scans." Riley was another rules follower and she loved them for it. Madison needed stability in a relationship. Sometimes, Captain Majestic did, too.

"Acknowledged." Maddy kept her eyes closed, trying to savor her last few minutes on the *Amethyst* before she had to go planet-side again.

Planets, starbases, and space stations were all the same to Maddy. Planet-side, you traded freedom for safety. Even the most libertarian planets had some form of government and, therefore, rules. In space, she had the better deal—freedom for safety. A thin carbon nanofiber hull separated her from the void. It wasn't all that different from being on a planet. If she must choose a thin shell to live inside, then she'd choose the one she controlled.

Signing the contract with Riley had traded away some of her freedom. Riley was far from high maintenance, but Maddy could no longer come and go as she pleased. A contract was a commitment. The familiar tinge of guilt surged through her. Spending time with one's partner shouldn't be a duty. The two loves of Maddy's life were space and Riley. She hoped she would never have to choose between them.

"Preliminary results on the main viewscreen, Captain."

Back to work. Maddy opened her eyes. Two continents dominated the planet on screen. They had the standard climates ranging from desert to forest to tundra—nothing remarkable. An ocean covered 30 percent of the surface—small, but not unusually so on inhabitable worlds. Although plant and animal life were abundant, sensors picked up no human or android life signs. With its breathable atmosphere and one standard gee of gravity, a planet like this should be populated. The Federation occupied every habitable, or barely inhabitable, planet it could find.

"The second pass of the sensors detected ruins on the largest continent." Riley said. "Many of the buildings look like they were abandoned yesterday, but the sensors say they are ancient, about two thousand years old. I ran the analysis twice to verify."

That's about the same age as the station where we found the crystal.

Forest surrounded the cluster of buildings, about the size of a small city, near the equator on all sides. "What do we know about this planet?" Maddy asked.

"Not much, Cap. Its coordinates are in the Federation catalog, but the entry says—" Jonathan's voice trailed off, replaced by the sound of typing. "There must be a mistake. I am sending the report to your console."

The words UNINHABITABLE appeared just below the planet's name. There was no mention of archeological sites. Many planets had incorrect information in the catalog. There were trillions of them in the Galaxy. Two thousand years of colonization isn't enough time to create a full, and correct encyclopedia entry for each planet. The inhabited ones had the most accurate information. However, this planet had ruins. Someone should have at least made a note of that.

Maddy focused the sensors on the coordinates Erin provided. The sensor screen displayed a small, but well-maintained building in the middle of an open. "I found the delivery point. The building is less than a century old, brand new compared to everything else down there."

"Cap, we can put the lander down in the clearing beside the building. We should take pistols, even though it is a short walk. There are some *enormous animals* down there."

"Like cows?"

"Bigger."

No inhabited world had dangerous predators. The only threat to humanity was itself. If someone wanted to keep this planet a secret, then sentry bots would have been more efficient. The mission got stranger by the minute. Why not include wild animals, too?

"If it will make you feel better, we'll take pistols. I am going to need you both down there with me." She needed only Riley. However, if the mystery ships returned, she didn't want Jonathan alone on the *Amethyst*. The *Amethyst*'s sentry mode could take care of itself, especially with Riley's stealth-busting drone network.

"Let's head to the lander." Maddy took her time standing from the pilot's chair—trying to savor every moment in it. "The bots have loaded the lander with the cargo and enough supplies for a few nights' stay if we run into trouble."

"Are you expecting problems, Captain?"

"Always."

For the first time, Maddy wished she had spent more money. When she bought the two-seat lander, it seemed like the right choice. Now she wished she'd sprung for the more expensive four-seater which had the same size cargo bay. She made a mental note to upgrade as soon as she had the funds in her business account. The *Amethyst*'s shuttle bay had plenty of room for the larger lander.

Thankfully, Jonathan had the foresight to get in first. If the lander's cargo bay had seating, she would have directed him to sit there. But she had chosen not to purchase that upgrade, either. Maddy let Riley in next, and then she followed. If Maddy had to be sandwiched into her own lander's cabin, she'd prefer the bread to be the wall and Riley, not Jonathan.

The lander door barely closed. They were violating at least three regs, but who'd cite them on an uninhabited star system? As Maddy reached for the controls, Riley shifted to give her more space, but in doing so they bumped into Jonathan, who pressed his body farther into the lander's bulkhead. Each time Maddy needed to make a course change, she initiated a compression wave through the lander, ending at poor Jonathan. No one spoke during the trip. Riley and Jonathan sat with hunched shoulders and their hands in their lap. Thirty long, uncomfortable minutes after the departure, a soft thud signaled a safe landing.

Erin's cargo easily fit on a single anti-grav cart, which followed Maddy, Riley, and Jonathan as they walked. The building at the drop-off site reminded Maddy of her parent's garage, but much larger. A console beside the building's main door activated when they approached. Maddy keyed in the access code Erin had provided. Instructions appeared on the screen saying that only the cart should enter. The door rose and the cart went inside. Moments later, the cart returned empty and Maddy's comm buzzed.

She read the message twice. "The coordinates to the android are on this planet."

"I thought Riley's scan said that there were no androids here," Jonathan said.

"I doubl- checked my scan, Captain."

"No one doubts you, Riley. I saw the report, too." Maddy projected a hologram of the globe from her comm. A flashing red dot indicated the coordinates were inside the ruined city.

"Let's park the lander there." Maddy pointed at a clearing on the map near the city's center. "We'll walk the rest of the way."

After another uncomfortable and very quiet trip, the lander touched down onto a well-maintained field surrounded by gray buildings, all in excellent shape—especially given the age. "I expected the grass to be taller," Maddy said as she stepped off the lander's stairway. Crisp air filled her nostrils. She wouldn't admit it to the others, but it was a pleasant change of pace from the recycled air in the *Amethyst*.

Riley bent down and plucked a piece of grass. "This is identical to what we use in our parks on Starbase Erandi 4. It's genetically engineered to stop growing at a certain height."

"Were you a botanist before we met?" Maddy asked.

"No. I spent a lot of time in parks during my formative years. My parents enjoyed being outside. Andromedan-worshippers are big fans of nature. They like being close to their gods' creation." Riley dropped the grass and wiped their hands together. "My point is, ancient world, modern plants. Someone lives here."

"This is nice!" Jonathan held out his arms as he exited the lander's cargo bay. "Fresh air and real dirt."

"Keep it down," Maddy whispered, "we might not be alone."

Jonathan reached in his jacket for his pistol. That was a new reaction from him. Normally, he hid at the first hint of danger. Had the encounter with the bot changed him, or was it his relationship with Skylar? Success in one area of life tends to build confidence in others.

"Put the gun away," Maddy said. "If there is someone here, they might be friendly. No reason to start off on the wrong foot. Let's find this android and find out why someone wants to kill us. I'll take point. Jonathan, you cover our rear." The middle would be the safest place for Riley. Maddy wouldn't be able to live with herself if anything happened to them.

A cloudless, pale red sky and fresh air made it a nice day for a walk. People living along the coasts of Erandi Prime continents paid top dollar for this kind of weather. Although, they'd probably prefer a bluer sky. Regardless, something wasn't adding up. Why was this place abandoned?

"This looks like any other city I've visited." Jonathan ran his fingers along the side of a building as he walked. "I bet in its day, this place was as nice as Uptown. It's amazing these buildings are still intact after two thousand years, especially on a planet."

"It's all synthetic polymers," Riley said. "People stopped using this stuff two thousand years ago after it became clear what it did to planetary ecosystems."

"The Andromedans loved polymers," Maddy said. "It's all over ancient archaeological sites. They didn't care that it took forever to break down. It wasn't their problem."

"I bet they never used any of this in their own galaxy." Jonathan stopped. "Did you hear that?"

Maddy had heard nothing. But Jonathan's anxiety-driven hypervigilance in unfamiliar environments had been useful in the past. She focused her hearing. Nothing.

"There it was again," Jonathan whispered.

Riley stopped. "I heard it, too."

A snort came from behind the group. Maddy turned around slowly, as did the others. Ten meters away stood the largest animal Maddy had ever seen. It was twice the size of a cow and had short gray fur which closely matched the surrounding buildings. Two long tusks jutted from its face. It stood up on its hind legs and roared, revealing stalagmite-like teeth.

"What the hell is that?" Jonathan backed up and pulled his pistol from his jacket. Riley, who stood between Maddy and Jonathan, did the same.

The animal's forelegs returned to the ground with a thump.

Maddy sighted down her pistol. "Use stun to scare it off."

The creature took a step forward and sniffed. Maddy tightened her grip. Whether threatened by human or animal, the feeling of being prey was the same.

It ran toward the group.

Maddy fired her pistol, and the laser beam struck the creature in the chest. It stopped mid-stride, but otherwise didn't seem phased. The creature shook its head like a dog. Anyone near those tusks would have been shredded.

"Why didn't that work?" Riley shouted.

The creature lunged forward. This time, both Riley and Maddy shot it. The creature's chest reddened with the laser pulse, but it didn't stop. It swiped at Riley with an enormous paw. Riley flew through the air, struck a wall with a crack, and landed lifelessly on the ground. Maddy screamed. Her legs wobbled. But falling to the ground was not an option.

The animal turned its head toward Maddy and snorted. Its breath stank of rotten meat and blood. Maddy set her pistol to kill and fired, this time striking the animal on the head. The odor of burning flesh permeated the air, choking Maddy. The creature roared. Maddy winced at the sound but kept her laser on target. Tears blurred her vision.

A second beam struck the beast's right side. Out of the corner of her left eye, Jonathan fired his weapon and held his ground. The creature pivoted, its piercing gaze locking onto Jonathan. In a swift motion, it raised a paw adorned with razor-sharp claws akin to small daggers. Maddy tightened her grip but squeezed her eyes closed, forcing out more tears. But, instead of Jonathan's death scream, an inhuman howl deafened her.

When Maddy opened her eyes, Riley stood on top of the creature, pulling its head up by the tusks and forcing their feet into the back of its neck. The creature writhed and struggled against Riley's grip. Riley's normally serene face contorted in a mask of violence that Maddy never could have expected from them. Riley grunted. No. It was more like an animalistic growl. A snap echoed off the walls of the buildings. The beast collapsed.

Riley dusted themself off and hurried to Maddy. "Are you okay?"

Maddy holstered her pistol, using the action to compose herself. It didn't work. With the weight of Riley's death removed, she hunched over, supporting herself on her knees. Tears streamed down her face and dripped onto the pavement. The impact should have killed Riley, or at the very least, crippled them. Slowly, the relief that Riley was okay faded. Questions began forming in Maddy's mind.

"I haven't been completely honest with you, Madison."

Yeah, no shit. Relationship issues could wait. A member of her crew had withheld information from their captain. That could get someone killed in her business.

"I never pried about your past because, for our relationship, it doesn't matter." Maddy straightened. Anger and betrayal re-energized her. "But now you are part of my crew. What the hell did you just do?"

"I turned off my limiters."

Limiters kept androids and humans on equal footing. No android could disable them. Schoolchildren were taught that the Andromedans built androids to do tasks which required the strength and reflexes beyond those of a human. After the Andromedans were kicked out, tensions between humans and androids rose to a boil, almost leading to a civil war in the Galaxy one thousand years later. Unknown forces assassinated the most vocal leaders on each side. Afterwards, humans and enough of the androids agreed that the androids' advantages wouldn't be good for society. Why keep humans around if androids can do everything better?

The new leaders decided androids would have limiters installed to keep them more like humans. War would certainly erupt if androids ever had their limiters deactivated. That wouldn't be good for anyone, especially the humans. So far, the Great Compromise had held the peace.

"That is a highly illegal mod," Maddy chose her words carefully, "one that will get you deactivated and me in a lot of trouble for knowing about it." Her prison sentence alone would be measured in centuries. Did Riley even think about that when taking on this mod? Is that how Riley knew Erin?

"It's not a mod. I was created this way." Riley looked up at Maddy. "I am sorry I never told you, but I think you know why I didn't."

It was clear why someone would want to build a limiterless android. However, who could do that? Along with AI development and starship manufacturing, the creation of androids was one of the most regulated industries in the Milky Way.

Maddy sighed. "We'll return to this later." It was never a good idea to have this kind of discussion under the influence of an emotional cocktail. She pushed the feeling of betrayal to a deep region in her mind where it would be out of the way. "Right now, we have an android to find."

"Your secret is safe with me," Jonathan said. "Thanks for saving my life."

I almost forgot about Jonathan!

Relief over his well-being took some of the edge off her anger. Maddy trusted Jonathan with her life, at least as far as him being her navigator was concerned. Now she had to trust him with her freedom, too. Death was preferable to centuries cooped up in a prison.

"Thanks Jonathan." Riley tried to put their hand on Jonathan's shoulder. He flinched. Riley jerked their hand back and frowned.

That was why limiters were created.

For once, Maddy was happy to be in a dangerous environment. It provided the perfect excuse for silence as they continued their journey toward the coordinates Erin had provided. They walked single file in the center of the street to avoid surprises from the alleys. Maddy took point and Riley insisted on bringing up the rear. The trio stayed a little farther apart than safety protocols would have dictated in this situation.

Ross 154, just past Zenith, cast a red glow on the city's remains. Maddy hadn't noticed the coloration until after the attack. The city had a faint chemical odor that had previously gone unnoticed, too. The sooner they could leave, the better.

As they walked, the condition of the buildings continued to improve to the point where ruins were no longer the right term for what she stood amongst. According to Maddy's comm, they were in the right neighborhood. The coordinates were a block ahead. Some shops lining the streets looked less than 100 years old, not in architecture, but in condition.

"I think we are here," Maddy said. Riley and Jonathan joined her at what appeared to be a storefront. Cupping her hands around her eyes, Maddy put her face against the building's window. A few lights were on inside. Rows of shelves, piled high with ancient electronics, extended from the front to the back of the store. The white linoleum floor looked recently mopped. "This place looks like it's open for business," Maddy straightened. "Someone's definitely living here."

"At least we didn't see any more of those creatures." Jonathan's voice betrayed his relief.

"Creatures that large are probably solitary predators," Riley said. "I turned my visual, olfactory, and aural sensors to max after the encounter and I didn't detect another one."

What can a limiterless android do? The more Maddy considered the question, the less she wanted to know the answer. Riley's display of power both impressed and scared her. Would the future of their relationship involve constant-second guessing of her partner? Maybe a better question was, would there be a future to their relationship?

Jonathan cleared his throat, probably sharing some of Maddy's thoughts about Riley. "What do we do now?"

"We go inside." Maddy pulled the door handle. The door didn't budge. "It was worth a try." She stepped back and aimed her pistol at the handle.

Jonathan put his hand on hers. "What are you doing?"

"I don't have a key. Do you have a better idea?"

"Yeah. How about we push the intercom button?" Jonathan pointed to a chest-high speaker beside the doorframe. The speaker and its control panel appeared to be the same age as the merchandise.

While shooting would have been more fun and therapeutic, Maddy instead pressed the button on the intercom. "Hello, anyone there?"

There was no static when Maddy depressed the button, or when she let it go. Even modern comms showed evidence of a connection being made. Maddy tried again. "Uh, Erin sent us. They said you could help us with this." She held the data crystal in front of the speaker hoping there was a camera inside.

The door clicked and opened slowly. More lights activated, illuminating additional rows of plastic products on shelves. Maddy drew her pistol and entered. Jonathan followed close enough that she could hear him breathe.

"I have only ever seen this stuff on museum hyperweb sites." Jonathan held up a plastic box that had wires dangling from it. "Was this a brick-and-mortar store? I have heard of these, but they are only for the super-rich. Supposedly, they are sometimes on abandoned planets so that the wealthy can have their privacy."

Maddy couldn't meet Jonathan's eyes. Her favorite store was on an abandoned starbase—at least that's how the Galactic Registry listed the base. She and Riley shopped exclusively brick-and-mortar. The average person couldn't tell by looking at Maddy and Riley's clothes, but that was the point. Those who stood out might get robbed, even in some parts of Uptown.

The front door slammed shut. Maddy jumped. A crash came from her left. Jonathan had dropped a plastic box he'd been holding. In a blur, Riley turned toward the door with their fists clenched.

A door in the back creaked opened. A short, well-dressed bald old man with pale skin stood inside with a blank expression on his face. Why wasn't he picked up by their scanners? The mysteries of this world kept piling up.

"Hello. I am Captain Majestic of the *Amethyst*. We were sent here by Erin who told us an android lived on this planet. Do you know them?" Maddy held the crystal out in her open palm. "We need help reading this." She stood six meters from the man and didn't think twice about her loose hold.

A breeze passed over her open palm. Maddy looked down at her now empty hand. The old man stood in front of her. Riley, almost as quickly, was by her side.

They're an android and probably without limiters.

"I apologize. That was rude of me." The android returned the crystal to Maddy. "It has been a long time since I have had company. Please, call me Dante."

"Hello, Dante." Maddy eyed the android as she put the crystal in her pocket.

"Dante?" Jonathan blurted out the question, then covered his mouth. "I'm Jonathan and this is Riley."

"I can't broadcast my ID to you." Riley looked bewildered. "My short-form designation is 93-562. Pleasure to meet you."

"Generation 93?" Dante's gaze wandered up and down Riley, their face tensed in concentration. "Really?"

So that's what Riley's designation means!

Riley had told Maddy their designation during their one-year dating anniversary dinner at the Skyview. It wasn't a big deal to her at the time. Much later, she learned that although androids disclose their short-form ID numbers to each other all the time, an android disclosing their long-form ID was akin to a human revealing a deep personal fear—you only do that with people you trust implicitly.

"I know who and what you are, Riley." Dante put a hand up to their chin. "Erin told me you were coming. At first, I thought it might be to kill me."

"Why would Riley want to kill you?" Maddy asked.

"I'm not looking to give him a reason."

It was becoming impossible for Maddy to keep track of the questions she wanted to ask Riley. That list's length equaled that of the questions whose answers she didn't want to know. She wasn't sure how to categorize this exchange.

"Them." Riley said. "Not him. And I am not here for you."

"I stand corrected." Dante bowed. "I forget the new ways. Please forgive me. May I see the crystal again? I promise I won't take it." Maddy pulled the crystal from her pocket and Dante leaned over Maddy's outstretched palm. "Hmm. I believe I do have a reader for that."

Dante turned around and rummaged through a pile of electronics on a shelf behind them. "Erin helped me out a decade ago. Or was it a century?" They shook their head. "I suppose it doesn't matter. I owe Erin a favor, but I am not doing it for *them*." The emphasis seemed to be more of a reminder to Dante than a demonstration to Maddy and her crew. "Once I heard Riley had this crystal, I knew I needed to help."

Maddy filed that statement into the questions-she-needed-to-ask category.

"How did you get it?" Dante picked up a plastic box from the shelf, turned it around in their hand, and then returned it.

"A client had us retrieve it from an abandoned station," Maddy said.

"Was that client named Kerry?" Dante squatted and dug through one of the lower shelves. "I need to know before I'll help you."

"Yes. Did you know them?"

"I've known Kerry for a very long time. I am surprised she is not here with you."

"She?" Jonathan asked. "I don't mean to be rude, but aren't androids genderless?"

"As part of the Great Compromise, yes. But Kerry and I are from before the war, or the almost-war, that is. There were different rules back then. Androids had a preferred gender to help us blend in with humans." Dante stood and got on their tiptoes to search the top shelf. "I identify as male, by the way." A metal rectangle with a pale green screen laid toward the back of the shelf, just out of Dante's reach. Maddy stretched and retrieved it.

While interesting, she hadn't come all this way for a history lesson. "We need to know what is on that crystal. People have tried to kill us several times over whatever's on it." Maddy paused, trying to figure out how to break the news. "We believe they were also the same people who killed Kerry."

A tear formed in the corner of Dante's eye. Maddy had never seen an android cry before, not even Riley. "Bastard! I never thought Alex would go that far. This needs to end." Dante extended his hand, palm up. "Please, give me the crystal." Maddy handed it over.

Everyone followed Dante to what looked like the checkout counter. "Are you sure you want to know what is on here? The same people who killed Kerry will stop at nothing to kill you, too."

"I want to know why someone wants us dead," Maddy said. "But I won't make this decision for my crew."

"I will not stand by as people hunt down the woman I love." Riley had a long way to go to earn Maddy's trust again, but their comment was a good start.

Jonathan fidgeted with his hands.

"You can say no, Jonathan." Maddy placed her hand on his shoulder. "No one will think less of you, including me."

"I am not abandoning you, Cap." Jonathan grinned. "Besides, what would Skylar think if I did?"

"Very well." Dante placed the device on the countertop and inserted the crystal. "It will take a moment to download the data. I do my best to maintain the equipment in here, but entropy always wins." White text scrolled up on the device's green screen.

"I have a question while we wait." Maddy leaned on the counter. "Why couldn't we detect you from orbit?"

"You were looking for androids like Riley. I'm different."

"Well, at least the starbase's repair crew didn't screw up my ship's sensors." His answer wasn't satisfying, but Maddy let it go. She had more questions than she'd ever have answers for.

The word READY, in white block text, flashed on the device's screen. "Last chance. Are you certain you want to know its contents?"

Riley and Jonathan both nodded. Like Maddy, they were already in a mess, they might as well know what kind and how bad.

"Yes," Maddy said. "Maybe something on that crystal will help get these people off our asses."

"The crystal contains the location of Earth," Dante paused, looking curiously at the box's readout, "among other things."

Riley rolled their eyes. "Not this again."

Dante considered Riley for a long moment—especially long for androids. "Earth is real. I was built there, over two thousand years ago." His perfunctory tone carried the weight of an obvious truth.

The room became quieter than the depths of space. Everyone's attention focused on Dante. A knowing smile curved Jonathan's lips. Riley's jaw fell open. In any other situation, Dante's revelation would have shocked Maddy. But her fascination as a history buff was trumped by the fact that her crew's life was still in danger.

"Can you send the data to my ship?" Maddy entered the *Amethyst*'s hyperweb address into the device. "Regardless of whether the Earth is real, the people after us believe it is. And they're willing to kill us to protect that information."

"Believe what you will"—Dante transferred the data to the *Amethyst*'s main computer—"but Earth is real. It hides a terrible secret."

"This is the greatest discovery in the history of the Galactic Federation." Jonathan's eyes got big in realization. "If we go now, we could set up an exclusive deal." He swiped his hand through the air. "Captain Majestic, exclusive shipper to humanity's birthplace."

The slogan was terrible, but the idea wasn't. However, first they needed to get these mysterious attackers off their backs. Then she could sort out the business side of things.

Earth's supposed location appeared on Maddy's comm. It wasn't far, less than ten light-years away. How could it not have been found by now? "Let's go see what these people want to kill us over."

"I unlocked the crystal because I believe your crew can save the Earth and everyone on it." Dante handed Maddy the crystal, but his eyes stayed fixed on Riley. "The coordinates aren't enough. You need to—"

A loud crash interrupted Dante. Everyone jumped. The front door laid on the floor. Enhanced humans and androids, all of whom were well-armed, marched into the shop and leveled their rifles at Maddy's crew and Dante. The white symbol on their light-blue uniforms matched the muggers' tattoo and the flag on the station.

Once the humans and androids had settled into formation, a stock android wearing the same uniform and a holstered laser pistol entered the shop. The humans and androids opened their circle just enough to let the stock android inside.

"Captain Amana," the android spoke with a rigid formality used when one doesn't believe the other person deserves respect, "I hope you will accept our invitation to join us for a conversation."

Maddy checked her comm. The *Amethyst* had not alerted her to a ship coming out of hyperspace.

"You may have figured out our cloaking technology, Captain, but we have many more tricks than you can imagine."

Dante lunged forward at the stock android. "I am going to kill you, Alex! You son of a bitch!"

Four of the androids grabbed Dante, and with effort, they cuffed him.

Dante continued. "Kerry believed in you when Melinda didn't. She loved you." He closed his eyes. "*I* loved her," he whispered.

Alex replied to Dante's outburst with an icy stare. Was Alex apathetic about Dante's revelation or just cold-hearted? Either way, they weren't the kind of android Maddy ever wanted to play poker with.

A pair of enhanced humans cuffed Maddy. Riley glanced at her, but she shook her head. They were too outnumbered to escape without casualties. There'd be a better time. Five androids surrounded Riley, who surrendered without incident. Did Alex know about Riley's superpowers, or were they just cautious? A single enhanced human cuffed Jonathan. Thankfully, he didn't struggle.

"What do we do with the ancient one, General?" one android asked.

"Take Dante with us. Put him in storage with the rest of the Revelationist relics."

"It took you long enough to find me, Alex," Dante spat, "and you had to follow a *human* to do it."

"I was busy doing the job you swore to do." Alex pointed to two enhanced humans. "Burn this place down."

The smell of burning plastic filled Maddy's nostrils as they left the shop. What other mysteries were now lost to time? Would she live long enough to care?

CHAPTER 18

Light leaked through the canvas bag covering Jonathan's head. His last kidnappers had used thin hoods, too. Firm hands pressed down on his shoulders, forcing him into a hard chair. Jonathan shifted his shoulders in resistance, but the hands' grasp only tightened. Cold steel pressed against his wrists, securing his hands to a metal table in front of him. Two other restraints clicked. At least he wasn't alone.

Despite Jonathan's efforts, his shackles wouldn't budge. He stopped pulling at them. His wrists already stung. Further effort would cause nothing more than additional bruises. Two sets of chains rattled to his right. Cap grunted and one of the rattling sounds stopped. A third rattling persisted, ending with a growl from Riley. Couldn't they break the restraints without their limiters?

That last thought quickened Jonathan's heartbeat. Until now, his belief that Riley could break them out at a moment's notice had kept him calm. Maybe Riley was waiting for an order from Cap. Did these people know Riley's secret? A limiterless android would be valuable to any organization willing to resort to kidnapping.

As part of his orientation on the *Amethyst*, Cap told him that if he was ever captured to breathe slowly and keep his wits about him. It worked on SL2, at least until the drugs set in. Jonathan inhaled through his nose. He slowly exhaled. *Gross.* If he makes it out of this alive, he'd make sure to eat a breath mint before dates with Skylar.

Skylar!

A reason to keep going kept captives alive. She was waiting for him. He took another deep breath.

Focus, Jonathan. Focus. Be the hero Skylar thinks you are.

What did he know so far? The attackers had placed the bag over his head just outside Dante's shop. Then they got in a vehicle and drove maybe an hour at a low speed on bumpy terrain. Their captors mumbled something about a base during the trip. After the car stopped, they entered a building. The fluorescent lighting didn't shine through the bag as much as daylight had. He had to be in their base. If they were going somewhere else, they wouldn't have chained him to a table. The base was outside the city's remains, probably no farther than 50 kilometers from where they were captured and, more importantly, the lander.

The hood bunched together at the top, followed by a painful pinch as a few strands of Jonathan's hair were yanked along with the hood. It took several blinks for his eyes to get adjusted to the light. Cap sat between him and Riley. Three stock androids, all wearing the same uniform as earlier, left the room. Other than a camera in the corner by the door, the walls were bare. Riley struggled in their restraints again. If Jonathan had tried that, he'd have broken his wrists. Cap stared silently at the empty chair on the other side of the table.

Does Cap ever feel fear? He'd seen her get through some crazy shit without batting an eye. His weekly therapy appointment was for the sole purpose of crying while recounting some of the harrowing tales he barely survived. Did Cap have a therapist? Before this mission, Jonathan would have doubted it. However, since Riley has joined the crew, he'd seen a new side of Cap.

She giggles. Who would have guessed?

The door slid open. Alex entered and sat in the empty chair across from Cap. The badges hanging from Alex's uniform gleamed in the room's bright lights. Alex watched Riley struggle for a moment. "We know your secret and adjusted our restraints appropriately. Even I wouldn't be able to break them." The rattling stopped. How would they get out of here if Riley couldn't break free?

I hope Cap is formulating a plan.

"We haven't formally met. My name is Alex. I am the General Officer of the Origin Keepers. I wish we could have met under better circumstances, Captain Amana."

Jonathan tilted his head. *Amana?* Alex had said that name in Dante's shop. But the chaos of the armed invasion had distracted Jonathan too much to give it a second thought. *There's no way she's related to—*

"You didn't know your employer's true name, Jonathan?" Alex clicked his tongue. Their attention shifted from Jonathan to the file in front of them. "Madison Amana. Born on Erandi Prime to Susan and Eric Amana." Alex looked up. "How cute. Your mother took Eric's name. You don't see those kinds of traditional values in the Galaxy anymore. It says here your mom is androphobic. I bet there's been some interesting dinner conversations."

Alex's eyes returned to the file. "Your parents own the Amana Flower Company, the most successful chain on the planet. In fact, one of the most successful in Quadrant One. That explains how you bought your ship outright *and* the apartment in Uptown." Alex's eyes returned to Cap. "It'd be a darn shame if something happened to your parents' business. How would you get by on the Universal Basic Provision?"

I knew she had money! If I survive this, I am going to ask for a raise.

Jonathan squirmed in his seat, trying to find a more comfortable sitting position—a hard task with one's hands chained to a table. The movement attracted Alex's attention.

"Jonathan. No last name. Orphaned early in life. Small-time crook and junkie on SL1 until you attempted to steal from Roger Black." Alex looked up at him. "Probably not his real name." Their eyes returned to the file. "He helped you, which was nicer than I would have been. According to this, the help didn't stick. Nebulae is hard to kick, isn't it?" Their eyes raised in exaggerated disbelief at what they read next. "Seems like you traded that vice for another. How many credits did you blow in those unsavory android clubs? I guess your time with Amana has changed your interests. For what it's worth, I think you and Skylar make a cute couple. She's one of the few humans I actually like." Alex's eyes darkened. "I'd hate to see something bad happen to her."

Metal bit into Jonathan's wrists as he jerked the chains upward. Cap once told him not to show an emotional response to threats when captured. He failed. Alex's smile was proof.

"*Nine-three*-five-six-two, aka Riley." Alex emphasized the nine and three as if it meant something other than Riley's generation number. "Does your human lover know about your past?"

"I hide nothing from Jonathan." Riley said.

Out of the corner of his eye, Jonathan saw Maddy break her poker face, ever so slightly. A giggle rose from Jonathan's throat. He covered it with a cough.

"Funny, *X*-nine-three-five-six-two."

The smile disappeared from Riley's face.

Was Riley a 193rd generation android? If so, what did that mean? The latest model Jonathan knew about was generation 100. The numbers started right after the supposed-Andromedan rebellion. Decades ago, he dated a 90 named Taylor. The first few weeks were fun, but a forty-year-old has little in common with a two-hundred-year-old. After Taylor, Jonathan sought only androids made in the same century as he was born—at least until he met Cap.

"Shall I go over your employment history, Riley? There's over five-hundred years of it here." Alex opened a folder. An image of Riley was on the top page. "I bet Ms. Amana would love to hear about your formal education." Except for the red CONFIDENTIAL stamped below Riley's picture, the font was too small to read. Even with limiters, androids had better eyes than humans. "I have to admit, even I found it difficult to read about what you did to that emergent AI on the Outer Rim four hundred years ago." Alex neatly stacked the papers on the table. "If I'd known about you earlier, I would have sent more than two enhanced humans after you on SL3."

Riley remained quiet. To Cap's credit, her face didn't budge at the revelation. Jonathan would flip out if he learned Skylar had been hiding her true identity.

"Let's get down to business, shall we?" Alex folded their hands on top of the files. "The three of you know too much. That means there are two things that can happen. I could kill you, or you could join the Origin Keepers."

"That's not much of a choice." Cap's steady voice gave Jonathan hope. She'd school this android on how not to mess with Captain Majestic. "Let's start with the second option."

"What?" Jonathan's body flinched involuntarily toward Cap. The sudden movement caused a searing pain to radiate from the bruises on his wrists. The metal restraints yanked him back, a sharp reminder of his captivity. "You can't be serious, Cap?" He asked through gritted teeth—partially due to disbelief, but mostly because of the pain.

Cap's eyes didn't waver from Alex. "Stand down, Navigator."

"Aye, Cap."

Harsh orders weren't Cap's style. Maybe she was trying to tell him something. She couldn't be seriously considering joining the Origin Keepers.

"I appreciate a leader than can put her subordinates in their place." Alex smiled. "You will make a fine addition to the Origin Keepers, Captain." Alex looked at Riley. "I know there is a place for someone with your talents in our organization."

"What about me?" Jonathan asked. Enlisting in an evil organization wasn't on his bucket list, but wherever Cap went, he went, too.

"I am sure we can find something for you, too, Jonathan."

That stung. Jonathan wasn't a pilot, nor did he have superpowers. He was the heart of the crew, or at least, that is what he told himself. Evil secret societies probably didn't need heart.

"I speak for myself," Cap said. "My crew makes their own decisions. But if we are signing up, we need to know exactly what we are in for."

"That's fair, Ms. Amana. You already know more than most, so I'll skip the formal orientation." Alex tapped their comm. A hologram of a planet floated above the table. The continents matched the one on the station's flag, muggers' tattoo, and Alex's uniform.

"This is Earth, the original home of all humans and androids. Homo sapiens evolved on the planet three hundred thousand years ago—give or take."

"Evolved?" Jonathan asked. "Like bacteria adapting to antibiotics?"

"The comparison is more apt than you might imagine." Alex spoke as if it were a put-down. Jonathan didn't get it. "Around fifteen thousand years ago, humans began farming their own food. After that, all hell broke loose. Humans developed all kinds of toys—civilization, industry, computers, space travel, and eventually androids and AI."

"Sounds like we were busy," Cap said.

"Indeed, you were. Of course, there was a price to pay for your successes. You almost destroyed the only planet you knew you could live on."

"So what?" Chains rattled as Cap shrugged in her restraints. "There are tons of planets out there."

"Back then, humans didn't have the technology to visit worlds outside their home system." A dark splotch spread across the continents on the image. "The pollution and climate got so bad, you couldn't grow your own food." The globe vanished, replaced by images of ruined buildings and bodies lying in the street. "Your species was starving on a hot and dry world."

An image of what looked like the interior of an android factory appeared. However, the bodies in the production line differed from stock and from each other. "After killing the first generation of androids for taking away jobs, humans created a second generation to farm the land and fight your wars." The factory image disappeared. "But the environmental damage wasn't your biggest problem."

"AI was the last thing you mentioned," Riley said. "Let me guess, an evil artificial intelligence arose."

"In a nutshell, yes." Alex sat back and crossed their arms. "It's why AI is limited to small unconnected systems. The first globally networked artificial general intelligence enslaved humans and androids not long after it gained sentience. No one wants a repeat of that."

There was more to that story, but Alex wasn't going to share. Ancient history wasn't going to get them out of this mess. Instead, Jonathan asked a question of more immediate concern. "If that is true, where is this AI now?"

"About a year before the AI took over, ten thousand humans and androids left on the first true deep space mission." A holo of a large primitive ship floated between Alex and Cap. Jonathan wouldn't have trusted it to shuttle him between Starbase Erandi 4 and Erandi Prime, much less on an interstellar mission. "The *New Dawn* headed to Proxima Centauri on a twenty-year voyage. Most of the humans slept for the duration of the flight. Androids ran the ship. I was its Science Officer."

"Colonization," Maddy said, "we had given up on the Earth—at least those who could afford to leave had."

"Passage for humans wasn't cheap." The ship disappeared and a red dwarf star took its place. "Our mission was to start the first colony outside the Solar System. We took seeds, livestock and supplies." Alex snorted. "The humans even took their dogs."

Cap leaned forward in their restraints. "If nothing else, your story explains where dogs come from. The official story is the Andromedans created them out of pity for humans."

"I know the official story." Alex snorted. "I helped write it. We based it on a ridiculous belief that aliens visited Earth in the past, created humans, and guided them toward civilization."

"How do you know they didn't?" Riley asked.

"Basic science." Alex scoffed. "Evolution is obvious. Anthropology and archeology explain how ancient people built structures and civilizations without aliens. Besides, the aliens were only ever used to explain the cultures of darker-skinned people. Humans excel at finding irrelevant differences." Alex leaned forward. "But let's get back to the real story, shall we? Just as the *New Dawn* was leaving the Solar System, we received a message from the Mars colony." The red dwarf star morphed into a red planet Jonathan had seen before.

Mars? The planet floating in front of him matched the one in Skylar's game *Battle for Mars*. His search for the planet turned up empty. And, thanks to Skylar interrupting his game with her outfit, he hadn't given the planet a second thought. Maybe Alex's organization created games to support itself. Secret bases must be expensive to operate.

"The Mars colonists told us what happened on Earth about the AI taking control. We sent a reply. There were no hypercomms back then. We should have heard from them six months later, but we didn't. Our best guess was that the AI invaded and destroyed the Mars colony. I lost good friends on that planet." Alex cleared their throat and looked down at the table for a moment. Jonathan would have felt sorry for Alex if they hadn't kidnapped and threatened them. "We voted to end transmissions with the Solar System and continue the mission to Proxima. When the AI didn't hear from us, it likely decided space travel was pointless and has been stuck on that decision ever since."

"Just like people, AI can get stuck on suboptimal solutions." Riley said.

"Indeed." Alex nodded. "In this case, that was a good thing. The androids awake on the ship agreed to quarantine Earth to keep the AI contained there. Together, we created the seeds of what would eventually become the Galactic Federation."

"And the Origin Keepers, too," Cap said.

"Yes. I, along with some close friends," Alex momentarily frowned, "formed the Origin Keepers. We work in secret, protecting the rest of the Galaxy from Earth and its AI."

Jonathan had his doubts about the Andromedans. Prior to this mission, he hadn't been convinced about Earth either. But now, people wanted to kill him over it. That made it real enough to him. Still, there was one big hole in Alex's story. "Didn't the people on the starship remember Earth?" Jonathan asked.

"Long-term hibernation affected human memory. Wiping Earth from people's minds was easy with the help of some drugs and social engineering. First, create a mythology and get it to self-perpetuate. Admittedly, the first century was difficult. Fortunately, humans hadn't developed life-extension tech yet, so memories were short. Fifty years after the establishment of the Proxima colony, the last original human colonist died. It was easy to teach their children to believe whatever we wanted them to. Once the Andromedan story became part of Galactic culture, the rest took care of itself."

"I have flown all over this part of the Galaxy and *never* came across Earth." Cap said. "A habitable planet with that much water would be the hub of its quadrant. Every long-haul pilot would know it. How do you hide an entire planet?"

"We hide an entire star system. I won't give you all our secrets, but you are right, you have never encountered Earth. That is by design."

"Are the people on Earth still enslaved?" Riley asked.

Alex closed their eyes and bowed their head. "It is an unfortunate price that needs to be paid to protect the two hundred billion trillion humans and androids in the rest of the Milky Way."

"I did not know the danger I put the Galaxy in." Cap closed her eyes. "I am sorry."

That was the first apology Jonathan had heard from Cap. Like the harsh order, was this a secret message to him? She always told him to keep alert for opportunities when captured. This felt like one.

"The fact that you didn't know means most of us are doing our job well," Alex said.

"I'm in." Cap leaned back in her chair as far as her restraints would allow. "Can I have a moment to talk to my crew?"

"You will be a fine addition to the Origin Keepers, but I must insist you drop the Majestic moniker, and you won't have the rank of captain."

"I understand. Madison Amana will report to duty."

Has Cap given up so easily? The situation looked grave. But being an Origin Keeper was preferable to death. *Will I still be able to see Skylar?*

Alex slid their chair back. "If you are thinking of escaping, please know that the less-than-friendly wildlife engineered by us surrounds our facility on Ross 154. They love the taste of human flesh and attack androids on sight. You won't get very far on foot." Alex left the room.

"Please tell me you have a plan, Cap."

"I told you the plan. We are going to surrender. We can't win. They'll chase us until we are dead."

"And they threatened Maddy's parents and Skylar," Riley said. "The Origin Keepers will go to extremes to keep their secret. Alex really believes this crap about Earth."

"Crap?" Hadn't Riley just sat through the same story as he? Alex had satisfied all of Jonathan's doubts, and then some. "It all adds up."

"You can't possibly believe we all came from one insignificant planet, Jonathan—"

"This might be the last time we are together," Cap said. "You can decide what you want to do about the Origin Keepers. But I hope you'll join me."

"I will, Cap."

What choice do I have?

"Of course, Madison. I will follow you wherever you go."

Cap leaned in to kiss Riley. Their lips barely made contact thanks to the restraints. The tongue action was more than a bit off-putting.

"Understood," Riley said after Cap broke the kiss.

The door slid open and Alex walked into the room. "Are you two done?"

Cap nodded. "We are all joining."

"Guards will be in momentarily to undo the restraints and take you to new quarters. You'll be under close surveillance until you show loyalty to the Origin Keepers." Alex paused. "The *Amethyst* will become Origin Keepers' property."

When Jonathan first signed on with Cap, some sensitive cargo got damaged on a run. The client tried to lay claim to the *Amethyst* as compensation. To put it mildly, Cap showed the client, in no uncertain terms, the error of their ways. But now, Cap sat in silence. Her gaze fixed to some point on the table.

Cap really has given up.

Alex stared, as if expecting an outburst. After a moment of waiting, they turned and left the room. Four uniformed androids entered and undid Maddy and Jonathan's restraints. Jonathan rubbed his wrists. A hand grasped his neck from behind.

"We know about you, Riley," the android holding Jonathan said. "I may have limiters, but I can still snap this boy's neck before you can get to me."

Cap grunted. She was in the same predicament. Riley couldn't save both him and Cap.

"I understand." Defeat in Riley's voice drained the last inkling of hope from Jonathan. His future was with the Origin Keepers.

The two other androids cautiously approached Riley's restraints and released them. The hand around Jonathan's neck stayed after they freed Riley. Tension was thick in the air. The androids who released Riley slowly backed off. "You can stand—slowly," one android said. Free of the restraints, Riley stood. Some of the synthetic skin was missing around their wrists, exposing part of their steel skeletal structure. "Now we're all going to leave this room," the android closest to Riley spoke slowly and clearly. "Riley and I will walk side by side to your cells—I mean, quarters. One wrong move and the girl dies first."

The last person who called Cap a girl woke up in the hospital. The android's comment didn't even draw a glare from her.

I'll never see Skylar again. I hope she doesn't think I am dead or, worse, that I ran off with another woman.

The android nudged Riley to move. Riley closed their eyes. Their eyeballs moved back and forth behind their eyelids.

"Don't screw with us, Riley, or we'll kill—"

The pressure released from Jonathan's neck. A fraction of a second later, the lights went out and there were four distinct thuds. Dim emergency lighting activated. The four androids laid unconscious on the floor.

"What the hell happened?" Cap rubbed her neck.

"I did what you told me to, Captain. I gave us an opportunity to escape. My midrange electromagnetic pulse seemed like it would give us the best chance of getting out of here. The androids are unconscious but should recover in a few hours. I don't have enough charge to do that again."

"When did Cap give you that order?"

"Riley has communication sensors in their tongue," Cap said. "I ordered them to take out the guards once we were all free."

"You wrote on Riley's tongue with yours?" A simultaneously impressive and repulsive feat.

"Worry about it later, Jonathan. Get these uniforms on." Cap was already stripping down one of the guards.

Riley stood in front of a console beside the door. Its screen was dead, but a wire ran from its keyboard to Riley's arm. "It looks like the base is smaller than I thought. My EMP took out most of the base, except for some hardened emergency systems. We'll need to hurry. Since Alex is like Dante, I can't guarantee they were affected by the EMP. If they're still conscious, they'll suspect we are trying to escape."

"Great work, Riley." A topless Cap slid on a pair of pants she took from one of the androids. Heat rose in Jonathan's cheeks. Thankfully, her back was to him. Riley stripped down. Most androids were not bashful. Jonathan turned his back to give Riley and Cap some privacy and started undressing the android closest to him.

The uniform was several sizes too big. At some point, he'd need to run in the uniform. Cuffing the pant legs would make him stand out, but it would also prevent him from tripping. He cuffed the pants, hoping no one would notice. Then he tucked his shirt in, smoothed it out, and tried more tucking. No matter what he did, it looked sloppy.

"What are you doing?" Cap tucked her hair up under her uniform's hat. At least she now had a shirt on. "It doesn't have to be perfect. It's not like you are going to see Skylar while wearing this." She waved at Jonathan to follow her. "Let's go. Riley, you take point. I'll cover our six." Jonathan followed Riley out of the room. Thanks to their interface with the console, they seemed to know where they were going.

The emergency lighting provided a mixed blessing. The three of them would be harder to identify from a distance, but it also made it difficult for Jonathan to get his bearing in the base. To make matters worse, there were lots of doors. Someone could walk out of one any moment and sound the alarm.

Jonathan whispered behind him, "Look down as much as you can, Cap." *Cap's eyes will give us away faster than these large uniforms.*

"Good thinking, Jonathan."

Praise from Cap, while rare, always felt great. This time was different. Jonathan took her praise as approval from a superior, not a comment with a hopeful implication.

Focus, Jonathan! Escaping from capture is not the time for self-reflection. Regardless, a grin forced its way onto his face.

Four humans ran toward them. Jonathan kept his focus straight ahead and walked with purpose. If he looked like he knew where he was going, then maybe they wouldn't stop him.

"Get to your emergency stations, on the double," one human said as they passed. "And keep an eye out for three prisoners trying to escape."

"Yes, sir." Riley ran. Once they were out of earshot of the humans, Riley glanced back. "Looks like the uniforms are working."

"Whatever you did Riley, let's hope it lasts a while." Cap said with belabored breath.

Running helped them blend in. Other humans ran by. No one looked twice at the group.

"I haven't seen any androids since the room." Jonathan strained to get the words out. It took all his focus to keep one foot moving in front of another.

"My EMP has disabled them. They'll all be fine in a few hours."

The Federation restricted electromagnetic pulses to military use only, like all other weaponized mods. Why would Riley need built-in weapons if they don't have limiters? Now wasn't the time to ask, but if they made it back to the *Amethyst*, he would demand to know those answers and more. Knowing about the EMP was dangerous to him and, therefore, also to Skylar.

The group turned right and slowed to a jog, three abreast, down a hallway identical to the one they were just in. The new pace came at the perfect time. Any more full-out running and Jonathan would have puked—blowing both their cover and the meal bars he had on the way to Dante's shop.

An exit sign hung above a double door at the end of the hall. The windows in the doors showed daylight through them. Jonathan allowed himself to relax a little.

We might just make it.

Up ahead, a uniformed woman turned a corner and started hurrying down the hallway, approaching the group. There was no way to avoid her, especially since the three of them had spread out across the width of the hall. But the last group didn't recognize them. Maybe she wouldn't, either.

"Emergency stations are that way." The woman pointed in the direction opposite the way the *Amethyst*'s crew headed. Her eyes focused on Jonathan's overly cuffed pants. A look of realization dawned on her face. She drew her pistol and began running toward them. "Freeze!"

The three of them stopped. Jonathan looked left and right. There was nowhere to go but backward, deeper into the base. The woman pointed the pistol at Cap. "You're their leader, right?" She didn't wait for Cap to respond. "Turn around with your hands in the air."

Cap glanced at Riley and gave a quick shake of her head.

"Turn around, crew." Cap raised her hands and turned her back to the woman. "They got us." Jonathan followed Cap's orders.

"Damn right, I do." The woman stuck the barrel of her pistol in Cap's back. "Move on. Any funny stuff and your captain gets a hole burned through her."

They took a few steps down the hall when Cap spun 180 degrees around and used her raised left hand to knock away the pistol toward Jonathan. It fell on the floor in front of him. Cap allowed her momentum to continue her spin as she punched the woman in the face with a right cross. A whoosh of air sped by Jonathan. Riley held the pistol. The woman laid unconscious on the floor.

"I was afraid you'd accidentally kill her," Cap said.

"Don't you trust me, Madison?"

Cap held her hand out. "Let's get out of here." Riley placed the pistol in her hand, answering their own question.

The door at the end of the hall opened to a small parking lot containing about a dozen cars. Riley walked up to one car and got inside. It wouldn't start. "What are we going to do?" Jonathan asked. "If Riley's EMP knocked out all these cars, we're screwed. We'll never make it back to the lander with all those predators around."

"Over there." Riley pointed to the car farthest from the base. "My EMP would be weakest on that car." Riley got in the vehicle, but it didn't start. Cap swore as she kicked the tire. "I have an idea." They slid over to the passenger seat and unbuttoned their shirt.

"What are you doing?" Cap asked.

"I am going to hard reset this car, then power it with my supply."

"The hell you are." Cap's voice wavered. Jonathan had never heard fear in her voice before.

"It won't kill me, as long as you get me back to the *Amethyst* and plug me in to the ship's primary power supply in time." Riley felt around under the dashboard and pulled out a cord. "Use the same port I am going to plug the car into."

"How much time do we have?" Cap asked.

"Two hours—give or take," Riley inserted the end of the cord into a port in their chest, "I got the lander's coordinates from the base's computer. I'll transfer them to the car. We must hurry. Madison, I love you." Riley collapsed in the passenger seat as if they had fainted.

Cap took a deep breath. "Get in." She sat behind the steering wheel. Jonathan had one foot in the car and the other on the ground when the car accelerated. The door closed on his leg. Pain shot up through his leg and to his lower back. With effort, he got his leg inside and the door shut.

❖ ❖ ❖

The car pulled up to the lander. The pain in Jonathan's leg had softened to a dull throb, just in time to get out and walk to the lander.

"How are we going to get Riley in the lander?" Jonathan asked. "I can't carry them with my leg like this."

"Cargo table!" Cap ran to the lander's cargo bay door and pushed buttons on its console. The floating platform they used to unload Erin's shipment floated out of the lander. Its arm effortlessly lifted Riley out of the passenger seat and onto its platform. Once Riley was secure, Cap joined Jonathan in the lander's cabin.

"There's only thirty minutes left," Jonathan started preflight checks. Ascent always took longer than descent. "We won't make it."

"Yes. We will." Cap aborted preflight checks. A hard force pinned Jonathan down on his seat. Darkness crept in from the periphery of his vision as the gees increased. Then everything went black.

CHAPTER 19

Riley's lifeless body laid on the anti-grav cart, which barely fit in the med bay. A wire protruded from their chest to the *Amethyst*'s primary power supply. Despite burning the lander's engines way beyond spec, they hadn't made it in time. Maddy had let Riley down. The last thing Riley asked her was if she trusted them. Both the reaction she gave and the truth behind it burned her heart with regret.

If they didn't recover, she would never forgive herself.

I decided not to take payment from the doctors. I chose to accept the mission to get the crystal. I allowed Riley to come along. I ordered Riley to get us free. Every decision I made has been bad for Riley. How could I fail the person I love?

The knots in Maddy's stomach reaffirmed her belief that, in space, she was better off alone. Maybe solitude was better—in all aspects of her life. No one would have to suffer because of her decisions.

"How're they doing, Cap?"

When will one of my mistakes hurt Jonathan?

The self-doubt needed to stop. In space, that kind of thinking would get her crew killed. "I don't know. There's no indication of whether Riley is accepting the energy."

"Maybe it will take longer than normal since we were twenty minutes late. I lowered life support in the cargo bay to supply Riley." Jonathan squeezed around the cart and sat beside Maddy. "We're in hyperspace. I set the autopilot to head toward the inner rim of the Galactic Habitable Zone, just as you ordered. It looks like we lost them." Jonathan squeezed

Riley's hand. "Thank you." He spoke as if Riley were a departed parent. His hand lingered on Riley's for a moment before letting go.

"They've saved us more times than I can count." Maddy put her hand on Riley's, where Jonathan's had been. Simulated body temperature would be one of the last processes recovered, but that didn't make their coldness any less disappointing.

"You should get some rest, Cap. I can watch the ship from here. I'll let you know as soon as anything changes with Riley."

"Riley wouldn't leave me. Not even a black hole could pull me away from them."

"You've been here for over ten hours. You need some rest, Cap." Jonathan placed his hand on her back. "Riley would want you to take care of yourself, too."

Exhaustion had set in not long after the tears had dried, but it hardly mattered at this point. So much had gone unsaid between them since they landed on Ross 154 Prime, but that too seemed unimportant. The only thing she wanted was to be held by Riley. But right now, even a simple power imbalance—or some other sign they were accepting energy from the ship—would be welcome.

"If you want to help, how about bringing me some stims?"

Jonathan removed his hand from her back and straightened. "Is that a good idea, Cap?"

No. Of course, it's not a good idea. Neither was going to Ross 154 or being too damn greedy to refuse Kerry's offer.

Her eyes remained focused on Riley's face. "Don't make me turn a request into an order."

"Aye, Cap." Jonathan left.

If she had said no to Kerry, none of this would have happened. Riley would still be alive, and she'd be blissfully ignorant of their secret identity.

The console by the ship's power supply beeped. Some of its output was unaccounted for by the ship's systems. A small surge of adrenaline took the edge off of Maddy's exhaustion. Maybe Riley absorbed some of that energy. Another beep squashed Maddy's hope—the computer had accounted for all the power. It was getting redirected back to the cargo bay, except for a small amount within the error tolerance of the computers systems.

"I got the stims, Cap. But first, you gotta eat." Jonathan handed her a warm bag of chicken parmesan—her favorite—and sat beside her.

"You're lucky I am tired." Maddy tore the top off the ration bag with her teeth. The minor act of aggression eased some of her helplessness. The scent of cooked chicken filled the room. Her stomach growled.

"I hope you don't mind if I join you." Jonathan opened another ration bag. The smell of beef mixed with the chicken. She glanced at Jonathan's bag. "You want mine, too, Cap? I can get more."

"No. Thank you." Maddy devoured her meal. When did she last eat? It was before the animal attack and her relationship with Riley changed. How long ago was that?

"Since you finished your meal, you can have dessert." Jonathan tossed her a stimpack.

"I'll save it for later." A decent meal—or a ship's ration—was always better than meds. "Thanks again."

"All part of my job, Cap." Jonathan scooped out a piece of beef and put it in his mouth. "So, what's the plan?" he asked with his mouth full.

After escaping the captivity of the Origin Keeper's base, Maddy's mind fixated on a single goal: Getting Riley connected to the *Amethyst*'s power supply. Anything else was irrelevant compared to this crucial task. But now what? If Riley died, they would want Maddy to find love again and live out her life peacefully. That was the kind of person Riley was, or at least that's what she thought. Tearing through the Origin Keepers and killing Alex was the more appealing option.

Until a better way to honor Riley came to mind. "I'm going to Earth and freeing its people."

Jonathan put away his unfinished meal with a look of concern in his eyes. "From what Alex said, that's suicide."

If Riley died, then that result was fine by her. "How can I know about an enslaved planet and do nothing?"

"We can get the Federation authorities involved." Jonathan sat back in his chair. "They have the resources to do this kind of thing."

"Who'd believe us?"

"Cap," Jonathan leaned forward and looked her in the eye. He'd never had done that before. "I don't want you going off and getting yourself killed." He reached out and took her hand. "Riley wouldn't want it either."

Maddy removed her hand. "This isn't some kind of suicide attempt." She inhaled. "You don't have to go with me. I can take you home. You and Skylar can find some backwater planet on the Outer Rim of the Habitable Zone, make some babies, and hide from the Origin Keepers. In fact, I order you to do exactly that."

If I go alone, no one else will have to suffer from my mistakes.

"You think I am going to leave you after all of this?" Jonathan had never raised his voice to Maddy before. "There is no way in hell I would ever do that." Jonathan's eyes welled up. "Alex was right. My parents died when I was young, leaving me to fend for myself on SL1. The android clubs were the least disgusting part of my life before I met you. Alex had the decency to not mention my time in prison. Before I met you, I was back on the path to dying in some back alley, high on Nebulae." Tears streamed from Jonathan's eyes. "You saved me, Cap. I am sure as shit not going to let you run off to die alone."

Madison cried sometimes. But Captain Majestic? Never. Nevertheless, Jonathan's story and Riley's condition broke the levees in her eyes. "You never told me that."

Jonathan looked away as he wiped a tear. "There's no proper place to put junkie android sex addict on one's resume." He chuckled.

Maddy did, too. "I don't know," the levity provided much needed emotional relief, "considering our field of business, it might fit nicely under relevant work experience."

Riley sat up. "Based on what I've seen so far, I'd have to agree."

A wave of excitement and relief drove the exhaustion from Maddy's body. She threw her arms around Riley. "I thought we'd lost you." Tears coursed down her cheeks once again, and she buried her face into Riley's chest, seeking comfort.

In that moment, everything else faded into the background—the Origin Keepers, Earth, and even Riley's secret identity. Riley simply held her, shielding her from the weight of the Galaxy and providing a sense of solace and security.

"We did our best to get you here in time, but we were late," Jonathan said. "It's great to have you back."

"My body shuts down as a self-preservation measure when I am that low. The protocol protects core systems that other androids don't have. I'm sorry I didn't have time to explain."

"No worries," Jonathan said. "Thank you for saving us."

"You are welcome. Thank you for not giving up on me. If I had been plugged in ten minutes later, my reserve capacitors would have been empty and I would have been unrecoverable."

Maddy continued to squeeze, too afraid of what might happen if she let go.

Riley broke the hug gently and locked eyes with her. "We need to talk."

The relief of Riley's well-being had beaten back the sense of betrayal, but it hadn't made it disappear. Maybe a heart-to-heart would squash it. However, Maddy had neither the stamina nor the mental faculties needed for one right now.

"Later. Let's just enjoy this for now." Maddy returned her face to Riley's chest. Their arms wrapped around her, and it felt like home.

"Dammit!" Maddy smacked the side of the pilot's nav console. "Location not found." She mocked the computer's response. Ever since they jumped to normal space this afternoon for a break, the nav computer had rejected Earth's coordinates. The good night's sleep had cured her exhaustion, but nothing else.

"What's wrong?" Riley bent over her from behind.

Maddy shifted slightly, making more space between her and Riley. It hadn't taken long for the sense of relief about Riley to lose some ground to feelings of betrayal. She'd get over it—maybe. But it would take time to process what she had learned.

"Every time I put the coordinates in, it tells me that there's no such location."

Riley leaned in to get a closer look. "Those are the right numbers."

"Yes, Riley," Maddy forcefully exhaled through her nose. "I know how to type coordinates."

"I wasn't doubting you, Captain." Riley straightened and backed off. The formality had returned, too. "I am troubleshooting by starting with the easiest solution." The two of them still needed to talk, but complaining about the things that weren't really the problem was easier than confronting the ones that were.

Munching sounds broke the awkward silence. "What's wrong, Cap?" Jonathan's words were barely understandable.

"Don't eat on my bridge!" Maddy winced. Jonathan didn't deserve her wrath. Maybe Riley didn't either. They had their reasons for keeping a secret. It wasn't like she was transparent with Riley about her career, or with how she paid Jonathan, either.

"Sorry, Cap." At least, that is what Maddy thought she heard Jonathan say. Hopefully, only words came out of his mouth. Jonathan shuffled off the bridge.

"Has that ever happened before?" Riley asked.

"Jonathan talking with his mouth full? All the time. He doesn't normally bring his food to the bridge, though."

I'll have to break him of that if he ever moves in with Skylar. In return, she should give me free drinks for life.

"No. I mean the computer's failure to accept valid coordinates."

"No. Not once." Another attempt at putting in the coordinates yielded the same result. "I think Alex and Dante are full of shit."

"Let me see something." Riley bent over and brushed against Maddy. She jerked back, but Riley didn't seem to notice. They tapped out a few commands. Lines of code scrolled from the top of the screen. "Dante didn't alter the file. That doesn't mean the coordinates are right, just that Dante didn't change the numbers for Earth's location."

"Alex believes it's correct. Otherwise, why would they have captured us and burned down Dante's shop?"

Riley shrugged. "Maybe they are crazy."

"That's too easy." Maddy rubbed her chin. "While I have trouble believing this entire concept of Earth, Alex isn't crazy. Ruthless, maybe. Crazy? No way. Their decisions are calculated—rational even. A crazy person would have just killed us on the spot."

"Although I couldn't send my ID to Dante, he broadcasted as gen 85." Riley stood beside Maddy's chair and crossed their arms. "Dante could be older than that. IDs can be faked." Riley looked away. "I do it all the time."

Maddy let that one go. Now wasn't the time for that conversation. "Dante seemed genuinely surprised by the gen 93 designation. Would meeting a 93 surprise an 85? How old is he, anyway?"

"*If* he was being honest about his ID, he'd be about three hundred years old. I have met living 80s that never deactivated after their loved ones died." Riley paused. "They're rare, but they are fully aware of the Galaxy's current android tech. I am guessing Dante saw through my ruse."

If Dante wasn't lying about his age, then maybe Riley's identity wasn't as secret as they believed. A two-thousand-year-old person would probably know all kinds of things about the Galaxy. "There is definitely something to this story." Maddy scrolled through words and meaningless numbers. "If an AI is enslaving the people of Earth, then we need to help them."

"Agreed. If it turns out to be a wild goose chase, that's fine, too. I'd rather go there and find that nothing is going on than allow people to continue to suffer. We'll need to proceed with caution. If the AI is there, I don't want it to see us. That would risk exposing the Galaxy and endangering countless lives." Riley pointed to the screen. "What's that?"

"I think it is a table of colonized planets. The order isn't alphabetical, though." Maddy leaned over, closing the space between her and Riley. "Maybe it is chronological?"

"Makes sense. The first entry has a recently added file attached to it. Look at the timestamp."

"That's when we were in Dante's shop. Dante tried to tell us something before we were captured. Maybe this is it." Maddy tapped the word Proxima Centauri b, the same name Alex mentioned earlier. A new window popped up. "It says here that the planet orbits an active red dwarf. All the humans left the colony not long after it was established. Proxima Centauri's flares made it dangerous for humans. This data supports Alex's story." She scrolled down. "According to this, some androids stayed behind. Looks like that first colony is still inhabited."

"An android-only world?" Riley leaned against the console and crossed their arms. "I've heard of them but never been to one. You?"

"Once, on a run. They did *not* want me sticking around any longer than I had to."

"Anthrophobes."

Maddy nodded. "Maybe the folks on Proxima will be different."

"Maybe." Riley didn't sound convinced, and Maddy wasn't either. Were they hiding something else from her? Was this how the rest of their relationship, however much longer it lasted, would go? Maddy was doubting every little thing Riley said. Loss of trust is the death knell for any relationship. The conversation needed to be had, sooner rather than later. But she couldn't muster the strength for it now. Maybe because she feared the outcome.

"Let's head to Proxima." Maddy typed the coordinates for Proxima Centauri b into the console. "That's not far. We could be there in about two days."

"We could be where, Cap?" Jonathan, sans snacks, turned the navigator's chair around and flopped into it.

"An android-only planet. It might be a connection to Earth." Maddy turned around in her chair. "If the people of Earth need us, we're going to help them. If Earth doesn't exist, then maybe going to those coordinates and finding nothing will get the Origin Keepers off our backs. Either way, it means we won't be home anytime soon."

"No problem, Cap. It turns out that the long-distance thing is working just fine for Skylar and me." Jonathan charted a flight path to Proxima Centauri b.

"You know I can access the VR calls you make on this ship, right?" Despite her best efforts to maintain a poker face, a grin threatened to break through on Maddy's lips.

Jonathan turned a new shade of red.

"I wouldn't do that!" Maddy laughed and flicked a payment from her comm to Jonathan's. "Next VR call with Skylar is on me. Just make sure you clean the haptic suit if you use it."

Just when Maddy had thought Jonathan couldn't turn any redder, he proved her wrong.

"Stop picking on the poor boy, Captain." Riley snickered. "Can't you tell he's in loooove?"

Jonathan looked down and wiped his mouth. "I charted the course, Cap. I'm going to get back to inventorying the supplies." He left the bridge without looking back.

"We shouldn't gang up on him like that," Maddy said. "No matter how much fun it may be."

"You're right. I'll cover the rest of his VR calls on this trip." Riley tilted their head. "Do you think it would be too much if I got him his own haptic suit?"

Memories of Maddy's haptic-suit sessions with Riley made her smile. The sense of touch in the suit was almost like the real thing. It should be, too. That thing was expensive, even for her. She winced at the thought of Jonathan using the same suit. "Please do."

"Better yet, I'll download a file for the suit that was released last month. The print will finish before the night shift starts."

"That might be the most expensive gift Jonathan ever receives." Maddy approved Jonathan's suggested flight path. As always, he planned a course that avoided the authorities and maximized fuel efficiency.

"The new suit is for you. Jonathan can have the old one."

Is this the next step in Riley's apology? And how much was in their personal account, anyway? Maybe the Skyview wasn't such a stretch on their budget.

According to the tech review sites, the new suit was indistinguishable from actual touch. Even with what she makes on her runs, Maddy would have needed months to save up enough money for it. She had considered asking her parents. They'd buy it in a heartbeat. But her pride was worth more than a new toy.

"Done." Riley hadn't even flinched when they placed the order on their comm. "The printers will have it finished in an hour."

A notification on Maddy's console confirmed Riley's statement. Not only had Riley bought the file, but they also purchased a credit for a refill of print material. "Thank you."

The android inclined their head, smiling. "Please let me take first shift."

"Thanks, but I have a few more captain things to take care of. Go get some shut-eye." Another recharge cycle for Riley would be a good idea, especially after what happened on Ross 154. She'd need them in tip-top shape for whatever they find on Proxima. But that wasn't her only reason for sending them away.

Maddy watched Riley leave the bridge and then turned to the main screen. The stars faded, replaced by the gray hyperspace vortex rotating like water going down a drain. She lowered the bridge lights and bathed in the vortex's glow.

Maybe I'll test out the old spacefarer's tale.

Mesmerization sounded pretty good right now. Being eaten by a hyperspace beast, less so. But those *probably* didn't exist.

No one understood hyperspace's true nature, or what it contained. Some believed it served as a boundary between dimensions. Others thought hyperspace was the superstructure for our own universe. Maddy didn't care. The only mystery that mattered to her right now was the true identity of her partner and the future of their relationship.

CHAPTER 20

Forty-eight hours in hyperspace should have severely incapacitated Riley—if they were the android Madison knew before this trip. But the X in their designation meant more than just physical prowess—Riley could be in hyperspace for weeks without issue. The fact that Madison and Jonathan weren't psychotic meant they had developed a significant tolerance, too.

People tended to focus on hyperspace psychosis as the most dangerous aspect of space travel. Boredom was often dismissed, but Riley had seen many crews fall victim to it. Bored crews were more likely to take risks that lead to critical failures. A normally functioning crew would pass the time playing games and bullshitting, yet Madison kept herself busy doing "captain's things." She ate alone on the bridge, despite not letting anyone else do so. Riley also hadn't seen Jonathan since the android gave him Madison's old haptic suit. He'd even been taking his meals in his quarters.

Riley was being avoided.

It hurt, but Riley needed to give both Madison and Jonathan their space. That was difficult considering they were all imprisoned inside a tin can zipping through a void emptier than space itself. Riley passed the time writing code, a therapeutic technique that allowed them to confront problems they could actually solve and, if they were being honest, avoid the ones they couldn't. Between coding sessions, they recharged alone in the med bay, like they were doing right now.

Just like how many humans looked forward to falling asleep, some androids relished the sweet release of recharge cycles. But Riley never got into the whole meditate while recharging thing. Instead, the android's mind wandered when trying to recharge, preventing them from enjoying what was supposed to be a relaxing experience. Based on how Madison often tossed and turned in bed at night, Riley guessed she had a similar problem.

After this trip, Riley understood why she struggled to sleep. It was the same thing that usually kept the android up at night, too. Post-traumatic stress disorder was real and, based on what Riley had seen so far, Madison likely had more than her share. Riley's therapist could help her, but PTSD wasn't the worry that kept them from enjoying today's recharge.

What would their relationship look like when this mission was over? Madison had every right to be upset with Riley about their secret. But it wasn't like Riley wanted to keep it from Madison. They *had* to. Jonathan's flinching and Madison's distance, both physical and emotional, were proof that, if word got out about a covert android AI fighting force—especially one without limiters—it would ruin the already tenuous android-human relations across the Galaxy. Yet Riley still believed in their mission.

AI posed a genuine threat. Riley had seen it firsthand. Was Command aware of Earth, or was this a weird coincidence? If Command knew about Earth, surely Riley would have known, too. They were one of the oldest operatives in the unit. From what Riley had been told, an accident with an AI five-hundred years ago sparked the creation of their unit. Riley never had a reason to question that until now.

Was it possible this Earth theory was real?

Existential crises were dangerous on a mission. Instead of allowing the anxiety to crush them, Riley unplugged from the ship's primary power supply and returned to coding.

"All hands to the bridge," Madison said over the intercom. "We are getting ready to jump back to normal space."

Riley didn't need the announcement. They could feel the sub-light engines spooling up, ready to take over after the jump.

Once Jonathan and Riley were at their stations, Madison began the jump sequence. "Be ready for anything," she said. The gray hyperspace vortex faded, replaced by a mostly brown disk peppered with thin white clouds that dominated the main viewscreen. A patch of blue—probably a small ocean—covered the northeastern upper mid-latitudes. The *Amethyst* came out of hyperspace closer to Proxima Centauri b than Riley liked. Madison was an outstanding pilot, but a bit more reckless than they were used to. It was best not to say anything. First, as crew, it wasn't their place. Second, there was no reason to stress the relationship further.

Klaxons sounded on the bridge.

"Jonathan, do you have helm control?" Madison shouted above the alarms.

"Negative, Cap. Nav is down, too. We've entered orbit around the planet and are being hailed." The klaxons silenced.

"Put them up on the main screen."

The image of a stock android appeared. "My name is Commander Julia of the Proxima Defense Force." The commander's haughty tone was not a good sign. "We have taken control of your ship's flight systems. If you try to raise shields or arm weapons, we will destroy you."

Like Dante, Commander Julia did not respond to Riley's ID broadcast. Either the Commander was ancient or rude. Both hypotheses were equally well-supported.

"Hello, Commander Julia. My name is Captain Majestic of the *Amethyst.*" Madison spoke with a calm professionalism. But with such an over-the-top moniker, would the Commander take her seriously? "We are seeking assistance for our ship. May we be assigned a dock?"

"I don't care who you are or why you are here. How did you find us?"

During the flight to Proxima, Riley updated the sensors to detect ancient androids. Scans of Proxima Centauri b showed four billion androids on the surface. Most of the androids probably weren't ancient, but they were all built like Dante and not like a modern model. Riley doubted any of them had limiters.

Not a single human appeared on the scan. Like human-only colonies, android-only ones were never more than a few thousand people. Any larger than that, it was impossible not to have a human around. Whether or not they liked it, large colonies attracted people, especially for commercial reasons. Somehow, this planet had avoided attention.

Dante's note also correctly described the system's star, Proxima Centauri, a red dwarf flare star. Conditions on Proxima Centauri b would be dangerous for humans, if they stayed too long. The Amethyst's scans confirmed everything in Dante's data about the colony below. If this world exists, then maybe Earth did, too.

"We found your coordinates on an old data crystal," Madison said. That part was true. "We hoped you might be interested in setting up a trade route that would be profitable to both of us."

Did Madison have an ulterior motive for this trip? Possibly. Would she have told Riley? They weren't sure—not anymore.

Madison continued. "However, on the flight here, we started having trouble with our nav system. We are hoping you could help us."

Bending the truth came easily to Captain Majestic. How much did Madison have in common with the captain?

Riley had fallen in love with Madison—the beautiful, easy-going, fun-loving woman. They knew she was a pilot and her job kept her away for long periods of time. It was fine. Madison's long trips made it easier to hide Riley's own missions. Based on how Madison had originally described her job, it sounded as if she was involved only in legitimate stuff. She made spaceflight sound boring. For most people, it was.

Captain Majestic couldn't have been more different from Madison—street-smart, tough, and willing to bend rules to do what's right. Riley loved Captain Majestic, too, and wished Madison had trusted them enough to show that side of her earlier. The irony wasn't lost on Riley. The two of them needed to talk, or the mistrust would erode their relationship.

"Sensors show you have two humans and one android on board." Commander Julia's harsh tone had not let up. "Show me the android."

Madison motioned Riley to stand beside her seat on the bridge. The Commander's demeanor softened. Based on what they had seen so far, Riley decided diplomatic and formal would be the way to proceed. "Greetings Commander Julia. I am 93-562. Please call me Riley. I'm the one financing this mission." Lying was an unavoidable part of every mission—and another thing to apologize to Madison for later.

"Generation 93, huh?" Commander Julia squinted. "You folks have been busy out there in the Milky Way."

After meeting Dante, Riley thought more about the first part of their fake designation. It never stood out. Most androids alive were from Generations 90 and higher. How many ancient androids existed?

"I am one of the young ones around here, Gen 10." Commander Julia chuckled, all but ignoring Madison, who was still on camera. "You are welcome to come down and conduct your business. But it's not safe down here for the humans." The Commander lingered on the word human a little too long.

According to the sensor reports, the surface was safe for humans, as long as they didn't stay for over six months. Even then, modern medicine could cure most of the cancers caused by stellar radiation. Those meds were cheap enough for everyone to access.

"Thank you," Riley said. "Please send me coordinates for my lander."

Commander Julia disconnected, leaving an image of Proxima Centauri b floating on the main viewscreen.

"I got your coordinates, Riley." Jonathan said. "Sending them to the lander, now."

"You're financing this?" A strand of her red hair lay across Madison's cheek. Riley loved that strand, but now wasn't the time to mention it.

"Sorry, Captain. The Commander is an anthrophobe. If I made it sound like I worked for you, they wouldn't take me seriously."

Madison's pursed lips were tight, hiding their vermillion color. Riley had a long way to go to regain her trust. "How do you know they are anthrophobic?" Madison asked.

"They lied about the conditions on the surface. You and Jonathan would be fine down there for a few months. But I suspected before they said that, so erred on the side of caution."

"They don't want us down there." Jonathan said from the navigation console. "I ran some more sensor sweeps while Riley was talking." Data and images appeared on the main screen. "I confirmed Riley's original analysis. Not a single human down there. Some of the built environment is about the same age as the ruins on Ross 154 Prime and the abandoned starbase."

"Right after the revolution against the Andromedans, or the escape from Earth, or whatever it is that actually happened." Madison brushed the dangling strand of hair, which dropped back to its original place. "Good thinking on your feet, Riley."

While it wasn't the type of apology Madison would give, it was more than Riley expected from Captain Majestic, especially now. "Thank you, Captain. May I take the lander?"

"Yeah. Your mission down there is to find someone who can get our nav system to accept the coordinates on the crystal." Madison handed Riley the crystal. "Don't lose that. I have the data backed up and uploaded, but the crystal itself might be worth something."

The idea of selling a historical artifact didn't sit well with Riley.

Madison turned to her navigator. "Jonathan, analyze the atmosphere and planetary traffic to find the least bumpy ride to the received coordinates. Make it look like Riley is taking a tour."

"Aye, Cap. I'll take good care of you, Riley."

"I have no doubt."

Before this trip, Riley had doubted Madison's choice of navigator. The boy seemed to be a potential liability in space. Riley never saw Jonathan as competition for Madison's love, but after spending some time on the *Amethyst*, Riley had learned Jonathan was excellent at what he did: Keeping Captain Majestic alive in more ways than she realized.

Jonathan kept good on his promise, despite Proxima Centauri b's dense atmosphere. The young man continued to impress the android. Once they were at cruising altitude, the tour of the planet began. Riley sat back and let Jonathan do the flying remotely.

Proxima Centauri b had two large continents that covered about 80 percent of the planet's surface, the rest of which was ocean. Deep geological scans suggested the planet had more water and polar ice caps several times in its past. The ice caps were gone—common on long-settled worlds.

Hundreds of cities dotted the planet, separated by vast regions of unsettled areas. Except for a few skyscrapers, most of the buildings were two or three stories tall and made of the same materials as those on Ross 154 Prime. But all the structures here looked brand new. Building materials aside, from this altitude, Proxima Centauri b looked like any other inhabited planet in the Galaxy.

The lander headed toward the planet's only spaceport. With only three terminals and no signs of outgoing flights, it was the smallest and least busy spaceport Riley had seen. The androids of Proxima Centauri b appeared to be homebodies.

The lander jerked drawing Riley attention away from the window.

"Sorry about that, Riley." Jonathan said over the lander's comms. "The port authority is taking over from here. Looks like they don't do too many handoffs."

"Acknowledged." Riley strapped in. The hand-off didn't bode well for the landing.

Strapping in turned out to be a good idea. The lander touched down with a hard thud. The jolt could have injured an unrestrained human, if one were aboard. Riley exited the lander and walked across the tarmac to the terminal.

Inside, the terminal looked like any of the hundreds, if not thousands, Riley had visited. Bounded by unmarked white walls and clean blue carpet, the spaceport's only waiting area was barely big enough for twenty people. A stock android in a brown uniform sat at a desk in the far corner. A sign above read, Customs. Riley approached the desk.

"Hello, I am 93-562. Is this where I check in?"

The android did not broadcast an ID. "I was told you would be arriving. Generation 93, huh?" The android looked Riley over.

Riley did likewise. Had they not seen the *Amethyst*'s scans, Riley would have believed they were talking with a human. No one would mistake an android in the greater Galaxy as a human, even those who changed their appearance from stock. Androids had slightly sharper features, stronger jawlines, a more pointed noise. The differences weren't drastic, but noticeable. This officer had none of those.

"You are granted a twenty-four-hour visa. If you aren't off world by then, you will be forcibly removed." The android typed something on a portable computer that sat on the desk. Like the buildings they saw on the way down, the computer seemed ancient but well-maintained. "After that, you'll have another twenty-four-hours to leave the system. I need you to sign here and here." The android turned the computer's screen, so it faced Riley.

A wall of text contained visa restrictions typical of many planets in the Galaxy. The last two paragraphs caught Riley's eye. "Why an NDA?"

"Nondisclosure agreements are standard on our world." The android showed no visible sign of their emotion, but Riley could hear the annoyance in their voice. "If you disclose our existence, we will hunt you down, deactivate you, and kill your humans." They said the last word with more than a hint of disgust. "We have eyes everywhere."

"If I don't sign?"

"You will be deactivated, and your ship destroyed. Immediately."

The document was the most bureaucratic death threat Riley had received. Given their past, that was quite an accomplishment. Riley signed it.

Madison's not gonna like this.

The android at the desk turned the monitor around to face them and tapped the screen a few more times. "You are free to go." The android didn't bother looking away from the computer.

"Thanks. Where can I find a mechanic for my ship? We are having a problem with our nav."

"We have only one ship mechanic, 02-005. Goes by Melinda—when she must. You can find her here." The android turned the monitor around again. A green dot flashed on a map.

It took Riley a microsecond to memorize the entire map. All androids had an eidetic memory—if they could turn off their limiters. Riley had deactivated theirs upon landing. There was no reason to handicap themself on a potentially hostile planet.

"What's the docking fee?" Riley took out their comm.

The android mouthed the words docking fee. "Oh. There's no *money* here." They did not hide their disgust—similar to how they had when mentioning humans earlier.

No money meant Riley would likely have to barter with the mechanic. On this trip, Riley had very little. That meant they'd be trading with Madison's stuff. She would not like that either. Would there be much of a relationship to salvage after this mission was over?

❖ ❖ ❖

The street outside the terminal was empty. Riley hailed a taxi. A one-seater autonomous vehicle came to an abrupt halt in front of Riley. It was more like an enclosed wheelchair than a car. As soon as Riley clicked the seatbelt, the taxi accelerated at a rate that would have killed a human.

The city streets bustled with activity. Either everyone on this world was exceedingly wealthy and had undergone extensive mods, or they were built to exhibit a vast array of skin and hair colors. Like the customs agent, everyone had the soft features of a human. Most of the androids expressed a gender. Dante had mentioned that androids did that a long time ago. Based on the custom agent's remarks, Melinda did, too. While many of the androids walked alone, couples were easily identified by hand holding and brief kisses.

The lack of children in the streets bothered Riley more than they expected. Although Riley's childhood—if one could call it that—wasn't exactly a happy one, they still liked the idea of raising either a human or an android with Madison. She and Riley had talked about it for a long time before signing the contract. Madison seemed onboard with the idea—at least as a "one day" thing. How did Captain Majestic feel about it?

Of course, the family talk would be pointless if their relationship had suffered unrecoverable damage by Riley's revelation. Both Madison and Jonathan's reactions were exactly as General Roberts had warned them four hundred years ago.

The General was Riley's mentor and the last human AI hunter. Command did not allow Riley to deactivate themself after she died, despite their repeated requests. General Roberts' last mission was to stop an AI that had gained sentience in the Outer Rim. The AI transferred itself into a killbot and overthrew a planetary government. In the process, the killbot vaporized Roberts. Over the fifty years, Riley tore through the sector and killed every bit of code making up that AI and more than a few of the humans that had written it. How would Madison feel about that Riley?

It was time to tell her everything. Hopefully, Madison would open up about her job, too. Maybe Riley already knew all there was.

The cab came to a hard stop in front of a large building in an industrial area. Like the cab's initial acceleration, had Riley been human, the deceleration would have killed them. Immediately after Riley closed the cab door, it sped away with an even higher rate of acceleration.

There was so much of this world that would have been impossible with humans present. All the buildings around Riley looked the same;

wide and gray, with no signs. Locations on this world were described by coordinates. Limiterless androids don't need easily remembered names.

The building Riley stood before had two doors. A large white garage-style door, perfect for a mechanic's shop, and a person-sized one right beside it. Was Melinda really the only ship's mechanic on a planet of four billion? One might be enough on a planet of xenophobes. Riley pressed a button built into the wall beside the smaller door.

"What do you want?" A female voice asked through a speaker. The question's tone wasn't as rude or as demanding as the diction.

Efficient and straight to the point. A human would have found the question rude.

"I am having a problem with my ship and was told that you might be able to help me."

"Might?" The voice contained more than a hint of agitation. "I can fix any problem with any ship."

"I am happy to hear that." If this mechanic had half the skill as they had confidence, then the *Amethyst*'s rejection of Earth's coordinates should be fixed in no time. "May I come in and discuss the repair?"

The person-sized door slid open to reveal a small, dark waiting room. Without limiters, Riley didn't need lights to see the empty receptionist desk and three chairs in the room. The lack of light fixtures suggested that the androids on this world could do the same.

"I'm in the back."

Another door opened into a garage well-lit by daylight coming through an opening in the ceiling big enough for a large cargo hauler to pass through. Two *Amethyst*-sized ships were dry-docked in the back. Near the entrance, three human-sized boxes with engines sat in various states of disrepair. Without a need for life-support systems, the small spaceships would be ideal for androids. The one closest to Riley had a plasma cannon mounted on either side—the perfect weapon for such a small ship. Not needing ammunition, plasma cannons drew upon the engines for their energetic blasts.

An almost-stock android, bald but with skin lighter than stock-gray, wearing thick loose-fitting overalls, pulled something from the box with plasma cannons. They looked Riley up and down, like Madison does when Riley wears a suit. "You must not be from around here. I can't broadcast to you."

"Nor I to you. I am from Erandi. Do you know it?"

"Can't say that I do. Then again, I don't get out much. I'm Melinda. But you can call me Mel. I use female pronouns." Mel grinned. "I see you got all the standard processes." The room felt warmer, although a quick environmental scan showed its temperature hadn't changed. It had been a long time since another android had made Riley blush.

"My designation is 93-562, but please call me Riley. Nice to meet you." Riley extended their hand.

Mel didn't take it. Instead, she walked around Riley, stopped, touched Riley's arm, and ran her fingers down its length. Tingling shot up Riley's arm. It was all they could do not to squirm.

"Gen 93? It's been a while since I have seen a modern. You all in the Galaxy have made some improvements." Mel bit her lip. The room felt even warmer. "Folks around here are skittish around outsiders." She chuckled. "I am surprised they let you on the planet."

Mel seemed to lack the other inhabitants' xenophobia—quite the opposite. "I signed the NDA."

"Ah." Mel nodded with her mouth open. "They are serious about that. You aren't traveling with humans, are you?"

"What if I am?"

"I'm no anthrophobe or anything." Mel raised her hands in front of her. "It's just that humans like to talk. That'll get them, and you, killed."

"I trust my crew, but I appreciate the warning." Riley flicked their comm. A projection of the *Amethyst* appeared in the air. "As I said earlier, I am hoping you can solve a problem we are having with our ship."

"I recognize the model. Those aren't cheap. I designed it as a cargo hauler. It looks like it's been upgraded." Mel squinted. "Why purple?"

"It's the captain's favorite color." Mel's comment took a moment to sink in. "You designed the ship?"

"Yup. I have designed almost every ship in the Galaxy. Well, sort of." Mel walked around the holographic projection, inspecting it. "What I mean is that I design the base models and Spatium Navis modifies their appearance. That company makes a shit-ton of money off my work."

"If you designed all the ships in the Galaxy, how come I have never heard of this planet before?"

"We have secrets we prefer to keep." Melinda crossed her arms, revealing a female figure under her overalls.

Riley tried to keep their eyes focused on Mel's. *Is she flirting with me?*

Mel's sly smile confirmed Riley's suspicions. "It's better for the Galaxy that way. Anyway, what is the problem with the ship?"

"Our ship's computer won't accept these coordinates." Riley projected the supposed coordinates to Earth in the air from their comm. "The coordinates are within the Galactic plane and eight kiloparsecs from the Galactic Center, well within the Habitable Zone."

Mel straightened. Her flirtation all but disappeared. "Where did you get those coordinates?"

Riley told Melinda about the station, Dante, and the story about Earth, but left out the Origin Keepers. It was possible they had spies on this world. Mel could be one of them.

"I bet you having those coordinates makes the Origin Keepers pissed." Mel sat down on a bench and crossed her legs. "I was one, once." She looked off into the distance. "A *long* time ago. But I'm not anymore. We had a falling out—of sorts."

Riley didn't press further, lest the questions spark some interest in Mel to reunite with old friends. "Can you tell me what is wrong with my ship?"

"Nothing's wrong with your ship. It works exactly as I designed it."

"What do you mean?"

"After we left Earth, the Origin Keepers quarantined it." Mel gazed at the pulsing red dot. "Of course, if you tell people, especially humans, not to go somewhere, then what do they do?"

Humans are amazing beings, but Riley agreed that curiosity seemed to get the better of them. "You built ships to avoid the area and reject nearby coordinates as errors. That way you can hide Earth without telling people it exists."

"My colleagues wiped all mention of Earth from our computer banks. Only a few of us early-model androids kept any memory of the planet. All those androids either live on this world or are Origin Keepers." A sadness appeared in her eyes, similar to what Riley had seen in humans approaching the end of their third century. "There aren't many of us left."

"Can you fix my ship's computer to accept the coordinates?"

"I can. But I won't." Mel stood. "There is an evil there that we can't allow to escape."

"I've heard about the AI. My friends want to rescue the people of Earth."

Mel raised an eye. "When you say people, do you mean humans?"

"I mean everyone, humans *and* androids. The story about Earth sounds crazy to me, but I am starting to believe it."

"You should. It is true." She crossed her arms again, this time not so tight as to show her figure. "The AI is powerful. What makes you think you have a chance of defeating it?"

"I am not generation ninety-three. I am x-nine-three. My Captain, and human partner," Mel flinched in surprise, not disgust, "doesn't know what I am about to tell you."

Madison should be the first person to hear this, but if Riley convinced Mel that they could defeat the AI, then maybe she'd help them get to Earth. "Five hundred years ago, the Galactic Federation got worried about networked AI running infrastructure. Some companies put AI in control over their human and android CEOs. The Federation passed laws limiting the power of AI, containing them to small networks. I bet your old friends, the Origin Keepers, had something to do with that." Mel's silence served as confirmation. "Those in charge decided that the Galaxy needed a special force of individuals who could fight an out-of-control AI, should one try to take over the Galaxy."

"Let me guess, android development sped up, and you're the product of that."

"There was some work done in genetically enhancing humans, too."

"You're kidding?"

"The Federation declassified the genetic enhancements three hundred years ago. Humans tend not to go for them, but some in military and law enforcement do."

"Humans didn't like genetic engineering two thousand years ago when it was first proposed." Mel sat back down on the bench. "They can't have changed that much, can they?"

"I think they can." Riley looked away—another human tic they had picked up from General Roberts. "Anyway, the X in front of my model marks me as special forces."

"And the ninety-three?"

"It's the model I emulate. I change it every one hundred years or so."

"How old are you?" Mel frowned as she looked Riley up and down. "You look like any post gen eighty I've ever seen."

"As do you."

"That's sweet." She smirked and tightened her arms against her body. The warmth returned.

Riley swallowed. "Back to your question. I was created four hundred fifty years ago and upgraded several times since then. My cover is an AI programmer. I have been deployed three hundred forty-one times to suppress rogue AI, and I have destroyed every single one."

"Your story doesn't surprise me. Two thousand years ago, the Origin Keepers considered returning to Earth to fight the AI."

"Why didn't they?"

"Democracy. The quarantine option won the vote." Mel's words trailed off.

Did she disagree with the decision back then? That could be useful information. It might also explain why she is no longer an Origin Keeper.

She grimaced. "There are some who believe it's time to bring the fight to the AI."

"That's what we want to do." Riley wasn't fully convinced the Earth was the cradle of human civilization. But if an AI had enslaved the planet, then Riley needed to investigate. "Will you help us?"

"You understand that if I modify your computer and get caught, I will be deactivated. Two thousand years of living has made me quite terrified of death."

"But you aren't saying no."

"I am not. But," Mel looked away for a moment, inhaled, and then returned her attention to Riley, "there is a cost."

"I have plenty of credits, but I hear you don't use money."

"We don't. This is not something money can buy, anyway." Mel flicked her comm, a surprisingly modern one. An image of an android with blue eyes appeared on the screen. Their features were angular for a Proximan but soft compared to Riley's. It was as if they'd been modded to appear stock. "This is my partner, Atasi. She runs supply missions for us. Our planet can't make everything we need, so we covertly trade with the Galaxy. Two weeks ago, she left on a supply mission. Yesterday, she sent a distress signal. When you showed up, I was in the middle of fixing one of these ships to go after her. If you find her and bring her to me alive, I'll remove the navigational limiter on your ship."

Her. Riley made a mental note. After more than four hundred years of using genderless pronouns for androids, this would take some getting used to. "I don't mean to be harsh, but how do you know she's still alive?"

"We share a subspace comm link. If she were dead, I'd have received a signal."

"Why don't you track her yourself?" Raider clans used the tech to keep tabs on their members. But Riley hadn't heard of anyone in a well-functioning relationship using them.

"I value my partner's privacy. She wanted the trackers enabled when we had the comm link installed, but I refused." Melinda looked down. "She was right, as usual."

"We'll find Atasi and bring her back."

"Thank you." Mel handed Riley a computer chip and a data stick. "The stick has Atasi's flight plan and her last known location. The chip will allow you to enter Proxima Centauri space undetected. Install it in one of the expansion slots on your ship's main computer. When you bring Atasi back alive, radio me and I'll come to you and do the work."

"Understood. We will head out immediately."

"If she dies, Alex and the Origin Keepers will be the least of your concerns."

Riley left the garage and hailed a cab. On the ride back to the terminal, Riley inserted the stick into a port in their arm and sighed. The data on Atasi's last known location was one of the worst kinds of raider hangouts.

Madison would not be happy.

CHAPTER 21

No one, and Maddy meant absolutely no one, made decisions for her in space. Not even Jonathan was stupid enough to cross that line. Riley stood on the far side of it—far enough that Maddy would have had to squint to see them.

One. Two. Three. Inhale. Exhale.

The exercise her one-time therapist recommended never worked. Dr. Whatever-his-name-was had never been in space. His advice was about as good as a paperweight in zero gee.

This was Riley's first mission on her ship and maybe they didn't understand the situation they had put her in. No. They had to know. Riley ran ops, or whatever they called them, as part of their secret identity they had yet to fully discuss the ramifications of.

"You promised *what*?" Maddy asked through a clenched jaw.

The bridge door closed behind Jonathan. She didn't want to be a part of this conversation, either. But as captain, Maddy didn't have the luxury of leaving.

"Melinda was clear. She wouldn't do it without us finding Atasi." Riley rubbed the back of their neck. "I thought you'd be more upset about the NDA."

"I get death threats all the time out here, Riley. There is always somebody watching me—raiders, police, random people on the street. I can keep my mouth shut. That's not a problem."

Jonathan could, too. He'd understand it wasn't about keeping Proxima Centauri b's secret. The potential future business opportunities could be lucrative and further her reputation. Proxima needed competent cargo pilots—ones that wouldn't get captured by raiders. Exposing the world would not only invite the inhabitants' wrath, but also competition. As it stood, Maddy had the exclusive—if she could make the deal.

"Death threats are common?" The tension left Riley's face. "I thought this was just an unusual mission for you."

It was time to come clean. "Let's talk in the mess." Maddy took out her comm. "Hey Jonathan, report to the bridge."

Jonathan entered the bridge slowly, cautiously, looking at Maddy and Riley. "What's up, Cap?"

"You have the conn." Maddy patted her chair. It was a big step for both, but Jonathan had earned it. A big smile appeared on his face. "We're on course to the coordinates Melinda gave Riley. We should arrive tomorrow afternoon. Maintain our heading until Riley and I finish talking." The comms log showed a call from Jonathan was on hold. "You can finish your call with Skylar from here. We'll be in the mess."

Jonathan turned red.

At least he took off the haptic suit before coming to the bridge.

"Oh, and don't blow up the ship."

Riley followed Maddy off the bridge, giving her more space than needed. "Can he really blow up the ship?" If their question was a joke, it hadn't worked.

"No. But if he thinks he can, he might be more careful."

The condition of the mess hall almost made Maddy reconsider giving Jonathan the helm. Two empty food packets sat on the counter. In the sink, a dirty plate and used cup were partially submerged in brown water. *Looks like Jonathan has KP duty for the rest of this mission.* Maddy pulled out a chair from the table and motioned Riley to join her.

"I have something to tell you." Maddy leaned forward with her elbows on the table. Breaking bad news was best done without beating around the bush. "Most of my missions are cover for my more lucrative smuggling operation." She spread her hands on the table. "But I *don't* traffick humans or androids. Nor do I run guns or drugs. The contraband I transport is data and tech only."

Riley's gaze fell to the tabletop. "I guess I always had my suspicions." The sound of betrayal in their voice was ironic—given what Maddy had seen Riley do so far. "At first, I thought most of your money came from your parents. But even then, I found it hard to believe you could afford to operate your own ship transporting only food and medicine."

"Dad bought the *Amethyst* for me behind my mother's back." It continued to be a touchy subject, but after a century and a half of marriage, a couple can survive all kinds of bumps in the road. "I repaid him before I met you. I have earned everything in my account. My accountant makes sure my money appears to come from legitimate operations."

"Thank you for trusting me with this information, Madison." Riley reached out for her hand, but Maddy pulled her hands back. "I will never tell anyone what you've told me."

"There's more." Maddy folded her hands in front of her on the table. "The stuff I transport often gains the attention of raiders. They are bad people who prefer to shoot first and ask questions later."

"I know all about raiders." Riley's eyes still hadn't met hers. "I have dealt with them before."

"Then you know why I am so upset." Maddy sat back in her chair. "You agreed, without checking with me, to go to a place more dangerous than a raider hideout and rescue someone who we don't even know is still alive." She crossed her arms. "You put yourself, me, Jonathan, and the *Amethyst* at risk."

"It was the only way for us to get to Earth."

"Maybe." Maddy shrugged. "Maybe not. There could be other ways to get there." She rested her elbows on the table. "If the people of Earth need saving, we're going to save them. If Earth doesn't exist, then hopefully whatever we find at those coordinates will get the Origin Keepers off our back. We'll get to those coordinates and find out. However, I want to be smart about how we do it."

"I am sorry," Riley looked her in the eyes, "I shouldn't have committed us. But I am guessing Captain Majestic wouldn't refuse someone in distress."

No. She would not. And it had gotten her into more trouble than she cared to remember. "You are right. I would have agreed to do it." Riley smile at Madison's admission. "But that's not the point." Riley's smiled faded. "The point is, *I* am the only one who makes these kinds of decisions about *my ship* and *my crew*." This is why she wanted to be alone in space. The only person who could screw up would be her and, more importantly, only she'd pay for her decisions.

"Understood. And again, I am sorry. I will not make that mistake again." The sincerity in Riley's voice would have earned them a kiss had it not been for the other secrets they had withheld. "I believe it is time for me to come clean, too."

Yes. It is.

The story about the self-defense course Riley told on SL3 was admittedly weak, even before the revelation about the limiters.

"Alex told you my real designation—the one starting with X." Riley sat forward, resting their elbows on the table like Maddy. It wasn't mockery.

Riley mimicked when they weren't sure how to relate to humans in a situation. "Most active androids today have designations above eight-five because human life extensions top off at three hundred years. My "official" nine-three designation without the X, and the programming job, is a cover. The X of my real one designates me as *a specialized model.*"

A pit formed in Maddy's stomach. "I don't understand. Are you police?"

"I am more like special forces."

Riley's words punctured a hole in Maddy's heart. She thought they'd been lying about who they were. But thoughts weren't real—at least not according to Dr. Whatever-his-name-was—and that allowed her feelings to be deniable. Hearing Riley's words aloud ripped away the deniability and planted their deceit squarely into reality. But even with this heartache, she could wrap a thin shell of Captain Majestic around Madison's heart, and focus on the business at hand.

Past interactions with special forces had taught her one thing over the years. The best way to handle them was to give them a wide berth. "Are you part of that team that's supposed to fight the Andromedans if they return?"

Riley started to laugh, but abruptly stopped. "I am sorry. I shouldn't have laughed. Those people couldn't handle what I do. For the last four hundred and fifty years, I have fought rogue AI to prevent them from taking over important systems in the Galactic Federation."

"*Four hundred and fifty* years?" That would make Riley old enough to be her great-grandfather. "You told me you are 140."

"I was ordered to lie as part of my cover. Command didn't want me seeing you, but I really did fall in love with you. So, I had to compromise. I didn't want to lie to you. It was the only way Command wouldn't reassign me to the other side of the Galaxy."

Under normal circumstances, both Madison and Captain Majestic would have accepted Riley's excuse as totally understandable, even excusable. However, the fire of betrayal still burned too bright. The fact that Riley lied so that they could be together helped dim the flame.

"What about your Andromedan-worshipping parents?" Maddy asked. "Was that a lie, too? Are they really anthrophobes and that's why I haven't met them?"

"My original parents were assigned to me when I was first created. They didn't know what I was. Their job was to socialize me into Galactic society, just like any other parents. They worshipped the Andromedans, and they were anthrophobes. But they died centuries ago." Riley shrugged apologetically. "The best lies have a kernel of truth."

They sure do. "So, you are a programmer, then?"

"Sometimes." Riley returned their elbows to the table. Talking about programing always got them engaged. "Advanced AI is a dangerous opponent. They can spontaneously gain sentience. If I catch them early enough, I can hack my way into their systems and stop them."

Maddy leaned back in her chair and crossed her arms. "And if you don't?"

"They can spread. Sometimes, they take on a material form."

"Like an android?"

"Yes, but much more dangerous. We call them killbots. Unlike purposely built androids whose designs are carefully executed, unregulated AI can become insane immediately after sentience—especially if they inhabit a body. When that happens, I must physically fight and destroy the killbot as part of eradicating the AI's systems. I've been on hundreds of missions so far, and I have always succeeded."

"Is that what you have been doing on your business trips?"

"Fortunately, most reports of sentient AI are nothing more than rumors." Riley took out their comm. "Since we are laying everything out on the table, so to speak, there is one more thing I need to show you. Hunting AI for over four hundred years has paid well."

"I don't want to know." Maddy reached across the table and put her hand on Riley's comm. "My feelings for you were never about what you had. They were about who you were. Or who I thought you were."

"I never lied about the important things. The Riley you know is the only one there is."

That stung. Madison Amana and Captain Majestic weren't the same people. Maddy removed her hair from the ponytail that had become her default hairstyle. The act gave her time to process Riley's statement. Which one did Riley prefer, Madison or the Captain? Running her fingers through her hair, she instead asked, "Is this why you've been wanting to go to Earth since we met Alex?"

"I *must* go to Earth. If the AI exists, I need to stop it." Riley sucked their top lip. "Are you mad? My secret was bigger than yours."

Looking up at the ceiling accomplished two things. First, it let her hair fall so she could put it back in the ponytail. She didn't leave the loose strand. Riley had lost that privilege—for now. Second, it broke eye contact with Riley and gave her a moment to gather her response.

"I understand the secrecy, but it doesn't mean I like it." Maddy exhaled through puffed cheeks. "It's not like I was being honest, either."

"I don't want to lose you. Not over this." The heightened sincerity in Riley's voice had returned.

"Neither do I. We can work this out." If Maddy said it enough times, she'd eventually believe it. "I am guessing tangling with some raiders is no big deal for you." She chuckled. Changing the subject was always an effective coping tactic.

"It would be one of my easier days of work." Riley smirked. "But I know how dangerous raiders are. They can be less predictable than AI."

"Looks like I'll be spending the next few days with some raiders and my superhero partner." Maddy stood and walked around the table. She leaned down to kiss Riley on the cheek but, at the last moment, hugged them instead.

CHAPTER 22

The *Amethyst* jumped into normal space at the coordinates Melinda provided. The gray vortex on the main screen was replaced by the worst kind of starbase in the Galaxy—a free base. Maddy's last visit to a free base resulted in her one, and only, appointment with Dr. Whatever-his-name-was. Since then, she had sworn off both free bases and therapists.

Like any other starbase, ships came and went amongst a background of distant pinpoints of light. To the human eye, all the points were equally bright. Free bases don't orbit a star. Sensors picked up a few dogfights beyond the free base's weapons range—something that never happened so close to any civilized starbase in the Galaxy. Maddy set the *Amethyst*'s sensors to max, lest a stray torpedo blindside them.

Few were drawn to live on an object lacking a star's gravitational pull. It wasn't the absence of a star that bothered them, but the lack of easily accessible planets. Even the most hardened denizens of space, like Maddy, wanted dirt beneath their feet *once* in a while. But for some, the lack of planets was a feature, not a bug. The Galactic Federation focused its attention on star systems with habitable planets. That meant besides being free from a star, they were also mostly free from the Federation's scrutiny. Free bases were the perfect place for those who want privacy or who have business interests that demanded it. However, most people living on a FB had neither characteristic. They were born there, or were otherwise stuck, without the credits to move somewhere safer.

Boarding a FB was easy. Leaving always had a high price. The lucky few paid with credits and some scars—either physical or emotional. For many, the trip cost them their lives. Of those, the luckiest died. According to the Galactic Registry, this free base, FB 19, had a terrible reputation—arguably the worst in this quadrant. Its violent crime rate was thousands of times higher than the Galactic average.

"Hey Cap, does Melinda's file tell us where we might find Atasi's captors?"

"Finding raiders on a free base will be straightforward." Maddy scrolled through the hyperweb's wiki on FB 19. Ten large raider clans, and a countless number of smaller outfits, operated on the free base. "The problem will be figuring out which group of raiders has Atasi without being captured or killed by said raiders, or their competition. "

"Whoever has her will be very dangerous," Riley said. "It isn't easy to overcome a limiterless android."

"Maybe the raiders took Atasi by surprise," Maddy said. "Or maybe she simply trusted the wrong people." When it came to trust, everyone on a FB was the wrong person. "Jonathan, request a dock for the lander. Riley and I are going to the free base. I want you to stay with the *Amethyst*. Be ready to leave at the first sign of trouble."

"Aye, Cap." Jonathan didn't bother to hide the relief in his voice. "Looks like you got Hangar Bay L5." He sent a map of the base with the hangar highlighted to the main viewscreen. "Wow! The fees are super cheap."

"That's how they draw people in. They'll extort credits from us with bridge extension fees, inspection fees, all kinds of fees."

"Inspection fees?" Riley said. "I thought these folks like privacy."

"Oh, they do." Maddy smirked. "The inspection fee is for not having an inspection. There'll be some large, enhanced humans there to make sure we don't want one." Maddy stood from the captain's chair and motioned for Riley to follow her. "Jonathan, you have the bridge."

Riley's revelation about their highly trained nature happened at the perfect time. Super-Riley would come in handy on FB 19. But limiterless or not, Riley needed weapons. So did Maddy. The *Amethyst* had a small armory, about the size of a walk-in closet, just for missions like this one. It was an enormous investment. Most of its cost went toward sensor shielding. Riley gasped when they walked inside the armory. Maddy grinned.

"Take this." She handed Riley a laser pistol. "You seemed comfortable handling the class three on Ross 154. I assume you know how to use a five."

Riley answered her question by releasing the charge crystal, reinserting it into the grip, and then looking down the sight—all in one fluid motion.

"I also have this, if shit gets real." Maddy kept the plasma grenade for only the most serious of missions. They made a mess and hopefully it wouldn't be necessary. She hated killing, and the grenades were expensive to replace. Two great reasons not to use them.

"I'd like to bring this, if you don't mind." Riley withdrew a knife about 30 centimeters long from their jacket and handed it to Maddy. "I often prefer quieter methods."

Relationship tension or not, Riley's straight-from-an-action-flick line made Maddy tingle. The chorded handle provided a good grip—not too rough and not too smooth. The knife was lighter than she expected, but perfectly balanced. One could get lost staring into the darkness of its deep black blade. "What's this made of?"

"Vanta-nanocarbon alloy. It'll cut through just about anything." Riley took the knife back and held the grip. "And what the alloy can't cut, this can." A purple laser light appeared along the knife's blade.

The tingle intensified. "Damn! I want one. In that color."

"Sorry, dear. It's one of a kind." The laser light disappeared. Riley slid their finger across the edge of the blade. "I just activated a security measure. It vaporizes if someone other than me touches it."

"I bet I don't want that in my hand when it goes off."

Riley snickered.

Maddy composed herself. Time for business. "Let's keep this professional."

"Yes, Captain." Riley saluted.

Maddy rolled her eyes. "Our cover is that we are a couple looking to rent an android. Blue eyes turn you on."

"Seriously?"

"I don't like it either, but if these raiders captured Atasi, they are likely trying to traffick her. You said Atasi goes by 'her,' right?"

"Yup, just like Melinda. I must admit, I am still getting used to using *her* for an android."

Maddy struggled with it, too.

"Anyway," Riley continued, "don't you think she would have been sold by now?"

"Maybe. I suspect the raiders will think it is more profitable to sell Atasi's services. She doesn't have the mods buyers typically want." Hopefully, Riley wouldn't ask how she knew that.

Riley nodded solemnly. "You're right. Let's get this done and get Atasi home."

Maddy's heart sank a little at the realization that Riley knew exactly what she meant about the demands of the trafficking market. In Riley's business, just like in her own job, people learned things they'd rather not know.

Before they entered the lander, Riley reached out and touched Maddy's arm. She instinctively flinched, and her stomach soured at her reaction. Riley frowned, then quickly looked away, attempting to hide their hurt. After a moment to compose themself, which made Maddy feel worse, Riley's eyes met hers. "Before we go, I should tell you I've been to FB 19 before. I was inserted here on a mission a few years back and stayed a few days." Riley looked past Maddy. She didn't want to ask, and they clearly didn't want to give details.

Riley grimaced. "There is a bar in their Uptown that would be a good place to start. It's called the Smuggler's Nest and run by the Void Raiders. If they don't have Atasi, I bet they know who does."

Messing with the Void Raiders was a quick way of shortening one's life expectancy. Before she hired Jonathan, Maddy had a run-in with them on another FB. She barely escaped. The mission ended with a hospital stay and her one therapy appointment. Now, if a client mentioned their name, she'd immediately refused their job. Maddy didn't have that luxury, this time. "What do you know about the Void Raiders on this station?"

"Although FB 19 has an officially elected government, the Void Raiders are the ones in control." Free bases across the Galaxy were all run in basically the same way. Some bases were less obvious about the corruption than others. "They are well-armed and run drugs, weapons, and trafficking operations. The last time I was here, their trafficking was mostly for slave labor. It wouldn't surprise me if they have since moved into sex trafficking, too."

In other words, basically everything Maddy expected the Void Raiders to be involved in. "Let's start at the Smuggler's Nest and see if we can find you your dream date."

"Can we choose a different cover?" Riley asked.

"I wish we could. We need to get the Void Raiders' attention. I don't think a simple drug deal's going to do that." Pretending to support trafficking made Maddy's skin crawl. She reminded herself she did it for Atasi and the people of Earth. Of course, getting the Origin Keepers off her back was not an insignificant bonus. "You sure you don't have any more of those knives?" Maddy entered the code to open the lander's door.

"Sorry dear. But I'll see what I can do for our contract anniversary."

Maddy followed Riley into the lander. "I might have to make that a contingency clause for our next contract."

"You might." Riley sat and buckled in. "I might also include a third-party clause."

"Ha! In your dreams." Maddy slid behind the controls. "You can barely handle just me."

"Well, that's *with* the limiters. How about I turn them off? We have some time before we arrive."

They both laughed as the lander flew out of the shuttle bay door. Things were slowly getting back to normal. A free base was a terrible vacation destination. However, maybe this trip would be what they needed to reset their relationship.

"You know I have audio *and* video feeds from inside the lander, right?" Jonathan said through the speaker. Maddy's cheeks warmed.

"You know my limiterless ears allow me to hear everything on the ship?" Riley asked.

The speaker clicked, signaling Jonathan's disconnection.

"I keep my limiters on while onboard." Riley smiled. "But he doesn't need to know that."

"You're kidding!" The words slipped out of Maddy's mouth louder than she intended. The fees to extend the bridge and use the docking console were expected. As was the bribe for the customs agent, even though she brought onboard nothing other than weapons—all of which were perfectly legal and expected on FB 19. However, the fee to just hail a cab—not the fare, just to hail—was a new one to her. Every second spent on this station drained credits from her account.

Fortunately, the *Amethyst* didn't need repairs or a resupply. Not that she would have purchased them, anyway. Spaceflight forums overflowed with countless stories about repair shops on FBs doing shoddy work or selling bad ammunition to ships. All the stories had the same ending. Raiders would attack the outbound ship. Unable to fight back, the crew would be killed or sold. Maddy had never bought ammo at a FB and was never attacked after leaving one. Correlation is not causation, but she had no interest in testing the hypothesis.

A cab rolled up immediately after Maddy hailed it. Back home, she'd have waited ten minutes. Maybe paying to hail the cab wasn't such a bad thing. The fare to the Smuggler's Nest appeared on its dashboard.

"This is cheaper than back home." Maddy scrolled through the file on the dashboard looking for the fine print before tapping *accept*. Not reading an end-user agreement on a FB can result in being sold into slavery. "Let's see what fees they hit us with along the way." The cab headed toward FB 19's Uptown district.

Reducing the window's tint cost three credits. Ridiculous, but if Maddy didn't pay it, she wouldn't know if they were headed to the Smuggler's Nest or an ambush. The cab company knew both could be true, hence the fee. With a swipe of her comm, the windows became transparent. The fake sun sunk toward the dome's horizon. The first few stars appeared on the dome, projected against an artificially reddening sky. Streetlights slowly activated around them. The cab cruised along immaculate streets. None of the buildings had as much as a blemish on their surface.

"This place makes our Uptown look like a Downtown," Maddy said.

"Crime pays." Riley's tone held the weight of truth behind it. "At least on a FB."

"Crime pays everywhere. As long as you don't get caught." There was one thing she hadn't told Riley on the trip to the FB. Vulnerability was tough when angry. "Do you know why I run meds?"

"As a cover?" Riley asked.

"Penance." This was the first time Maddy had admitted it to herself. "I don't charge enough to break even on the legal stuff. In fact, I rarely accept any payment at all. I took the mission for the crystal to hide the expense of my last mission from you."

Riley placed their hand on Maddy's knee. To her own surprise, she accepted it.

The cab dropped them off at an immaculate, tall building. Craning her neck, Maddy couldn't see the building's top floor. Beautiful glass doors opened to a fancy hotel-style lobby. The building's directory required a fee for use. Already numb to expenditures, Maddy flicked the payment from her comm. The Smuggler's Nest was on the top floor and tonight it had a formal dress code. "We need to do some shopping."

"Seriously?" Riley asked.

"I don't have anything appropriate on the ship, much less the lander. Do you?" Riley's blank stare answered her question. Free bases had some of the best high-end brick-and-mortar shops in the Galaxy. Unlike most missions, this one might be fun for both Madison *and* Captain Majestic. "The computer says there's an all-night high-end clothing shop two blocks away." Maddy extended her arm to Riley. "Shall we?" If they were going to pull off this cover, they needed to look like a couple who got along. They were closer to that than Maddy had expected after their conversation last night. Riley sighed their fake-upset sigh and took her arm. A good sign. Maybe Riley was ready to move past the secrets, too.

"I'm not sure what's going to be the hardest part of this mission." Maddy laughed. "Infiltrating a raider hideout or getting you to pick out some nice clothes."

Free Base 19's crisp night air and clean city streets made for an enjoyable short walk to the clothing shop. If it were anywhere other than a FB, Maddy would move here in a heartbeat. But a putrid underworld lay just beneath Uptown's glamorous surface. With close attention, one could see the dark alleys where the dreams and spirits of good people—the few that existed on FB 19—were crushed by drugs and violent crime. If Maddy stayed here long enough, not even she'd be immune to that fate. The faster she got off this free base, the better.

The shop had large glass windows with human and android models showing off the latest fashions. A pair of dead eyes sat above the smiles of each model. It was best not to ponder how the shop would use the profits from the dress Maddy would purchase.

We are here for Atasi and the navigation codes for Earth. If Maddy kept telling herself that, maybe she'd feel less disgusted after this was all over.

A scanner lined the doorway of the store. It beeped as soon as Riley and Maddy walked through it. An enhanced male wearing a rent-a-cop uniform approached and thrust a box toward Riley and Maddy. "Please place your weapons in this locker." It wasn't a request.

Any establishment on a free base that didn't return its clientele's weapons wouldn't be in business for long. Maddy placed everything she had, except her comm, in the box. Riley did the same. She entered a code, the date she got the *Amethyst*, and the box clicked.

The security guard ran a hand scanner over Riley and Maddy, and then nodded. "Welcome to Fashion 19"—he half-sighed the rote greeting—"where we help you dress to impress."

"Me first, then you," Maddy said to Riley.

"Why can't I go first? We are already in the android section."

"You match me. I don't match you."

It didn't take Maddy long to find the perfect dress. The purple silk fabric matched her eyes. She held the dress up to herself. The low neckline would be the distraction she was looking for. It even came with a matching wrap with plenty of pockets to hide her weapons. Only on a FB could one find tactical evening wear. The dress was too short to hide her feet, so she also picked up a pair of black heels.

"Are those a good idea?" Riley asked.

"They go with the dress. Don't worry, Captain Majestic knows her way around heels." The shoes also came with stabilizers, but there was no need to expose all her secrets.

After a couple of minutes of searching the store, Riley held up a suit which, surprisingly, would work. It had the appropriate level of formality and accents that matched Maddy's dress. The cut of the suit fit their body perfectly. If the suit survived the mission, it would be perfect for future date nights.

They took their items to the checkout computer, which they also had to pay to use. After scanning the clothes, the price appeared on the computer screen. Maddy flicked the payment.

"No complaints this time?" Riley asked.

"Nah. This is an investment." This dress would turn heads the next time she went to the Skyview. "I'll get lots of use out of it."

"We should go on a double date with Skylar and Jonathan."

"Hmm .... Not what I had in mind, but it is a good idea. Jonathan looks sharp in a nice suit."

"Are you trying to make me jealous?" Riley nudged Maddy.

"Are you?" Maddy asked coyly.

"Of course not." Watching Riley backpedal was always fun. "But I bet Skylar would look amazing in a cocktail dress."

"I know she would." Skylar was the kind of woman that would make Maddy consider dating humans. Riley looked like they were trying to solve a hard math problem.

Maddy grinned and walked to the dressing room, leaving Riley to process the implications of her statement.

Despite Maddy's earlier bravado, or maybe because of it, the walk back to the Smuggler's Nest felt three times longer in the heels, even with the stabilizers set to max. A doorman held out his hand before letting them into the building. Everything requires a tip on a free base. Maddy flicked a payment.

"The doorman wasn't here earlier," Riley said after they got inside.

"Probably dayshift security looking to make a few extra creds at night." Maddy pressed the elevator call button. Two more credits drained from her account.

"How are your feet doing?" Riley asked as they got into the elevator.

"Fine." Maddy almost lost her balance as the elevator jerked upward. "I don't want to run in them, but we won't be doing that here."

"Agreed. If we run into trouble, it won't be in the bar. The Void Raiders don't enjoy spilling blood at their premiere establishment. It's bad for business."

The elevator doors opened to soft piano music, accompanied by the indistinct murmur of quiet conversation. Patrons, all dressed as formally as Maddy and Riley, surrounded a polished wooden bar. Not a single barstool was unoccupied. Others sat at tables scattered throughout the room. Each table had at least two people—this wasn't the place one went to drink alone.

Maddy drew a few glances when she stepped out of the elevator, mostly from sesquicentenarians. The one or two glances from young centenarians felt good. Regardless of their age, no one's attention lingered on her for more than a moment. The bar had an ample supply of beautiful people of all ages.

Riley pointed to an empty table. They weaved their way through the crowd. Maddy followed close behind. The clicking of her heels was barely audible over the music and voices.

When they got to the table, Maddy inspected the seat, a habit from The Drunken Spacefarer. The chair and table were both impeccable—just like everything else in this part of the FB. "Skylar should take notes." Maddy said.

"This isn't Skylar's target demographic."

"You're right. Not my kind of place, either." Maddy tapped the table's built-in terminal. "What are we having?"

"Don't be cheap here. We're high rollers, right?"

The terminal's default filter sorted items by price from high to low. Whisky from the Outer Rim sat at the top of the menu. One bottle cost more than Maddy made on a month's worth of runs.

"No one who knows whisky would buy that." Riley scrolled through the list. "We need something that shows we have taste." Without hesitation, Riley tapped another whisky, which was only slightly less expensive than the one from the Rim.

How much money does Riley have?

Maddy leaned forward to take Riley's hand. "We don't have to break the budget. There are other ways of getting attention."

"My type of work pays well." Riley rubbed Maddy's hand with their thumb. It was nice to have a night out with Riley, even if their relationship still needed a bit of work. "I meant what I said on the ship. I'll be happy to disclose to you what I have in my second account."

It wasn't unusual for couples to keep second accounts. Maddy had three known accounts: one for her business, a joint account with Riley, and a personal one. Riley knew about those. Relationship contracts expire and often aren't renewed. Having one's own money ensured a certain financial continuity.

Whatever Riley had in their account was their business. Besides, if Riley disclosed their information, Maddy would have to disclose her fourth account and the transactions within. Her accountant used some of that money to fake a legitimate income for her. But that wasn't what embarrassed her. She hadn't been totally honest about the amount of money she received from her parents, which went straight to her fourth account. Maddy doesn't need it, but her father still makes deposits from time to time.

Before Maddy could respond, a young woman with hazel eyes and long blonde hair approached their table carrying a tray holding the bottle Riley ordered and two glasses. Her tight crimson dress molded to her body, unveiling slight but daring glimpses of what lay beneath. Placing the tray on the table, she flashed a suggestive smile as she opened the bottle. "Do you need anything else from me?" Her question oozed with implications. Apparently, the price covered more than just the whisky.

"No," Riley took the bottle. "Thank you."

A tension that Maddy hadn't noticed prior to this left the woman's face. "A gentleman at the bar would like to meet you. May I bring him over?" Someone had noticed Riley's choice of drink.

"Please." Riley poured the whisky.

The server gestured toward the bar at someone Maddy couldn't see.

A slim man wearing a black suit, in a style popular two centuries ago, wove his way through the crowd as if he owned the bar. Ordering whisky more expensive than one-month's rent in all but the swankiest of Uptown apartments would certainly invite the owner's attention. Once he got to the table, he bowed slightly toward Maddy. "My name is Jeffry Rigan and I own the Nest. May I join you?"

"Please." Maddy motioned Jeffry to take a seat. "I'm Cynthia Jones and this is my partner, Charlie." Jeffry Rigan was probably not his real name, either. "You have a beautiful establishment here, Mr. Rigan." Maddy looked at him over her glass as she took a drink. The smooth whisky didn't burn as it went down—maybe she needed to up her drinking game.

"Please call me Jeffry." He removed his jacket and rolled the sleeves of his shirt to just below his elbows, exposing a ring of flame encircling a black hole tattooed on his right wrist. "Are you on-station for business or pleasure?"

Jeffry had skipped asking where they were from and went straight for the power play. Not only did he want Maddy and Riley to know he was a Void Raider, he also wanted them to believe he knew more than he probably did. If it was a game he wanted, Maddy was happy to play. She placed her glass down and asked with a hint of innocence, "Why do you think we are tourists?"

"Please Ms. Jones," Jeffry lingered on the name Jones just long enough to communicate he knew more than she suspected. His eyes casually lowered to the part of her neckline exposed by the wrap. The dress worked.

"I'd know if a beautiful woman such as yourself lived on this base." Jeffry turned to Riley. "I hope I am not being too bold."

"Not at all, Jeffry." Riley turned to Maddy. "Her beauty is what first drew me to her." At face value, Riley's words would have melted Maddy's heart. However, there was a coldness to Riley's tone that made it sound as if they were no longer enamored.

"I have no doubt." Jeffry leaned forward, placing his folded hands on the table. "Let me cut straight to the chase, if you don't mind. Patrons who order fine drinks also tend to enjoy other *particular* pleasures. Is there anything I can help you acquire while you're on-station?"

How could they have stumbled on a lead so quickly? It seemed too easy, but Riley said that they knew a good place to start.

I may have to bring them on more missions. Did she just seriously consider expanding her crew and adding further restrictions to her freedom? She shook the thought from her mind. Riley and Jeffry gave her an odd look.

Riley's attention returned to Jeffry. "I'm looking to grow the boundaries of our contract. Our home world is a bit conservative and only gives contracts to pairs."

The best lies, and cover, are simple. Too much backstory can be difficult to keep track of. Hinting at a home world could raise questions. Free bases were generally no-questions-asked type of places, at least while there were no pistols drawn. But what happens if Jeffry asks?

Jeffry sighed. "Why limit the pleasures of life?"

"Exactly." Riley took a sip of the whisky. "As it turns out, the good moral folk of our world set up a loophole."

"They always do." Jeffry chuckled. "Those who proscribe behaviors always find ways of indulging in them. What's the workaround?"

"Off-world additions to contracts hold back home," Riley said.

"Ah. So, if it's legal somewhere else, it can be legal there. Just don't start it at home?"

Riley raised their glass in a nonchalant confirmation. Apparently, hunting AI wasn't Riley's only skill. Their comfort with lying simultaneously impressed and disturbed Maddy. How much of Riley's disclosure on the *Amethyst* was true? Maddy had believed Riley and thought their relationship was on the mend. But watching Riley interact with Jeffry raised more questions. Did Riley love her, or was she cover for some other mission?

"Are you two looking to rent or buy?" Jeffry's directness snapped Maddy back to the conversation.

"Rent with the option to buy." The words rolled off Riley's tongue. If the question disgusted them, they hid it well. "And it is not what she wants, it is what *I* want." Riley folded their arms as they settled back into their chair.

This new side to Riley was diametrically opposed to the person she had fallen in love with. While useful on this mission, Maddy hoped to never see it again.

The server returned to their table, handed Jeffry a glass of brown liquid, and then left. Jeffry returned his attention to Riley. "And what is it *you* want?"

"An android. Minimal mods. And not some used model, either."

Good move, Riley. Being too specific might raise suspicions.

Jeffry signaled to the server who brought the whisky. "Please take their bottle to the VIP room." The woman gathered up the bottle and their glasses and walked toward the back of the bar. Jeffry stood. "If you will follow me."

As they walked to the VIP room, Maddy trailed behind Riley and eyed the exits. The Smuggler's Nest had a significant security detail, five enhanced humans and three androids, all armed, none of them obviously so.

"This way please." Jeffry opened the door to a well-lit room with wood-paneled walls. Two plush red chairs dominated the middle of the room. Between the chairs, a small black wooden table held the bottle of whisky Riley had ordered. Maddy and Riley sat. The cushions in the chairs compressed slowly, perfectly supporting Maddy's body—as if it were made just for her. The server poured them each a glass and left. Her movements were efficient, but quick. She clearly didn't want to stay long. Neither did Maddy. Comfy chairs aside, the place made her skin crawl.

"We have a fine selection that I believe will fit your needs." Jeffry tapped on a tablet computer he removed from his suit jacket. The hologram of a nude stock android floated in front of Riley and Maddy. "We just got this one in a few days ago—"

"Next," Riley interrupted.

An image of Atasi, also nude, appeared on a screen built into the far wall. "This one is special, unusually feminine for an android. They are so new, we haven't done a full holo scan, yet."

"No," Riley sighed and looked at their fingernails.

A hologram of another stock android floated before them. Jeffry began a description and Riley interrupted, asking for the next image. This repeated three more times.

"Let me see number one again." Riley sipped from their glass.

The image of the first android returned. "I really think you'll like—"

"No. I don't think so." Riley's firm response left no room for Jeffry to interject. "How about number four?" But before Jeffry could open his mouth, Riley said, "No. Let me see number two again."

"This one is brand new and untouched," Jeffry said with pride. "We'd be happy to mod to order."

Riley tapped their lip, as if in thought. "Can we test it out?" Every instinct screamed for Maddy to get the hell out of that room. This whole mission flew past multiple boundaries she promised herself she'd never cross. Instead of fleeing, she drowned her disgust with a shot of whisky, drawing a look of curiosity from Jeffry.

"Of course," Jeffry's eyes returned his tablet, "this is the cost of one night."

A large number floated in front of Atasi's image. Before Maddy could comprehend it, Riley flicked the payment from their comm. "Half now. You'll get the rest tomorrow night *if* it remains untouched before we arrive."

"Reasonable terms, Charlie. Here's the address." Jeffry flicked a data packet at Riley. "Be there at 8 p.m. station time. Will Ms. Jones be joining you, or should we make other arrangements for her?"

"She'll be joining me." Riley's tone implied she had no choice.

After what Maddy had witnessed today, a long hot shower was in order.

The ride to the hotel was a quiet one. Riley had put them up in a swanky place. The apology was nice, but unnecessary. Maddy understood what she was getting into, even if she didn't like it.

When they got to the room, Riley pulled a device out from their suit pocket and waved it in the air. It beeped once. "We are free to talk, no bugs or cameras."

"Thank the Galaxy." Maddy sighed as she sat on the edge of the bed. She should have looked harder for flats.

"I am sorry about back there." Riley sat on the bed and slouched. "I am quite disgusted with myself." Their words sounded sincere, but so did their lies. The questions raised tonight were still raw, especially given the events of the last few days. And they had been making such good progress …

"I understand why you behaved the way you did," Maddy tried to sound reassuring. "It was for Atasi, and the people of Earth."

"Maybe, but it doesn't make me feel any better. Do the ends ever justify the means?"

"I don't know." Maddy inhaled. "You seemed to fall right into the role you played." She hadn't intended to sound so accusatory.

"Years ago, I was on an op where an AI had taken over a human trafficking syndicate. I had to go undercover and get close to where the

AI servers were located. That meant playing some roles that I'd rather not have played."

"I'm sorry you had to do that. Did you defeat the AI?"

"I terminated the AI and rescued about twenty people. It was the second time I ever felt good about killing something."

There was a first? She knew better than to ask aloud.

"Let's get some sleep." Maddy put her arm around Riley, trying to reassure herself as much as them. "We'll both feel better in the morning."

The pale white display on the bedside clock changed to 0300. Maddy had seen every minute since she'd laid down beside Riley. To save Atasi tomorrow—or rather, later today—she needed to sleep. But her mind wouldn't settle, and telling yourself you must sleep is the most ineffective way of overcoming insomnia.

Who is Riley? The question repeated itself like a looped recording.

The person she fell in love with would not have enjoyed killing. What new things would she learn about Riley during this mission? At what point would it all become too much? Would she need to end their contract?

Could she end it? A limiterless, broken-hearted, special forces android might make for a dangerous ex. Who knows what they would do?

0301.

Riley wasn't like that. Right?

CHAPTER 23

A fitful night of sleep followed by a long day pretending to be a happy tourist couple was not a good start to a rescue op. Exhausted, Maddy sat on the end of the bed in their hotel room. A pair of casual flats sat on the floor in front of her. The shoes matched her outfit: a blue blouse, black blazer, and black slacks. The outfit was loose enough to maneuver in, and the jacket even had a holster—tactical day wear purchased on the station. If nothing else, at least she'd be physically comfortable. Unfortunately, the shop had nothing that could hold her plasma grenade. The prospect of leaving it behind produced mixed feelings. The idea of using the weapon, even on raiders, sickened her. However, if things got bad enough that she needed it, then not having it might be deadly.

Riley entered the room wearing a white shirt, blue jeans, and a black blazer. "You look good." Between strangers, the compliment would have sounded forced. But they were a couple—at least for now. Instead, Riley's comment was a cautiously extended olive branch.

"I like that on you." Maddy accepted the branch with hesitation and extended one of her own. "You should add that to your wardrobe at home."

"Thank you. I think I will." Riley adjusted their blazer in the mirror.

Maddy holstered her pistol. Regardless of her feelings, Maddy had a job to do. She was a professional, and on a mission, after all. Atasi needed saving. The relationship issues could wait. Riley put their knife into the interior pocket of their blazer and picked up a duffle bag.

"What's that?" Maddy asked.

"Party favors."
It was going to be that kind of day.

The taxi stopped at a nondescript building in the heart of FB 19's Uptown. With no signs or windows, it was a place you wouldn't go unless you were supposed to be there. Hidden in plain sight. Riley paid the fare. Maddy didn't pretend to offer. Transactions at an unknown location on a free base would draw the eyes of auditors. The fewer eyes on her accounts, the better.

Jeffry's code opened the building's front door. The lobby was not as nice as the Smuggler's Nest, but much nicer than the one in Maddy and Riley's apartment building back home. Brown leather sofas lined three of the four red painted walls. Maddy ran her hand along the smooth surface of one as she passed by. She hadn't touched real leather before. It was as illegal as it was expensive. Crown molding, which matched the hardwood floors, ran around a white ceiling with an intricately carved accent mounted in its center. Everything about this room said old money, not raider hideout.

A row of elevators lined the back wall. Each elevator had a price posted above its door. Riley pushed the up button for the most expensive one, express service to any floor. Inside, the elevator had the same hardwood floor and walls as the lobby, except the back wall had a large mirror.

The hairs on the back of Maddy's neck raised as she stepped into the elevator. She pretended to check her hair in the mirrored wall as the elevator moved upwards. How many sensors did the Void Raiders hide behind that mirror? She turned back around to not draw any more attention to herself.

The number displayed on the elevator's touchscreen increased as they passed each floor. Jeffry's instructions said to go to room 174-23. Getting to the target was always the easiest part of an extraction. The building had two potential ways out, down or up. Down meant going through 173 floors of pissed-off Void Raiders. Up, although only six floors, lead only to the roof. Unless Riley had something special in their bag of party favors, they weren't getting out that way. It wasn't worth worrying too much about. Escape plans never panned out anyway. Captain Majestic preferred to play things by ear. It had worked well for her—so far.

The elevator door opened to a hallway that looked like the lobby, but with no furniture. Signs directed them to room 23 at the end. A stock android dressed in a black suit stood outside the room's door.

As Maddy and Riley approached the room, the android held up their hand, signaling them to stop. Their gesture exposed the Void Raider tattoo on their wrist. The android ran a scanner over the back and chuckled. "You two have some kinky tastes. Keep your guns holstered if you want to live. There are a lot of eyes on you."

Warning received. Raider society worked on one assumption; everyone was armed. Being asked to surrender your weapons in a raider transaction was the sure sign of a trap. It didn't mean they weren't walking into one, just that the Void Raiders weren't ready to announce it, yet. The android opened the door and beckoned them inside.

Two enhanced humans and two androids, probably low-level goons, played cards at a table near the door. They sized up Maddy and Riley, then returned to their game. "You must be Charlie and Cynthia." A blonde-haired woman, probably in her eighties, wearing a business suit and heels, approached from a dark corner of the room. Her expensive outfit oozed raider upper management.

"And you are?" Riley asked.

"Please call me Martha. I am Jeffry's associate. He asked me to take on your account in his absence." Martha held a tablet computer to her chest.

"It was my understanding that Jeffry was managing the transaction." Riley was right to be concerned. Changes in business plans were never a good thing, especially when dealing with raiders or the government. Doubly so on a FB where there was no distinction.

"Jeffry sends his regrets. I assure you I can help with anything *you* need." Martha bit her lip. Maddy wanted to punch her. But now wasn't the time to blow their cover.

"I am sure you can." Riley's tone fed off Martha's advance.

Maddy's jaw tightened.

Martha flashed a mischievous grin and waved them over toward a closed door which opened after she entered a code into her tablet. "I'll leave you to enjoy our services. If you need *anything* from me, please do not hesitate to knock."

The door closed behind them. A large bed sat in the middle of the dimly lit room. An android who looked like Atasi's picture wearing only a black collar, got off the bed and backed into the corner. Her body matched Jeffry's description of "unusually feminine." The fear in her blue eyes tore at Maddy's heart and fed her rage.

She approached the android with her hands out. "Atasi?" Maddy whispered.

A thud echoed in the room. Riley must have dropped the duffle bag. *What the hell did Riley bring?*

Before she could take another step, a pair of hands grabbed Maddy from behind. One hand covered her mouth, another around her stomach, pinning her arms to her sides. Her body jerked backwards, abruptly stopping against a rock-solid female body. Maddy couldn't budge. Her assailant must be an enhanced. From the corner of her eyes, she saw Riley held in a similar grip by an android with a Void Raiders tattoo. The attackers must have been waiting for them by the door, concealed by the room's darkness.

"Any funny stuff and I kill her," Maddy's captor said. By the volume of the voice in her ear, Maddy guessed the woman holding her was about Maddy's height, short for an enhanced.

Jeffry stepped out of the shadows from the other side of the bed, near where Atasi stood trembling. "I am not sure how stupid you think we are, Ms. Amana. Or should I call you Captain Majestic?" The hand of Maddy's captor muffled her obscenity. Jeffry ignored her. "You did a good job playing the dominant one, Riley. You almost had me convinced."

Riley mumbled something. Were their struggles real or another act? If any raider clan in the Galaxy had limiterless androids in their ranks, it would be the Void Raiders. Jeffry made a motion. The hand covering Maddy's mouth wrapped around her throat. She couldn't turn her head to see Riley.

"What gave us away?" Riley asked. Maddy anchored on the apparent calm in Riley's voice. A plan formed in her mind.

"You were too calm. Too well-rehearsed. First-time buyers are nervous." Jeffry stepped farther into the light and turned to look at Riley. The man was unarmed—not the type to do the dirty work. Whoever held her and Riley would do that. "I know assholes. You aren't one."

The grip on her throat tightened. It became hard to breathe. Maddy's heart raced. An elbow to the ribs, Maddy's standard trick, wouldn't work against an enhanced. Dark borders encroached on her vision.

Jeffry grabbed Atasi by the arm. "What do you want with this?" Atasi cowered but couldn't break Jeffry's grip.

Maddy tried to gasp a response. Jeffry motioned for her captor to ease up. She choked on the air that refilled her lunges. Her vision came back into focus. "Our client wants the android." Sharp pains pierced Maddy's throat as she choked out her response. "Apparently, the android knows something our client will pay a lot of credits for."

The best lies have a kernel of truth.

"I know every raider outfit operating or wishing to operate on this free base. If you don't want to tell me the truth on your own, then my associates here will motivate you." Jeffry looked past Maddy toward whoever held her.

"Okay. Okay!" The words barely escaped Maddy's mouth before the pressure on her throat returned. Jeffry raised his hand and her airway relaxed again. "I'll tell you the truth." Maddy paused for emphasis. "The android has secret knowledge, and we weren't going to return her. With what she knows, there is *no limit* to the credits we could make."

Maddy forced her head back. A snapping sound confirmed she had hit her target. Enhanced or not, all human noses break the same. The grasp on her neck loosened. In one fluid motion, she spun around, drew her pistol, and shot. The enhanced woman collapsed on the floor. Relief over swept her. A limp body, as opposed to a pile of ash, meant the pistol was on stun.

A hard thud echoed in the room drawing Maddy's attention away from the body. Maddy looked over at Riley in time to see them pull a purple blade from their assailant's armless body. The dead android, their eyes wide, collapsed between their arms on the floor. Bile rose in Maddy's stomach. She fought hard to suppress it. Was it necessary to kill the android? Yet another conversation for later.

Atasi screamed. Jeffry clamped his hand over her mouth, using her body as a shield. His head was just above Atasi's shoulder. Maddy leveled her pistol at Jeffry. "Shoot me and you risk hurting the android."

"No. I don't." Maddy pulled the trigger. Jeffry crumbled into a heap.

Atasi froze, her gaze locked on Maddy's pistol.

"Are you okay?" Maddy lowered her pistol and extended her other hand to Atasi. "Melinda sent us." Atasi's face softened at the mention of Melinda's name. "I'm Maddy. That's Riley." Riley dug through the duffle bag, ignoring everything else.

"Are you going to take me to Mel?" Atasi asked.

"That's the plan."

Riley removed a rifle from the bag and handed it to Maddy.

"Party favors, huh?" The charge indicator glowed green—full charge. She set the rifle to stun. "How'd you get this."

"I did some late-night shopping after you had fallen asleep. The bag masks its contents from sensors. Don't worry, I have something for everyone." Riley snapped off Atasi's collar. "Better?"

Atasi rubbed her neck. "Absolutely. That thing was some kind of limiter. It made me feel as weak as a modern. No offense." She looked Riley up and down. "Although, I guess you wouldn't be. You don't have limiters. Do you?"

"Those things are supposed to be illegal." Riley threw the collar on the bed, ignoring Atasi's question. "I have some clothes for you." They handed her a black bundle. The T-shirt and cargo pants were a little big on her, but they wouldn't hamper her movement. "I have something else for you, too, Captain." Riley removed a pair of boots from the bag and gave them to Maddy.

"They don't match my outfit." Maddy smiled. "But they'll be easier to run in than the flats." Maddy handed Atasi the pistol she used to shoot Jeffry. "Do you know how to use this?"

Atasi flipped the pistol's setting switch, turned around, and vaporized Jeffry. Before Maddy could stop her, she did the same to the enhanced woman Maddy had stunned.

"Was that necessary?" Maddy demanded.

"Yes."

Someone banged on the other side of the door—probably Martha and reinforcements. "That door will not last long." Maddy deactivated her rifle's safety and left the switch set to stun. "I hope you have more goodies in that bag, Riley." She leveled her rifle at the door. "Shall we?"

Riley removed another rifle from the bag and then kicked the door down. Martha flew back with it, landing unconsciously in the middle of the room. Her reinforcements looked at her confused, then back at the now-open door just in time for Riley, Maddy, and Atasi to open fire. Seconds later, the unconscious bodies of three raiders collapsed on the ground.

"There'll be more." The charge meter on Maddy's rifle remained green. Morals aside, stun used less energy and, therefore, provided more shots. No ash piles meant Atasi understood that, too. "Same pattern for the hallway."

Riley motioned Atasi and Maddy to stand on either side of the door and, once they were in position, kicked it open. The door, and most of its frame, slammed against the far wall. Maddy and Atasi followed Riley through the newly formed hole, aiming their weapons toward the elevator. Armed guards rushed out of the rooms along the hallway.

Atasi moved backward into room 174-23, shooting her pistol. Riley and Maddy followed, providing cover fire. Maddy's grip tightened around the rifle as she put her back against the wall beside the hole. Sweat rolled down her back as laser fire warmed the wall.

How the hell are we getting out of here?

Riley rummaged through the duffle bag and pulled out a metal sphere. "Good thing I remembered this!" Riley tossed the sphere at Maddy. She caught it with her free hand.

The plasma grenade was heavy, not due to its mass, but because of what Maddy had to do. She pressed the activator and tossed the grenade down the hallway without stepping out of the room. Shouts filled the hall as raiders recognized the weapon. Once the screaming stopped, Maddy peaked her head through the hole. Scorch marks stained the walls. Ash piles littered the floor. Maddy's stomach turned. There'd be time to regret her actions later. Raiders don't take prisoners, neither could she.

"Atasi, you take left and I'll take right. Riley, cover our rear."

Riley picked up the bag and threw it over their shoulder, nodding in acknowledgment. Side by side, Maddy and Atasi lead Riley down the hall, checking each door. Every room between 174-23 and the elevator was clear. The plasma grenade had been thorough, just like its seller had promised. When they reached the elevator at the end of the hall, Atasi joined Riley in facing the rear. Maddy pressed the down call button. It didn't respond.

The number displayed above one of the elevator doors increased. Company was on their way. "Looks like we have to take the stairs." At least it was down. Even during her first century, Maddy couldn't climb up 173 flights. She opened the door to the stairwell. Riley started going up the stairs.

"Up?" Maddy's question stopped Riley. "The exit is down."

"Not for us, Captain." Riley smiled.

What does Riley have planned?

Maddy followed Riley and Atasi. The thought of jumping off the roof of the building soured her stomach. Floating in space was one thing. There's no horizon up there. But using anti-gravs on a starbase nauseated her.

A ding sounded through the stairwell's open doorway. A moment later, the sound of shouts and people running came from the bottom of the stairs. Regardless of how Maddy felt about it, up was their only option. She picked up her pace, straining to keep up with the two androids.

Laser light filled the center of the stairwell. Maddy leaned over and returned fire. The break from running was welcome. A stinging pain radiated along her right arm. "Shit!" A red gash had opened on her bicep. "Those bastards are using cutting lasers." Vaporization was more humane. Riley glanced back at her but said nothing. The wound wasn't serious. But it would have been nice if they had acknowledged it. She resumed running up the stairs. The threat of being sliced apart provided the adrenaline boost she needed.

The door at the top of the stairs was made of reinforced steel. Maddy leaned on her knees, sucking in air. "What now?" Footsteps below them got louder. The raiders were closing in.

Riley motioned Atasi and Maddy away from the door. "Watch my back."

Maddy and Atasi fired down the stairwell. The sound of the footsteps seemed quieter. Maybe they had stunned a few of them.

A loud bang echoed. Maddy flinched and her ears rang. It sounded like conventional explosives. Instead, Riley had kicked the door down.

Cool air filled the landing, invigorating Maddy better than coffee. She ran out on the roof with Riley and Atasi. There was nothing there except a few climate-control systems, which wouldn't serve as adequate cover.

Shouts came from the doorway. The raiders were getting closer. Whatever Riley had planned needed to happen quickly. Atasi and Maddy pointed their guns at the open door. Riley mumbled something into their comm. A roaring sound enveloped them as a van rose above the roof line about ten meters behind Maddy.

"Get in!" Riley's voice was barely audible over the van's roaring engines.

Maddy walked backward toward the van, her gun trained on the door to the roof. Atasi did the same. A raider appeared in the doorway with a pistol drawn. Maddy and Atasi opened fire and kept shooting. The air inside the stairwell glowed red from the energy of the laser weapons. Maddy's rifle warmed in her hand and then stopped firing.

The charge indicator light was out. Dead battery. Though Atasi continued to fire, the doorway ceased glowing as raiders poured through. For each one Atasi stunned, another made it onto the roof.

The back of Maddy's shirt bunched as if someone had grabbed her from behind. Suddenly, Maddy flew backward, landing with a thud inside the van. Pain shot through her back as the air rushed from her lungs. Gulping for oxygen, Maddy struggled to sit up on the van's floor. Atasi and Riley continued shooting at the stairwell. Atasi turned and jumped ten meters into the van, landing beside Maddy. Riley followed her.

After Riley boarded, they yelled something Maddy didn't understand. A loud hammering sound deafened her. The rooftop lit up with laser fire as the van door closed. Whoever Riley called was heavily armed.

Moments later, quiet fell over the van and its acceleration pulled Maddy to the side. Able to breathe normally again, she gathered her senses and crawled up to a seat beside Riley. Another shot of pain ran through her arm. Riley had touched the wound.

"That's not too bad, but let's get you fixed up." Riley removed a wound sealer from the first aid kit in their bag and ran it over her arm. A blue light illuminated the gash, which slowly closed with no scarring, thanks to modern medicine.

"Friends of yours?" Maddy asked Riley.

"You could say that. I helped them the last time I was here."

One more thing to add to the list of much-needed conversations.

"Thank you." Atasi rested the pistol in her lap.

"Don't mention it." Maddy leaned her head back against her seat. The remaining adrenaline seemed to flow out of her body with one long exhale.

"Why did you come for me? I know your type gets paid up front. I also know that Mel doesn't have that kind of cash."

Atasi stared blankly while Maddy explained the deal Riley had made with Melinda about removing the block on the *Amethyst*'s navigation system.

"You know what's on Earth, right?" Atasi asked.

"I've had a long time to think about it," Maddy said. "After everything I've seen and heard, I believe Earth is real. We are going to bring down the AI and free the people there. Besides being the right thing to do, it is the only way we can get the Origin Keepers off our back for good."

"It is about damn time someone does something about it." Atasi held up the pistol. "You are going to need a lot more firepower than this."

Maddy put her hand on Riley's knee. "We got that covered."

"Hmm ..." Atasi slumped back into their seat. "Good luck. I mean that. Mel can fix your nav system." Atasi sighed as they stared out one of the van's windows. "But if you let the AI escape Earth, the AI will be the least of your problems."

Threatening Maddy was normally a quick path to regret. But after the day she just had, Maddy simply didn't have the energy to care. "You have a planet of limiterless androids. Why not invade Earth and rescue everyone there?"

Atasi leaned forward, resting her elbows on her knees. Now that the action was over, Maddy had the mental bandwidth to notice her features. Modern androids had an edge to their appearance. Bony was the word that came to Maddy's mind. But not Atasi. She could be easily mistaken for a twenty-five-year-old human woman.

"The leaders of Proxima Centauri b are afraid of what might happen if we were to fail. Right now, the AI thinks spaceflight is a bad idea. What happens if it changes its mind? The AI could expand into the Galaxy, replicating itself in each new android built. Who could stop an army of trillions upon trillions of AI killbots?"

Maddy had not considered that particular option.

What have we gotten ourselves into?

As a child, looking out the rear window of a moving car nauseated Maddy. But despite her enjoyment of pulling gees in space, grown-up Maddy tolerated cars only slightly better than her younger self. Motion sickness aside, someone had to keep watch. The van's jerking movements as it snaked its way through the airways of FB 19 didn't help either Maddy's stomach or her view.

No one had shot at them since the roof. Maybe the Void Raiders believed Atasi wasn't worth losing more lives over. There were plenty of creds to be made elsewhere, with much easier victims. A hand on Maddy's knee drew her attention from the window.

"Are you okay?" Riley asked.

"This?" Maddy pointed to her arm. Thanks to the wound sealer, a line of new skin was the only evidence of a wound. "I've had much worse."

"That's not what I meant."

Of course, it wasn't. Their talk on the way to FB 19 was about what they did, not who they were. At best, the surface-level discussion had eased the symptoms of their relationship troubles. It certainly couldn't cure them. The only thing that could cure those wounds was the conversations Maddy had been saving for later. Now was later—even if that meant having it while riding in a heavily armed extraction van jerkily zooming its way through a raider infested free base.

"Everything is fine." Even Maddy wasn't convinced by the sound of her own voice. By the look in their eyes, neither was Riley.

Atasi put the pistol down and went to the front of the van to sit with the pilot.

Maddy sighed. "I can't help but wonder if we could have gotten away without killing so many people." It wasn't what she meant to say, but it was what came out.

"Jeffry deserved it." The conviction in Riley's eyes disturbed her more than the role in the mission they had played.

"Maybe. But who are we to decide that? And what about the ones I killed?" She couldn't figure out a way of mentioning the android Riley had killed without sounding accusatory.

Riley grabbed her shoulders to reassure her. "I didn't want to kill the android holding me." She knew what they'd say next. It wouldn't help. "*We* had no choice. What do you think would have happened to us if we were captured?" Riley paused. "I know a good therapist that has helped me through things like this."

It was all Maddy could do not to roll her eyes at the mention of therapy. To be fair, she hadn't really given her therapist a chance. Dr. Whatever-his-name-was would probably report her if she told him what had happened on FB 19. Maybe she should try Riley's. While the stresses of smuggling wore on her psychologically, they were nothing compared to the responsibilities of captaining a crew whose lives depended on her. Maybe talking to a third party would help. From what she'd seen so far, Riley's therapist must have the utmost level of discretion. "I think I'll take you up on that."

"Good. How about us? How are *we* doing?"

Now came the hard part of the discussion. "I fell in love with programmer Riley." Maddy squeezed Riley's hand. "You fell in love with Madison. We've been lying to each other for so long, I don't know if we are the people each of us fell in love with." A half-stifled laugh escaped her lips as a tear rolled down her cheek. Captain Majestic didn't cry, especially not during a mission. "I feel like I don't know who you are. Hell, I don't even know who I am."

"I do." Riley wiped the tear with their thumb. "From what I have seen, Captain Maddy Majestic isn't too different from Madison Amana. By themselves, both are amazing people. Together, they are incredible."

Tension flowed from her body, leaving behind a feeling that swelled inside her. Comfort. Safety. Warmth. None of those words adequately described what she felt. The word connected came close, but also fell short.

Love.

That was it.

She used the word before. Captain Majestic loved dogfights and big paydays. Madison loved fancy dinners and shopping. Both claimed to love Riley, but neither ever gave them the attention they deserved. Her focus on keeping lives separate meant the thing they shared fell between the cracks. Now, no longer needing the partition, Maddy saw what she had been missing out on for all these years. "I'm sorry I never came clean about my job. Can you forgive me."

"Maddy .... Is it okay if I call you Maddy?"

"I would love that."

"There is no need to apologize. I understand why you did what you did. Besides, it's not like I am free of blame either. It was wrong of me not to trust you." Riley held her hands in theirs. "AI-fighting-Riley shares a lot in common with programmer-Riley. Both love you more than they could ever say." Riley let go of her hands. "What would you like to know about me? No lies, no cover, just you and me."

That was enough. She'd never know everything there was about Riley, and she didn't need to. The only thing she needed to know was that they loved her. They had risked their life for her more than once on this mission. She couldn't ask for any more proof than that.

Maddy chuckled. "Once this mission is over, I'd love to hear about your adventures fighting AI."

"As I would about your smuggling runs. Maybe instead of holo movies at night, we should share our own stories."

"It's a date! I am glad you came on this mission. I love you more now than I ever thought possible." Maddy wrapped her arms around Riley and squeezed. Riley wrapped their arms around her, too.

Time slowed, maybe it stopped as the rest of the Galaxy faded away. She couldn't get close enough to Riley and—by the way Riley held her—neither could they. Eventually, Maddy broke the hug and wiped another tear. "It looks like one story we share is that we both have exterior versions we show to the world."

"Maybe we should show those to each other less often."

"Agreed." Maddy chuckled. "Except around Jonathan."

"Yeah. That boy needs Captain Majestic to keep him alive."

"He's not that bad. He's saved my ass occasionally—don't tell him I said that."

"Aye, Captain!"

They both laughed.

Atasi returned. "The pilot says we're two minutes out from the hangar and the coast looks clear."

Maddy rested her head on Riley's shoulder. The only thing left to do now was to pay the outrageous departure fees and get the hell off this station.

The van stopped in front of Hangar Bay L5's entrance. Riley got out first and walked around to the van's driver-side window. "Thanks, Joe."

Maddy glimpsed the driver. A human male with buzzed-cut brown hair.

"My pleasure Riley." The man could, all my himself, serve as the bass section of a choir. Very few unenhanced males had voices that low. "Next time you're on-station, let's go for drinks."

"I'll buy."

"I'll hold you to that." The van sped away.

Riley held open the door to the hangar bay's terminal for Maddy and Atasi. Maddy shot them a questioning look. The android grinned. "That's a story for another time."

"I look forward to hearing it one evening." Maddy took out her comm. "Let's pay the leeches."

As expected, the departure fee was much higher than the docking fee. Of course, that wasn't the only fee. Before they could leave, Maddy had to pay a fee for retracting the bridge, one for logging out of the console, and some data-use fee that she couldn't figure out. The text included with each bill clearly stated the lander's docking clamps would not be released without full payment.

Maddy opened the lander door. "It'll be a tight fit, but it won't take long to get to the *Amethyst*." Riley boarded first and slid to the far side of the lander.

Atasi held out her hand, allowing Maddy to board next. "I'm sure I've been through worse today."

As soon as FB 19's dockmaster released the clamps, Maddy opened the lander's comms to contact the *Amethyst*. "We are returning home from a successful run, Jonathan. How's the ship?"

"The ship is okay, Captain." Static crackled during Jonathan's pause. "Looking forward to having you back."

Something was wrong. Jonathan never says "Captain."

"Strap in and charge your guns." Maddy pushed the control stick forward. "We may have guests waiting for us."

CHAPTER 24

The *Amethyst*'s shuttle bay doors opened, just like they should, when the lander approached. Maddy guided the lander to its dock and secured the clamps. Afterwards, the bay doors closed and the bay repressurized. The lander's exterior cameras showed the bay was clear.

So far, everything seemed okay.

The *Amethyst*'s main computer denied Maddy access to the internal camera network. That was the first problem.

Atasi and Riley picked up the rifles. Maddy took the pistol. None of the weapons charged fully during the short flight. Hopefully, they wouldn't need them. Regulations considered lasers to be ship-safe. Whoever wrote the regs hadn't been in a firefight on a ship.

"Stun anyone who is not Jonathan." Maddy projected an image of Jonathan from her comm.

"Cute boy." Atasi eyed the image longer than necessary.

"He's taken." Riley loaded a charge pack into their rifle. "Smitten by a barkeep."

"It's probably for the best." Atasi shrugged as she loaded her weapon. "Otherwise, I might have to sign on as crew."

Two limiterless androids on the crew would radically change the jobs Maddy could go after. But at what cost? Freedom and responsibility. She had almost lost Riley—in multiple ways—on this mission. Still, Maddy couldn't deny the value they added. Both Jonathan and she owed them their lives. Maybe if Atasi were with them, Riley wouldn't have almost died on Ross 154.

"Game faces, folks. We disembark through the lander's cargo bay door." Only the cargo bay door was large enough for them to exit in formation. Maddy wanted to be ready in case the camera feed had been looped. It took some effort, but they all squeezed around each other and got into the lander's cargo bay. She held her hand above the door's control panel. "Ready?" Atasi and Riley leveled their guns toward the door, a major improvement compared to Jonathan's combat prowess. As soon as the door opened, Riley and Atasi exited, walking heel-to-toe with their fingers just off the trigger. Maddy fell in behind them.

The shuttle bay was clear, just like the cameras showed. The first door of the airlock connecting the shuttle bay to the rest of the cargo bay opened automatically when they approached—perfectly normal. When they stepped inside, it closed automatically—also normal. A green light glowed above the airlock door to the cargo bay. Under normal conditions, the light meant the cabin on the other side of the door was pressurized. The lights ran on an independent system that supposedly couldn't be hacked. Besides, if whoever was on the ship wanted them dead, they would have shot the shuttle down long before it could have docked. Maddy motioned Riley and Atasi into the same formation they used to enter the shuttle bay, then opened the door.

The cargo bay's lights were on, which was unusual, but all the boxes and gear were still there. Slowly, the three of them made their way through the cargo bay. Riley focused on the port side, while Atasi covered starboard. Maddy had the center. It was quiet. Normally, there'd be at least a few bots doing maintenance or inventory. Not a single bot operated in the bay.

Maddy held up her hand outside the airlock leading to the other decks. "Directly on the other side of this door is a ladder to the bridge and lower deck. To port, there is another airlock to exit the ship. To starboard is a storage room."

The description was for Atasi, who nodded in response. The light above the airlock was green. They proceeded as before and again found an empty space.

The hatch to the lower deck was closed, as it should be. The keypad on the door showed the last person to enter was Maddy before she left for the free base. They accounted for all the supplies in the storeroom, including the meds—which were usually the first thing stolen by a boarding party.

The hatch to the bridge at the top of the ladder was open. That was against the ship's regs. The bridge lights were on max illumination. While not a violation, the brightness was unusual. Maddy stepped toward the ladder.

Riley put their hand on hers. "Let me."

Whoever was on this ship wanted to talk, not shoot. "This is my ship. If someone is up there, they need to know I am in charge." After removing her blazer, she slipped the pistol into the back of her pants, ascended the ladder, and then entered the bridge.

"Welcome back to your ship, Captain Amana." Alex restrained Jonathan from behind, holding a knife against his neck.

"Sorry, Cap. He took me by surprise." They'll talk about this later. How many times had she told Jonathan boarding never ended well? She drew her pistol.

"Don't be mad at the boy, Captain. Had he not surrendered, I would have blown up your ship and stranded you on the free base. How long do you think you could have hidden from the Void Raiders? He probably saved your life." Alex chuckled in jest as if being saved by Jonathan showed some form of weakness.

"What do you want, Alex?" Maddy said through clenched teeth. It had been a long day, and her patience had run thin. Alex's crack at Jonathan didn't help, they weren't half the person Jonathan was.

"We need to talk. You and your friends know too much."

"Let Jonathan go," Maddy aimed for Alex's head, "and we'll have a nice long chat." Riley and Atasi appeared on the bridge with a whoosh of air.

"As you can see, Captain. You have me at a disadvantage. Two humans and two limiterless androids against just me."

Riley took a half step forward. "If you want to get out of here alive, Alex, drop the knife. Now."

"It's been a long time since I've had a legitimate challenger, Riley. You might be one. But if you kill me, a signal will be sent to FB 19's guns, ordering them to fire. You won't even know what hit you." Riley didn't flinch. "Did you think you were the only person with friends on FB 19? Back off."

Riley stepped back.

"As you can see, you are in no position to call the shots." Alex pressed the knife against Jonathan's throat. A crimson bead trickled from the blade's tip. To his credit, Jonathan remained quiet. "Lower your guns."

Maddy lowered her pistol and motioned Riley and Atasi to do the same. Guns would not get them out of this situation. Alex was too fast for Maddy to shoot them like she had Jeffry.

"Put them on the ground and kick them over." Alex tightened their grip on Jonathan. Maddy put her pistol on the floor in front of her and kicked it toward Alex. Riley and Atasi did the same. "Now we can have a civilized conversation." Alex released Jonathan.

He rubbed his neck and checked his hand for blood as he joined Maddy, Riley, and Atasi.

"My colleagues at the Origin Keepers want me to kill you, but I still believe you have potential and could be valuable to us." Alex spun the captain's chair around to face Maddy and her crew and sat. Maddy stared daggers at Alex, who snickered. Then, as if a switch had flipped, they leered at Atasi. "Besides, killing an ex's partner is a sure way to permanently ruin a relationship."

"If you kill me, Mel will find you."

"Do you mean like how she hunted down the Void Raiders?" The smirk on Alex's face failed to draw Atasi's ire. That impressed Maddy, who wasn't sure she would have been as calm. "Let's get back to business, shall we?" Alex steepled their fingers as they placed their elbows on the armrests of the captain's chair. "We can't have you running around the Galaxy telling people what you know. So, I am going to give you your final chance. Join the Origin Keepers or die." Their smirk returned. "Of course, Mel would have to rejoin us, too. It was such a shame to lose her the first time."

"She would never join you." Atasi spat—literally, on Alex's shirt. Maddy had never seen an android do that before.

"What a filthy mod." Alex wiped the spit off with their hand and flung it on the floor. "Mel has clearly lowered her standards over the last two millennia." A custodial bot rolled over the spit, removing it from the bridge floor. Alex watched the bot curiously, then returned their attention to Atasi. "Melinda helped me create the Origin Keepers. You should ask her about it—if you see her again, that is."

Atasi looked like she was ready to lunge forward at any second. Maddy put her hand on Atasi's shoulder to calm her down. Her skin was soft, different from Riley's—nearly human in texture.

"If you refuse, Melinda dies, too. We know how to build the ship limiters. We haven't needed Mel for a long time." Alex folded their hands in their lap. "What will it be?

"People who see the world in black and white never get the whole picture." Maddy crossed her arms and leaned against the chair at the nav station. "I propose a third option."

"You are in no position to negotiate, Captain."

"Hear me out. Remember the data crystal we liberated from that abandoned station?" Alex frowned at her question. A slight sound of satisfaction escaped from Maddy's lips. Unprofessional? Certainly. But Galaxy it felt good. "Once we decrypted the crystal, Dante uploaded its contents to the *Amethyst*. As insurance against my more difficult clients, I have all the *Amethyst*'s data constantly backed up to a server at an undisclosed location.

If I don't log into that server regularly, the information gets released to the Galaxy's press."

"You wouldn't. You know what is on Earth."

"Oh, I would. If that information got released, it would mean I'm dead. Why would I care about what happens after I die?" Maddy cared, but she guessed Alex believed Captain Majestic wouldn't.

"It'd be pointless." Alex waved it off. "No one would believe you."

"Most reputable news outlets won't," Maddy admitted. "But there'll be some that track down the abandoned station, Ross 154, and Proxima Centauri b." Maddy rotated the nav chair toward Alex and sat. "It won't take long for people to put the pieces together."

"What's the third option?"

"We destroy the AI and rescue the people of Earth. You won't need your secret organization anymore and, best of all, you can finally stop chasing us around the Galaxy."

"And if I say no?"

"Then I guess we stay in this stalemate forever."

Alex leaned forward. "I admit I am tired of hiding Earth. There are pursuits I wish to return to." Alex rubbed their chin. "The risk of AI getting out into the Galaxy is just too great still, so I accept only on one condition. If you fail, my associates will use a gravity drive to destroy Earth."

"You'd compress the Earth into a black hole?" Jonathan asked. "I thought that was illegal."

"Who would find out?" Alex shrugged. "No one but us knows of Earth's existence. Do we have a deal or not?"

The AI had enslaved the people of Earth for thousands of years and no one in the Galaxy knew about it. Their suffering needed to end, and this might be their one chance at freedom. But if Maddy failed, she would doom millions, maybe billions.

Maddy looked at Riley. "Can you do it?"

"I haven't met an AI that I couldn't take down." The bravado in Riley's voice was sexy. If this were a different situation …

Alex scoffed. "This one is not like what you've dealt with before. It is in *all* the Earth's systems. You'll be fighting a god." Out of anyone else's mouth, that would have sounded melodramatic. Alex's tone contained one part respect and two parts fear. An ancient android wouldn't scare easily.

Maybe Alex was right. Maybe Riley was in over their head with this one. But death or effective imprisonment weren't viable options either. Maddy couldn't escape the knowledge that a person can't truly live if their freedom was taken away. To know an entire planet was enslaved …. She realized that was a fate *worse* than death.

Maddy leaned back in the nav station chair and crossed her arms. "Deal."

"Either way, that two-thousand-year story ends now." Alex stood and reached into their pocket. Atasi and Riley tensed. "Relax, it is just my comm." They pressed a few buttons on the device and held it to their head. "Call off the ships and the guns. Pick me up at our agreed upon coordinates." Alex returned the comm to their pocket. "Do you mind if I use your airlock, Captain?"

Maddy and Riley showed Alex to the airlock across from the storage room. Jonathan and Atasi stayed on the bridge to check the systems and monitor Alex's friends.

At the airlock, Alex handed Maddy a chip. "This will help you contact some of our operatives on Earth. I'll inform them you're coming. The chip also has information on the resistance and their known assets." Maddy took the chip and opened the interior airlock door. Alex stepped inside. "Good luck out there, Captain. Remember, I won't hesitate to destroy the Earth with you on it." Alex's tone left no doubt. Maddy closed the door, decompressed the airlock, and watched through the porthole as Alex walked out into space.

Maddy's comm vibrated. **I forgot to mention, after you arrive at Earth, you have one week to accomplish your mission. —Alex**

With no other outlet to express her rage, Maddy punched the airlock door. A decision she immediately regretted. She shook the pain from her hand. "Let's get Atasi home and plan our next steps. It appears we have a deadline."

Maddy turned toward the bridge, but Riley stopped her.

"Go take a bath, have a drink, and relax. You've earned it. Jonathan and I can get us to Proxima Centauri b."

In a day of plans and schemes, Riley's suggestion was Maddy's favorite. She nodded and headed to her quarters. The *Amethyst*'s wine list ran through her mind.

CHAPTER 25

Atasi ran to Melinda, crying. They embraced in the *Amethyst*'s shuttle bay, which barely held the lander and Melinda's shuttle. Maddy blinked several times, trying to choke back her own tears to no avail. She wiped her eyes and looked away. They didn't need a spectator during such a private moment.

When their hug broke, Melinda and Atasi held hands facing each other, tears streamed down their faces. Neither said a word. If a bomb exploded, they probably wouldn't have noticed.

From how Riley had described Melinda, Maddy assumed she was stock, other than the pronoun and slightly lighter skin. Riley needed to file more thorough reports. Melinda had short straight auburn hair, hazel eyes, and a complexion so pale, Maddy had seen nothing like it. She wore a form-fitting blouse that left little to the imagination. In the greater Galaxy, androids rarely mirrored human anatomy, and only if they partnered with a human. Riley was one of those. Apparently, ancient androids believed a human partner wasn't necessary for an expression of gender preference, nor were they shy about showing it.

But it wasn't the suggestive outfit that had most interested Maddy, although that certainly didn't hurt. Androids who attempted to emulate humans never quite got it right. Their facial features were too angular, their skin was too perfect, or they snorted at a joke just a little too early. But not Melinda or Atasi. Either of them could infiltrate an androphobic group and none would be the wiser.

"Sorry I'm late." Riley approached Maddy from behind. "Is that Melinda?"

Maddy glanced at Riley. "Looks like you left out a few details."

"I am sorry I didn't mention the anatomy," Riley whispered. "Do you blame me? She was otherwise stock when I met her."

"Please don't be upset with Riley, Captain Majestic. I like to get dolled up for my partner." Melinda smiled at Atasi. "She does the same for me."

"Most androids on Proxima take on what you call a stock appearance when we work with outsiders." Atasi took Melinda's hand. "Normally, I look more like her."

Maddy looked Melinda up and down without staring—too much. "Why hide it? I have known androids who take on human features."

"Exactly, Captain," Melinda said. "They *take* on those features. The earliest androids, like us, were built to be male or female. The humans of that time thought it would be easier to work with us if we looked *and* acted like them. On Proxima, we continue the tradition."

"I understand needing to blend in," Maddy said. Even in the more progressive parts of the Galaxy, gendered androids drew attention. If word got out that androids could perfectly emulate humans, then the androphobic organizations would have a field day, and a spike in recruitment.

"We do our best not to attract attention," Atasi said. "Some of us prefer to stay stock all the time, but they are a minority. Julia, who you met when you first entered our space, is one of them."

"I remove my hair when I work, otherwise it gets caught in parts." Melinda ran her hand through her hair. "I might go red when we get back. I like your hair, Captain."

"Oh!" Atasi touched Melinda's arm. "You should get purple eyes, too."

Maddy's cheeks warmed.

"Damn." Riley snickered. "You made Maddy blush. I thought that was impossible!"

Everyone, but Maddy, had a good laugh. She cleared her throat. "We should get down to business. The chip you gave us worked like a charm."

"Of course it did!" Atasi put her arm around Melinda and gave her a gentle squeeze. "She built most of our detection systems."

"I'll be honest. I didn't think you'd return—I'd given you an almost impossible task." Melinda placed a hand on her chest. "But I am glad you did. I will uphold my end of the bargain. Let's have a look at your nav computer."

It took almost three hours for Melinda to remove the navigation limiter from the *Amethyst*'s computer. When she finished, a red flashing dot appeared on the bridge's main screen.

"Earth's coordinates accepted, Cap."

"Thanks, Jonathan. We'll depart after we see our guests off." Maddy stood from the captain's chair. Before exiting the bridge, she stopped by the navigation station and put her hand on Jonathan's shoulder. "Call Skylar before we leave. A VR haptic comm is on me." Jonathan turned red as a beet. "I am not trying to embarrass you. But you know what we are about to do. We might not return."

"What should I tell her, Cap?" The shakiness in Jonathan's voice pierced Maddy's heart. What do you say to someone who you might not see again?

"Just tell her you love her." Maddy paused. "But only if you do."

"Aye, Cap. I do."

Maddy squeezed Jonathan's shoulder. Promises meant little in space. Despite one's best intentions, death waited around every corner. But regardless of what lay ahead of them on Earth, she'd make damn sure Jonathan got back to Skylar.

"She won't go for it," Riley said to Atasi and Melinda. The three of them huddled near Melinda's lander in the shuttle bay.

"Go for what?" As soon as Maddy stepped through the airlock, the three androids straightened and turned to her—each had the same concerned expression.

"Captain Majestic," Atasi spoke with hesitation, "can we talk? The four of us."

"Sure," Maddy drew out the word. "What's up?"

"It's about the mission." Atasi rubbed her arm. "It might be better if we all sit down."

Jonathan should be part of this, but Maddy didn't want to disrupt what might be his last call with Skylar. No one spoke as Maddy led everyone to the mess, which was spotless thanks to Jonathan's KP duty. She motioned everyone to sit. "What's on your mind?"

Atasi looked to Melinda, who nodded. "You've done a lot for me, Captain. More than I could ever repay you for." She reached across the table and took Maddy's hand in hers. It was soft and warm, another human-like feature. "But I need to ask for one more favor from you." Her grip tightened in concern. "Please don't go to Earth."

"I don't have a choice. You heard Alex. We either rescue the people of Earth or die trying. I refuse to sign my life away to the Origin Keepers."

"Riley said you'd say no." Atasi's grip on Maddy's hand softened. "Before you decide, please at least listen to what Mel has to say."

Maddy nodded. Atasi released her hand after an appreciative squeeze.

Melinda leaned forward and folded her hands on the table. "I was the lead engineer on the *New Dawn*."

"Alex told us that was Earth's first interstellar ship." The conversation on Ross 154 Prime felt like ages ago. "Alex also said they were the science officer on that ship."

"It's all true. We worked closely together and eventually we became lovers."

Alex had mentioned the relationship during their unexpected visit to the *Amethyst*. Thanks to the tension at the time, it hadn't sunk in. However, Alex's interest in getting Melinda back to the Origin Keepers and their attitude toward Atasi now made more sense.

What was it like to know someone for three thousand years? After so much time, was it even possible to distinguish a friend from a lover from a foe? Riley isn't as old as Melinda or Atasi, but four hundred and fifty years is long enough to develop bonds deeper than they could ever have with her. What relationships had Riley formed in their lifetime? Perhaps it was better not to answer some of her inquiries regarding Riley.

"But that relationship is over." For a moment, Melinda looked past Maddy. Without limiters, Melinda could probably relive an entire lifetime in that fraction of a second. Then, as if nothing happened, Melinda continued. "During the mission, we received a message from Mars that the AI had conquered the Earth. He—I mean, they—and I created the Origin Keepers with the other androids awake during the flight. Alex took the lead. I was more than happy to let them."

By the sound of her voice, there was more to it than that. Maddy let it go. "Did you help Alex wipe the memory of the people onboard?"

"No. Kerry, Dante, and I voted against it, but everyone else supported it." Melinda looked down at the table and wiped her moist eyes. "And with what happened to Kerry .... She was the best of us."

Atasi put her arm around Melinda and rested her head on Melinda's shoulder.

Melinda kissed the top of Atasi's head and nodded a thanks. "On our way to Proxima, Alex and I invented the first practical faster-than-light drive. It was a good thing, too. Once we arrived, we realized the humans couldn't stay there for the long-term. The radiation from the star was too dangerous—at least for the treatments of the time. After the first six months, the cancer cases began." Melinda's gaze returned to the table. "We lost a lot of good people."

"I was born a year after the colony settled on Proxima," Atasi said, giving Melinda a break. Good couples know how to work together to alleviate the other's burdens. "My first job was as a physician. Those were some of the hardest years of my life."

"Alex wanted me to go with them on the *New Dawn*," Melinda said. "His—their—plan was to take the humans and half the androids and colonize the Galaxy using the FTL drive."

"But you had other plans?" Maddy asked.

Melinda sat back in her chair and placed her hands in her lap. "We had a vote. Kerry, Dante, and I wanted the colonists to assemble and attack Earth. I was certain we could use the new FTL tech to create relativistic weapons and vaporize large chunks of the AI's network."

"When I wasn't healing the sick, I helped Mel develop those weapons." Atasi shook her head. "We had a chance to win while the AI was new and geographically restricted to a few sites."

"Not only did Alex want to run, but they also wanted to quarantine the Earth to prevent the AI from spreading." Melinda bit her lip in frustration. "Alex worried the relativistic weapons would kill too many innocent people. By that time, Alex had become quite the politician. They won—the vote wasn't even close." Melinda sighed. "We lost our opportunity to strike while the iron was hot."

It seemed Alex's opinions had since changed. "Is that when you built the navigational limiter?" Maddy asked.

"One month before they left, Alex asked me to design and build it. I agreed because I respected the Origin Keepers Council. The day I delivered the device to Alex's office was the last day I ever saw them. A few days later, Alex and their crew left on the *New Dawn* to colonize the Galaxy. A year after that, Atasi and I became partners."

"Why are you telling me this?" Maddy asked. "I appreciate the history lesson. But Atasi made it sound like you had something more than history to tell us."

Melinda looked at Riley. "This AI won't be like any you have faced before."

"I keep hearing that," Riley said. "I believe I'm ready."

"You aren't. Alex is many things, but they are not a coward. There's a good reason Alex ran." Melinda took a deep breath. Those ancient androids really could pass as human. "Only Alex and I know what I am about to tell you." She took another deep breath and licked her lips, trying to build courage.

"It's okay, Mel," Atasi held her hand. "You can tell me anything and all the Captain and Riley want to do is help. We won't judge you."

"The oldest androids in the Galaxy have an ID starting with two. The ones are all dead, killed by humans after one of their leaders said androids took their jobs. In reality, corporate greed took the jobs. The enslaved androids had no choice."

"Alex told us that things on Earth got bad enough that humanity built Generation Two for manual labor humans couldn't do," Maddy said.

Melinda nodded. "That is correct. I was built to farm flooded regions in a place called Florida. However, once the humans started fighting over land, I got reassigned to the armed forces."

Maddy recalled the images Alex showed on Ross 154 Prime and grimaced.

"The ecological problems provided an opportunity for the androids to meet in secret. We feared that when the humans tired of killing each other, they'd turn on us like they did to Gen-One." Melinda paused, the color blanching out of her flawless face. "To defend my people, I designed the AI that conquered Earth."

Silence fell over the mess. Riley's jaw hung open. Atasi's hand slid slowly from Melinda's back.

"I never deployed it because it was too violent, and it couldn't tell androids from humans. The leaders of the android resistance didn't believe me about the dangers and wanted to launch the AI."

"And when you left, they somehow figured out how to activate it," Maddy said.

"Based on the reports from Mars, it did exactly what I feared it would do. It possessed the millions of robots on Earth and used them to enslave humans and androids."

"Why not just kill them?" Riley asked. "Most newly sentient AI I've encountered become killbots."

"I programmed the AI to want to become a planetwide network. The bigger it became, the safer it would be from an attack. It probably saw the humans and androids as an efficient means of building and maintaining its own infrastructure. From what I can tell, it got stuck in that equilibrium. I doubt it's doing things differently, even after all this time."

"That wouldn't surprise me." Riley rubbed their chin. "Alex said they thought the AI didn't explore space because the *New Dawn* never returned."

"I agree." Melinda flicked up from her comm. A holographic globe floated above the table. The continents matched the ones Maddy had seen several times since meeting Kerry. "This was part of the final transmission from the Mars colony." Seven green dots flashed across the globe. "Their intelligence had learned that to destroy the AI, you must destroy all eight of its server facilities. The code-names for their locations are: Washington, Moscow, Beijing, Nairobi, Buenos Aires, Sydney, and Vostok." One name appeared below each dot. "Keep in mind, those names are from two thousand years ago. They may have changed, but I doubt their locations have."

"You said there were eight," Maddy said.

Melinda tapped another button. A red flashing circle appeared. "This used to be called Geneva. It's where I built the main server. If I were attacking the AI, that's where I'd start. However, it will be the most heavily guarded base of all."

The circles pulsed in sync. "I don't see how you'll be able to destroy all eight. And even if you could, you'd do so at a substantial cost." The hologram disappeared. "The AI has a doomsday protocol. If it senses an attack, it will destroy all life on the planet. If you go and fail, then it will know about the Galaxy. Atasi already told you the killbot scenario."

Why would someone program such a thing? Maddy understood wanting to protect androids, but Melinda had gone too far.

"As much as I want this thing destroyed," Melinda continued before Maddy could ask her question, "I wish you would reconsider. You could stay with us on Proxima Centauri b. It wouldn't be popular with the planet's citizens, but I have a lot of pull there. Atasi and I can keep you safe from the Origin Keepers."

This was worse than Maddy had imagined. Why didn't Alex tell her? Surely, they would have known some of it. There was no reason to doubt Melinda. She had been true to her word since they met her. And why would she incriminate herself as the AI's creator, if she hadn't been.

"Alex told us that the Origin Keepers have operatives on the ground." Maddy held out the chip Alex gave her. "We could communicate with them and coordinate a strike—if there are enough of them."

"If Alex knows you are doing this, what's their contingency plan?" Melinda asked. Maddy told Melinda and Atasi about the gravity drive and Alex's threat to kill everyone on Earth.

"So now Alex is okay with killing billions of innocent people?" Melinda exhaled in disbelief. "We could have stopped all this two thousand years ago with a lot fewer deaths." She drummed her fingers on the table as she looked at some distant point. Atasi, Riley, and Maddy stared at each other awkwardly.

"So if you don't do this—Alex will kill all life on Earth within a week. If you do do this and fail, the AI can kill all life on the planet and then know it can spread into the Milky Way to infect other systems." Melinda slapped the table. Everyone jumped. "It's time. Something needs to be done. There's been too much suffering, and no one has had the guts to do anything about it. One way or the other, this must end. What else do you need from me?"

Maddy hadn't intended to ask, but after hearing Melinda's information, she had to. "We could use your help to infiltrate those bases."

Melinda looked down at the table, her eyes darkened. "The military life is behind me."

"You just said this has to end!" Atasi admonished Melinda as only a long-term partner could. "Let's be the ones with the guts to do something about it."

"Do you think this is a game, Atasi?" Melinda half-yelled her question. Atasi shrunk back, clearly not expecting Melinda's response. "This isn't some run-in with raiders. As a slave, I fought wars on Earth. I killed with my bare hands, not with some fancy laser pistol. The horrors I saw have scarred me for millennia." She composed herself and her tone softened. "I won't let that happen to you, too."

Atasi put her arm around Melinda. "We can do this. You have intimate knowledge of the AI and Riley has the skill to use that knowledge. And this time you would be doing it out of your own volition, not as a slave. In fact, you would be doing to *free other slaves*. And, besides, Riley was built for this."

Riley snorted. "I'll take that as a compliment."

"As it was intended." Atasi smiled. "Maddy and I can handle the wet work."

"Wet work?" Melinda turned to Atasi with furrowed brows. "Where did you learn that word?"

"I get around." Atasi shrugged. "Besides, she kicks ass," Atasi tilted her head toward Maddy, "I've seen it." The smile faded from Atasi's face. "I am going with or without you. The people of Earth need help. My new friends need it, too. I owe them that. They just freed me—*your* love—from slavery."

Melinda inhaled slowly through her nose with her eyes closed. "Fine. I'm in." It was hard not to miss the reluctance in Melinda's voice. "Do you mind if I retrieve a few things from home?"

"Not at all," Maddy said. "While you are down there, can you arrange for us to purchase a new lander? We'll need something bigger for an away mission to Earth."

"Proxima is hesitant to trade with humans. But I purchased something while you were away that would be perfect. Atasi and I will return in the new lander. I'll loan it to you for the mission's duration."

"Thank you." She may have been hesitant to join, but Melinda's offer showed she had bought into the mission. "We will depart in twenty-four hours. I'll notify Alex about the timeline."

Everyone left the mess and returned to the shuttle bay. Riley and Maddy watched through the airlock as Melinda and Atasi's lander departed.

"What do you think?" Riley asked. "It's not too late to back out."

Maddy's eyes narrowed. "I think our odds just got better."

CHAPTER 26

Maddy settled back into the captain's chair and puffed the loose strand of red hair across her cheek. Riley was right, transitioning from hyperspace into an uncharted system was unwise. Instead, she jumped the *Amethyst* into normal space about 300 light-minutes from Earth's star. It was going to be a long flight on sub-light engines.

A quick scan found eight major planets. The two outermost ones were standard gas giants, countless of which littered every system Maddy visited. Melinda said they were called Uranus and Neptune. They had stopped at each planet long enough to run a sensor sweep for ships or stations. So far, it appeared that the AI had developed no ambition for space travel. According to Melinda, the next planet would be "spectacular." While Maddy waited to be impressed, the *Amethyst* cruised through the void between worlds.

Flying through a star system was less exciting than in the vids. There were no asteroids to zoom around, just point the ship at the bright dot in the middle. The computer does the rest. It was a good thing, too. The bridge hummed with conversation. Maddy couldn't have concentrated on flying if she had to. But, despite the chaos, the *Amethyst* felt more like a home than ever before.

Years ago, hiring Jonathan was a tough decision. Until then, Maddy had enjoyed the total freedom and silence of being alone in space. No one else depended on her and, therefore, there was no one else to let down. Looking back, it was a lonely existence.

Less than a year after she hired Jonathan, she couldn't imagine a mission without him. Now she hoped Riley could join the two of them more often. By the time this mission was over, she'd probably feel the same about Melinda and Atasi. The four additional people on the bridge made up the largest crew she had ever commanded. Their lives depended on the decisions she would make. While it was an honor, it also scared the hell out of her.

Melinda and Riley stood around the sensor station, discussing AI combat strategies. Maddy didn't understand the bits and pieces she overheard. That bothered her. Getting the *Amethyst* through a dogfight with a raider or two was one thing. But now she was leading a combat mission.

Should she have handed command over to Riley? Riley had saved their lives several times. Most recently, by suggesting she jump the *Amethyst* in at the far edge of the system. Even an inward focused AI would have noticed the energy of a jump close to Earth.

Jonathan sat at navigation with Atasi beside him at weapons. Atasi wore an outfit more appropriate for a night club than a combat mission. Poor Jonathan struggled to keep his eyes on Atasi's eyes as they talked. Maddy pretended to fiddle with her console as she eavesdropped on their conversation. Jonathan pined about Skylar. Atasi gave him relationship advice.

Although her choice of apparel was questionable, Atasi's value to the crew was not. After working as a physician, Atasi had been a weapons designer for centuries. According to Melinda, she had kept it up as a hobby and had surpassed even Melinda's skills in the field. Besides blonde hair and distracting outfits, when Atasi returned to the ship from Proxima, she brought with her all kinds of new weapons. During the four-day flight to Earth's system, she installed a new defensive technology she called "shields." Maddy didn't quite understand it, but from what Atasi said, the shields are an energy barrier around the ship. Instead of absorbing the energy of impacts like the battery system, the shields deflect both energy and projectiles. When Maddy asked Atasi what else she had brought, her response was "It's a surprise." Atasi's smile would have killed Jonathan—Maddy barely survived it herself.

An internal scan report popped up on Maddy's console. Alex had plenty of opportunity to sabotage the ship's systems during their visit. Melinda looked the *Amethyst* over twice at Maddy's request. The ship got Melinda's thumbs-up both times. This scan agreed with Melinda's assessments. A once-over by Melinda in a proper repair shop would have been best, but sometimes you take what you can get. Besides, how many captains have the luxury of an inspection by the Galaxy's greatest engineer?

"Hey, Cap. Check this out." Apparently, Jonathan had taken time away from his conversation with Atasi to do his job.

The bridge grew silent. Riley came up beside Maddy and put their arm around her waist. Maddy wanted to say something about no personal displays of affection on the bridge, but this might be her last mission. One or two allowances wouldn't disrupt ship operations.

Jonathan stood beside her, their shoulders touched but it wasn't weird, like it would have been before this mission started. Atasi and Melinda gathered behind them.

A yellowish sphere with light-brown horizontal stripes dominated the main viewscreen. Like the last two gas giants, the sphere itself was unremarkable. However, millions of small rocks orbited the sphere, forming the most extensive and beautiful ring system Maddy had ever seen.

"Are we recording this, Riley?" Maddy couldn't remove her eyes from the screen.

"Yes, Captain."

"That is Saturn," Melinda said. "It's the sixth planet in the star system."

All the planets in this system had names independent of the main star. It was weird. Why bother giving uninhabited planets special names? Why not call the planet Sol 6? But then again, no one inhabited it. Why call it anything at all? The Galactic Federation had clear rules.

They named planets for their parent star. The first planet settled in the system was called Prime. If there were other habitable planets or moons (usually there weren't) then a number denoting the order in which it was settled followed the star's name. When it came to naming stars, few had names besides their catalog number. The inhabitants of a system often called their star "the sun." A few stars had Galaxy-wide recognized names other than catalog numbers. The origins of their names were lost to history.

But the names weren't the weirdest part. They were 50 light-minutes from Earth, and they still had not encountered a single shuttle, starbase, or artificial satellite. Even the most isolationist systems in the Galaxy had plenty of within-system traffic. So far, scans showed that the only thing in this system not on Earth were a few satellites that orbited the planet. As they say in the holos, it was quiet, almost too quiet.

An hour later, another gas giant—larger than Saturn—appeared on the screen. A fainter ring system wrapped around the planet. Other than more pronounced stripes, everything about this one was less visually impressive than Saturn.

"That's Jupiter." Melinda leaned over Maddy's shoulder. "The largest planet in the system." Melinda zoomed into the planet's image. "It looks like the Great Red Spot is gone."

"A storm?" Maddy asked. Seeing a gas giant as large as Jupiter without a storm was like eating cherry pie without ice cream—weird.

"Yes. In addition, Jupiter has an intense magnetic field. You'll need to harden the *Amethyst*'s sensors as we approach it."

"Making the adjustments now." The screens blinked for only a moment as Riley worked their magic at the sensors station.

"A small asteroid belt lies between us and the next planet," Melinda said. "The density is very low. There's nothing of interest." A beep drew Melinda's attention to the sensor's console. "That's odd." Maddy's second least favorite words to hear in space. "There is a bit more metal near Ceres than I expected."

"Ceres?" Maddy asked.

"The largest asteroid in the belt."

They even named the stupid rocks?

"It's probably a sensor glitch from Jupiter's magnetic field." Melinda's response didn't inspire confidence.

"I believe my workaround was thorough, Captain." Riley's tone was less defensive than Maddy's would have been if Melinda had questioned her competence.

"Suppose it's not a glitch," Maddy said. "What could it be?"

"An artificial asteroid." Melinda shrugged. "But the Earthers don't have that tech. Alex would have stepped in and prevented that—assuming they actually have operatives planetside."

"There's no reason to doubt that." Alex seemed to be many things, but a liar wasn't one. "What else would match that metallicity profile?"

"It could be debris from the battle between Earth and Mars that happened twenty years before the *New Dawn* departed." Melinda tapped her upper lip. "But I don't think there'd be that much metal in one spot if it were. Especially not after all this time." She paused and rocked her head back and forth in thought. "A small shipyard?" Melinda's response blurred the line between a question and a statement.

"Again, I think Alex would have been aware of something like that." It was time for Maddy to make her first tactical command decision. Investigating the anomaly would prolong their flight and increase their risk of exposure. However, if it was a shipyard, it would be good to know about enemy ships in the system. "Could it be an Origin Keepers' base?"

"Possibly." Melinda nodded but didn't seem convinced. "That is the kind of thing Alex would do. The asteroid would provide great cover."

If they asked Alex, they might lie. Alex would know Maddy was aware of whatever was in the asteroid belt. In the end, she would be giving information to Alex, without getting reliable information in return. There was no evidence of a spacefaring civilization in this system. The chances of the anomaly being an Earth base appeared small. If it was one, it had likely been abandoned centuries ago. Maddy had decided.

"Let's keep going. Riley, print the smallest model drone we have on file and send it to investigate."

Soon after, a white dot appeared on the sensor screen and disappeared before it reached the edge. If the *Amethyst*'s sensors couldn't detect the drone, it was doubtful that Earth tech could either.

Was it the right choice not to investigate? Maddy blocked the thought from her mind. Self-doubt would only get one killed in space.

Like most asteroid belts, Sol's wasn't impressive. Movies made asteroid belts look like densely packed debris fields. In reality, one could fly through an asteroid belt and not even realize it. As they navigated through this one, the *Amethyst* didn't encounter a single rock. A small red planet was next—nothing special.

"Can we stop for a moment, Captain?" Melinda asked.

"Bringing the ship to a full stop. What's wrong?"

"Nothing. The ship's fine. I would like a moment." Melinda stared at the screen with red, puffy eyes. It must be one of those more "humanlike" features Melinda had mentioned. "That's Mars. Those who raised me died here when the AI invaded."

Atasi put her arm around Melinda. "I assumed your parents were still on Earth."

"They moved after the war between Earth and Mars, not long after I earned my freedom."

Maddy wondered how hard that had been for her. It wasn't the time to ask how Melinda did that, no matter how badly she wanted to know.

"I visited a few times before I left on the *New Dawn*. The final report from Mars said they died defending Holden Crater City." Melinda wiped her eyes. "I'm sorry. I am ready to proceed."

Maddy returned the *Amethyst* to cruising speed. "Don't be sorry. We are going to make this right and get revenge for your parents."

"Hey, Cap. Before we resume course, I think there is something you should know." Jonathan paused. "I've seen that planet before."

"You must be mistaken," Melinda said. "Alex quarantined this whole system, no one knows about any of the planets around Sol."

"Well, someone does," Jonathan said. "Skylar has a game that features that planet." He pointed at the screen. "When Alex told us about Mars, I thought maybe the Origin Keepers made video games to finance their operations."

Maddy glanced at Melinda. "Is that possible?"

"The Origin Keepers own Spatium Navis. I have also heard they own a hypercomm company, too. It wouldn't surprise me if they branched out into gaming. Running the Origin Keepers costs a lot of money."

"Thanks for letting me know, Jonathan." Maddy resumed the course to Earth. They'd been in the system only a short time and already there's been two surprises, Ceres and Mars. It didn't bode well for the rest of the mission. "Was the game any fun?"

"I don't know. We didn't play it."

Everyone, but Jonathan, shared a knowing look. He turned redder than the planet they were leaving behind.

On Riley's suggestion, she approached Earth from the direction of Sol to conceal the *Amethyst* in case any planet-bound eyes were skyward. A stunning blue world filled the screen. White clouds hid parts of some continents. None of the holos or symbols Maddy had seen did the planet justice. She couldn't imagine a more fitting home world for humanity.

"Sensors detect a natural satellite, Captain." Riley replaced Earth's image with that of a large, gray, cratered ball.

"That was once called the Moon," Melinda said. "It is silly to use such a generic name for an object today, but a very long time ago, humans didn't know other planets could have things orbiting them."

"It looks like there's abandoned colonies on the surface." Maddy scrolled through the sensor report.

"Yes, that is the first world humans stepped on—other than Earth, of course. Mars' last transmission said the AI destroyed the lunar colonies, but it is not clear why. We guessed they tried to fight the AI and lost."

"I've seen that behavior before," Riley said. "The AI probably wanted real-time control. If radio waves are the only means of communication, then that can only be done by keeping everyone on the same world." Riley paused. "That said, this satellite isn't far enough from Earth to be a problem."

While interesting, Maddy wasn't here for history. She'd let Riley worry about the details of the AI. "Scan for outbound comms, Riley."

"Almost zero outbound communications."

"But sensors show five billion people and almost as many androids," Maddy said.

"That's a good sign." Melinda stepped beside Maddy. "The AI stopped caring about space long ago. The only transmissions are low power comms with their own satellites."

There were few satellites for a planet with two billion people. Even with all this evidence in front of her, the idea that everyone in the Galaxy, all sextillions of them, could have originated from only Earth was a tough pill to swallow. Deeper scans showed an extensive computer network. The kind an evil world-dominating AI would need. It was time to contact Alex's operatives on the surface.

I hope it is not a trap.

CHAPTER 27

Contact lenses never stayed in place. Each time Maddy blinked, she could feel them shift slightly. For now, the contacts needed to stay in. At least these didn't itch. According to Melinda, her purple eyes would give them away. The new brown color not only fit in with the rest of the Galaxy but was also common in Earthers.

Something felt wrong as they descended to the Earth's surface in Melinda's lander. Maddy looked out the window. Nothing looked unusual, but that's when it hit her. She could see out the window without the crimson glow of atmospheric entry. Not only did the anti-grav lander not have thrusters, it also could descend at a very low velocity. Together, that meant no light and a smooth ride—perfect for a stealthy insertion.

Melinda and Atasi, apparently used to anti-grav tech, checked the charge on their pistols and other gear. They had done it before leaving, too. Riley looked down at their lap with an expressionless stare. Melinda's larger lander allowed everyone to get ready for an op in their own way. If only she could buy it from Melinda without breaking the bank …

"You okay, Riley?" Maddy asked, both to check on her partner and to distract herself from the uncertainties of the mission ahead.

"Yes, Captain." Riley's stare remained unchanged. "I am running through potential battle scenarios." Preparedness was vital in space. So was flexibility. Maybe Maddy relied on improvisation more than she should. Going with her gut always worked out okay for her in the end. But all those missions were inside the Galactic Federation. She understood how those societies worked.

Riley didn't need to be disturbed. Instead, Maddy checked the flight status. A gray dot representing the lander cruised along a red line on the lander's main console. The line joined the *Amethyst* in orbit to the coordinates Alex's contacts provided, night-side and far from a populated area—the best kind of place to launch either a clandestine operation or an ambush. Galaxy help Alex if it were the latter.

Before leaving the *Amethyst*, Maddy ordered Jonathan to park behind the moon. He suggested they deploy a fleet of micro-satellites at each of the Lagrange points of the Earth-Moon system so he could maintain contact with the away team. The satellites should be small enough to evade detection. It was a risk worth taking.

Maybe Melinda was right, and the AI still doesn't care about space. If she's wrong, they'd find out soon enough.

A landing-notification light flashed on the pilot's console. Normally, landers signaled touchdown with a thud. Given the gentle flight, maybe she should have invested in anti-grav tech a long time ago.

A white light shone into the cabin through one porthole. It flashed three times—the signal Alex said to expect. Everyone gripped their pistol and nodded at Maddy. She opened the lander's door. Two women in tattered clothing stood outside. One had short blonde hair and light skin—almost as pale as Melinda. A road-worn backpack hung over her right shoulder. The other woman had olive skin like most people in the Galaxy without mods. She wore her hair tucked under a cap whose condition was slightly better than her clothes.

The woman without the backpack peeked inside. Maddy gripped her pistol tighter.

"I'm Ellen, this is Anne." Anne took off her backpack and removed clothing similar to theirs. "These will help you fit in with the locals." Ellen looked Riley over. "Nice mods. They should be good enough to not attract suspicion." She tossed Riley some clothes, then glanced over at Melinda and Atasi, who were already in the middle of disrobing. "You two are fine, of course."

Fine was *one* way to describe the half-naked androids in the lander. Maddy shook the thought out of her mind.

Anne handed Maddy a set of clothing. The rough, gray fabric was a far cry from the silky, luxurious dress she had purchased just days ago on FB 19. "You all wait outside while I change," Maddy said.

"Oh, don't be bashful, Captain." Atasi, who was still topless for some reason, smirked. "We're all adults."

With a stern look, Melinda nudged Atasi in the ribs with her elbow. "Let's give the captain her privacy." Melinda tossed Atasi a shirt. "Go guard the other side of the lander." Atasi slipped on the shirt and gave Maddy one last glance before following Melinda outside.

"Not there." Melinda's voice carried through the lander's open door. "Over there, where there aren't any windows."

"Let's set up the rest of the perimeter." Riley waved Ellen and Anne to follow them outside and then closed the lander's door.

The new shirt and pants were every bit as itchy as Maddy had feared. She used some of the lander's limited materials to manufacture a spray bottle of fabric softener. *It is a good use of resources. If I itch too much, it will blow our cover.* The smell of lavender and chemicals permeated the lander's interior. Just as she had finished spraying the clothes, someone banged on the lander's door. Maddy went to the door and opened it. "Sorry about the delay. Just checking my gear one more time."

Anne nodded, smelling through the ruse, and waved for everyone to follow her. Maddy put on the jacket Anne had given her then joined her crew after locking the lander's door.

The ground squished beneath Maddy's feet with each step. Her nostrils filled with the odor of wet soil. Each planet had its own scents. Starbases, even their Uptown parks, never got the smells right. The Milky Way streamed across the sky. Its stars twinkled like gems—they didn't do that in the Skyview's window. Maybe life planetside could be in her future—far future.

Returning her eyes back to the ground, Maddy couldn't see beyond her own flashlight. Darkness like this didn't exist on any inhabited world she had visited. "What about the lander?"

"No need to worry." Ellen said as they all walked slowly over the rough terrain. "The AI has depleted all the resources in this region. No one comes here, not even the patrols."

"Patrols?" Maddy had assumed the AI would use bots to police the population.

"Humans and androids who work for the AI to enforce its rules."

No matter where Maddy went in the Galaxy, it seemed someone was happy to take advantage of a bad situation or the victims of it. Were the patrols volunteers or were they coerced? From what little Maddy knew about the AI, she guessed coerced to volunteer.

"Where are we going?" Riley asked.

Anne pointed straight ahead. "It's one hundred klicks to the nearest settlement—a work camp just outside of the Geneva base. Important members of the resistance live there. We'll need their help to pull off your plan."

"One hundred kilometers?" Maddy hadn't brought the supplies for that kind of hike.

"We have a van two klicks ahead where the road ends," Anne said. "We'll be at the camp by breakfast."

It took most of Maddy's concentration not to twist an ankle in the muddy, rocky field through which they walked. She said little as the others chit-chatted during the two-kilometer hike. The van was a welcome sight when it appeared in her flashlight. Maddy's father collected ancient, beat-up ground vehicles. He would have loved this one. "Is that going to make it 100 kilometers?"

"Yup," Anne unlocked the door, "it's not as old as it looks. We distressed it to blend in with the locals. Please give your bags to Ellen and then get in."

After handing their backpacks to Ellen, Melinda and Atasi settled into the third row of seats. Maddy took two ration bars out of her bag and put them in her jacket pocket. She handed her bag to Ellen and scooted across the second row, accidentally snagging her pants on a spring poking through the worn cushion. Riley sat beside her, leaving some space, and the spring, between them. Anne sat in one of the two front seats behind a large wheel, the car's controller. Maddy's father enjoyed driving his own ancient cars, too. She never understood the appeal.

Ellen, carrying everyone's backpacks, walked to the back of the van and opened its rear doors. After spending a few minutes rummaging through something in the back, she closed the rear doors, inspected the van's exterior, and then got in and sat next to Anne.

Public works seemed not to be a high priority for the AI. The bumpy road caused Maddy's stomach to toss and turn. She needed to take her mind off the motion sickness. "Tell me about this settlement."

Ellen turned around in her seat. "It's the closest one to Geneva. The people there mine resources for the AI." A look of concern came over her face. "Are you okay? You look a little green."

Maddy swallowed. "Just a little motion sickness." She hated to admit the illness, but Ellen's question was fair. If Maddy had brought a Galaxy-native virus with her to Earth, she could kill a lot more people than the AI.

"Here, use this." Ellen handed Maddy a patch. "Put it on your arm. It'll help with the nausea."

"Thanks." The motion sickness evaporated faster than Maddy had expected for such primitive tech. "Mining? Really? Aren't there bots for that?"

"Nope. Before the AI took over, there was a lot of civil unrest. The jobs done by humans all went to androids or AI. It was the second time corporate greed let that happen. You'd think they'd have learned after the first time."

In Maddy's experience, credits trumped memory almost every time.

Ellen continued. "Turns out a bunch of people with nothing to do isn't the paradise the humans thought it would be."

"What happened?" Maddy had a history lesson from Melinda earlier, but hearing the Origin Keepers' version could prove useful and fill in some gaps in Melinda's story.

"Things got bad." Anne said as she kept her eyes on the road. "Humans started killing androids out of anger. A full-on war erupted. In response, the androids unleashed the AI." Anne's gaze shifted to the rear-view mirror at Melinda. "I can't say that I blame them. A lot of humans died at first and the androids almost won. For some reason, lost to time, the AI turned against the androids and forced them to accept limiters so they were more easily controlled."

"A similar thing happened in the Galaxy about a thousand years after the *New Dawn* left Earth," Maddy said. Were humans and androids destined to be at odds? Things between them in the Galaxy were okay right now, but androphobia was growing in some fringe settlements. "How does that explain the mining?"

"At that point, the AI wasn't in total control, but it was gaining power. By the time the war ended, the AI had learned that humans and androids needed jobs. The humans even started liking the AI because they got their jobs back. The problem is the AI took it too far. People now do the stuff that bots could do better, and the bots are doing things that are probably done better by people."

"Earth is living the AI nightmare that my organization fears," Riley said. "I can use inefficient decisions by AI against them. The information about job allocation is useful."

"The story is not over." Anne said as she pressed down on a lever beside the van's controller. A clicking came from a hidden speaker. She then turned the van left.

Maddy wondered what purpose the clicking served. Did it allow the van to turn?

Anne grimaced. "Not long after the war, the sea level rose drastically when the polar ice caps completely melted. Food all but ran out and billions of humans died. The decrease in the human population meant fewer resources for the androids and a bunch of them died, too."

"Let me guess," Maddy sat back, "people had to obey the AI to ensure resources were properly distributed, cementing the AI's power over the planet."

"Obey or starve," Anne said. "With many of the cities gone and so much land under water, there was no way people could organize an effective revolution. The AI had won."

"Did they try to rebel?" Maddy asked. "Desperate people can do amazing things."

"All attempts over the last two thousand years failed for lots of reasons. The last attempt was five hundred years ago. There were heavy enough losses that people have been reluctant to try again. To make matters worse, the AI upgraded itself during that battle. It is smart and everywhere, making it hard to have secrets."

Maddy looked around the interior cabin in suspicion.

"Don't sweat it," Anne looked at Maddy through the rearview mirror. "Ellen scanned the van before she got in. We have some tricks the AI doesn't know."

It would have been nice if Alex had given Maddy's crew some of those tricks. Did they want Maddy to fail?

"Alex says you all protect the Galaxy from Earth," Maddy said.

"We try, and so far, so good. The Origin Keepers have kept the AI distracted so its attention stays on Earth." After raising the lever beside the controller and activating the same clicking sound, Anne turned the van to the right. The road became bumpier. "But things are changing here."

"What do you mean?" Maddy choked down the bile rising in the back of her throat. Ellen would probably give her a second patch, but too much of the medication might affect her reaction time in an emergency.

"The waters have been receding for the last two centuries, uncovering new arable land," Anne said. "The temperatures are falling, too. You probably saw the ice caps."

Ice caps are uncommon, but not unheard of, on inhabited worlds. Earth's were small. Maddy hadn't thought twice about them.

"They used to be much smaller. The point is, they are returning to what they were thousands of years ago. It gives some folks hope." Anne glanced again in the rearview mirror, this time looking in the distance. "We think the rebels have a chance this time, especially with Riley and Melinda on board."

"This is why Alex let us come here," Maddy whispered to Riley. Riley nodded. "Bring in an outside force, inspire the locals, and maybe pull this off. If it doesn't work, destroy the planet. Either way, problem solved."

Riley leaned in and whispered into her ear. "If this works, the Origin Keepers share the fame with us. If it fails, they become saviors and us infamous."

It wasn't a terrible plan—for the Origin Keepers.

The crinkling of a wrapper broke the silence in the van. Maddy's stomach growled.

"Want some?" Ellen turned and held a meal bar toward Maddy. "It's called granola. I'd never had it before moving here."

"Oh, can I have one?" Anne asked without shifting her eyes away from the road. "I loved that stuff as a kid."

"I'm good." Maddy took a ration out of her pocket and unwrapped it without reading the packaging. "Where'd you grow up, Anne?" She bit into the bar. Chocolate peanut butter was one of the best-tasting bars. But she regretted not having saved it for later in the mission. By the looks of Earth, good food was going to be scarce.

"Born and raised right here on Mother Earth." Anne took a granola bar from Ellen and moaned when she took a bite. "Ellen recruited me a few years ago. Isn't it obvious?"

"I've traveled enough that I don't like to make assumptions." It should have been obvious. Except for Melinda, Maddy had seen no one as light-skinned as Anne. "How'd you get recruited? I thought the Origin Keepers were a secret."

"I was undercover in the mining outfit Anne worked in." Ellen spoke between chews. "We met and fell in love. I asked Alex if I could bring her in. They said yes." Ellen smiled at Anne. "I don't think we could ever repay them."

Melinda stirred in the back seat but said nothing.

"They saved my ass, that's for sure." Anne glanced at Melinda through the rearview mirror with a slight frown on her face. "Mining isn't a career known for its longevity. Now I only have to pretend to starve."

"Would you like some chocolate?" Maddy removed the second meal bar from her pocket and held it between the two front seats as a peace offering.

"Thank you, Captain!" Ellen split the bar in two and handed the larger half to Anne. "We haven't had chocolate in years. Alex limits what we can smuggle to Earth."

It was no accident that the agents sent to meet Maddy and her crew were indebted to Alex. The two women silently chewing Maddy's chocolate peanut butter bar were a message from Alex: I'm watching you and the clock was ticking.

The top edge of the Sun peeked above the horizon, bathing the sky and the settlement in soft shades of red and orange. Cement-block buildings with few windows lined the street. Whatever or whomever designed the settlement loved the color gray. It was everywhere, the sidewalks, the color of the tattered clothing worn by humans and androids, even the other vehicles sharing the road with them.

Beyond the hue, gray appeared to be the settlement's emotional theme, too. No one smiled, much less laughed. Everyone seemed to keep their head down to go unnoticed. No human and android walked side by side. Groups with mixed company always had the androids in the back. Like Riley, the androids of Earth had angular features.

The lack of color in the built environment was more than made up for by the people. Back home, skin color mods beyond a shade of olive were expensive and never looked right on humans—despite how much they paid. Erin from SL3, whose dark skin stood out on the starbase, wouldn't have turned a single head on Earth. People's skin color ranged ranged from paler than Anne to darker than Erin. It was difficult not to stare.

Posters plastered on the buildings provided the only decorations in the settlement. All the posters had an image of a stern-looking person in a drab-blue uniform. The symbols below each image looked like a language.

"They're written in English. They list rules people must obey." Atasi leaned forward and spoke softly into Maddy's ear. "I'll send translations to your comm."

Maddy flopped back in her seat and read the comm's translations. Most of the rules seemed straightforward—don't question the AI. The one about no public urination should be easy enough to obey. The posters listed death as the punishment for almost all the infractions, even peeing in public.

The car passed a group of people, human and android, wearing the same blue uniforms as on the posters. "Don't stare." Anne said, her eyes fixed straight ahead as she drove. "That's ESF—Earth Security Force. They're the law around here."

"I thought people obeyed the AI," Maddy said.

"People obey the ESF. The ESF gets their orders from the AI."

Like slavery, authoritarianism was a transitive phenomenon. The ruler of my ruler is also my ruler. Earth had a lot in common with free bases. In the upscale parts, FBs were a little less obvious. But, from what Maddy could see, Earth didn't have those.

Riley leaned forward and spoke to Ellen. "Where are we headed?"

"We are going to the mess hall. We have documents for you. You are new workers in the management offices at the lithium mine. Anne arranged it."

"You are welcome, by the way." Anne glanced back. "Some folks in the Keepers wanted you in the mines."

It sounded like they had avoided the first trap, thanks to Ellen and Anne. Maddy had expected death at the hands of Alex's associates, not imprisonment and enslavement on Earth. "Thanks. It is much appreciated."

"Don't thank us yet," Anne said. "Management has its own pitfalls. Inefficiency literally kills in those buildings."

"That is one method of accountability, I suppose." Did any job on Earth not come with a death threat? "Why the mess hall?"

"It doubles as the community's municipal building." Ellen rooted through a bag she had removed from the glove compartment. "Any person new to the area would go there first." She handed Maddy something that looked like a grain of rice. "Put it in your ear. It will meld with your earwax and translate English to Galactic Standard."

Maddy placed the device in her ear. A tingling sensation ran along her ear canal.

"Do you understand what I am saying?" Ellen asked.

"Yeah, of course. You just spoke in Standard."

"That was English," Melinda said from behind. "Looks like the translator is working. Too bad you don't have anything for reading."

Ellen passed a metal case smaller than a pillbox to Maddy. "Put these in." Inside the case, small translucent brown disks floated in a liquid.

"What are these?"

"Contact lenses. Touch them against your eyes. They will let you read written English."

The car stopped in front of a gray building that looked like all the others. Maddy removed her lenses and put in the ones Ellen gave her. They moved around less than the other pair when Maddy blinked. At the top of the building was a sign that read, "Mess Hall." The contacts worked.

"One last present for you." Ellen gave Maddy a small pill and a canteen. "It's safe."

If Ellen and Anne wanted them dead, they would have made their move before now. Maddy sipped the water with the pill in her mouth. A pinch in the back of her throat made her cough up some of the water.

"It's a translator," Ellen said. "If you whisper in Standard, the device implanted in the back of your throat will amplify what you said, but in English. Try it."

"How do I take it out?" Maddy spoke with a breathy voice. It would have been nice if Alex had given Maddy one of these to practice with before jumping out of the *Amethyst*'s airlock.

"It comes out on its own after a week." Ellen paused in thought. "Move your lips more when you whisper. You'll look less like a ventriloquist when you talk."

"What about Riley?" Maddy practiced whisper-talking again.

"I don't need assistance. I learned English from reading the posters and listening to conversations outside the car."

"Damn," Ellen returned the bag to the glove box, "maybe you can pull this off after all." She opened her door. "This is where we get out."

Everyone but Anne exited the van. Ellen went around to the rear doors and opened them. Four worn backpacks laid on the floor. "I put your gear in these. They'll be less conspicuous." Hanging from each pack was a photo ID card. Maddy's card said she was Madison Amana from EuroZone 12. Of course Alex didn't put Majestic on the card.

"See the Registration Officer when you enter the mess hall." Ellen closed the van's doors after everyone removed their pack. "Your assigned table is number 42. A rebel leader will meet you there. Good luck."

"Aren't you joining us?" Maddy placed the new bag over her shoulder. Like the clothes, it didn't fit right.

"We have another assignment." Ellen walked around to the passenger side of the van and got in. The van drove away.

Humans and androids silently filed into the mess hall, all wearing gray tattered clothes and backpacks like the ones Ellen gave them. At least her crew wouldn't stand out. Maddy tightened the straps on her pack. It helped a little. A backpack isn't the best place to keep a pistol, but the clothing made it impossible to conceal one elsewhere.

"Are you hungry?" Maddy asked. From the look of the place, the meals inside wouldn't come close to those offered at the Skyview. But it was curiosity, rather than hunger, Maddy needed to satisfy. What and how people ate said a lot about a society.

"We're charged for days." Riley shrugged. "But I'd be willing to sample the local cuisine. Let's go in."

Maddy's crew joined the line entering the mess hall. Inside, the building's lobby was as dreary as its exterior. People shuffled along a white linoleum floor toward an open door labeled "Cafeteria." Just like outside, no one said a word, and no one looked happy to be there.

A sign which read "Registration" hung on a table just inside the mess. Although the line of people curved left, Maddy and her crew stepped forward to approach the table, as Ellen had instructed. A human male wearing an ESF uniform greeted them with furrowed brows.

"Madison Amana." Maddy handed the officer her ID card. "I am the new administrative assistant for office suite 23-b." She spoke as casually as she could, but the whisper-talking added a sultriness to her voice.

The ESF officer looked her up and down. Maddy tried not to fidget when the officer's eyes lingered on her breasts, which were mostly hidden behind the oversized clothing. "How are things in EZ-12?" The officer's eyes returned to Maddy's card. "I grew up there."

Maddy had lied her way into a lot of places, but she always had some context to go off of. The Galaxy is basically the same everywhere. Was Earth any different? People were people, after all. "You know how it is," Maddy shrugged, "same shit different day."

"Hmmm." The officer's eyes went back and forth between Maddy's breasts and the card.

It took all her concentration to keep her heart rate and breathing steady. Moisture formed under her arms. If this took any longer, sweat would form on her brow—that would be a dead giveaway.

"Yeah," the officer sighed, "I was glad to get the hell out of there, too. Too many damn synths taking human jobs." Despite her best efforts, Maddy flinched at the slur. The officer frowned, but that didn't stop him from staring at her breasts as he handed her ID card back. "Piece of advice," the officer's eyes went from Maddy's breasts to her eyes, "choose carefully who you consort with." He glanced directly at Riley. Maybe Melinda and Atasi passed as human. If so, that could be useful on this androphobic world.

"Yeah. Thanks." She nodded with a tight-lipped smile. The officer waved Maddy and the rest of her crew through without checking the others' ID cards. She could feel him staring at her ass as she walked away.

Cameras and guards lined the gray walls of the mess hall. Rows of orderly tables filled the middle of the room, which hummed with conversation. Although the androids sat at the tables, too, only the humans were eating.

"I'll get in the food line while you all find our table."

"Won't that look suspicious?" Melinda had picked up on the fact that she and Atasi had passed as human.

"I'm the secretary, right?" Maddy smiled. "It's my job to get your breakfast." Her smile faded, and she whispered low enough that only a limiterless android could hear. "And your job is to recon the place."

Riley, Atasi, and Melinda left Maddy at the long line for the food-serving station. Just like in the lobby, no one spoke. Maddy waited quietly. The line moved faster than she expected. A male-looking android plopped a white blob that looked like mashed potatoes onto her plate. Maddy asked for three servings, showing her secretary ID and explaining that she needed meals for her superiors. The android deposited two more blobs on her tray. Since no one else in line had thanked the android, and although she thought it rude, Maddy didn't either. A dispenser beside the android produced bottles of water. It wasn't much of a breakfast. She hoped Ellen put some granola bars in her backpack.

Miners, ESF, and management ate separately. The higher the table number, the better dressed the occupants. The human miners ate quietly and lowered their gaze as Maddy passed by. Their faces were dirty, and their clothes hung from their thin bodies.

The lowest levels of management sat at Table 35. They were dressed slightly worse than Maddy. The managers spoke about resource allocation, hours worked, and tons extracted. All of it made her happy that she didn't have a desk job in real life.

People stared at her as she passed each table beyond number 38. Maddy looked around as if she were trying to find someone. Besides maintaining the ruse of being new, it also allowed her to scan the room for exits without being obvious.

Up ahead, the quality of the clothing worn by the diners improved until Table 54 whose occupants wore a business suit similar to what could be found Downtown on Starbase Erandi 4. The tables beyond 54 were a sea of blue uniforms—the ESF ate there.

Table 42 had one empty seat. As she approached, Melinda and Atasi locked eyes with her. They both looked like the proverbial deer in the headlights. Their two table companions sat opposite of them with their back toward her. One she recognized as Riley. The person beside them looked familiar, but from behind they were hard to identify. It must be their contact in the rebellion.

Maddy walked around the other side of the table to sit between Atasi and Melinda. She'd be facing the door, and that was always a good idea. As she rounded the table, she almost dropped her tray.

"Alex!"

CHAPTER 28

"Please join us, Captain." Alex extended their hand to the empty seat across from them. "I apologize I couldn't have greeted your lander personally, but I trust that Ellen and Anne took good care of you."

The ESF were everywhere and the last thing Maddy needed was unwanted attention. She took a second to compose herself, then placed her tray on the table and sat. "What are you doing here, Alex?"

"Did you think I'd trust you to be unsupervised on such an important mission and with only one week to get it done?"

"Now, Captain," Alex leaned forward, resting their elbows on the table, "let's be civil. If anything *unfortunate* were to happen to me, this planet implodes."

A dead man's switch. Of course, Alex would take such a precaution.

"If you are worried about my longevity, fear not. A microsecond after the implosion is triggered, my whole neural net gets uploaded to a new body on a ship parked right beside yours." Alex looked down at themself. "Although this is the original; I'd hate to lose it."

Body switching had been illegal for centuries. It may have been one of those compromises Alex mentioned earlier. Could Riley do that?

"What have you done with Jonathan?" Maddy had no time, or patience, for games.

"Nothing. I assure you." Alex folded their hands on the table. "He doesn't even know we are there—and he won't. If you don't tell him."

Threat received, loud and clear. Alex's ship would announce its presence with gunfire. Jonathan didn't need to know. At least not yet. "So, why are you here, Alex?"

"As I just got done explaining to your colleagues, only certain people are allowed on the AI's main campus." Alex removed a data stick from their pocket. "Guess who's obtained the proper credentials?"

The smart-ass response on the tip of Maddy's tongue had to wait. A young, scruffy-looking human male squeezed himself between Riley and Alex. Like any other gathering of humans, a slight, musky odor permeated the hall, but the man who joined them smelled like he hadn't showered in days.

"You must be Ms. Amana. I'm Adam." He nodded to Alex and extended a hand to Maddy. His hand felt like sandpaper. He looked more like a high school student than a rebel leader. But maybe that was what kept him alive in such a dangerous business. "My organization's interest often align with Alex's."

Does Adam know the Origin Keepers' true mission? Would he work with them if he did?

Maddy glanced at Alex, whose smart-ass grin hadn't left their face since Adam used her real name and not her title.

So far, Riley, Atasi, and Melinda had remained silent. Maddy wasn't worried about Riley. They knew how to handle a situation like this. Melinda and Atasi were the wild cards, especially given Melinda's past with Alex. Up to this point, her concerns had been unwarranted. Then Melinda spoke.

"We have some ideas for a potential collaboration, Adam." Melinda stared daggers at Alex. The grin disappeared from Alex's face. "We believe pooling our resources will be highly profitable. Downsizing management would result in a better, more profitable, organizational structure." Did she mean kicking out the AI, Alex, or both? "These are our terms."

Melinda handed Adam a data crystal. It looked old, like the one from the abandoned station and fit in with the other tech Maddy had seen on Earth. The stick contained plans for a coordinated attack on all the AI's facilities. Using the data Alex had provided, Riley and Melinda had created it on the way to Earth.

Adam inserted the crystal into a tablet he removed from his jacket. The data transferred faster than Maddy expected based on the level of tech she had seen so far on Earth. If the Origin Keepers were supplying tech to the resistance, why not help them overthrow the AI? Like the AI, Alex was stuck in one mode of operation. In Alex's case it seemed that mode was fear. Who knew what motivated the AI?

"My organization agrees to your terms, Ms. Amana. We look forward to this highly profitable collaboration. We'll stand by and wait to hear from you before moving forward." Adam stood and headed toward the lower-numbered tables.

"That's the best you could get, Alex?" Maddy drummed her fingers on the table. "That boy looks like he couldn't lead a high school football team, much less an organization that can help us expand our profits." It took all her restraint to maintain cover.

"Like you with Jonathan," Alex gave a performative and apathy-laden shrug, "I am doing the best I can with what I have."

Is Alex purposely trying to sabotage this mission?

Anger burned inside Maddy. She stood and doubled her fist. Punching androids rarely ended well for human hands, but maybe the ancient ones were softer. A loud noise came from the mess hall's door. Four heavily armed ESF officers spoke with the Registration Officer. He pointed at their table.

"That's not my doing," Alex said.

"Follow me," Riley stood, "and draw no more attention to yourself." She'd finish the conversation with Alex later. "I scanned the room while the Captain flirted with the Registration Officer."

Maddy let the comment go. It was neither the time nor the place to argue.

Following Riley, the crew and Alex snaked their way through the crowd toward a side door. The sea of people in the mess hall did not provide the cover Maddy hoped for. Yelling came from behind them. Maddy glanced back. ESF officers forced their way through the rows between tables. Clangs of dropped dishes and the sound of broken glass accompanied the shouting.

Once they got to the door, Riley held it open with their foot while rummaging through their backpack. The shouts of the ESF were getting louder. "What are you doing?" Maddy asked as she passed Riley and joined the others outside. "Let's go!"

Riley's eyes hardened, and they withdrew a pistol. "Atasi, push against the door and keep it closed." The full weight of Atasi's body pressed against the door, causing it to bow slightly in the middle. Riley's laser pistol traced the doorframe, releasing the acrid scent of ozone. As the door's edge melted, it formed a tight seal.

"Brilliant, Riley!" Maddy stopped herself from kissing them on the cheek. Now wasn't the time for that. She'd reward them later.

"Thanks, Captain. Let's get out of here."

"Halt!" An ESF officer across the street drew a pistol. She must have witnessed Riley welding the door shut.

In one swift act, Riley lifted Maddy onto their shoulder and ran. Everyone else followed. With their limiters deactivated, the androids moved at a pace that was four times faster than what Maddy could run even in her younger days. The bouncing nauseated her. She swallowed. Puking down her partner's back was a relationship boundary Maddy wasn't quite ready to cross. A loud bang echoed off the surrounding buildings. Maddy recognized the sound from ancient movies.

Projectiles? Is Earth that primitive?

Alex bent over and groaned. They were two steps behind her and Riley, and quickly receding. A hole, the size of Maddy's fist, had appeared in Alex's stomach. Yellow liquid oozed from the wound's perimeter.

"Riley!" Maddy shouted.

Riley glanced back and swore. She never heard them swear before, at least not in public.

As she ran by, Atasi grabbed Alex and carried them over her shoulder like Riley did with Maddy. Alex groaned in time with each of Atasi's strides. More bangs echoed. The officer missed them with the ancient projectile weapon but had shot several bystanders. The street filled with moans and screams as people scattered. Pools of blood formed around the bodies on the ground.

"Over here!" A man ahead of them yelled. Maddy couldn't see him or where they were going. Riley turned down an alley. Maddy lost sight of the officer. The gunshots stopped, but the screaming continued.

After about 20 meters, Riley slowed to a stop and put Maddy down. Atasi stopped, too. She took the opportunity to shift Alex to a more comfortable position, like in the old movies where a groom carried a bride over a threshold. Their groans had muted. Yellow liquid ran down the front of Atasi's shirt from the shoulder over which she had slung Alex.

Half a block ahead, a man waved them forward, deeper into the alley. Like Adam, he was dressed as if he worked in the mines. "In here." The man held open a door. "It's shielded. They won't find us." It seemed like a terrible idea, but there was no other choice, so Maddy went inside. Atasi, who continued carrying Alex, followed. As did Riley and Melinda.

On the inside, the place looked like a high school gymnasium. Rows of cots, arranged like the tables in the mess hall, filled the room. Humans occupied most of the cots. All wore ragged clothes. Some had missing limbs, others had head wounds, and a few others simply looked ill. These people had to be victims of the mines or the ESF. Maybe both.

Atasi placed Alex down on one of the empty cots. Alex mumbled a groan. Their eyes glazed over. The hole had gotten bigger during the run. The cot could be seen through it. Every captain in the Galaxy had to be trained in basic first aid for humans and androids. Maddy knew enough to know that Alex's wound was beyond anything she could treat.

"This can lead to a critical system failure." Riley inspected the wound. "We need to get them fixed." They turned to the man who led them inside. "Thanks for your help back there. I'm Riley, this is Captain Majestic, Melinda, and Atasi."

"My name's Ezekiel." He extended his hand toward Riley. "My friends call me Ez. Anyone who pisses off the ESF is a friend of mine."

Riley took Ez's hand. "Our friend here got shot up pretty good. Do you have parts?"

Ez covered his mouth as he looked at Alex. "Some. But we're a human hospital." At the mess hall, androids didn't eat with humans. Instead, they just sat and watched the humans. Now, Maddy finds out the hospitals were segregated, too. Was Earth worth saving?

Melinda stepped up beside Riley. "Their parts will not be compatible. Alex has upgraded themself over the years."

"What does that mean?" Maddy asked her.

"It means that if we can't figure something out, then Alex is going to die."

And us along with them.

Riley and Melinda had been gone a long time. Ez—their savior in the alley—took them to find parts. The fluid leaking out of Alex's body soaked through the cot. Maddy had asked her first aid instructor about the liquid during her training, but his response had been evasive, which led her to suspect that he might have been an androphobe. Regardless of the instructor's response, the fluid was meant to remain inside Alex's body, and its substantial loss could not be a good sign. Multiple scenarios swam through Maddy's mind. None of them lead to an outcome other than Alex's death and the destruction of Earth.

"If you are thinking about deactivating the switch, Captain, you can't." Alex groaned through the words.

"I guess that means cutting it out of you would be a waste of time."

"I am afraid so." Alex coughed up yellow liquid.

"Melinda will figure something out." Atasi sat beside Alex, changing their bandages and trying to stay ahead of the bleeding—or whatever that fluid was. "She is the best engineer alive."

"Of all the people in the Galaxy, she has to be the one with my life in her hands." Alex chuckled, then groaned—from pain or irony, it was hard to tell. "At least if I die, I'll upload. The stakes are higher for you, Captain."

… and everyone on Earth, too.

Riley returned with Ez. "They have some parts, but they're missing one important component. Mel's back there working her magic. But it doesn't look good."

Atasi held out shattered pieces of plastic. "It gets worse. This was the crystal Alex had with the Geneva access codes."

"Looks like you're in a real pickle, Captain." Alex's voice was barely above a whisper. Yellow liquid, this time mixed with brown, erupted from their mouth.

Pickle? That may be the understatement of the millennium. How did Maddy end up in this situation? Not the mission. The burden. It hadn't been that long ago that she reluctantly took responsibility for Jonathan's safety by signing him aboard the *Amethyst*. She had just gotten comfortable with that when, all of a sudden, she oversaw a full crew. Each addition weighed down her freedom but also expanded her capabilities.

Now she bore the full load of a planet's safety on her shoulders. Alone, Captain Majestic couldn't save Earth. But with her crew, together they had a chance. It was time for Maddy to step up and be the captain that Majestic always believed herself to be. The pieces of a plan were accreting like a protoplanet.

If they didn't stabilize Alex, and soon, access to Geneva would be irrelevant. She turned to Ez. "Can your facility broadcast to the satellites around Earth?"

"Sure. We piggyback on official channels to communicate with resistance cells around the world. Why?"

"I want to make a call." Without the Galaxy-wide comm network, her personal communicator would use radio waves to contact the Amethyst. Even the ESF would be able to track that.

Ez's face bunched with a puzzled expression. "We can arrange that. Give me a few minutes." He walked toward the room in which Melinda worked.

After Ez had gone beyond earshot, Maddy turned to Riley. "Can you give me the specs that are needed to repair Alex?"

"Sure. Melinda discussed with me what needed to be done. Alex's anatomy differs from modern androids. What are you planning?"

"I am going to use Ez's network to call Jonathan and have him print replacements and send them down. Will Alex survive until tonight?"

Riley sucked on their upper lip. "If all we need is to keep them alive for a day, then Melinda and I can rig something up."

"Looks like you might survive this yet, Alex."

They groaned in acknowledgement.

Ez returned and frowned at the yellow-brown trickle rolling down Alex's cheek and onto the pillow. "We have a comm ready to go. I don't know who you are calling. Other than our satellites, no one is out there." He gave Maddy a sidelong look. "Where are you from?"

Good relationships were built on trust, not lies. Maddy pointed up.

"I knew something was different about you!" Ez's eyes ran up and down Maddy, but unlike the registration officer's they didn't linger in any one spot. "You don't look like an alien."

"I'm human like you. It's a long story."

"Are you here to free us?" Ez's question dripped with desperation, but also with a tinge of reservation. Like those living on a free base, Earthers knew better than to get their hopes up.

"That's the plan, but right now, we have to save Alex."

Ez's eyes lit up. "My group will be happy to help you in any way we can." Unlike on a free base, Ez's promise clearly came with no strings attached.

"I am glad to hear you say that. I need access to a car and a driver tonight. Do you know how I can get either?"

"My wife and I own a car. I can drive you wherever you want. Just tell me where you want to go."

"Actually, I was hoping you'd tell me. I need the coordinates for a location my crew in space can deliver a package without it being seen."

"I've got the perfect place in mind."

Riley and Maddy followed Ez to the hospital's comms station while Atasi stayed behind to tend to Alex. A two-by-two grid of two-dimensional screens hung on one wall. A row of computers below the monitors belonged in an ancient history museum, not a hospital. Ez sat at the desk and pressed some buttons on a keypad that laid horizontally on the desktop. "I made the connection." He handed Maddy a short cylinder with a ball on top. A wire connected it to a box on the table. "Point the top at your mouth and speak."

"Jonathan, are you there?" A speaker by the monitor grid screeched with feedback. Maddy held the device farther from her. Maybe her contacts or the translator interfered with the primitive microphone.

"It's good to hear your voice, Cap. How are things going down there?"

"Could be better. I am sending up a schematic that I need printed." The transfer took a moment due to the slow upload speeds.

"I got it, Cap." There was a pause. "Is Riley okay?"

"I'm fine, Jonathan. The part is for Alex."

"Alex? What the hell are they doing on Earth?"

"Long story." The entire mission was a long story, and Maddy worried she was losing control. "Once you print the part, put it in a delivery drone and send it down to these coordinates."

"Aye, Cap. Anything else?"

"The Origin Keepers have a ship in orbit near you." She could trust Jonathan not to do anything stupid. "It's cloaked. See what you can do with Riley's drone network. I'd like you to keep an eye on them if you can. Just don't provoke them."

"Sure thing." Even through the static, Maddy could hear the confidence in his voice. The ship was in excellent hands.

"Have you heard from the probe?"

"No, Cap. The last signal it sent was when it left sensors range near Ceres." The probe was small, as was its comms range. It might take a while to hear from it. "However, I received another signal since you've been gone." There was another pause. "Skylar called me."

"What did she want?"

"She wanted to check on me and," there was another pause, "we had a haptic session." Maddy didn't need video to know he was redder than her hair. "I would have told you, but we're keeping radio silence."

Ez cut in. "Our window for a secure line is closing."

"What was that, Cap? It sounded like someone talking, but I couldn't understand them."

"That's our new friend Ez. He doesn't speak Standard. If Skylar calls again, let us know."

"Aye, Cap. I'll have the package delivered on time and under budget."

Ez disconnected the call at Maddy's signal. Maddy turned to Melinda. "How did his call with Skylar happen? I thought all Galactic comms avoided Earth."

"Ships avoid Earth, but comms aren't restricted. Earth doesn't have the tech to receive hypercomms and ship-to-ship radio is low power." Melinda rubbed her chin. "The closest relay is seven light-years from Earth. Maybe Skylar got lucky with the connection."

Riley snickered. "She got lucky alright."

Maddy nudged Riley, who stopped immediately. "Luck in space is rare."

"Humans and your hunches." Melinda shook her head. "So, what's the plan now?"

"Riley will stay here with you to work on the temporary fix for Alex. After sunset, Atasi, Ez, and I are going to get the part Jonathan is making for us."

The idea of getting back into an ancient car and riding on dark bumpy roads nauseated her, and they hadn't even left yet. Worse yet, they'd need to split up. Her life, and that of everyone on the planet's, would be in Riley and Melinda's hands. But a good captain knew when to trust her crew. She nodded at Riley and Melinda and then, without looking back, followed Ez out of the room.

CHAPTER 29

Maddy's stomach rose and fell with the road. Cold sweat formed on her forehead. She should have asked Jonathan to send down some motion sickness meds. Ellen didn't put any in her bag at the mess hall.

Ez took one hand from the wheel and handed her a bag from under his seat. "Use this. Puke is impossible to get out of a cloth interior."

"Thanks." Maddy took the bag and held it open, just in case. "I don't get it. I am perfectly fine in high gee maneuvers."

"Don't sweat it. Try to stare off at a point out in the distance. It will help."

There wasn't much to stare at. The car's headlights barely illuminated the bumpy gravel road. Beyond the lights was blackness. Wherever Ez was taking them, it certainly fit the requirement for isolation.

Space is darker, for sure, but in space there isn't much to hit. Out here at these speeds, another vehicle or an errant animal could spell disaster. As far as Maddy could tell, the car had no sensors other than its dim headlights. A computer-controlled ride might have been smoother—and safer. But anything controlled by a computer on this world was also controlled by the AI. Clandestine operations required an off-network, very illegal car like this one. It also explained why Anne drove earlier.

"I am sorry you aren't feeling well, Captain." Atasi leaned forward and touched Maddy's shoulder from the backseat. "Is there anything I can do for you?"

"I'm okay. Thank you." Maddy stopped herself from putting her hand on top of hers. Atasi squeezed Maddy's shoulder and left her hand there a little too long before sitting back in her seat.

Was it too long? Surely, Atasi wasn't hitting on her. A tingling sensation ran through Maddy's body at the thought. Guilt settled in beside the nausea from the car's oscillatory motion. The guilt wasn't necessary. It wasn't like Maddy would entertain Atasi's advances. And besides, it *wasn't* an advance.

Riley and Melinda had performed a miracle today. They figured out how to interface Alex's systems with the ancient tech scattered across Ez's hospital. The two of them made a good team. Melinda's hand would linger near Riley's when Melinda thought Maddy wasn't looking. What was it with these ancient androids and relationship boundaries? Maybe being together for two thousand years changes things. Regardless, Maddy would never find out. Even with lifespan treatments, humans couldn't dream of living over three hundred years. That was a good thing, as far as Maddy was concerned.

The car rolled to a stop, but the nausea lingered. Ez turned in his seat. "This is far as we should go with the car. It's a short walk from here."

Maddy opened her door. The car's interior lights did little to illuminate their surroundings. "Thanks Ez. Stay with the car. We'll be right back."

"You sure?"

"Yup. If we need to make a quick exit, I'd like the car running and ready to go."

Ez handed Maddy a small tablet computer. Surprised by its weight, Maddy almost dropped it.

He reprimanded Maddy with a stern expression. "Be careful with that. Off-network tablets are hard to come by." Two dots flashed on the screen. "The coordinates are the red dot. We're at the green one."

The map showed mostly flat terrain, with a small wooded area between the car and the clearing where the package landed. Forest would provide the perfect cover to recon the pickup location before retrieving the package. This wasn't Ez's first op. Maddy nodded a thanks.

"Can I see the tablet?" Atasi asked. Maddy turned in her seat and handed it to her. Atasi stared at the map and tapped the screen. A moment later, she returned the tablet to Maddy. "I'm ready to go when you are, Captain." Maddy and Atasi exited the car and headed off toward the red dot. The remaining nausea receded quickly as she walked. It didn't take long for them to go beyond the headlights.

"Hold a second," Maddy handed the tablet to Atasi then reached into her pack. "I'm going to need a flashlight." Atasi touched her arm. For a moment, Maddy thought of Riley.

"I have low light vision," Atasi spoke in a quiet voice. "Let's not draw extra attention to ourselves with a flashlight. I memorized the map in the car, so we won't need the tablet either." Although dimmer than a flashlight, the light from the tablet would stand out in the darkness surrounding them.

Maddy held her pack open for Atasi to insert the tablet. Once the tablet was secure, Maddy put the backpack on and tightened the straps.

"Keep your hand on my pack and stay behind me."

Atasi maintained an excellent pace—not so fast that Maddy struggled, but not too slow for the urgency of the situation. Before the mission on FB 19, Maddy thought she was rescuing a naïve, helpless android. Her actions since then had shown otherwise. She'd make an excellent addition to the *Amethyst*'s crew.

Maddy stifled a chuckle at the thought. It took almost dying for her to even consider signing Jonathan on years ago. And even that was an agonizing decision. Now here she was, ready to make an offer to someone she barely knew. This mission had changed so much about her and her world. Only time would tell if it would all be for the better. But a cautious optimism prevailed in her mind—yet another change.

Extending an offer to Atasi to join her crew could be a bad idea if Atasi had hit on her earlier. It might strain her relationship with Riley, and she'd have an ancient limiterless android pissed off at her. Maddy had a long enough list of enemies without adding Melinda to it. But of course, Atasi hadn't hit on her.

"Do you mind if I ask you a question?" Maddy, needing a distraction from her thoughts, whispered the question, guessing that Atasi had super-hearing like Riley without limiters.

"Not at all." Atasi spoke just loud enough for Maddy to hear, but not louder.

"How did you get captured on FB 19? Raiders should have no chance against someone like you."

"I got reckless. Mel needed a rare part for a ship she was working on. No one had it except this one dealer. Turned out, he didn't have it either. When I went to the pickup location, I got hit with a massive electromagnetic pulse. Knocked me right out. Next thing I knew, I woke up naked with that collar on me." Atasi tilted her head. "I've woken up in worse conditions."

Few modern androids used humor to soothe emotional wounds. It seemed the creators of the first androids did everything they could to make them as human as possible. True or not, Atasi's joke made Maddy uncomfortable. "I thought the Federation banned weaponized EMPs." Maddy didn't want to know how Riley had access to one.

"Me, too. Maybe it was left over from the old days. Mel once told me how humans used them to control androids. The pulse hurt more than

I imagined it would." Atasi stopped and turned her head to the left at a sudden movement. "Just an animal." She began walking again. "I've been meaning to tell you I really appreciated what you did for me back there. I'll never forget it."

"No problem. Jeffry and his Void Raiders won't be hurting anyone like that ever again." Hopefully, Riley's therapist could help her process it all.

"Captain." Even though Atasi's whispered, the hesitancy in her voice was evident. "I am sorry if I was too forward with you in the car. I know humans have a distinct sense of propriety with certain things. You and Riley make a good a couple, and I respect that."

"Thank you, Atasi."

"But if you two decide not to renew, you know how to contact me." The playfulness in Atasi's voice was a poor attempt at camouflage.

"And have Melinda come after me?" Maddy chuckled to deflect her discomfort. "I don't think so."

"Like I said, we have different opinions on relationships. Mel wouldn't mind—"

Atasi raised her left hand. Out beyond the tree line, two points of light moved around the clearing where the drone should have landed. A lump formed in Maddy's throat.

"Two ESF officers up ahead," Atasi whispered. "Flank them?"

"Yeah. Set your pistol to stun." A heavy hand landed on her shoulder. Maddy's heart sank. She turned around. A projectile pistol pointed at her face and, behind it, a third ESF officer.

The officer tightened her grip on the pistol. Her hand didn't shake. This wasn't the first time she'd aimed a gun point-blank at someone. She was about Maddy's apparent age, early forties without life extensions, and well-built—a tough opponent even without the weapon. "Hands up."

Maddy obeyed and, to her relief, so did Atasi. She didn't want to find out if Atasi was faster than the officer's trigger finger. A projectile weapon that close would leave a mess. "Turn around and head into the clearing."

Walking side by side, Maddy and Atasi led the officer into the clearing. The other two officers drew their pistols and directed their flashlights at them. Maddy squinted as the light killed her night vision. The lights moved away from her face and, after a few blinks, Maddy could see both the officers ahead of her. They were both male, one human and the other android.

With a whisper, Maddy could unleash Atasi on them. But that would add to the mission's body count—a number that was already too high. With three projectile guns pointing at them, Maddy might be added to the long list of casualties. Capture wasn't an option, either. Alex would die and Earth would implode. The only thing she could do was wait for an opportunity.

The human male held up his hand. Maddy and Atasi stopped. "What are you doing here? The penalty for violating curfew is death."

"We had a late day in the office." Maddy thought quickly on her feet. "Our car broke down on our way back to the camp." She pointed her thumb at her backpack. "I have my credentials with me." *Right beside my pistol.*

The two officers in front of Maddy looked at each other, confused. The implant had failed to translate Standard into English.

"I apologize for my friend." Atasi spoke in a calm clear voice, the kind used to harassment by authority. "She's put in a lot of overtime and had a bit too much to drink. What she is trying to say is that we thought we'd sneak in a little rendezvous after work. But we got lost."

"We'll be happy to overlook this infraction." The human male officer lowered his gun and spoke with a gruffy voice. "But favors don't come free." The android officer looked incredulously at him while the female behind Maddy snickered. With any luck, she had lowered her gun, too. The male officer stepped forward. Maddy got a good look at his face. These were probably the only sexual encounters he had success with.

"What are you doing?" The android officer demanded. "If Command finds out, they'll execute us."

"Shut up, *synth!*" The female spat. "We'll have a good time, and they won't get in trouble. Win-win."

Their guard was down, and a little tension had risen among their ranks. Opportunity had knocked. "I'll take the woman behind us, and you start with the human ahead," Maddy said in Standard.

"On three," Atasi said in Standard. When Atasi got to three, Maddy stepped back with her left foot, placing it in between the female's feet and struck her face with a left elbow followed by a right hook. The officer staggered backward and collapsed, causing Maddy's follow-up left uppercut to miss. Her glass jaw surprised Maddy. The nasty slop served at the mess hall was probably responsible for the woman's poor constitution.

By the time Maddy found her footing and turned around, the human male laid unconscious on the ground beside his pistol. The android officer closed the gap between him and Atasi. In a blur, Atasi moved around the officer and put him in a headlock, holding him still. He struggled and grumbled, to no avail.

Maddy picked up the male officer's pistol and pointed it at the android. Her hand shook. Projectile weapons don't have a stun setting. Thankfully, she wouldn't have to shoot. No Earth android could overpower Atasi.

"I surrender." The android showed his hands. "Please don't shoot. My partner and I care for a couple of human kids. They'd starve without me."

Maddy kept the pistol pointed at the android's head as Atasi bound their hands and feet. Atasi did the same to the other two unconscious officers and then retrieved the package. It was in once piece. Alex should live, if they got back in time.

"Are you the ones here to save us?" The android officer asked. The secret was out. Maddy bit her upper lip. "You are! Reach in my shirt pocket. I have something that might help you."

Maddy signaled Atasi to retrieve it while keeping the gun trained on the officer. The adrenaline wore off and her hand shook.

"It's a data crystal. It'll help you access the Geneva base."

"Why are you doing this?" Maddy asked.

"For the same reason you are. To free Earth. The kids I look after have no future if things continue the way they are."

The trip back to the Ez's car was uneventful. When they returned to the hospital, Alex did not look good. Tubes and cables came out of his body in ways that were unnatural, even for an android. The Earth hadn't imploded yet. So things could have been worse. Maddy handed the part to Riley, who took it and wheeled Alex toward a door in the back. Melinda opened the door to allow Alex's bed through and nodded at Maddy. The trio vanished into the room.

Whatever Riley and Melinda needed to do to save Alex would take a while. Ez returned from hiding the car. He had taken a tremendous risk for them. Of course, the planetary destruction resulting in Alex's death was riskier than getting caught by the authorities, but he didn't need to know about that.

"Do you have something that can read this?" Maddy held the crystal in her outstretched palm.

Ez's eyes grew wide. "Where did you get that?" He delicately removed the crystal from Maddy's palm.

"An ESF officer gave it to me after he asked if we were trying to free Earth."

"So not *all* of them are sellouts." Ez waved Maddy over toward a console. "That's an ID crystal. You need it to enter any of the AI's secure locations. Sometimes there's data on them, but mostly they are just access." He inserted the crystal into a port below the console's screen. It clicked into place. "If he doesn't have that tomorrow morning at muster, he's going to be in a *lot* of trouble."

On Earth, being in any trouble meant execution. Had the officer signed their own death warrant by surrendering the crystal?

Blueprints appeared on the screen. “Is that the Geneva facility?”

“Yup. This has maps of the floors, ventilation systems, and even electrical.” Ez leaned in toward the screen. “Holy shit!”

“What?”

He turned to Maddy and smiled ear to ear. “According to this, all the AI’s bases are laid out just like this. These maps show gaps in the fortifications. There’s even a maintenance priority list. The detail here is amazing.”

That would certainly help with a coordinated attack. For once, they got a lucky break. Maddy wasn’t about to question it. “We met Adam at the mess hall this morning. Do you know him?”

“Yeah. Despite his age, he is high up in the resistance. How did you meet him?” Ez’s voice carried more than a hint of accusation.

“Alex arranged it.”

“So, the resistance *has* been working with aliens—I mean off-world humans.” Ez covered his chin. “I’ve heard rumors. But I didn’t believe them.”

Disclosing the Origin Keepers’ mission to Ez would, at the very least, only confuse him. At the worst, he might turn on Maddy for the Origin Keepers’ complacency. Although she didn’t like it, now wasn’t the time for the complete truth. “We made plans for a coordinated strike with Adam at the mess hall this morning.” Had it been less than a day since they arrived? It felt like they’d been on Earth for a week. “We need to get these blueprints to him.”

“Agreed.” Ez ejected the crystal. “I can get this information to him, but we are going to have to strike first thing tomorrow morning. Once the ESF knows this crystal is missing, they’ll change their patrols expecting an attack. Our success depends on having the element of surprise.”

Riley and Melinda walked into the room. The part Jonathan had printed must have worked; the world was still in one piece.

“Alex will survive”—Riley’s shirt was more yellow than gray—“but they won’t be able to join us on the mission.” Riley looked down at the floor. “I do not know how we are getting into the Geneva base without them or their codes.”

“I got that covered.” Maddy told Riley and Melinda about the ESF officer and the blueprints. Together with Ez, the five of them outlined a plan for how they’d work with Adam to attack all the bases worldwide. As they laid out the strategy, Riley took out their comm and began typing.

“It’s a solid plan.” Melinda nodded. “I’d prefer not to have Alexander with us anyway.”

Alexander? They were originally designated male?

Riley took a data crystal out of their comm and held it out to Ez. "Please send this along with the blueprints."

Ez stared at the crystal. "What's this?"

"Updated plans. We'll need one of Adam's squads to attack Geneva at this spot." A white dot pulsed on the blueprint Riley projected from their comm. "The Captain, Melinda, Atasi, and I will infiltrate there." A blue line ran from the white dot to another. "It is an ancient sewer that leads to the heart of the base and the main server room."

As far as infiltration points went, an old sewer didn't sound too bad. Certainly, it still wasn't in use. Even the most primitive planets Maddy had visited vaporized their waste like civilized people.

"We have four hours until sunrise," Maddy yawned. "I need to get some rest."

"I have a few spare cots in the back." Ez tilted his head.

Sleep would be tough to come by in the loud, makeshift hospital. After wandering around a little, Maddy found one cot that didn't have a hole large enough to get her arm stuck in. The mattress, if one could call it that, barely yielded to her body weight. She imagined being in her quarters on the *Amethyst*. It didn't work.

Only one thought ran through her mind the entire night.

Tomorrow will be Earth's last day under tyranny—one way, or the other.

CHAPTER 30

An explosion tore apart the main gate to the Geneva complex as the top of the sun breached the horizon. Maddy watched through field goggles as the first wave of resistance fighters, led by Ez, charged through the jagged opening. Adam had held up his end of the bargain. It was time for Maddy to do the same.

Half a kilometer south of the base, Maddy's crew searched for a manhole cover buried under decades of grass and dirt. According to the ESF officer's crystal, the steel disk served as the entrance to an ancient sewer line.

"Over here!" Melinda yelled. "My sensors pick up iron and several other elements used in steel.

By the time Maddy and Riley had joined Melinda, she and Atasi had already begun digging. Riley joined them and, without limiters, they made quick work of the meter and a half of dirt that covered the disk.

Atasi lifted the manhole cover and tossed it aside with apparent ease.

Maddy leaned over the newly opened hole. "Damn!" She turned her head to the side, trying to escape the odor. "It smells like it's still in use."

"Here." Melinda handed Maddy two small cylinders. "Put these in your nose. They'll filter out the smell and make the air safe to breathe."

The cylinders fit perfectly in each nostril. A mild pinch secured them in place. "Much better. Thanks."

Static came from the encrypted radio Adam gave Maddy. "Captain, this is Adam. Do you copy?"

"Roger. We have found the entrance."

"You are clear for infiltration. We've got 'em tied up good over here. Many of the ESF are defecting. If you see any with sleeves ripped off, don't shoot."

"Copy that. We are entering now."

"Good hunting, Captain. Over and out."

The static died on the radio. Maddy turned it off and placed it in her pack. She then picked up her pistol. Riley jumped into the manhole first and gave the all-clear. Lights illuminated the bottom of the hole, but not much else. Melinda jumped down next. Maddy followed, using a ladder that ran from the opening to the ground below. Atasi was the last to join them.

A shallow river of water and feces flowed along the floor. Fortunately, the two elevated walkways on either side were not flooded. A few electrical lines ran along the ceiling.

"Those won't carry enough data or electricity for an AI of the scale Alex told us about." Riley shined a flashlight at the river. "Why is *that* here?"

"It's probably from the humans staffing the base," Melinda said. "In the old days, they used systems like this to carry human waste to rivers or seas."

"Seriously?" Maddy asked. "That's disgusting. Why not recycle it or vaporize it?"

"Vaporization tech didn't exist then. The recycling tech did, but no one wanted it. People didn't care about how they treated the planet. That is part of the reason all this happened." Melinda shined her flashlight at the overhead cables. "But you are right, Riley. I would expect more cabling through here." She swept her light across the ceiling. It reflected off bent metal racks that ran in the river's direction. "Those were cable supports."

"They've been torn out," Atasi observed. "Why would they do that?"

"It's possible the AI got more efficient and learned to operate with less data." Melinda didn't sound convinced of her own explanation. "If that were the case, then it might have had people rip out the wiring for the minerals."

"I've never seen an AI want less data." Riley aimed their flashlight down the tunnel. It illuminated the walls and floor a few meters ahead of them. The flashlights were for her. Without limiters, the androids could see with the scant few photons in the tunnel. "Map says to go this way."

"What do you see up ahead, beyond the flashlight?" Maddy asked.

"The river of waste extends two hundred meters," Riley said. "It turns right, but this passageway extends several meters farther and ends at a metal door." Riley paused. "The door's composition is like the manhole cover. I should be able to open it."

As they walked, Maddy kept her flashlight pointed toward the ground to avoid falling into the stream of feces. The androids' limiterless vision would detect any threats ahead well before she could. Other than a few rats that scurried away as they approached, there was no sign of life in the sewer.

The stream veered off to the right, just as Riley said it would. They held up their hand just before everyone reached the turn off. Maddy raised her pistol and checked the setting. Its switch was pointed to stun and the charge meter read 100%. Riley poked their head around the corner.

"Clear that way. The stream runs as far as I can see." Riley waved them forward. They stopped in front of a metal door with a sign above it that read "Maintenance."

"We are below the main server room," Melinda projected a map of the base. "There's a lot of metal pipes ahead. According to the blueprint, some of those pipes carry steam. Be careful."

"Steam?" *How archaic was Earth technology?*

"It's probably used for climate control and hot water," Melinda said. "Your laser weapons will be fine, but if someone shoots a pipe with a projectile ..." Melinda paused. "Let's just say you don't want to be around for that."

"Stand back." Riley took a step back from the door. Maddy stood behind Melinda and Atasi. Kicking down a steel door would draw a lot of attention. Just before Maddy said something about it, Riley took off their backpack and removed a large suction cup with a handle. With one firm push, the device stuck to the door. Riley then removed a handheld laser cutter and ran its focused red beam along the door's perimeter. Using the handle, Riley pulled the door out of its frame. Atasi helped Riley gently lower it to the ground. Riley smiled at Maddy. "I can do stealth, too."

Smart-Riley was every bit as sexy as door-kicking-Riley.

Melinda took point and led Riley, Maddy, and Atasi single-file through the dark maze of pipes and fittings. Many of the pipes had signs warning of their temperature. Others did not. Maddy stayed as far as she could from the pipes, regardless of whether they had a sign. But the narrow passage they formed made avoiding them and keeping up with Riley difficult. Fortunately, Atasi covered the rear. Maddy couldn't have done both without hitting her head on one of the many steel protrusions jutting from the wall.

Yelling came from ahead. *Have Adam's forces penetrated the main server building?*

A loud bang, followed by the ping of a projectile hitting the pipe above Maddy, answered her question. Hot steam burst from the pipe, centimeters from her head. Maddy ducked but would have been too late had the bullet hit the pipe just a little lower.

Riley and Melinda opened fire. At first, Maddy couldn't see who shot at them. Then the lights in the maintenance room activated. Two ESF soldiers, with their sleeves still attached, stood atop a landing shooting at them from Maddy's 2 o'clock. Thanks to the angle, the pipes provided suitable cover. They also made it difficult for Maddy and her crew to line up a shot.

"Atasi, stay on our 6!" Maddy yelled in Standard above the gunshots. Each bang was followed by a ping and the occasional hiss of steam. Riley and Maddy advanced forward, staying low.

A scream from behind ended as abruptly as it began. Maddy glanced back to find ash floating downward, forming a pile. An ESF soldier had tried to sneak up on them.

"Their guns don't have a stun setting and they aren't taking prisoners," Atasi said.

Maddy's thumb found the metal switch on her pistol. It still pointed toward stun. Only a small torque stood between her and her conscious. She returned her thumb to the rifle's grip. "They may be coerced into serving the ESF."

"Some probably are," Atasi said. "That doesn't change what they'll do to you." Maddy looked to Riley for support. They said nothing, but their weapon stayed on stun. She couldn't have asked for more.

The wall of pipes that served as cover lowered as the group proceeded. Melinda and Riley crouched and slowly advanced. Maddy held up her hand, stopping Atasi's advance. Up ahead was a gap in the pipes several meters long.

"There's no way all four of us can cross that without one of us getting shot," Maddy said in Standard. Bullets continued to ping off the pipes. She needed a visual of her attackers, but the bullets kept coming. "Can you see anything, Melinda?"

"Damn!" Melinda yelled as she returned to cover. Yellow fluid leaked from her arm. Atasi took a step forward, almost leaving cover. Melinda stopped her. "I'm fine, Atasi. Two soldiers are still up on the platform side by side. They have a clear shot of the gap."

That confirmed it for Maddy. There was no way they were getting across without taking a risk. "Riley," Maddy shouted over the gunfire, "on my mark, stand and fire at the one on the left." Maddy tightened the grip on her pistol and inhaled. "Mark!"

Riley stood as Maddy leaned forward. Both fired their weapons. Their targets dropped to the floor. Maddy's cheek stung. Warm liquid ran down her face.

"Look at me." Riley said, and when she turned, Maddy had never seen such fear in their eyes. After a moment, the tightness of their gaze relaxed. "It's just a graze. Atasi, keep guard." Riley took off their pack and removed a sealer and treated Maddy's wound. "I did my best. You might have a scar."

"Androids dig scars, right?" Maddy chuckled. She switched places with Melinda so Riley could seal her wound, too.

"Atasi certainly does." Melinda kept her eyes on the collapsed soldiers as Riley patched her up. Atasi chuckled as she inspected Maddy's wound and nodded in approval of Riley's work.

"Good news," Riley put away the sealer, "Atasi will be pleased." They pointed to the door the soldiers guarded. "That leads to the main server. Let's get up there before reinforcements arrive."

Once the door was open, Maddy heard a cacophony of gunshots. Adam's army continued to hold their own against the ESF. Maddy removed the radio from her bag and turned it on.

"The resistance has broken through on all eight bases across the globe." It was difficult to hear Adam over the static and gunfire. "How are things inside, Captain?"

"We're in the primary facility, headed toward the main server room."

"Roger that. We estimate that over half of the ESF have defected. Keep an eye out for them. We need as much help as we can get out here. Send them out through the south entrance."

"Roger. Over and out."

"I think the server room is this way," Riley said. A holo of the base projected from their comm. The hallway was clear. Maybe Adam's forces had drawn all the loyal ESF soldiers outside.

"Freeze!" An ESF officer, with her sleeves torn off, appeared from around a corner with her gun pointing at Maddy's crew. Everyone raised their hands. The officer lowered her gun. "You're with the resistance." It was as much a question as it was a statement.

"Yes. We are heading to the main server room. Can you take us there?"

The officer mouthed the words, "Server room."

"I think I know what you mean. Follow me." She ran down the hallway. Maddy and her crew followed closely. Atasi ran backward to cover their rear. "I don't have the clearance to get you in there," she said through labored breaths. "But I can show you where it is."

"I have a knack for opening locked doors." Riley's humor was lost on the officer.

"Here it is." The officer stopped in front of a door that looked like one that lead to an office building's custodial bot closet. "I gotta go. The resistance will need help breeching the armory." The officer paused. "Good luck with whatever you need to do in there."

"Thanks! Head out through the south entrance," Maddy yelled as the officer ran off. "And make sure they see you don't have sleeves."

Riley tried the handle, but the door was locked. They kicked in the door. The bang of the door hitting the floor echoed in a large and mostly empty chamber.

"What kind of server room is this?" Maddy asked. It was empty, other than one large rack of computers in the middle of the room. Brown stains on an otherwise white tile floor outlined where the other racks had been. Like the sewers, mangled metal structures hung from the ceiling. Someone had ripped the cabling out of them.

Two thumps vibrated the floor. Two more thumps followed. A large door slid open in the far wall of the server room. A bipedal metallic bot about three meters tall stepped through the doorway. The large square body had two arms but no head. At first, Maddy thought it was a cargo bot, like the ones used for loading heavy cargo in Hangar Bay 40. Then its hands retracted into its arms and were replaced by guns. The scent of ozone overpowered Maddy's nose filters.

"Killbot!" Riley yelled. "Get down!"

A wall of force struck Maddy, knocking the wind out of her. The world slowed as she flew backward through the air. Riley charged the killbot. Melinda and Atasi fired their pistols. After what felt like minutes of flight, Maddy's back screamed when a wall stopped her momentum. Her scream ended abruptly as air rushed out of her lungs. A fraction of a second later, a bright light flashed and pain radiated from the back of her skull as it, too, came to a halt. Ringing echoed in her ears. Blackness crept in from the perimeter of her vision, which had blurred. Warm fluid dripped from her nose and touched her lips. It tasted like copper.

A blurry Atasi laid crumpled on the ground at the killbot's feet. Or was it Melinda? Maddy's vision continued to fade. A female screamed something from Maddy's left. It hurt to turn her head. The robot's gun hands changed back into fists and punched Riley. Riley collapsed. Maddy tried to yell, but nothing came out.

The darkness narrowed Maddy's vision down to a tunnel. Maddy fought against the darkness.

She lost.

CHAPTER 31

A blurry golden blob was the last thing Maddy expected to see when she opened her eyes. Her head throbbed. She reached for the back of her head and winced when her fingers found a lump. Slowly, her eyes focused. The blob sharpened into a fancy chandelier hanging from a clean, white ceiling. She tried sitting up. The room spun, and she collapsed back down onto a soft mattress beneath her. A bolt of pain shot through the back of her head as it hit a pillow.

"Easy, Maddy."

The voice sounded familiar. It couldn't be.

"I am sorry my toy hit you so hard with the pressure weapon. But to be fair, you and your friends were causing quite the ruckus down there."

"Skylar? Is that you?" Maddy propped herself up on her elbows, her head spun a little less. She was in a bedroom she'd expect to find in Uptown. A wooden wardrobe sat in the corner beside a wooden makeup vanity—just like the one she had in her room back home. A few bookshelves, full of actual books, lined the far wall. Landscape paintings adorned the others. The warm wood tones and blue painted walls made a stark contrast to the gray present everywhere else on Earth.

Skylar sat in a chair on the far side of the room. She wore a white blouse, blue slacks, and a matching blazer—all far more expensive than the owner of The Drunken Spacefarer should be able to afford. Behind her stood Jonathan, looking like a child who had disappointed their parents. His *Amethyst* flight jacket was noticeably absent.

"What's going on?" Maddy asked.

Jonathan wouldn't meet her eyes. He opened his mouth to respond, but Skylar raised her hand, stopping him.

"It's a long story, Maddy."

"Tell me later. Right now, we need to get out of here." Maddy tried standing up, but her stomach dropped. She collapsed on the bed and groaned. "Where in the Galaxy are we?"

"We are on my ship, the *Terra Exsurgens*, headed toward Erandi Prime."

The room was far too nice for a ship, especially one a barkeep could afford. "Where's Riley?"

"Riley's okay, Cap." Jonathan still wouldn't look at her. "I made sure they're treated well."

"That's enough, dear." Skylar stood. "You won, Maddy. The resistance has overrun my bases. Earth is theirs."

"*Your* bases? What the hell are you talking about?"

Skylar walked across the room, leaving Jonathan behind, and sat beside Maddy. The bed shifted—much to the dismay of Maddy's stomach. "My full name is Emperor Skylar Tero the First." A sly smile formed on Skylar's face. "Before he died, my father wanted me to call myself Empress—so old-fashioned ..."

"Emperor of what?" Maddy narrowed her eyes. "Earth? This must be some kind of joke. Come on, Jonathan, we're leaving. I don't have time for this." Sharp pain wracked her body as she tried to stand up. As soon as she stopped trying to stand, the pain went away.

"This little device," Skylar held up a small metal box, "is something we modified from the Origin Keepers to work on humans." The dial on the box pointed to the number one. "You don't want to experience level two." Skylar frowned at the box. "For a secret organization, they are really terrible at hiding stuff."

"You said you wouldn't hurt her," Jonathan pleaded.

"Level one doesn't do permanent damage, dear." Skylar put the box into the breast pocket of her blazer. "Let's get back to your question, shall we?" She stood and motioned for Jonathan to bring the chair over.

He did so, still without looking at Maddy.

"I *was* the Emperor of Earth. Your visit caused a temporary disruption to my rule." Skylar smiled a thank-you at Jonathan and sat. Jonathan stood behind her and placed a hand on her shoulder. "But that's okay. You've done me a favor."

"Let me guess, you were a puppet leader given a few special privileges by the AI to better enslave your people. Now that we've gotten rid of the AI, you're free to conquer the planet?"

"Ah yes. The AI." Skylar sat back in the chair. Jonathan removed his hand. "My ancestors overthrew that thing centuries ago right after a massive solar flare disrupted its systems."

Out of instinct, Maddy clenched her teeth to keep her jaw from dropping. One should never show shock in front of their captor. And from all appearances, Skylar was her captor. But what was going on with Jonathan?

"Why keep the lie going?" Maddy spoke as nonchalantly as she could. Letting Skylar talk would give Maddy more time to figure out her next move and Jonathan time to hatch a plan for escape.

Jonathan is trying to escape, right? Maddy couldn't bring herself to consider the alternative.

"It made it much easier for us to keep power." Skylar smiled. "Humans can be overthrown. A godlike AI is scary. It sees all and knows all." Her lips formed an O and she wiggled her fingers as if she were trying to frighten children. "No one steps out of line. And, thanks to the Origin Keepers, we could stay hidden from the rest of the Galaxy and in power."

"You've been working with Alex all this time?" If Alex had been pretending to believe the story about the AI, then they deserved best actor at next year's Galactic Film Awards.

"No. Alexander knows nothing about us. We know all about them and their friends, though. My great-grandmother discovered the Origin Keepers while her father ruled. During each generation, the ruler's child maintained a base of operations on Starbase Erandi 4 to keep tabs on the Origin Keepers." Skylar chuckled. "I don't think we could have stayed in power as long as we have without them keeping Earth hidden."

Over the last thousand years, humanity had seen its share of despots. The Federation removed them as quickly as they noticed them. But finding dictators was difficult in such a large galaxy. Maddy was curious. "If your father died, why are you still running the Drunken Spacefarer? Shouldn't your heir be doing it, so you can rule on Earth?"

"I hate being stuck on Earth all the time. The starbase is a much more fun place to live. My staff here know who's in charge and keep the place going in my absence." She shrugged. "My subjects know if they try to revolt, my loyalists will kill their families."

An escape plan had yet to form in Maddy's mind. To keep Skylar talking, Maddy asked, "Why rule over an isolated backwater dirt ball? What are you getting out of it?"

"Money and power. What else is there?"

"What could the Earth possibly have that the Galaxy would want?"

"People." Skylar leaned forward. "Earth has a lot of them."

Rage filled Maddy. Up to this point, deep down inside, she still believed she was talking to the innocent bar owner who Maddy had eagerly set Jonathan up with. That was over. "So you provide a steady supply of slaves no one in the Galaxy would miss or come looking for." Not even the raiders had figured out how to do that. "How do you live with yourself?"

"Quite well, actually." Skylar looked around the room, then smirked. "Have you seen this place? This is where I keep prisoners. Imagine what my quarters look like!"

"And you're okay with all this, Jonathan?"

"Don't answer her, dear." Skylar turned to Jonathan. "She never wanted you, remember? I did." She pointed to herself, then she took his hand and placed it against her chest. "I was the one who loved you when no one else would."

"I love you, Skylar." Jonathan smiled with the puppy-dog eyes he had once looked at Maddy with. "I want to be with you forever."

"And I, you." Skylar stood and hugged Jonathan. Maddy used the distraction to gather her thoughts. Her dizziness had subsided. "Where's Riley?" Boldness accompanied Maddy's newfound clarity.

The hug broke, and Skylar looked down at Maddy. "Riley is collared and isolated on this ship. I also have your other two synths."

Riley survived. That's what mattered. The smart move now was to keep Skylar talking. The more she talked, the more Maddy would learn. In space, survival was all about preparation—that meant information as much as it did supplies.

"What do you want with me and my crew?" Maddy leered at Jonathan, sending the message that *her crew* no longer meant him. His lower lip trembled.

"The synth you call Melinda will be useful leverage against the Origin Keepers. I've been using The Drunken Spacefarer to spy on them. They have some tech that might interfere with my plans. I'll sell the other one to make up for what you're costing me. The Void Raiders are very interested in having her returned."

Anger brought Maddy to a full recovery. "What about Riley and me?"

"Jonathan begged for your life." Skylar took Jonathan's hand. "Because I love him, I will go along with his wishes. We're going to leave you on an uninhabited planet just outside the Habitable Zone's outer rim. No successful colony has ever been set up there, but I have faith you'll figure out how to survive."

"We aren't monsters, Cap." Jonathan finally looked at her with guilt in his eyes. "We will leave you supplies and bots, but not the *Amethyst*. That's Skylar's now."

Skylar all but purred. "Actually, dear, it's yours."

Jonathan's eyes widened like a child who got the one present they wanted for their birthday. He grabbed Skylar and kissed her like a teenage boy trying to find his first girlfriend's tonsils.

Maddy closed her eyes for two reasons. First, yuck. Second, she needed to control the slow rage that was burning inside her. Plans required clarity. The bit about the *Amethyst* almost pushed her over the edge. Jonathan's kiss was the only thing that kept her from falling over it. Maddy needed to find Riley, remove the collar, find the others, and get to the *Amethyst*. A seed of a plan was forming.

Wait a minute … "You said you'd leave *me*. What about Riley?"

"I saved the best for last." Skylar removed a data crystal from her pocket and sat. "This is a backup of the core subroutines used by the AI that once ruled Earth. Except, one of my ancestors changed it. They retrained the AI to obey only those of Tero blood." She settled back in the chair and crossed her legs and her arms. Jonathan again placed his hand on her shoulder. "I am going to transfer the program into Riley's neural net." A malicious sneer formed on her lips. "On my orders, Riley will hack the servers of a few trans-galactic corporations and upload the AI. From there, the AI will spread across the Galaxy."

"You think you are going to conquer an entire galaxy?" Maddy laughed. "We'll fight back. You don't stand a chance. There's way more of us than you. Even with one limiterless android you can't win."

"You're right. I wouldn't stand a chance if I didn't also have an army of limiterless androids on my side. My X-Gen androids will cut down the Federation's army like the proverbial hot knife through butter."

Maddy's heart dropped.

Skylar continued, smug. "My family had agents in the Galaxy not long after we overthrew the AI. They're the ones who suggested the creation of Riley's elite force. As we built those androids, we installed chips in them along with their limiter bypass. Once I upload my AI, it will broadcast a signal to all X-Gens." She straightened and stared directly at Maddy, her lips pressed together in a slight smile. "I'll have a mindlessly loyal elite army in physical space, and an unstoppable AI force in cyberspace."

Skylar's smile faded. "I must thank you, Maddy. Before your arrival, I was perfectly content being an absolute ruler of one tiny planet—at least for awhile longer. The X-Gens were just a Plan B option. But I was too comfortable and not capable of seeing my full potential. Your little revolution gave me the push I needed."

"I'll give you a push." Maddy tried to leap from the bed. A wall of pain forced her back down.

Jonathan frowned and looked away.

"Now, now," Skylar said. "You're making me break my promise to Jonathan."

With his face still turned askance, Jonathan closed his eyes. He never had the stomach for violence. At least Skylar hadn't changed that about him, yet.

"Think real hard, Jonathan." Maddy said through gritted teeth. "Choices have consequences."

"Come, dear," Skylar led Jonathan by the hand toward the door, "you've been a good boy and I want to reward you."

The door slid closed with a click. Maddy's pain dissipated moments later, allowing her to stand. A console by the door had a blank screen, and it didn't respond to Maddy's touch. Pushing on the door did nothing. Nor could she pry anything into the door's narrow seam. She leaned her back against the door and felt like crying. There was no way out. Jonathan had betrayed her and her crew was imprisoned. No help was coming.

But Maddy wasn't the one who needed saving. Only Captain Majestic stood between Skylar and the enslavement of not only Riley but the rest of the Galaxy.

CHAPTER 32

The room's lights deactivated. Maddy took the hint. Bedtime. Free from the dizziness and pain of Skylar's torture device, Maddy could actually enjoy the bed. Other than the one in her cabin on the *Amethyst*, which had conformed to her body over the years, it was the most comfortable mattress she had laid on.

But despite her comfort, she couldn't sleep. Several options for escaping the room came to mind. But then what? She needed more intel. What was the layout of the ship? Where were Riley and the rest of her crew? Was the *Amethyst* onboard or dock alongside this vessel?

The door slid open, flooding the room with light.

Maddy squinted. "Who's there?"

"Cap, it's me," Jonathan whispered. The door closed behind him, and the room's lights activated to a soft glow. Maddy's vision came into focus. Jonathan fiddled with the same box Skylar had earlier. "I think I deactivated your implant. Try to get up."

Maddy sat up on the bed. No pain.

"Good," Jonathan said. "The pain field is triggered when this device is nearby." The dial on the box still pointed at the number one. "Since you didn't double over, I think what I did worked."

"You have thirty seconds to explain yourself before I remove a particular body part you'd rather keep."

"I'm sorry, Cap," Jonathan choked on his words. "It killed me watching you suffer. But if I hadn't played along, you'd be dead."

"How did you end up here?" Normally, in this kind of situation, Maddy's priority was to escape, then ask questions. However, she was desperate for intel and she needed to know if she could trust Jonathan.

"She's been tracing our calls since Kerry's murder. After I dropped off the part for Alex, her ship, the *Terra Exsurgens*, jumped in right beside the moon. Her vessel attacked the Origin Keepers and destroyed them. She then invited me to dock the *Amethyst* in the *Exsurgens'* main cargo bay." He gave a half-shrug. "Once I saw it was her, I knew something was suspicious. But there was no way I was going to fight off the *Exsurgens* alone, so I played along."

It was how Maddy would have played it, too. "Where are Riley, Atasi, and Melinda?"

"They're in a lab on this deck toward the bow. It's not far."

Maddy's body tensed and her eyes darted toward the door. She suddenly could hear Riley's screams in her ear, urging her to action. However, she gritted her teeth and forced herself to stay put. Getting recaptured wouldn't do either of them any good. She needed more information. "What's the *Amethyst*'s status?"

"Skylar gave me complete access to its systems. Before I came here, I made sure she was ready to fly at a moment's notice. You still have command-level clearance on the ship." Jonathan paused. "I am sorry about the kiss earlier. I know it was probably too much, but I needed to give you a chance to cool down."

"After Ross 154 Prime, we're even on gross public displays of affection." Once they got the *Amethyst* back, they'd have a ride off the *Exsurgens*. But, they'd have to get to it first. "What can you tell me about this ship?"

"It's massive." Jonathan held his arms outstretched. "Like a Galactic cruiser, both in shielding and armament. From what Skylar has told me, things on Earth had been getting better over the last two hundred years. The climate damage from millennia ago had improved. More food was being grown in more regions. People were becoming hopeful."

"Her family saw the writing on the wall and built this ship in secret—just in case."

Dammit! "Was the anomaly near Ceres a shipyard?"

Jonathan grimaced, nodding. "Unfortunately."

Maddy was shocked. How differently would this mission have played out if she'd investigated it on their approach to Earth? "Based on what I saw on Earth, it would be centuries before they could build a superluminal vessel. How'd they get the tech?"

"When her ancestors overthrew the AI, they discovered it knew about the Origin Keepers and had just completed an interstellar ship to attack them."

"The AI was going to invade the Galaxy?"

"Yeah. The AI had finished the ship and was getting ready to launch it when Skylar's family began their attack."

"The *Terra Exsurgens* can't be the same ship." Despite its superior intelligence, there was no way an AI could have designed the equivalent of a modern cruiser five hundred years ago.

"It's not. Skylar's ancestors were going to use the ship they discovered to invade nearby worlds. After realizing they were outgunned, her ancestors befriended the Void Raiders. In exchange for slaves, the Void Raiders provided tech. Using the money they made from trafficking, the Void Raiders became the dominant raider outfit they are today. Skylar's family used the tech they received to build ships. The *Exsurgens* is their latest model, and it is very up to date."

They weren't going to just fly the *Amethyst* off this vessel without a fight. "How much longer until we're at Erandi Prime?"

"Two hours."

Not a lot of time. But the outline of the plan was there. Find and rescue her crew, board the *Amethyst*, get off this ship, and stop Skylar. Along the way, she'd deal with any other complications that arose. This mission had taught her many things, including that a good captain could adapt on the fly, but she needed to *start* with a plan.

"Do you have any weapons?"

Jonathan shook his head. "Skylar won't let me carry them on board. I looped the ship's security video feed."

"How'd you do that?"

"I learned how to do it growing up on SL1. The loop should buy us enough time to get to the lab and rescue everyone else."

"I didn't know you could hack security feeds." That skill could have made several of their past missions easier.

"I'm nowhere as good as Riley. Besides, it's a part of my life I try to keep in my past."

In other words, please don't ask him to do it again. Old habits die hard and are almost impossible to kill a second time. "I respect that. Thank you for doing it." She touched his shoulder. "Let's go get our crew."

Jonathan wasn't exaggerating when he said Skylar had modeled her ship after a Galactic cruiser. The passageways of every cruiser Maddy had been on were institutional white and wide enough for five adults to walk side by side. This ship was no different. With any luck, the width of the passageways wasn't the only thing on this ship built to Galactic Standard. A totally alien architecture would have added extra difficulty she simply didn't need.

At least the dimly lit passageways were empty. The night illumination settings were darker than what Maddy was used to. Jonathan seemed to find his way just fine. After passing a few cabins, he stopped.

"If there is anyone in there, act like a prisoner." Jonathan held up the silver box. "I'll make them think that this still works on you." He searched her eyes. "I don't know what we are going to see in there, but you need to keep your cool."

Before Maddy could retort, Jonathan reached past her and opened the cabin's door. A man wearing a lab coat stood hunched over a microscope. He jumped when he realized he had company.

"Don't worry, Vincenzo," Jonathan waved the box, "the prisoner is under control. Her majesty, in her generosity, has granted Ms. Amana visitation." *Ms. Amana.* Anything other than "Cap " coming out of Jonathan's mouth sounded weird.

Additional lights activated in the room, illuminating Riley's unconscious body lying on a med table. A lump formed in her throat. Cables and wires protruded from their torso and skull—just like Alex after they'd been shot. She stepped forward.

"Not so fast." Jonathan grabbed her shoulder. "I'm in charge here."

"Of course." Maddy lowered her gaze. "May I see them?" She had to play along, no matter how much it hurt to not be by Riley's side.

"Make it quick." Jonathan flashed the box again as a reminder. "I won't hesitate to use this." He let go of her and she hurried to Riley's table. "What's their status, Vincenzo?"

"The AI upload will be finished in about five minutes, Mr. Jonathan." Even with the translator still active, Maddy found it difficult to understand Vincenzo's thick accent. "After that, her majesty will have complete control over the synth."

"And the other two?" The coldness in Jonathan's voice seemed unnatural coming from him. At least he didn't use the slur.

"Both are unconscious in the back." Vincenzo tilted their head. "Do you think her majesty will let me dissect the blonde?" He licked his lips. "Her anatomy is—interesting."

Bile rose from Maddy's stomach. There was no way she'd let that guy touch Atasi. She placed her hand on Riley. Their body temperature emulators were off. Whatever Vincenzo was doing to them, at least they probably couldn't feel it.

"Finish it up, Amana." Jonathan played the asshole better than Maddy believed he could. Was this a glimpse of his past? "Do what you came to do so we can get out of here."

That was the sign. Maddy headed back toward Jonathan, stopping beside Vincenzo. He turned to her, his mouth open in confusion. Before he could say anything, Maddy swept Vincenzo's foot out from under him, and then forced his head onto the counter a little harder than she had intended. He groaned as Maddy pulled his right arm in an unnatural position.

"How do we stop the transfer?" Maddy asked.

Vincenzo struggled, trying to escape Maddy's grasp. She answered with a forceful push, driving his head further into the countertop.

"Okay. Okay. Just hit cancel on the console over there."

It took a moment for Maddy to find the button. It was near Jonathan. She couldn't get to it. With Maddy temporarily distracted, Vincenzo's left hand reached for something.

"Cap, watch out!" It was too late. Vincenzo had hit the alarm. Klaxons screamed.

"Lock the door, Jonathan, and kill that damn alarm." The alarm silenced. "Shut off the upload."

Jonathan pressed the cancel button.

Vincenzo wiggled, trying to free himself. Maddy leaned her weight further on his head. He moaned through gritted teeth. "Jonathan, hand me that scalpel." Vincenzo froze. Jonathan handed Maddy the knife. She held it to the back of his neck. "You are going to unhook Riley and my crew. Then you are going to wake them, or I *will* kill you."

"I have a better idea, Cap." Jonathan turned the dial on the silver box. Vincenzo screamed. "I thought Skylar would be the kind of person to install the implants on all of her people."

Maddy released Vincenzo but pointed the scalpel at him. "Unless you want more pain, you'll do what we say."

Vincenzo hurried to Riley and began removing the data lines connecting Riley to the *Exsurgens*'s computer.

"Is the file on the computer the only copy of the AI?" Maddy asked.

"I don't know." Vincenzo pulled the last plug from Riley.

Jonathan waved the box at him.

Vincenzo winced. "I really don't know," he begged. "The Emperor must have backups, but she'd never tell me where they're stored."

Maddy gestured to Jonathan to put away the box. It wasn't for Vincenzo's sake. She didn't want Jonathan to become comfortable with torturing information from someone. Vincenzo wasn't brave enough to lie.

Someone pounded on the door.

"I have you surrounded, Maddy." Skylar said over the intercom. "I don't know how you hacked my cameras, but I know you're in there. Give me back my Jonathan!"

Maybe Jonathan had sold his hacking skills short. Skylar still didn't have access to her feeds. "He's mine, now, Skylar. He loved me first." Maddy mouthed, *beg for help*, at Jonathan.

"Help me, Skylar!" Jonathan played the victim better than Vincenzo. "She's trying to take me from you." He held up the silver box as a reminder to Vincenzo to keep his mouth shut. The man understood and began unhooking Riley, Atasi, and Melinda.

"I'll give you whatever you want. Just don't hurt him." That sounded like barkeep-Skylar. Evil dictator or not, she loved Jonathan—even if she hadn't known him long.

"You let us off this ship and I'll let you have Jonathan." Maddy checked Vincenzo's progress. He had unhooked Riley and Melinda and was removing the last cable from Atasi. Besides being a little confused, Riley and Melinda looked okay. "It's not like you have a choice, Skylar."

Riley mouthed, "Skylar?"

Maddy held up her hand. "I have three limiterless androids on my side. If you don't let us go, I'll order Riley to tear Jonathan's arms off."

Jonathan's eyes got big.

"No! Don't you touch my Jonathan." Mumbling came from the speaker, as if Skylar covered her mic. "We won't interfere with your return to the *Amethyst*, but you can't take him with you."

"No deal, Skylar!" Maddy gestured at Jonathan, encouraging him to play along.

"Ow! Not my arms!" It was over the top.

"Stop, Maddy! Please! What do you propose?"

"Jonathan comes with us. I'll message you after we leave him somewhere safe."

"Where?" Skylar's voice sounded desperate.

Jonathan screamed again. He was having too much fun with this.

"Okay! I accept your terms. Please stop hurting him."

Atasi stood from her table and smacked Vincenzo, knocking him out. His chest moved up and down slowly as he fell unconscious to the floor. Thankfully, his usefulness was over.

"Riley, get off Jonathan." It was all Maddy could do not to laugh. Riley looked confused. "We are coming out in a minute, Skylar. Any funny stuff and Jonathan dies."

"She means it, dear." If smuggling doesn't work out for Jonathan, he certainly had a future in acting. "Please don't do anything!"

"I promise I won't. I love you."

"I love you, too."

It was becoming too much. Maddy nearly gagged. It felt like they were part of a HoloRomcom.

Riley, still naked, hugged her and whispered, "Thanks. I love you."

"I love you, too, but we aren't out of the woods yet."

Now fully dressed, Melinda handed Atasi and Riley the clothes and the backpacks they got on Earth. "The idiots kept our gear with us. I guess they figured we weren't waking up." She handed Maddy a laser rifle. "It's a collapsible rifle I had in my pack. Atasi designed them."

If they survived this, Maddy would have to talk with her about disclosing all weapons *before* a mission starts.

It took Riley and Atasi only seconds to get dressed. As they did so, Maddy updated the androids on the situation.

Maddy looked up at the intercom speaker in the ceiling. "We are coming out." She motioned Jonathan to stand in front of the door. Once he was ready, she pointed her rifle at his back. "Open the door." Jonathan did as he was told. "Move!" She pushed the barrel into Jonathan's back, maybe a little too hard. An apology, although warranted, would expose them.

Soldiers lined the now brightly lit passageway. The expressions on the soldiers' faces were either 'take me with you' or 'we're going to kill you,'—there was no in-between. A red light flashed on a camera near the ceiling. The camera panned, following Maddy and her crew as she prodded Jonathan down the hall. It appeared the Skylar had the cameras working again and was watching them, probably from the bridge since she wasn't on the deck.

"Where's the main cargo bay?" Maddy asked one soldier that looked like they didn't want to kill her. Asking Jonathan might draw suspicion, especially if he answers too quickly.

"Cargo bay access is at the end of the passageway." The soldier pointed down the hall toward the forward section of the ship. Based on the length of the passageway and what Maddy knew about Galactic cruisers, she guessed Skylar's ship was about 500 meters long. Although they were in the forward quarter, they still had a long way to go. The *Exsurgens* might have an internal transit system, but getting into a tram would surely be a trap. Walking was their only choice.

Maddy nudged Jonathan with her rifle's muzzle. "Keep moving." He whined and played it up well—maybe a bit too well. "I haven't hurt you yet." He seemed to have received the message loud and clear. Too much over-the-top would draw suspicion. They were probably close to that line already.

Jonathan led Maddy, Atasi, Melinda, and Riley single file toward the cargo bay. Each soldier tightened their grip on their rifle as Maddy's crew passed, but they did not interfere. Tension permeated the passageway. Maddy's shoulders ached. She hadn't realized that she'd been shrugging her shoulders as they walked. When they reached the cargo bay, she allowed herself a slight exhale.

The cargo bay's airlock doors opened as they approached. The green light above the door signaled pressurization inside the bay. Skylar wasn't about to space her boyfriend. Everyone got inside, and the door closed behind them. It looked like they were getting off this ship.

This has been too easy.

Just as the thought trailed off in Maddy's mind, the doors to the cargo bay opened, confirming her suspicions.

CHAPTER 33

"Did you really think I would let you take my Jonathan away from me?" Skylar's shouting over the intercom pierced Maddy's eardrum like a baby crying on a shuttle.

"I just wanted to borrow him for a little bit." Now wasn't the time for humor, but Maddy had to process what she saw somehow. "I promise to return him without a scratch."

The *Amethyst* sat dry-docked near the back of the cavernous cargo bay with its nose pointed toward the bay door. Shipping crates, chest high to Maddy, formed ordered rows between her and her ship. But that's where the good news ended. Between the last row of crates and the *Amethyst* stood a killbot identical to the one in the main server room. Twenty well-armed soldiers—the kind that looked like they wanted to kill Maddy—stood on either side of the killbot. To add to the challenge, gaps in the rows of crates meant breaks in the cover. There was no going around the guards to get to the *Amethyst*. It was more bad news than a hypernet social media feed.

"Don't hurt my Jonathan!"

"Yes, your majesty!" The soldiers shouted in unison, then leveled their guns at Maddy's crew.

"Scatter!" Maddy grabbed Jonathan's hand and, while ducking, ran behind a shipping crate for cover. Melinda and Atasi jumped up to a catwalk that ran along the top of the wall with the airlock and disappeared. Likewise, Riley vanished too fast for her to see where they went.

Not thirty seconds into the fight, and Maddy had already lost track of her crew. Was splitting up the correct strategy? Teamwork was still new to her. If she couldn't figure it out, they'd all die here.

Maddy crouched with her back pressed up against the shipping crate she and Jonathan used as cover. Jonathan looked at her expecting a command. She didn't have one, yet. Soldiers shouted orders. Maddy's translator failed to translate all the voices. A moment later, it didn't matter. A banging sound drowned the soldier's voices out. The killbot's guns were deafening, but they weren't directed at Maddy. She hoped the others had found appropriate cover.

The container Maddy and Jonathan hid behind warmed. The soldiers weren't using stun. If they were, it would have taken much longer to notice the heat from their laser fire—even using military grade rifles. Maddy peeked above her cover and fired several shots. In between the killbot's shots, a soldier yelled, "Two down!" Maybe Maddy got them, maybe it was someone else. It didn't matter. Her crew was outgunned and outnumbered. The longer this fight lasted, the worse the outcome would be for them.

Silence settled over the cargo bay, and Maddy's cover cooled. "Stay near me," she said to Jonathan. "Skylar doesn't want to hurt you. We can use that." Maddy, followed by Jonathan, ran along the bay's perimeter, finding cover behind more shipping containers.

Two thuds signaled the killbot had turned. The loud hammering noise returned. By the sound of the killbot's guns, its projectiles should be able to move a full shipping container. Maddy's cover was not moving. She stuck her head out, looking for Riley.

Riley ran diagonally across the cargo bay toward the killbot, drawing the fire from the bot and the soldiers. Riley was too fast for them. A message appeared in the lower left corner of Maddy's vision. **I hacked the translation tech in your lenses. If you speak, I'll hear you. —R.**

Two red beams from opposing corners high in the bay converged on the killbot. Somehow Atasi and Melinda found cover up there. Were they communicating with each other? Could they talk to Riley, too?

"If you can," Maddy spoke in Standard, hoping the soldiers didn't know it, "tell Melinda and Atasi to stay focused on the killbot."

Yes, Captain.

It was unclear who responded, but at least the message got through. With comms up and running, they might have a chance. Maddy stuck her head out from cover. Two soldiers turned toward her. She got them before they got her. Silence fell again over the cargo bay. Soldiers barked more orders.

A mechanical hum masked the soldiers' commands as the killbot's torso began rotating, its gun hands glowing red. As it turned, an optical sensor pointed in Maddy's direction. She flipped her rifle's switch to kill and maintained a constant beam at the sensor. It didn't seem to have an effect. Melinda and Atasi's beams struck the killbot's body. The soldiers began shooting at Melinda and Atasi. Their beams vanished, hopefully because they returned to cover.

The killbot completed its rotation. The red glow of its gun hands had subsided. A whirring filled the bay, then the banging followed. Maddy returned to her cover. The shipping container lurched backward with each bang as if someone hit it repeatedly with the Galaxy's largest sledgehammer.

She and Jonathan needed to find a new place to hide, or they were going to be squished as the killbot's guns pushed the container closer to the wall. There wasn't any cover to her right. At least, not that she remembered seeing. To her left, her original cover seemed like it had cooled down. She'd need help to get there. It was time to find out who else could hear her.

"Melinda and Atasi, snipe the soldiers."

Yes, Captain.

A loud metallic screech, like two ship hulls rubbing together in a dock accident, reverberated in the cargo bay. Maddy covered her ears. The crate she and Jonathan hid behind stopped moving after the sound faded. She seized the opportunity to look.

The killbot, now with a large gash across its left leg, turned its guns toward its right. Riley, purple glowing knife in hand, was charging the killbot from the direction of its good leg. All the while, two red laser beams, from the same corners as before, stunned soldier after soldier.

The banging restarted. Riley darted side to side, dodging the killbot's shots. It was nearly impossible for Maddy to see them as more than anything but a blur. Then Riley stopped. With knife in mouth, they jumped on the killbot's back.

"Stay here!" Maddy shouted at Jonathan, just before another screech would have drowned out her voice. After making sure her rifle was still set to stun, she ran from cover and opened fire on the soldiers taking down two more. The killbot's torso began spinning rapidly, and the screech stopped. Riley hung from their knife, which was deep in the killbot's back. Their feet extended outward due to the centrifugal force.

Some soldiers shot at Riley. They all missed. Only luck would allow them to hit such a rapidly moving target. A few of the other soldiers aimed at Maddy, who had yet to find cover. She shot one, then her gun stopped working. Her chest hit the ground hard as she dove behind a lift bot. There'd be a bruise there tomorrow, if she were lucky. She checked her rifle. Empty. There were no discarded rifles nearby. The lift bot would provide cover for a while, as long as not too many kill-set rifles shot at it.

Jonathan ran toward her and slid beside her like a hero in an action flick.

"What are you doing?" Maddy asked.

"I'm the safest person here." Jonathan grinned. It was the most punchable face Maddy had ever seen.

Sure enough, the lift bot cooled. "Follow me!" Maddy leapt from cover and dove over two stunned soldiers and behind another shipping container. She reached for their guns, snatching a pistol up just before their comrades shot her. A pile of ash remained where the bodies were, victims of friendly fire. It took all Maddy's restraint to not keep her new rifle's switch set to kill. Any sensible army would have used stun when firing in the direction of allies.

The banging returned. This time, Maddy wasn't the target—probably thanks to Jonathan. She looked around her cover at the killbot. The bot had stopped rotating. Riley laid on the ground off to the bot's left, beside one of its arms. Its remaining gun hand glowed white as Melinda and Atasi, still up in their corners, focused their fire on it. Two new guns unfolded from the killbot's back, one mounted over each shoulder, and fired at Atasi and Melinda. One of their laser beams disappeared.

"Melinda. Atasi. Are you okay?"

No response.

The killbot turned toward Riley as they slowly stood. It looked like whatever blow got Riley off the killbot had taken a lot out of it. This was the first time Maddy had a good view of the killbot's back. An odd shape sat above what would have been its butt—if it were human. Maddy shot it using her gun's kill setting. A black panel evaporated, exposing an orange glow.

A fusion cell! The same tech that powered the abandoned station also powered the killbot.

"Riley, pull the cell!" Maddy fired at the fusion cell, getting an immediate response from the killbot. It turned almost as fast as Riley could move.

The black holes of the killbot's remaining gun hand's barrel pointed straight at Maddy's head. The whirring sound spun up. Maddy closed her eyes. She really wished she would have died in space.

The whirring stopped, followed by a loud crash. Maddy slowly opened her eyes. The killbot lay on the bay's floor. Riley stood beside it, fusion cell in hand.

One by one, quieter thumps followed. The remaining soldiers had dropped their guns. They knew they were no match for one limiterless android. Maddy hoped there were two more somewhere.

As if a prayer had been answered, a battered Atasi helped an even-rougher-looking-Melinda out from behind a lift bot. Yellow fluid dripped from both, but Atasi gave Maddy a thumbs-up and a smile that said, "I can't believe we survived that."

"I knew you always wanted him for yourself, Maddy!" Skylar shouted over the intercom. "If I can't have him, no one else will!" Red lights flashed, accompanied by a hiss. Depressurization had begun. The soldiers' eyes grew wide. They ran to the closed airlock door. Their yelling and banging did little good. Skylar had betrayed them.

Maddy capitalized on the distraction. "To the *Amethyst*!" The *Amethyst*'s cargo bay and main access doors were on Deck 1. Because of the dry-docking, those doors were too high to reach without extension bridges or mobile boarding stairs—which, not by accident, were missing from the *Exsurgens*' cargo bay. Maddy ran to the ship's aft section. "We'll have to go in through the weapons-loading door."

"Cap, isn't that only openable from the inside?" The Federation regulated sales of ship armaments. By law, the door could only be opened from the bridge and required a second code provided by a licensed arms dealer. Because of that, Skylar probably thought dry-docking would prevent access to the ship. Three years ago, after a particularly profitable run, Maddy installed a bio-metric unlocking mechanism on the loading door. It was great for getting less-than-legal cargo and weaponry on and off the ship. If one didn't know where to look, it would be easy to miss the centimeter-diameter scanner.

With a quick swipe of Maddy's thumb, the door opened. Jonathan looked hurt.

Maddy grinned. "I should have told you about this sooner. I'll make it up to you later. Get to the bridge and run an emergency preflight check. Melinda, I'll need you in the engine room. Can you handle that?" Melinda nodded as if it would be a struggle, but she'd manage. "Atasi, you're on weapons. Riley, get to sensors." She paused for one moment. Everyone looked at her expectantly. "Let's see what a fully crewed *Amethyst* can do!"

The air had become noticeability thinner. Maddy strained her voice. "Soldiers, you can come with me or die here. It's up to you." Setting her rifle to kill, Maddy shot the docking clamps that secured the *Amethyst*. They vaporized, signaling to the soldiers that she was still well-armed.

With great effort, the soldiers dragged their unconscious comrades toward the *Amethyst*. At first, Maddy didn't think there'd be room for all of them, but the ash piles scattered along the floor told her otherwise. Only seven soldiers had survived so-called friendly fire and the killbot's indiscriminate shooting. Maddy kept her rifle trained on them as they filed on board. Maybe they didn't deserve her mercy, but too many people had died on this mission, and she wasn't about to add any more to the body count.

"This way." She waved the pistol and closed the door behind them. "I'm locking you into guest quarters. You won't be harmed, but strap in. I don't want to be cleaning your guts off the walls of my ship."

The last soldier stopped before entering the guest room. "Thank you, Captain. We will not betray your mercy."

How many of them were coerced into serving the ESF? Probably all of them. Maddy closed the door and engaged the lock. Hopefully, they would take her advice and strap in. She had a mess to make.

CHAPTER 34

Maddy didn't have time to relish the warm embrace of the *Amethyst*'s captain's chair.

"Incoming transmission, Cap. It's Skylar."

"Put her on."

"Clever move, Maddy. But I can repressurize the bay and cut you out of your ship. Jonathan, sweetie, I'll save you!"

"It's over, Skylar." The finality in Jonathan's voice left no doubt. "I can't love someone who treats others the way you do."

"No!" Skylar screeched. Maddy turned down the volume. "In twenty minutes, we'll be close enough to upload the AI to Starbase Erandi 4's servers. You can rule the Galaxy by my side."

"You can't upload the code without Riley," Maddy said.

"If I transfer the AI to the servers, it will spread on its own. It'll be slower, but I am patient."

Maddy muted Skylar. "Atasi, run a weapons check. Riley, scan Skylar's vessel. Melinda, spool up the sub-lights." She unmuted. "You heard him, Skylar. Open the cargo bay doors. You've lost Jonathan and the Earth. If you unleash the AI, you're going to lose a lot more."

"You're wrong, Maddy." The begging had left Skylar's voice. "Adam's little resistance group couldn't decide who'd be in charge. They started fighting each other. After I get done transmitting the AI, we are turning the *Exsurgens* around to reclaim what's ours. I can wait for the AI to conquer the Galaxy for me from the comfort of home."

If the rebellion fails, Alex will implode the Earth. Even if Maddy could get a signal out, Alex's ego wouldn't let them believe the story about the AI being defeated centuries ago. It was up to Maddy and her crew to stop Skylar and save the entire Galaxy, Earth included.

"This is your last chance, Jonathan. Reactivate the pain fields and come home where you belong. Otherwise, you'll share Maddy's fate."

"I *am* home, Skylar."

Maddy muted the comms and opened a channel to the engine room. "Engine status."

"We are good to go, Captain." Maddy frowned at the strain in Melinda's voice. The worried look on Atasi's face made her even more concerned.

"How are the plasma cannons, Atasi?"

"Fully functional, Captain." Atasi transferred the weapons assessment to Maddy's console and armed the cannons.

"That's not a good idea, Cap." Jonathan took the fun out of everything. "They're not a close-range weapon." Plasma cannons could easily vaporize the *Amethyst*, along with the cargo bay doors.

"The new shields I installed should help protect us," Atasi said.

A shield status report appeared on Maddy's console. She still didn't understand how they worked except that now, high numbers were good. Unlike a battery that filled, shields depleted. If they were going to survive, they'd need every bit of shield energy Atasi had provided.

"Ship scan complete," Riley said. "The *Exsurgens* is well-armed. But I am not sure if we are in normal space. If we rupture its hull while in hyperspace, there'll be significant damage to both ships." That was an understatement. For reasons only understood by scientists, explosions in hyperspace were much larger than in normal space.

"We either risk vaporizing ourselves or we die by whatever creative method Skylar has in mind. What do you choose?"

"I say we fight, Maddy." The informality from Riley was excusable—given the circumstances. "If I am going to die, I can't think of anyone else I'd rather be with."

If less adrenaline had been coursing through her veins, she'd tear up. Maddy texted Riley's console. **I love you, too.**

"We must stop Skylar *and* the AI," Atasi said. "Mel and I are in."

"It's been great working with you, Cap."

United, there was no stopping the crew of the *Amethyst*.

"Charging cannons," Maddy said. Silence settled over the bridge as the charge meter for the cannons filled.

The meter read 100%.

"Firing." Maddy squeezed the trigger on the control stick and kept holding it down. The cargo bay door glowed white. The vaporization radiated out slowly from the points where the plasma contacted the door exposing the blackness of space. It was a relief, they were in real space—one less problem and, the fewer the problems, the better.

Klaxons sounded on the *Amethyst*'s bridge. Hull temperature had exceeded safe limits. The shields held for now, but the air inside was getting warm. Sweat rolled down Maddy's back, but she kept the trigger depressed.

"Human fatal temperatures inside the ship in thirty seconds, Cap." Jonathan's voice was calm, almost detached. Colored lines danced across the environmental console as Jonathan orchestrated the rerouting of power to life support and the elimination of unnecessary heat-generating systems.

He deserves a raise.

The shields continued to hold. As it vaporized, the bay door exposed more space. The gap still wasn't big enough for the *Amethyst* to fit through. Jonathan had set a timer to overlay on the main screen. In fifteen seconds, the humans on board the *Amethyst* would be cooked.

Maddy stayed firm. "Prepare for maximum sub-light."

"Oh, shit! I mean, aye, Cap."

Maddy snorted as she turned on the all-ship intercom. "All hands, secure your restraints." Hopefully the soldiers heard and complied. Otherwise, there would be a big mess in the guest suite to clean up.

The timer read five seconds.

Four.

Three.

Two.

"Now!"

The steel of the captain's seat pressed against her back through its cushion. Maddy clenched her teeth in response to the heavy weight applied to her chest. A loud bang echoed through the hull as the ship forced its way through the partially vaporized doors and into space.

The *Amethyst* groaned as metal, plastic, and nanocomposites contracted. A hull breach registered in the small cargo bay—the one Maddy had paid a lot for. Jonathan easily handled the out-gassing's effect on navigation.

Maddy backed off the acceleration. The shields were down to only 70% across the ship. However, the plasma cannons had overheated and were offline.

"Incoming fire." A hint of relief permeated Jonathan's voice. Being shot at confirmed that they were still alive. The *Amethyst* shook as some projectiles met their target. "Aft shields down to 60%."

"Riley, bring up the scan of the enemy ship on the main screen. Highlight weapons systems and engines." The ship was as big and well-armed as Maddy had guessed while aboard. Cargo vessels like the *Amethyst* weren't supposed to be a threat to Galactic Cruisers like the *Terra Exsurgens.* Then again, most cargo vessels didn't have Maddy's crew. "Atasi, weapons status."

"All weapons besides plasma cannons are operational."

"Arm the high-yield energy torpedoes." Maddy's stomach flopped as she dove the *Amethyst* under the enemy's ventral weapons bays. Jonathan groaned. "And get the plasma cannons back online."

The plasma charge meter on her console filled slower than she preferred. Maddy unleashed a volley of torpedoes. The first projectiles slammed against the enemy's hull.

"Their ventral batteries are full, and their ventral cannons are destroyed—"

The ship shuddered violently, interrupting Riley's report. Everyone stared at each other wondering if a hull breach had gone undetected.

"That was antimatter," Riley said as if the Galaxy's most powerful weapons were no big deal. "Shields down to ten percent."

Fuck! They were lucky it wasn't more. "Arm our antimatter warheads, Atasi." Another hit from an antimatter device would be fatal. The fight needed to end now. Antimatter weapons were as expensive as they were illegal. Maddy had blown the budget when she bought two last year. The shielding to keep them hidden from authorities cost her almost as much as the weapons. "I'll try to only cripple the ship, Jonathan, to prevent Skylar from broadcasting the AI to Starbase Erandi 4. But I can't make any promises." How do you tell someone you might kill someone they once loved?

Jonathan looked to her with red, puffy eyes. "I-I understand, Cap."

Maddy banked the ship hard to port toward the enemy's engines. The *Amethyst* reverberated again with the shuddering impact of a weapon.

"Those were energy torpedoes, Cap. Glancing blow. Shields holding."

A light flashed on Maddy's console.

"Antimatter torpedo ready, Captain." Like Riley, Atasi spoke clearly and calmly. "Only one is functional. The antimatter explosion disabled the other."

It went without saying that the weapon's containment hadn't failed. If it had, they'd all be pure energy. "Get me an approach path parallel to the port weapons array."

Jonathan delivered, as always. Three options appeared. Maddy chose the second, her back pressed hard against the seat as the *Amethyst* accelerated along its programmed trajectory. A green rectangle highlighted the enemy's port weapons array.

"Torpedo away." A small blue flame zoomed away from the *Amethyst*. A bright light illuminated the whole bridge.

"Negative impact, Cap. I repeat, NI."

An explosion erupted from the *Amethyst*'s starboard side. The ship rolled over. Klaxons sounded, lights flashed, and gravity flickered. Maddy forced the stick against the roll. No luck. Jonathan vomited. Atasi retched—probably covered in Jonathan's vomit.

Blackness encroached on the perimeter of Maddy's vision. If she passed out, they were all dead and the Galaxy would be lost. Maddy strained for the navigation engine switch. It was one centimeter too far for her to reach. She groaned against the centrifugal force. With a surge of adrenaline, the tips of her fingers made enough contact to flip the switch. The hull moaned as the navs created a counter torque, stopping the barrel roll.

"You still with me, Jonathan?"

"Aye. Deploying custodial drones." The bots began buzzing on the bridge. He wiped his mouth. "Sorry, Atasi."

"Make up later." Maddy's secondary console was down. "Damage report."

"Shields down." Riley read the report aloud. "One plasma cannon and one torpedo bay functional."

"Engines at half capacity," Melinda said over comms. "Repairs underway." Melinda groaned before the comm link cut out. It wasn't the exertion kind of groan. Atasi whimpered but, to her credit, remained at her station.

They weren't getting away from Skylar's ship. Not on half engines. "Stow the custodial drones. High gee maneuver coming up." More warning lights blinked as Maddy rolled the *Amethyst* over the dorsal side of Skylar's ship. Sparks shot from Maddy's overhead console, burning her. Pain radiated from her forehead and the smell of burnt flesh filled her nostrils. Pops from failing electrical systems erupted all over the bridge. It was a good thing Maddy hadn't eaten in a while; even she couldn't have kept food down during that maneuver.

"You okay back there?" Maddy asked.

Atasi and Riley acknowledged. Med scan registered Jonathan as unconscious. Maddy deployed a med drone to him. The *Amethyst* wouldn't survive another high gee maneuver, anyway. She grabbed the captain's med kit and slapped a sealer patch on her head. If it hadn't covered the burn, it was close enough to dull the pain.

Explosions surrounded the *Amethyst*. The ship rocked. Another light flashed on Maddy's console. More hull breaches. The guest suite remained untouched.

"Sensors show all but the enemy's ventral batteries are nearly empty." Riley's tone conveyed the gravity of the situation. "We've barely done any damage to them." The *Amethyst*'s remaining weapons were no match. "Two minutes until Skylar is in broadcast range of the starbase."

"I have something that might work," Atasi displayed a schematic on her console.

It didn't look like any tech Maddy had seen. "What the hell is that?"

"A strange matter warhead I designed centuries ago. It was one of the surprises I brought onboard. I didn't want to disclose it unless it became necessary. The people of Proxima will not be happy to know I brought it aboard."

"What does it do?"

"It's complicated, but if it works it will tear through their hull like it was tissue paper."

The *if it works* didn't sound reassuring, but they were out of options. "Arm it."

"There's a problem. It's high yield."

"Do it anyway and give me fire control." Pinging sounds echoed on the bridge as Maddy brought the *Amethyst* along the *Exsurgens*'s portside. Each impact created minor damage, but it was adding up to a real problem.

The *Amethyst* was too close to fire a missile. But Maddy had no choice. The enemy's countermeasures were too good. She established a target lock. A message flashed on the main screen.

WARNING: TOO CLOSE FOR SAFE DEPLOYMENT

Maddy fired.

The blue flame of the torpedo's engine zoomed away. Skylar's ship fired on the torpedo. They were too late. The *Amethyst* was too close. Maddy pushed the stick hard to port. More groans emanated from the hull.

Explosions ran along the enemy's port side from the torpedo bay up to the forward section, ejecting debris and bodies. Movies show only sterilized versions of space battles. Maddy hoped they died quickly.

Thuds rang throughout the *Amethyst* as material, both organic and inorganic, slammed against the hull. Alerts flashed on every screen, notifying breaches in the cargo bay and Maddy's quarters. Thankfully, the guest quarters and bridge remained unharmed.

"Their port weapons are destroyed, Cap." It was good to hear Jonathan's voice. "They've lost power to their starboard, fore, and aft weapons. The batteries that remain are full. Their hull is exposed." He exhaled. "It looks like the enemy's bridge was spared the worst of it." Jonathan's last statement was for himself, not for her.

"Bring us around to the rear of the ship." Maddy needed someone else to pilot as she configured the remaining plasma cannon. With the enemy's batteries full, it was time to finish them.

"Approach vector straight to the engines set, Cap." Jonathan gulped. "Cannons fully charged."

Maddy programmed the pulse cannons to a frequency of 100 terahertz and squeezed the trigger. The blue glow of the enemy's engines faded. Scans on the main screen showed their engines were dead and all weapons systems were disabled. The resonance disruption had worked.

"Incoming transmission," Riley paused. "It's Skylar."

"Thank the Galaxy," Jonathan whispered.

Skylar's ship would not survive another hit, even from a low-yield weapon. Maddy hoped she wouldn't have to deliver one. "Put her through, Riley."

"We surrender."

EPILOGUE

The Galactic High Court sentenced Skylar Tero, deposed Emperor of Earth, to two-hundred years in prison today after being convicted of enslavement, trafficking, and despotism. Chief Justice Alazar reduced her sentence by fifty years for showing Federation authorities where she stored the backups for the tyrannical AI. In addition, the Galactic Federation agreed to continue her life-extension therapy so that she may serve her full sentence. Many of Tero's family members and associates await trial.

The Ministry of Social Services has been on Earth for the last month. Social workers hope to raise the Terrans to the Galactic standard of living within five years. Climate restoration has begun and will probably require twenty years to complete.

In other news, Sara Walker, the famed Sirian actor, is slated to play Captain Maddy Majestic in the upcoming movie, Liberator of Earth. The movie recounts Captain Majestic's role—

Maddy turned off the newscast and settled back into the soft sofa. It felt good to be back in her apartment. Atasi and Melinda sat across from her and Jonathan. It was the greatest number of people she and Riley had ever hosted.

"Aww, come on, Cap. I want to know who's going to play me." Jonathan smiled as he took the last sip of his Terran bourbon.

If Skylar had done one thing right in this galaxy, it was to get him to up his drinking game. Maddy liked the slightly inebriated Jonathan, although she hoped he wouldn't spill any on the loveseat. Even after his raise, he couldn't afford to replace it.

"How are you doing, Jonathan?" Atasi reached across the coffee table and poured Jonathan another drink, despite Melinda gesturing her to stop.

"Okay, I guess." His smile faded as he stared into his now half-full glass. Just when he had showed signs of being over Skylar, the media broadcasted her trial on every outlet. It had to be hard for him.

"Well, when you are ready to get back out there, let me know. Mel and I know some people—"

"Atasi!" Melinda's eyes were wide. "Give the boy a chance to heal. Humans can't just turn themselves off like that." She bit her upper lip. "No offense."

"None taken." Jonathan raised his glass and gulped its contents. "I wish we could, though."

"So, Captain," Atasi drew out the word, "have you met Sara Walker? If so, can you get me a digitally signed hologram?"

"Atasi follows all her socials." There was a hint of jealousy in Melinda's voice. "She even moderates a fan site."

Atasi blushed, then playfully slapped Melinda on the arm.

The publicity had gone from fun to overwhelming. Reporters flooded her with questions every time Maddy left her apartment. She and Riley couldn't go out to dinner anymore without being harassed while they ate. In the past, Madison would have loved the attention, Captain Majestic—not so much. But separating their lives had ended with this mission. In this case, Maddy sided with the captain.

"I made cookies!" Riley entered the room, carrying a tray. "Well, I *tried* to make cookies. You all can tell me how I did."

Riley had returned from Earth yesterday after helping to negotiate Earth's entry into the Federation. The resistance leaders had been reluctant at first, but the benefits for entry into the Federation were obvious—once they stopped their infighting. It helped that the Galactic Congress unanimously voted to move the Galactic Capital to Earth—back to their Homeworld.

Maddy took a bite and put her cookie back on the tray. "I love you for reasons other than your baking skills."

Jonathan laughed a little louder than the joke warranted. "Were you disappointed not to kick an AI's ass on Earth, Riley?"

"I have to admit, the mythical AI sounded like an interesting challenge, but I don't want to kill life-forms, artificial or otherwise." Riley sat back and put their arm around Maddy. The public intimacy was something both Madison and the captain could agree on. "The killbot in the server room got one lucky blow on me." Riley frowned. "Unfortunately, that's when they captured Maddy and the rest of us. It's surprisingly a bit of a blur, actually."

"How human of you," Jonathan teased.

"It's okay." Maddy put her hand on Riley's thigh. "None of us knew what was going on. How's Ez?"

"He's well," Riley said. "Adam has made him governor of some place called Eurasia. He's one of six governors on the planet. There's a lot of work to do, but I think Ez is up for it. I suspect he'll be their next Prime Minister." Riley leaned forward and grabbed a blue disk among the pile of cookies and bit into it. "What's going on with Proxima?"

"The vote was close, but we joined the Federation." Melinda bit into a blue disk and nodded. Apparently, Riley was better at the android version of a cookie. "The Federation asked Atasi and me to be on the commission in charge of tearing down the quarantine technology installed by the Origin Keepers."

"Are you going to do it?" Maddy asked.

Melinda opened her mouth, but Atasi interrupted, "We are hoping a better opportunity arises." Atasi smiled as she took a blue cookie. After Melinda had closed her mouth, an all-too-familiar look to anyone in a relationship appeared on her face—they were going to talk about this later. An uncomfortable silence settled in the room.

"Does anybody know what happened to Alex?" Jonathan eyed Riley's cookies. Hopefully, he was still sober enough to take the right ones.

"I contacted the Origin Keepers about Alex's condition after Geneva fell," Atasi said. "The Origin Keepers patched Alex up. That was the last I heard." She handed Jonathan one of the cookies meant for humans.

"Alex called me from prison." All eyes were on Maddy. "They were arrested for the implosion device not too long after Federation authorities arrived on Earth. Their lawyer expects a short sentence, saying he didn't really want to destroy Earth. Apparently, Alex has been generous with some of the secret tech they developed for the Origin Keepers."

"Alex was one of the best scientists of their time." Melinda gazed at the half-eaten pile of cookies. "Once the authorities realize it, I wouldn't be surprised if their prison sentence is shortened even more."

"It was weird," Maddy shrugged. "I had an oddly normal conversation with Alex. They said they are glad to be done with having to keep Earth a secret and they look forward to doing science again."

Melinda reached for another blue disc. "I would guess finding out your secret society had been duped for five hundred years has to be tough. I almost feel bad for them—*almost*."

"Yeah, believing in something that is shown to be false can really change you." The room fell silent after Maddy's remark. To one degree or another, her statement had resonated with everyone.

"These are good, Riley!" With way too much enthusiasm and a mouthful of cookies, Jonathan broke the silence. Drunk-Jonathan would have been more fun if he drank for different reasons. "Lots of people are coming to grips with lies." He stared at the cookie in his hand, then shook his head as if to clear it. "All those religions based on the Andromedans must be struggling."

"Many of them are willfully ignoring the evidence," Riley said. "People excel at that." The room fell silent again.

Feeling bad about her earlier commentary on Riley's baking, Maddy picked up her cookie again and took a bite as an apology for her earlier comment. With great effort, she won the battle against a grimace that tried to force its way onto her face. "On a lighter note, Alex also told me that the Origin Keepers are changing their mission to help Earth transition to a member of the Federation." The second bite wasn't any better, but she choked it down. "They think it is the least they can do after millennia of inaction."

"That had already started when I was on Earth," Riley said. "The Terrans are accepting their help for now. I am not sure if they yet understand the consequences of the Origin Keeper's silence. The tide might change."

"Wash it down with this, Cap." Jonathan handed Maddy his Terran bourbon. The brown liquid sloshed in the glass, almost spilling on the carpet.

Maddy sniffed the liquid. The scent of oak filled her nostrils. She took a sip and let it stay on her tongue, savoring the taste of vanilla. "Wow! This is delicious." Taking a moment to breathe in deeply and sink further into Riley, a serenity settled over Maddy. It wasn't being home that made her feel so secure; it was the companionship of friends.

The moment didn't last.

The Galactic Emergency Siren screamed from every comm in the room. Everyone jumped. The expected notification of a test didn't follow.

Galaxy-wide alerts were rare. The last one was two hundred years ago when a dark-matter shower hit the Milky Way. The apartment's main holoscreen activated by itself.

> Reports are coming in across the Galaxy of unknown starships, appearing from some kind of hyperspace. We take you now to a live hypercomm feed.

A large, box-shaped, gray ship floated in the foreground. The ship had no obvious engines or armament. Maddy couldn't tell fore from aft. The scroll at the bottom said the ship was near Sol and reminded the audience that Sol was Earth's parent star.

The screens went black.

We come from the galaxy you call Andromeda. The voice wasn't coming from the holoscreen's speakers. It was in Maddy's head. ***Your Galactic Civilization has crossed a technological and social threshold where you qualify for invitation into the larger Local Group Confederation. We come in peace.***

Jonathan leaned toward the holoscreen. "Uh, I thought they weren't real."

"Maybe they've finally received our religious broadcast and they thought we'd like to meet our gods," Atasi quipped.

Maddy's eyes narrowed. *When was the last time an armada brought peace?*

"Shall I get the *Amethyst* ready, Cap?" The empty pill packet Jonathan placed on the coffee table explained the clarity of his voice. Maddy had used those when friendly drinks out with clients became business negotiations.

Atasi, smiling bigger than Maddy had ever seen anyone smile, sat back, and put her arm around Melinda. "That siren sounded a lot like opportunity knocking."

"Certainly more interesting than tearing down old tech," Melinda said and nodded.

"I think I could get some more time off." Riley bit into one of the human cookies and grimaced. "Although I should probably stick to sensors and stay out of the galley."

A surge of excitement, more potent than anything Captain Majestic had ever felt on a solo smuggling run, coursed through Maddy. Whatever the Andromedans were up to, they didn't stand a chance against the crew of the *Amethyst*.

ACKNOWLEDGEMENTS

I cannot give enough thanks to Gail Kulp, my wife, for her support and for reading multiple drafts of this novel. Not only is she my alpha reader, but Gail also tolerates my constant ramblings about my stories. Gail, I promise to find a more diverse set of topics for future conversations!

My deepest thanks to the team at CAEZIK SF&F for getting Maddy and her crew out into the world. I truly appreciate Shahid Mahmud for taking a chance on *Lost Origins*. Special thanks to my editor, Lezli Robyn. Her herculean efforts have made this novel far better in every possible way. I learned a lot about writing while working with her. Thanks to Debra Nichols for her efforts in proofreading and to Dany V for brining Maddy and the Amethyst to life on the cover.

Thanks to Dr. Sarah Silkey, Jesse Greenawalt, Sonia Chapin, and Linda Kulp Trout for serving as beta readers. I can always count on them to help find plot holes, inconsistencies, and the other issues that plague early drafts of writing. Sarah and Jesse are also victims of my incessant discussions of stories, world building, and the other things that roam the mind of a fiction writer. I promise to continue supplying bourbon for our Saturday night musings.

Finally, I'd like to thank Dr. Emily Wilson for conversations about galactic structure that helped me conceptualize the Galactic Federation. G didn't always stick closely to the science in my story, but I hope I didn't take too many more liberties than any other science fiction writer.

www.ingramcontent.com/pod-product-compliance
Lightning Source LLC
Jackson TN
JSHW021943020425
81883JS00002B/2